FIRESTORM

The Remarkables have gathered into a long wall, and they talk among themselves with crisp chittering sounds. Their eyes are looking upwind.

The orange flames are moving toward us. I never imagined the fire was so large. The wide valley is filled with tinder, and I can hear the fire working and smell it, and the ash and smoke make my nose sting.

Briar screams, "Move! We're moving! Go!"

He's downwind—a tiny furious shape throwing up his arms, his rifle in both hands—and his voice is thin and shrill.

Someone closer says, "We should go back."

I recognize the voice, turning to the Remarkables now.

"Better to retreat." It's Talker, voice rushed and panicked. "We can't cross in time, Ranier!"

Ask your bookseller for these Bantam Spectra titles
you may have missed:

LIFELINE, by Kevin Anderson and Douglas Beason
THE TRINITY PARADOX, by Kevin Anderson and Douglas Beason
NIGHTFALL, by Isaac Asimov & Robert Silverberg
FELLOW TRAVELER, by William Barton & Michael Capobianco
CONSIDER PHLEBAS, by Iain Banks
EARTH, by David Brin
SLOW FREIGHT, by F.M. Busby
SYNNERS, by Pat Cadigan
RENDEZVOUS WITH RAMA, by Arthur C. Clarke and Gentry Lee
RAMA II, by Arthur C. Clarke and Gentry Lee
THE GARDEN OF RAMA, by Arthur C. Clarke & Gentry Lee
THE REAL STORY, by Stephen R. Donaldson
FORBIDDEN KNOWLEDGE, by Stephen R. Donaldson
WHEN GRAVITY FAILS, by George Alec Effinger
FIRE IN THE SUN, by George Alec Effinger
THE EXILE KISS, by George Alec Effinger
THE HOST, by Peter Emshwiller
THE DIFFERENCE ENGINE, by William Gibson and Bruce
  Sterling
DESOLATION ROAD, by Ian McDonald
THE SINGERS OF TIME, by Frederik Pohl and Jack Williamson
THE FACE OF THE WATERS, by Robert Silverberg
UNIVERSE 1, edited by Robert Silverberg and Karen Haber
HYPERION, by Dan Simmons
THE FALL OF HYPERION, by Dan Simmons
RUSSIAN SPRING, by Norman Spinrad
RAISING THE STONES, by Sheri S. Tepper
SHIVERING WORLD, by Kathy Tyers
STAR OF THE GUARDIANS, VOLUME 1: THE LOST KING, by
  Margaret Weis
STAR OF THE GUARDIANS, VOLUME 2: KING'S TEST, by
  Margaret Weis
ON MY WAY TO PARADISE, by Dave Wolverton
SERPENT CATCH, by Dave Wolverton
STAR WARS, VOLUME 1: HEIR TO THE EMPIRE, by Timothy
  Zahn
STRANGER SUNS, by George Zebrowski

THE REMARKABLES

✛

Robert Reed

SPECTRA TM

BANTAM BOOKS
NEW YORK • TORONTO • LONDON • SYDNEY • AUCKLAND

To Dave and Sonya,
Jim and Dee
Thank you

THE REMARKABLES

A Bantam Spectra Book / March 1992

ISBN 0-553-29362-1

Published simultaneously in the United States and Canada

Bantam Books are published by Bantam Books, a division of Bantam Doubleday Dell Publishing Group, Inc. Its trademark, con-
sisting of the words ''Bantam Books'' and the portrayal of a rooster,
is Registered in U.S. Patent and Trademark Office and in other
countries. Marca Registrada. Bantam Books, 666 Fifth Avenue,
New York, New York 10103.

THE REMARKABLES

1
GOOTTICH

He has a boyish face, round and smooth, with tiny eyes lost against the pale pink skin. His hands are huge, stubby fingers wearing fancy rings and his broad fingernails changing color and their gloss every few moments. Goottich isn't talking just now. He has paused, and I feel odd: numb; out of balance. He nods and grins at me, and he sips something from an icy glass that seems to disappear inside his enormous hand. The glass has to be there, I tell myself, but from my perspective it looks as if Goottich's fingers are curled around nothing and he is happily sucking on the air and his thumb joint.

I haven't heard from Goottich in ten or twelve years.

We last met at a terraformers' conference—my last conference—and we struggled through several conversations. That's all. Goottich is ridiculously wealthy, I remember, and he has few social skills. I can't even remember what we talked about, not to save my life. Yet last night he squirted this message to me, and my house is playing it back while I eat breakfast. He began by saying, "How are you, Ranier? My good, good friend." It was a strange moment. "I understand you're in retirement," he continued. "A man of means and luxury? Well, I have an offer to make, something very special, and I hope you're sitting down. Are you?" A momentary pause. "I was wondering, Ranier. Would you like to join me and some other friends on a trip? A trip to Pitcairn? Would that interest you at all?"

That was when I became numb, in an instant, and

Goottich decided to wait a moment, sipping at his drink and enjoying the imagined suspense.

Pitcairn? Is he serious?

"I mean it," says the recorded image. Then suddenly he laughs, big square teeth filling the vast mouth. "Not an easy thing to organize, as you must well know. Do you know how long I've been making appeals to the Pitcairns? Years. I can't count them, and that's just to get permission to visit their planet. I had to find one grove, one group of Pitcairns and their Remarkables, who would officially invite me and my friends. They're a legal colony, after all, and they have their rules." He makes a frustrated sound, then continues. "I had to prove that I'm worth inviting, and who knows how they pick and choose? All you can do is list accomplishments and your genetics, then prove that you've got noble aspirations and can arrange your own transportation. Then you've got to be patient. You wait and wait, and one day comes a sputtery message from one of their homemade transmitters. Some grove has decided that you suit their needs, and can you bring along several friends? They need a variety of guests. A genetic mix. Which is why they invite anyone in the first place. For our genes. Genes are what they're really interested in."

I halfway nod and shift my butt against my chair.

Then Goottich says, "I thought of you at once, Ranier. Your family came from New Emerald, right? So you've got a tolerance for high-gravity—"

Pitcairn? I'm thinking. He means it!

"—and besides, you seem like someone who'd enjoy this opportunity. Am I right? Does this interest you at all?"

"Oh, sure," I whisper.

Goottich leans back in his oversized chair. I can see past him, making out the distant walls and the high arch of a ceiling. That must be his home, I decide. That one room is larger than my entire house, and maybe he's anticipated that thought. "I can afford everything," he assures me. "Hiring the torchship, buying its fuel, and paying for everyone's insurance policies. In case of mishaps, and so on. Money is not a problem for me." He resembles an enormous self-satisfied eight-year-old boy. Lifting a hand, he scratches his smooth cheek with a purple nail. Then the nail turns lime green, and he says, "But I think it's important, even vital, that everyone puts something into this venture. Do you understand? That's why I'm asking you and everyone else to pay a set fee. A fair amount, I believe. Nonnegotiable. And nonrefundable."

I feel tension building in my shoulders and back.

"One million and one credits," says Goottich, smiling again. "And because we're on a strict timetable, I'm afraid I'll have to have your commitment within seven days. Seven days from the time of this broadcast."

I expected a greater amount, the truth told. I almost relax, sitting forward and taking a few deep breaths while Goottich sips at his drink. Glancing at my breakfast, I feel no appetite. One million and one . . . an arbitrary figure. A number that would appeal to a clever eight-year-old. But I do see Goottich's point. Why should he have to supply everything? Why not ask his "friends" to drag up small fortunes . . . and I start to wonder about his timetable. Why does it have to be so quick? Seven days isn't long, not for this kind of decision—

—and he says, "I'm sending you background information, probably more than you need. It tells about the grove that's sponsoring us and about the specific offer. It's an extraordinary opportunity, Ranier. Almost unheard of. We'll be accompanying a *passion* into the Pitcairn interior, and I'm sure you know the significance of that! A rare, rare honor, my friend."

I shiver.

"I'll look forward to your answer. And I really hope you agree to go. It should be quite an adventure."

On a passion?

I hug myself, staring at the blackened screen and unable to decide what to think about anything. It's too much, too sudden. Then my house asks me if I wish to see the rest of Goottich's message—the promised background material—and I shake my head, saying, "Not yet. Just dump my breakfast."

The house removes my plate and cup.

Then I rise on shaky legs, walking toward the big transparent wall overlooking my lake. Its water is dark blue in the morning sunlight, and calm, and I press my face against the wall. My breath bounces back at me. It tastes humid and warm and really quite sour; and quietly, in a slow voice, I tell myself, "I could afford it. If I want. If I decide to take the risk, I could."

* * *

There is a dear old twist of wisdom.

"Space," it says, "is a conspiracy of vacuum, clean and pure, cheated at every turn and between."

In the earliest age of spaceflight, before people learned that wisdom, Earth and Luna built giant torchships designed to jump from star to star. What they didn't realize was that interstellar space was cluttered with jupiters and smaller worlds, sunless and almost invisible. Each world had its own Oort cloud of comets and grit. Those early torchships collided with the grit, and a lot of them were destroyed outright. Even the survivors suffered horrid damage. Some crews did manage to reach the nearby stars, but they didn't dare turn and come home. Too hazardous. They built sloppy little colonies on the various worlds— all harsh and lifeless—and after a few generations the colonies were dead. Too few resources; too many demands. Visions of some interstellar empire were finished. Public opinion said that torchships were expensive devices for killing brave and talented people, and no more should be built. It was better to stay home and make improvements on the local property. Thus began the terraforming of Mars and Venus and the moons of Jupiter.

In those next centuries humanity filled the solar system, mastering the business of making dead worlds Earth-like. Artificial suns were built from durable fusion reactors; artificial atmospheres were encased inside monomolecular roofs. Eventually settlers moved into Sol's Oort cloud, then places beyond. The grit and snowballs that had destroyed torchships were rich in organic matter, and the sunless worlds were perfect homes for the persistent. By expanding steadily, in numbers and in space, humanity conquered huge volumes. And still does. The human Realm is a vibrant, almost perfect sphere nearly twenty light-years in radius. A trillion trillion citizens live on the terraformed worlds and comets and inside the robot-built enworlds; the cheated vacuum is a functional paradise, in effect, full of green places and warmth with no end imaginable.

In my own mind, now and again, I picture humanity as a living firestorm. From my home on Rye's World—on the brink of the frontier—I can look back toward Sol and picture the sky filled with creatures like me—coherent, creature-like flames, oxygen-fired and short-lived—and like a

firestorm we spread outward, never resting, striving to en-
gulf everything we can reach, and illuminate all the
rest. . . .

I have been "retired"—as Goottich put it—for nine years.
It's unusual for a person of my age, scarcely a century
old, but I do have resources. I can afford to be an ex-
terraformer. My family were among the first to emigrate
to Rye's World; we purchased substantial tracts of raw
land near the equator. It's some of the best ground, much
of it beside the new-made sea, and I've inherited a portion
of it. New immigrants are coming every day, fleeing the
crowded worlds deeper in the Realm. They gladly pay giant sums for tiny lots. If I wait another fifty or hundred
years—approaching honest old age—I can make many
fortunes. But if I sell maybe half of my holdings now, in
these next few days, I can easily dredge up the million and
one credits.

That's all I think about. I'm watching Goottich's background material, and I feel as if I'm in a daze. Words and
images wash over me, unabsorbed. Sometimes I feel
happy, almost to the point of tears; and other times I notice my hands shaking, even when they clasp hold of one
another.

Pitcairn is the strangest world known to humankind.
It is named for an ancient torchship. *Pitcairn* was the
last and largest torchship built by Earth, and it's the most
famous of the bunch. Named for the wealthy ocean-state
that financed the project, it was designed to make a one-
way journey to a distant G-class sun. Giant free fall mirrors had found a single Earth-class world orbiting that
sun. The world was green-blue and well watered, a tiny
ice cap stuck on its northern pole and an atmosphere
showing abundant oxygen. A small colony, self-contained
and determined, might thrive on a living world. That was
the logic. Domes and closed ecosystems wouldn't be required. People could work in the open and reproduce rap-
idly, and with a reasonable growth curve they would
create a stable, substantial population in no time.

The ancient *Pitcairn* was the finest of its kind. Its hull
was shrouded in hyperfiber armor; its forward-seeing sen-
sors watched for any cold grit. With just a little luck,

thought its proud owners, humanity could plant itself into a second nest. Wasn't that worth the risk?

But in midvoyage some cold chunk of debris slammed into the hull, breeching it. All communication with *Pitcairn* was lost, and its crew were assumed to be dead. Nobody on Earth realized that the torchship was mute, not destroyed. Nobody guessed that the survivors managed to reach the green-blue world and make landings, taking everything useful down with them. Since metals were scarce in the Pitcairn crust, they adapted with ceramics and tough plastics and the odd native woods. To breathe the thick atmosphere, they devised durable filters worn in the throat. And to keep their crops and livestock from being poisoned by the alien environment, they constructed greenhouses and sealed barns and tried their best to breed toughness into every creature brought from distant Earth. Including themselves.

Pitcairn is still the only world known with a complex and wide-scale biosphere. Giant multieyed telescopes have looked fifty light-years in every direction; but Earth-class bodies are among the rarest in nature. Too many bad things can happen to planets, apparently. Fickle suns and asteroid impacts can sterilize in a moment. It's not just torchships that face hazardous voyages.

Earth and Pitcairn. They are the two exceptions. And like Earth, Pitcairn has intelligent life. Abundant and important. And when the first settlers found them and realized what they were, they named them something eminently suitable:

Remarkables.

I send word of my acceptance to Goottich, plus a first installment, and I promise the rest of the credits once my lawyers manage the file work. The real estate market is proving a little weaker than I had imagined. Buyers are available but not hungry, and I've had to offer up more of my inheritance than I'd planned.

Is this really worth doing? I ask myself. Again, and again.

The richest nearby world, New Albemarne, built and launched the *Pitcairn II* when I was a boy. It was the first mission to that sun since the original *Pitcairn*, and I still remember the wave of excitement when everyone in the

Realm. I've always had boyish dreams of adventure, wondering about that strange green-blue world. *Pitcairn.* A lost colony existing in harmony with an intelligent alien species; the strangest place known to science, inside the Realm or out. The boy in me had vowed to go there someday. In my youth it had been my biggest dream, either asleep or awake, untold hours spent wondering: *If only I could, what? What?*

But should I let the boy inside me rule me now? There are reasons—good ones—not to risk any trip. Not to Pitcairn, not anywhere. I have taken time to list each reason, giving them values and comparing them with a second, more positive list.

That alien world does intrigue me. Its inhabitants have always intrigued me. Besides, I remind myself, my "illness" has been under control. At least most of the time. Several of my physicians, hearing about the trip, have even suggested that I'll be safe from the symptoms on Pitcairn. Alien nervous systems . . . I might not be sensitive to them. . . . The place could be a paradise for me, I tell myself, and not going there would be the crime . . . !

No, I will leave.

It's decided.

I have sent my acceptance to Goettich's home—a nondescript address in the local Oort cloud—and now I make ready. I book passage on a small shuttle; we are to meet on New Albemarle. I wonder who else Goettich considers his friends, what kind of group is being assembled . . . and I instruct my house to pack for me, just a minimum of possessions. (The Pitcairns themselves will supply everything once we arrive.) I find myself moving from room to room, sometimes pausing, sometimes giving more instructions as they occur to me. What should the house do should friends call? Or my family? And what about the lake? I decide to let my house oversee the weekly poisoning of the water; the lake is easily contaminated by windblown seeds and spores and whatnot. And the house should also keep the rocky ground plucked bare of weeds. Use the household robots, if necessary. "Particularly after any rains."

The house says, "Yes, sir," with its colorless voice.

"I don't know when I'll be back. Not exactly," I make the statement, then I'm very much aware of the silence. But what can my house say to me? Good luck? Have a pleasant trip? I programmed it not to make small talk, believing that otherwise I would grow attached to that hint of a personality. It is a circumspect machine, officious and pleasantly simple; and I assure it, "I might return any time."

"Yes, sir."

"Keep everything as it is."

"Yes, sir."

Then I look at the high thin sky, wispy clouds being driven by strong winds . . . and my eyes shut of their own volition, a faint distant pain making me straighten and shiver for a moment, just a moment, before I can breathe deeply again, feeling the familiar heat percolating out from my head. . . .

2

RANIER

"Perfection," says one old wisdom, "is the average."

Gene-tailors say that quite a bit. In other words, what works in nature is what is common. What is average. Things ordinary are as close to perfect as possible.

I am perfect in size and build. *Ranier Lu.* I have an average face and long, uninspired blond hair that seems perpetually unkempt, and inside me are a stew of youth-enhancing genes keeping my tissues and organs vigorous. Resilient. My most individual feature is my gaze—green eyes of an uncommon brightness, piercing according to some friends—and that's a familial trait. We bought the genes that cause these eyes several generations ago, on New Emerald, in an attempt to melt into the general popula-tion. Otherwise I'm mostly old-fashioned, a slightly ma-nipulated example of my successful species.

I'm riding the shuttle, making my way from Rye's World to New Albemarle. It's a short voyage and a little ship, empty but for me, and I spend my time restudying the background files, plus other historical texts. And I'm using the on-board exercise equipment, almost without break, working my muscles through resistance and electrochem-ical means.

Pitcairn is a massive world.

And I've spoiled myself on Rye's World, its half-standard gravity making my limbs thin and the bones weak. I need every minute of work that I can get now, then every wak-ing moment on board our torchship. And even then I'm not sure I'll be ready.

Goottich says this will be physically taxing. *A passion is*

a critical coming-of-age event for the aliens, the Remarkables, combining biology with religious overtones. People
accompanying the *passion* can't use airplanes or any other
mechanical tricks. They walk and carry their supplies on
their backs, and I knew this before now. I knew it, but I
never imagined myself involved in a *passion*. I find myself
preparing like an athlete readying himself for some ultimate contest. Training hard, I visualize mountains and
thick forests, muddy trails winding up harsh slopes and
barren vistas covered with rock and ice.

I train my body and my mind. Goottich has warned me.
"There's not much time. We have to reach Pitcairn and
our grove by early summer." At first I blamed Goottich
for this rush, but now, reading the files, I decide that the
Pitcairns and Remarkables are responsible. Either they
don't appreciate the transit times from the frontier, or they
have other agendas.

Pitcairns *and* Remarkables.

I continually remind myself: I can't think of one without the other. The human descendants and those bizarre
aliens . . . two species, intelligent but otherwise wholly
unalike . . . and I can't separate them in my mind. Odd
as it seems, they are one unit. A union. Symbiotic partners
in every real sense.

The symbiotic ideal is part of my training too. I have to
condition myself, making ready for the new reality. "I'm
to join a *passion*," I whisper again and again. My arms
jerk against machine-controlled pressure; legs thrust as
electrical impulses trigger exhausted muscles. "I'll become
part of the symbiosis," I say. "Soon," I say. "Partners with
aliens," and my legs thrust again.

Partners.

It is too strange a notion to accept with ease.

"I'll be a symbiont," I mutter to myself. "The smaller
partner in the grand partnership."

It doesn't sound very human, does it? To share your future with a different species? Particularly a species like the
Remarkables. . . .

. . . yet that's what lies at the heart of it.

A marriage, biological and profound, and like all mar-
riages there is that palpable hint of being everlasting. . . .

* * *

The first two missions to Pitcairn made holos. Everyone everywhere has seen images of the adult Remarkables. Adults are giants, rootbound and incapable of mobility. They rely on their symbionts to help feed and care for themselves. Their natural symbionts are pseudomammals, colorful and simpleminded. The first Pitcairns named them cretins. *Cretin* is an ancient word meaning stupidity, which is true enough. But cretins are also tough and fast organisms, genetically quite plastic and fitting into a variety of ecological niches. Moreover they are loyal to their home groves—a driving and obsessive loyalty—and throughout their lives they fish and hunt and work fearlessly to protect the towering Remarkables.

We don't know much about their mutual histories. The common guess is that cretins descended from smaller otterlike creatures. Millions of years ago, probably behind the tropical shorelines, the original Remarkables were tiny versions of today's. Less successful, much less intelligent. But the otters began to live inside the groves. They found shelter among the upturned tendrils, and maybe they were sloppy eaters. They brought home Pitcairn mussels and fat-rich fishes, and sometimes the Remarkables could snatch up scraps. That's how symbiotic partnerships often begin—a casual relationship, supportive but not essential—and it evolved to the present day.

Remarkables have unique nervous systems built from proteinaceous crystals, efficient and quick. Their ancestors would have been much the same, only simpler, and the best guesses place them on high rocks and cliff faces, mostly out of reach of their enemies. Like now they fed partly on sunlight with the help of purple bacteria flowing through them. And like now they lured pseudoinsects and pseudobirds into their grasp, tricking them with nectar baits and birdlike songs.

The otters and primitive Remarkables must have prospered. Their ties became more formal over the millennia; both species could afford to grow larger, their food supplies more and more dependable. Giant otters could range far offshore and inland. And larger Remarkables could pump more bulk and energy into their swelling minds.

It was a division along lines of talent.

A true symbiosis was formed after countless generations of helping one another, both species reaching a point

where they couldn't survive without the other. A cretinless
grove would starve, unable to lure ample prey by itself.
And by then their cretins were eating rich nectars for their
subsistence, their bodies unable to synthesize all sorts of
essential vitamins.

This was the world discovered by the Pitcairns. And of
that history too we are left with guesswork. Besides a few
vague stories, nothing remains of those early times. The
colony did thrive for several generations; that much seems
certain. But then came feuds, perhaps even a civil war,
and there might have been fights with the nearby groves.
The agricultural system collapsed. Earth-born species went
extinct—the cattle and wheat, and so on—and the native
species were inedible. Even toxic. There was a protracted
famine, hundreds dead and the colony itself crushed. The
few survivors had no choice. They fled to a nearby grove,
using crude nets to fish the reefs. They brought their catch
to shore and left it. As a gift; as a plea for help. The Remarkable nectars, unlike everything else, were edible; the
aliens learned how to mix the sugars and amino acids to
fit human guts. And in the end the grove took pity on the
tiny humans, accepting the fishes and giving nectars in
return.

For a long time the survivors lived nearby, growing in
numbers and building larger boats. The quality and quan-
tity of nectar improved with experience, and the people
became superior fishermen. Both sides grew increasingly
comfortable with one another; and eventually the Remarkables invited the people to come inside the grove itself. For the first time. They allowed them to live as cretins
lived, sheltered by the high tendrils and eternally watched
by the strange alien eyes.

A new symbiosis had begun.

And for two hundred centuries the Pitcairns have been
on the slow rebound. They live in only a fraction of the
total groves, but their numbers are substantial. They've
developed a culture of devotion to their home groves—
they seem as loyal as any cretin—and to them it is a perfect, natural arrangement.

While my ancestors were spreading across the galaxy,
filling empty cold worlds with themselves, a different kind
of people were marrying an alien biosphere, using crude
tools and their backs . . .

. . . and for my life I can't decide which is the greater accomplishment.

It's morning, ship-time, and I'm approaching New Albemarne while eating breakfast, feeling a nervous knot just behind my sternum.

New Albemarne is the largest moon circling the local Jupiter. It is blessed with an abundance of metals—always a plus in interstellar space—and it already has a billion residents. The globe seems perfectly green under the light of its false sun. I can just see part of its ocean, salt water kept at Earth-norms and choked with tailored seaweeds and other crops. Most of its cities are bunched near the equator, but eventually they'll reach more than halfway to the poles. That's the pattern repeated time after time on terraformed worlds. And between the cities I see the young forests and carefully managed farms with dark spots scattered here and there. Those spots are the New Albemarne mines—hyperfiber shafts reaching down into the mantle, sucking up ores along with the plastic rock—and sometimes I see flashes as giant ingots are launched by railguns, meant for the people who build enworlds and other wonders.

Every now and then I feel New Albemarne. Just a little. A sphere of cool pain, then it's gone.

I have appointments scheduled with several specialists. Maybe new tricks have been invented since my last visit, I tell myself. There's always room for hope. Then afterward I'll meet with Goottich and the others, helping with any final arrangements.

I keep wondering who else has joined Goottich. How many other friends does that overgrown child possess? My shuttle is tilting, starting its approach, pressing belly-first into the first high traces of the atmosphere. And again I feel the familiar dull poke of pain. Not my pain, no. It's the misery of the world under me. The green ground is sick with life, and I find myself lifting my hands in front of me. I obscure my view of New Albemarne, even though it does no good. I know it, but I can't stop myself.

Maybe an alien world won't touch me.

I keep telling myself, "It won't. Different physiologies, and it won't. It can't!"

Pitcairn.

Who deserves going there more than I?

* * *

I was a boy when *Pitcairn II* made its voyage, and I was a young man—a mildly gifted student, the truth told—when the torchship made its second voyage. The last one. I was attending the university in New Albemarne City, and I can remember friends and myself talking about the possibilities of an alien world.

"Imagine what a laboratory it would make!"

"Think how it might revolutionize terraforming!"

But when *Pitcairn II* returned, the second mission finished, it brought the disappointing news. There would be no more scientific explorations of Pitcairn. Its people and the Remarkables had made their decision. Each grove re-peated the same key phrases; it was obvious that they were communicating with one another. By radio, perhaps, and by direct contact. Pitcairns had studied their rights ac-cording to the old Pitcairn charter. They knew that they owned their solar system to the outer fringe of its Oort cloud. Every comet. Every bit of grit.

In the future, they decreed, only little groups would be allowed to come, sponsored by human-inhabited groves, and the terms of the visits were clearly outlined. Pitcairns would exchange glimpses of their scenery and lives for new genes, their own gene pools extraordinarily shallow. Oth-erwise the Realm's citizens should keep their distance, please. And trespassers would be prosecuted.

A few dozen groups have visited Pitcairn. And mean-while I grew up and became a modestly successful terra-former, yet dissatisfied, and I tried something wrong. Something that was stupid, in retrospect. That a cretin, in the word's original sense, might have tried.

Afterward I went into my retirement on Rye's World. My childhood home. And that's where I have remained since.

Visitors to Pitcairn have written books. Books are the only way to enjoy the place vicariously; holo cameras are never allowed anymore, nor any other fancy recording tricks.

I've enjoyed some of the books. In places.

Most of these tourists have done manual work on the big fishing boats, the bulk of their time spent at sea. Others have lived and worked in factories near the grove boundaries. No one has been inside the groves themselves, and of course that hurts each account. Every book hammers hard on the same points. That being Pitcairn is hard work and sometimes boring. That they're happy people on their own terms, and thoroughly odd, and their desire for privacy seems to be innate.

It is odd, I have thought. People travel so far and come away feeling dissatisfied. I hope that's not my fate too. But we'll be on a *passion*, I remind myself.

Only a very few tourists have been invited to tag along on *passions*; and according to Goottich's files, theirs were anemic little ventures. The groves were in the tropics, the climates mild and the routes well established. The worst hazards were blisters where feet wore against the stiff Pitcairn boots. But our *passion*—I think this with a swelling pride—is much more involved. Our grove is among the most isolated. People have lived there for only ten or so centuries, and the *passion's* holy ground—our eventual destination—is a long ways inland, set at the base of a great mountain named Au.

This will be an ultimate adventure, promise the files. Harsh country and wild rivers, I'm thinking. I try to imagine how it will look and feel, and taste, and how I will write my own book when I return. Perhaps it will be a best-seller. If so, I think, I can make back my inheritance . . . or maybe double it. If I have a story worth the telling, that is—

—and now my shuttle bucks ever so slightly, absorbing the impact of the thickening atmosphere before tilting and diving hard for the green ground.

3
NEW ALBEMARRE

❖

People don't change as much as places change. New Albemarre City looks nothing like I remember, but Goottich is the same. I see him standing on the balcony of his hotel suite, speaking to the other guests—a giant figure with that changeless face, boyish and comically round, and the giant hands dancing in front of him. No rings tonight, I notice. And no colored nails either. He pauses when he sees me, and he says, "Ranier," with his voice glancing excitement. "We started without you. I hope you don't mind."

"Sorry," I offer. "I was delayed."

"I'm sure," he says. A hand gesture, and he says to the others. "Introduce yourselves, I guess. This is Ranier Lu."

"Hello," says a pretty-faced man. "I'm Bedford Yultur Means, and this is my wife. Effie."

I give a quick nod and say, "How do you do?"

"Goottich says you're a gene-tailor," Bedford reports. "Am I right? And retired now?"

"Yes."

His wife is small and quite lean, saying nothing in an obvious way. Bedford is holding one of her hands as if to keep track of it for her, and she seems nervous, particularly in the large dark eyes. She blinks too much, and she doesn't quite look at anyone.

"Effie and I map comets." Bedford names his employer—one of the giant terraforming corporations—then adds, "I know Goottich through work. His family buys our surveys."

"Reasonable," I allow.

Then he grins and says, "We're also ministers in the Unity Church." And as if to prove his claim, Bedford draws a circle in the air.

"You're certified terraformers?" I ask.

"Everyone is," says Goottich. "In one way or another."

I didn't know.

Goottich grins, square teeth gleaming in the dim light.

"Everyone here," he says, "and everyone who turned me down. In fact, I was just commenting on that fact. Just before you came. The grove that's sponsoring us? It made that a precondition. I could only invite other terraformers, and naturally I thought of you. My friends."

Another woman makes a sound, quiet but disagreeing. She is buxom and strong. Her ancestors probably came from a high-gravity world. Maybe even from one of the little jupiters where airborne cities ride on the winds. More than anyone else, she seems suited for Pitcairn. At least physically. But like Bedford's wife, she doesn't seem to be enjoying herself. The strong face almost frowns, eyes squinting, gazing indifferently at the sky.

It's clear tonight, the sky washed by the city lights. Six of us are out on the balcony. The two women, Goottich, myself and Bedford, and another man. A quiet man, older and sitting away from the others.

I can see Rye's World, tiny and ruddy. The other major moons are out of sight. Taplan's World. Aoif. The jupiter itself is a black water almost directly overhead, a sphere of compressed darkness; its belts and tireless storms are invisible under starlight. Where's Pitcairn star? It would be appropriate to have it presiding, but I recall that it won't rise for a little while.

Bedford is telling the strong woman, "Introduce yourself, miss. If you'd like."

I make a mental note: Bedford is pushy.

"I'm Pachel," says the woman. "Pachel Joon."

"She's a native of Albemarine," says Bedford. "Aren't you?"

Pachel shrugs and says, "But I'm not really a terraformer," and gives me a grudging stare. "I work for the New Albemarine government. I'm an administrative consultant, a bureaucrat. . . ."

"But you've had the training," Goottich adds.

She halfway nods, telling me, "I help set public goals

and priorities. I have to anticipate the influx rates of immigrants, and my office tries to decide where they will best
fit. What regions have the most room and tolerance, that
sort of thing."

Rachel has a bureaucrat's clothes, professional edging
toward drab, but I notice something more. Something out
of character? Little twists of metallic silver speckle her
skin. It's an odd bit of tailoring, and flashy. Will Pitcairns
like this? I wonder. They're going to get some speckled
babies.

I remark, "This will be quite a change for you."

She says nothing, hands together and her mouth pressed
shut. Finally she tells me, "It's a great opportunity," with
her voice flat and colorless. "I'm thrilled."

Goottich, ignoring the voice, says, "I knew Rachel in
school. We were classmates at the university."

The woman gives a little nod, nothing more.

Bedford looks at me, the pretty face smiling. "Effie and
I are *fascinated* with Pitcairn. It's so different. Just its
presence . . . it's quite a challenge for us. For any Unity
believers."

Unity. It's a widespread religion, and old. It believes in
the perfection of Nature and the dominion of humanity
over Nature . . . and I don't say anything. I remember my
manners, simply nodding and offering a watery brief smile.
"Alien intelligences living in tandem with human beings." Bedford shivers and grins. "Of course when my good
friend Goottich made his offer, we jumped at it."

Effie is conspicuously quiet.

"What about yourself?" he asks. "Why are you here,
Ranier?"

I can tell them about my boyhood dream, something
everyone would understand . . . or I can mention my illness and my hope of hopes that alien lifeforms will provide
a cushion for me. A substantial buffer. But there's too
much seriousness here, and instead I say, "I'm hungry for
a nice long vacation," and I smile with intensity. "Deep
water, sandy beaches, and a chance to enjoy my retirement—"

"On Pitcairn?" snaps Effie. "That's silly!"

Bedford shakes his head. "I don't think there are any
beaches . . . at least where we're going, I mean . . ."

Then the older man says, "I think he's teasing us," and

chuckles. I nearly forgot he was here. I look at him, and he says, "My name is Lumiere. It's good to meet you."

Lumiere has the puffy, too-youthful face of someone who has suffered through too many free-radical scrubs. He explains that his specialty is building atmospheres on the raw, newly settled worlds. His voice is pleasant, slow and measured. Turning to the others, he says, "I'm sure Ranier knows just what's involved." Then he stands, approaching me and offering his hand. It feels cool and too dry. I keep wondering about his age. He says, "I'm glad you're here, sir." He smiles brightly. Serenely. His happiness seems to percolate into me, and I give a little laugh, relieved to find someone who recognizes my humor.

"Actually," he adds, "I'm the only one of you who didn't know our host. I met him today."

It's hard to think of Goottich as a host.

Goottich approaches, saying, "He heard about my plans, and he came to me this morning. Out of the proverbial blue." The man seems pleased with himself and everything. He looms over us, his back to the city, and he hasn't stopped grinning since I arrived.

The truth told, I really don't know Goottich. Maybe Bedford does. And Pachel. But for me he's just a face and a name. We've had those few halting conversations, probably about terraforming, and the details are completely lost to me.

What I do remember—and for no clear reason—is that moment when Goottich was on my home screen. That moment when he paused to drink, and I couldn't see the glass in his hand. Not to save my life.

That's bothering me now.

I don't know why, but somehow that image makes me nervous.

Goottich talks about everything—the torchship he has leased; the Mount Au grove of Remarkables; the juvenile Remarkables that we will accompany; and another brief introduction into *passions*. I scarcely listen, absorbing key phrases and filling in the gaps for myself. What interests me are the other people. I watch them, trying to measure them. Why are the women so indifferent? Am I going to be able to tolerate Bedford? What is Lumiere's reason for being here? He hasn't explained, has he? And of course there's Goottich, linchpin to everything. A giant fleshy linchpin. I wonder about his physical conditioning.

New Albemarine City stretches out below us. I lived here, eighty years ago, and since then it's quadrupled in size. This entire world no longer seems like part of the frontier. The terraformer in me knows the signs. Mature trees break up the sharp edges of apartment buildings, and the buildings themselves show different designs. Different fashions of architecture. Different generations standing side by side.

Most frontier worlds, like Rye's, have empty stretches of ground, no soils and no established waterways.

But here everything feels established. I can just make out the shimmering ribbon of the Albe River. It winds through the center of the city, and it appears old and stately, helping the illusion of a naturally Earth-like planet. That river might be millions of years old, not hundreds. I presume that the species diversity on New Albemarine is nearing its limits. Only so many species fit into a finite environment; the factors are mathematical and rigorous. And typically after the limits are reached—after a few centuries of saturation—the human populations keep expanding, pushing aside others. The oldest terraformed worlds are quite simple places. As is Earth. Terraformers with a dark humor like to joke: "We work to make the universe safe for apartment buildings." It's a joke I've told myself. Many, many times.

Goottich is talking about the juvenile aliens now. Only the oldest and largest juveniles travel on a *passion*. We will help care for them. They will bask in the sun and try to commune with their god, the All-Answer—

"A lovely name," Bedford offers, his voice rather patronizing.

His wife says, "Shush," and tugs at his hand.

"*Passions* are more biological than theological," Goottich speaks with sourceless authority. "We'll be near the northern border of the Remarkables' range. It's a wet and rather marginal climate for them. They have to send their juveniles on long *passions* in the summer. The interior is dry then. Even hot. Everything I read convinces me that there are biological triggers involved. The juveniles bask in order to initiate their maturing process . . . and the All-Answer is just cultural noise."

Biological triggers? I wonder what would initiate adulthood in Goottich, and I laugh to myself.

He sees my smile and smiles back at me. He probably thinks that I'm agreeing with his perceptive diagnosis.

Effie coughs.

Goottich turns toward her, and she blurts, "You must be hugely wealthy." Her skin is dark, her eyes big and doll-like, and the voice is quite tense. Too quick and sounding practiced.

Bedford stirs, saying, "Dear . . . ?"

"You actually own enworlds," she persists. "Don't you?"

"Thousands!" The big man is happy to boast. "My family and I . . . well, tens of thousands of them, yes! Stretching from here back to New Emerald. All varieties, all sizes."

Enworlds are enclosed artificial worlds—cylinders and wheels and zero-gee spheres—built from the available materials. Typically hyperfiber braces ceramics and metals, and people live inside them. An enworld can be parklike for the wealthy tenants, or it's packed with bodies. There are countless billions of them scattered back toward Earth, each worth a small city; and Goottich's family owns a lucrative sliver of those billions. He's wealthy enough that I doubt if he knows how much he is worth.

"Rainer? Did I mention?" Goottich waits for my gaze. "I'm now in charge of terraforming in my family's new enworlds. Since we last met face-to-face, I was promoted."

"Congratulations."

Rachel makes a harsh little noise, and I'm not sure anyone else hears her. Her face hints at anger, or maybe it's mistrust. Or maybe nothing. My strongest impression is that she wants to be elsewhere, anywhere, and why would you pay money if you're going to leave your heart at home?

"I was wondering," says Effie. "Since you are so blessed, moneywise—"

"Effie," warns her husband.

"—you might want to reconsider—!"

"Dear?!" Bedford tells her, "We've talked this though, I thought. We decided—"

"Forget it," she snaps. "Never mind! I'm sorry . . ."

There's an uncomfortable silence. Goottich looks at everyone, and I can't read his expression. He seems quite pleased, but at first I don't know why. That he has money? That he's been promoted? Then I realize that it's something else. It's the sense of power. Sure. He can cause people to spend their savings, and he enjoys that sense of control. He reminds me of a little boy with trapped flies. We will do what he wants, and that's supremely satisfying for him.

Lumiere breaks the silence.

Rising to his feet, he approaches me and says, "Look over there." He points at a cloud, water rich and low to the horizon, and rising above it is the bright yellow-white star nearest New Albemarine. It is Pitcairn's sun, and I say: "Sobering, isn't it? We'll be there soon."

Pachel gives a sly smile, then jokes, "Unless we collide with a comet or something."

"Don't say that!" Effie moans.

I laugh at the bleak humor, and so does Lumiere.

Then again everyone is silent, but in a different way. It's a happier flavor of silence, more comfortable and long lasting.

Our little meeting finishes now. Goottich has outlined our schedule for the next days, and he gives us our room numbers in this hotel—at his expense, he mentions—and he suggests that we exercise as much as time allows. Each room has equipment. Our torchship will be likewise equipped, but most of the journey will be spent in cold-sleep. We're going to cross light-weeks of half-charted space, the torchship never moving more than a fraction of its top speed. Impacts won't be an issue; he repeats this promise several times. Then he makes a show of smacking his own belly, boasting, "I'm in the shape of my life. I've been preparing for this for years."

I'm feeling wonderful. As the evening draws to a close, I can't remember when I last felt this good. I'm standing by the railing, looking down at the moving skimmers and the tiny shapes of people walking, and sometimes I smell flowers and the scented insects that fly at night, and sometimes I catch a whiff of perfumes rising from warm bodies. I breathe deeply through my nose and hold my breath, and I grip the railing with both hands, cherishing the moment.

I was visiting specialists today.

I don't believe in their medicines. These last years have proved to me that physicians know little, that what they call medicine is oftentimes just magic swirled with sweet hope. But today one of them tried something new, and the effect was immediate and profound. Promising, I felt, and still holding intact.

Plus there's the prospect of this trip. That's also helping my mood, I'm sure.

But mostly it's how ordinary I feel, my illness in remission. New Albemarine is just a green world, and I might be anyone. Life everywhere, intense and conflicting and oftentimes in misery—

—and I'm immune to that misery.

Lumiere comes up beside me, waits a moment, then says, "This is really happening, isn't it?"

I turn to the old man. "Yes, it is. Hard to believe, but it's real."

And if anything he seems happier than I. Grinning, he stares at the nearby sun, the puffy face tired and the tired red eyes damp, the chapped lips trembling and his breath old and sour. I smell his breath for a moment, then I turn and smell the city again.

✦

The Old Ones speak in sound and scent and in motion, swirling and swirling to make a portion of their words, and they must be speaking underground too. Through their soil, through their roots. Which makes it harder to understand the story. Which makes us angry because we are part of the story, we are set at its center, but of course the Old Ones insist on telling it fast and by every means. It is a tale meant for adults, and juveniles like us must work just to absorb a tiny, tiny sliver of the whole. It is a huge and incredible story. I know from watching the nearby adults. They listen and watch and absorb, and they keep silent and still. The entire grove is transfixed, but I feel nothing except stupid. And it is worse because some youngster beside me whines, "I don't understand any of this, Talker! What kind of story is this, Talker?"

It speaks with sound and with motion.

Just with motion, I say, "Quiet." My inner tendrils jerk and point, warning the child not to test me. But it says, "I know about stories of the Past and stories about the Now—"

"Quiet," I repeat.

"—but what sort of story is this? Of things not yet? Of the Future? Only the All-Answer sees such things!"

The stupid child is incapable of silence. I ignore it and concentrate on the Old Ones above me. Concentration is one of my great talents. I have many talents, but this is the rarest. Adults tell me so. I am the only juvenile in their shared memory who has learned to speak the human tongue so well. I have trained my mouth to push out the syrupy words, achingly slow and simple, and of course my siblings are jealous of me. I enjoy their jealousy. "You are wasting your talents, Talker," they say. They tease by saying, "Talents without common sense," and then they laugh. But in times like this, in the midst of things they cannot comprehend, they seek me out and pester me. They believe I have answers, even when I have none. Even like now, when I am lost too.

The Old Ones sing, louder and now louder still, and the air itself is more story than breath. More of the Future than of the Now.

Their story has fractured into many lines. Plots interweave until I cannot keep track of any one of them. Humans weave dense blankets from fibers. This story is like a human blanket. I am part of those fibers, and so is every juvenile. We are tied together and lost inside the Future, and nothing makes sense. I have missed something, I think. Something essential. The Future looms before me, solid and alive and infinitely strange, and the Old Ones talk without pause, using every kind of voice.

That stupid child pushes up next to me, clinging with its inner tendrils. "But what what what are they telling, Talker? Have the Old Ones gone insane?"

Sometimes I do wonder.

But I say, "No!" with motion and sound. I say, "They have reasons, always, now *quiet*!"

"But you are in the story, Talker! It is more about you than anyone, Talker!"

I say nothing.

"And these humans too. Who are these strange humans, Talker?"

I cannot concentrate. I who have taught my young mouth to speak human words. I who think swiftly and clearly, better than any of my siblings. I feel lost. I feel quite foolish. Am I really so important to this insane story?

"And why why why why why are there so many futures, Talker? Why why why why why?"

"Because the Old Ones cannot know what will happen," I assure. "Only the All-Answer sees what is to come!"

"The All-Answer," echoes the child.

"Yes, the All-Answer. Who knows how you will die and I will die, and when. Who sees perfectly and eternally—"

And suddenly the Old Ones are silent. A screaming quiet

fills the grove, and I am scared. I shrink with my fear, as does every juvenile. We shrivel and wave our stinging tendrils at nothing, and after an instant the Old Ones speak in one great booming voice. They say, "Listen to us and not yourselves, little ones." Their words are simple and slow. "This is a great story, and true, and it belongs to you. Particularly those of you meant for this summer's *passion*."

I know this. I was paying attention!

But then the Old Ones say, "You were not listening either, Talker. Were you listening—?"

"Yes, yes!"

"Quiet!" they scream, using sound and their swirling tendrils.

And I shut my mouth, obeying them.

And they say, "We will begin again, and listen. Listen. How does it begin, Talker?"

"Humans," I say. "Coming from the green heart of the sky."

"Guests of the grove, yes," say the Old Ones. "Six of them, and this is what we know of them."

I concentrate.

"And this is how they begin the story."

Humans. The Future is full of them, I think. Even more than the Now, I think. Incredible as that seems . . .

4
THE SPIT

❖

Bedford prays, drawing furious little Unity circles in the air, and sometimes Effie helps him with a few of her own. Pachel prefers a different course, cursing the weather. How much longer are we going to be stuck inside these fucking clouds? She hates this shit, being blind. Feeling trapped. And then we're in the open, just an instant later, and the green-black water is beneath us and the mountains are straight ahead.

I'm sitting between Pachel and Goottich, energy belts lashing me to my seat. My hands are wrestling in my lap. My mouth comes open of its own volition, saying nothing. I feel cold. The mountains are sudden and steep, covered with spongy green rainforests; wave after muscular wave collapses against the rocky coastline. Suddenly the wind gusts, twisting the shuttle sideways and making its engines whine. I half breathe and shut my mouth to hold my heart inside me. Then the rain thickens, and it's as if we're flying inside some opaque gray-black oil. And I'm thinking, when I can think, how fear isn't the worst part of being afraid. What I hate more is not knowing how I might act or what I might say. Being terrified is like having a stranger inside my skin, and I despise it. It stinks and I want it over. Now.

Pachel moans and grabs my wrist, squeezing hard.

Then we pass out of the rain and see the steep mountains beside us, almost close, and through the transparent hull I can make out the juicy inflated leaves and dark limbs interwoven into a canopy. The shuttle maneuvers to the right, following the slope. On our left is the deep and long greenish bay with the telltale spit reaching halfway across the bay's mouth. Beyond the spit are smoother mountains of a different color. A deep bruise color, dark and purple, and I keep staring at it. I don't even want to blink.

Remarkables, I'm thinking. *That's the grove, right there . . . !*

Pachel jerks my arm, her strength enlarged with adrenaline. "See? On the spit? Isn't that the fort . . . where we're starting from . . . ?"

I nod and manage a soft, "Yes." Then I have an idea. I lift my free arm and smile, waving at the distant grove. At the aliens.

Effie notices and asks, "Can they see us? Really?"

"Absolutely!" Goottich assures us.

Lumiere says, "Amazing. . . ."

I continue waving. "Hello," I say without sound. Smiling at the purple grove, I say, "Hello, hello. Hello, Remarkables. Hello."

One of the giant freezer ships is docked and being unloaded. Our shuttle is making its turn for our approach, and we pass the ship and the pier and the tiny blurred figures scattered everywhere, unloading bundles of fishes and chunks of butchered air-breathers, everything thrown onto wide motorized belts. This is the lifeblood of the grove. Belts carry the frozen meats to the land, up into special thick-walled buildings. The buildings are sealed, I remember, and flooded with microwaves, then back doors are opened and the defrosted meats are loaded onto smaller belts that radiate into the grove. One belt runs parallel to the high-tide mark. I can make out the biggest fishes, their colors washed out and the sightless eyes dull, and sometimes a Remarkable reaches down with a tendril and claims a meal for itself, or maybe for a neighbor unable to reach.

We fly beside the grove. A blotchy mantalike fish is lifted high, vanishing into the tangled canopy, and I wonder how it is to live like them. They're rooted into one place, standing beside the same neighbors century after century. I wonder how it shapes Remarkable psychology . . . if that's the proper term. Cooperation must be mandatory. Privacy is impossible. Remarkables can't steal or horde. They lack the opportunity. And how do they perceive creatures with lesser morals? I swallow with a dry throat, considering the possibilities.

Adult Remarkables resemble trees at first glance; every account says so. Their trunks are dark purple edging into blackness near the base, and their long muscular tendrils are bright, seemingly lit from within. Some tendrils carry stingers toxic to local foes. Most are used to grab food from the air and the motorized belts. I think of willow limbs, watching tendrils swirling back and forth. Then suddenly they don't look like trees anymore. A switch is tripped in my brain, and I'm thinking of squids. Strange-shaped titanic squids have been pulled up from the sea and shoved tail-down into the thick black soil. The tendrils join at a mouth filled with razor teeth—just like with squids—and they move like animals move. There is a power and energy to them. And there are the eyes too. The famous, famous eyes. Each adult has several dozen of them, each one a meter or two or three in diameter. Black as a raw comet. Perfectly round and lidless. And it seems as if they are staring at me. All of the sudden. Countless thousands of them . . . I can feel their stares. . . .

I swallow again and press against the energy belts, too excited to sit still. This isn't any terraformed world, and what my intellect knows is being realized by my emotions. At last.

We move away from shore now, dropping all the time, and I glance back over my shoulder to see more. The canopy parts for a moment. I find the sharp-cornered suggestion of a building. A house? Some Pitcairn lives between those thick purple-black trunks. What did the background files say? The Mount Au grove has eighteen thousand Pitcairns, plus more than one hundred thousand Remarkables. This is the northern part of their range, but the seas are among the richest anywhere. Plenty of upwellings. An abundance of nutrients.

A little boat chugs across the bay, shouldering aside the waves, and I notice how the waves aren't as rough behind the long spit. The sea winds and currents are blunted. We pass over the boat, not moving fast anymore. A flock of pseudobirds is straight ahead—gull-like and white with long narrow wings—and we close on them. The bay lifts, and the autopilot keeps us on course. We slam into the gulls. They crumble and spin back overhead with a thin sudden rain of blood and feathers. There is no sound, no sense of impact. Then Lumiere says, "Too bad," with a quiet, respectful voice.

"Time for their peace," Bedford offers. It's the standard Unity prayer for the dead.

And I feel nothing. Instinctively I brace for the cold sensation of others' pain, and there is none. Either every last gull died immediately, or for some reason I can't feel them.

I hope they're in agony, the truth told.

I turn and look back at the bloodied flock, then the Remarkables. A purple shroud covers the mountainsides, rising and rising until lost among the quick-moving gray-black clouds—

—and we hit the water, jerking hard and the syrupy green waves rising on all sides and then collapsing. For an instant we're submerged, the shuttle expending its momentum and then finding its buoyancy; and we bob to the surface and hold steady, seawater flowing from the hull, making the outside world blur and waver.

Pitcairns are strange, strange people.

Every account written and every one of the old holos makes the same ringing point. Remarkables are aliens; their peculiarities are justified. But the humans among them seem worse, being human. They have faces and human voices and genes born from a common origin, and they insist on not being like us. It seems like a point of pride.

Pitcairns are independent and stone-faced and oftentimes cold to outsiders. They've never shown interest in the Realm or any history but their own. They've acquired no technologies from us. When told that they were worth billions of credits—the approximate early value of their solar system, not including Pitcairn itself—they merely shrugged their shoulders and turned away. Not one thought to ask, "What's a credit?" It just didn't occur to them.

They live to serve their grove. That means Remarkables and their fellow Pitcairns. Some researchers, playing with the data brought home to date, have decided that part of Pitcairn behavior is explained by culture. Remarkables have replaced cretins with people, and they have fostered

a culture that embodies cretinlike devotion. On the other
hand, however, Pitcairn genetics are crazily narrowed.
Each grove's people came from a tiny initial population,
and those populations rarely mix. Any two residents of a
grove are closely related. Brothers and sisters share fewer
genes than they do. In earthly lifeforms this kind of relatedness is found only in social insects, bees and ants and
such. And since working for the common good will benefit
your genes, just as it does the genes in a hive or nest . . .
well, it's a strong selection force. Altruism becomes the
norm. Pitcairns are hard-wired to labor and sacrifice for
the grove's successes, and the Realm and credits and other
worldly affairs make no difference to them.

The little Pitcairn boat pushes against our shuttle, wood
moaning on hyperfiber, and we file out into the rain. We
wear useless rainshields. There's too much moisture or the
atmosphere is too thick, distorting the force fields, and
everyone is soaked in an instant. I've never known such
rain, thick and cold and driving into my flesh. I bend under it, breathing in gasps and moaning aloud.

A figure waves at us: my first Pitcairn, I think. Goottich
jumps across. The Pitcairn is wearing a green plastic poncho sprinkled with patches, heavy dark galoshes set apart.
Goottich is down, and a brown hand now waves at me. My
timing is lousy. I jump as the boat drops into a trough,
and the strong gravity slams me onto the slickened deck.
I slip and nearly fall, and the man grabs me and jerks me
upright. A narrow weathered face gives me a quick scan.
Then he says, "Back," in Pitcairn, shoving me aside.

Dozens of cages are stacked on the deck and lashed in
place. I'm standing beside them while Pachel jumps, then
Lumiere, and then a wiry strand of something caresses my
face. I wheel around and find a head-high cage filled with
crabs and trilobites. Their antennae reach between the
cream-colored plastic bars, armored bodies scuttling about
on jointed legs, and I smell them. It's a fishy stink, and it
isn't. It smells like nothing I know, but my mind calls it
"fishy," because that's what it anticipates.

Everyone is across, and somehow the rain worsens. I
hear the boat's engines working as we back away from the
shuttle, and the thick air blows with force. I bend at the

knees. I breathe too deeply and cough hard, and suddenly I realize that I've been shivering for a while.

The Pitcairn man leads us along the deck, not speaking.

I notice coiled ropes and sometimes knots in the ropes, and I stop to study one complicated knot. Pitcairns don't have static seals or other tricks. They actually tie things to other things, and that seems infinitely exotic. Wondrous.

The wind ebbs. For a moment, no longer, I hear a strange bright convoluted roar against my face. I'm following the others, keeping low and groping for handholds, and I realize that I'm hearing the grove itself. The Remarkables are singing. Speaking. Whatever it is. I cock my head to listen, and marvel, then a new gust hits and obscures everything, the raindrops driven into my pores and my blood. Wouldn't it be ironic? After so much preparation and money, the travel and the sleepless anticipation . . . wouldn't it be ironic if I was swept overboard and drowned?

So much and then nothing.

I hunker down and drive with my shivering legs.

Remarkables might be geniuses. No one knows. Not even the Pitcairns, if their pronouncements can be believed.

Scientists on the early missions managed to make sonic probes of the adults, mapping organs and counting neurons. The best computers in the Realm have roughly the same memory as the largest Remarkables, and that's caused some experts to claim they're enormous data sinks coupled with some limited powers of reason. Organic computers, in other words. The aliens have no sense of planning, no real concept of self. That's become the general consensus throughout the Realm. I have heard every opinion—I've held all of them myself, one time or another—but most people want them to be alien in a manageable way. Benign and imaginable.

Pitcairns don't seem to bother with questions about intelligence.

What matters is the symbiosis, the linkage of both species, and they claim that it's foolish to try deciphering a Remarkable's mind.

"Help them and help yourself."

That's the Pitcairn ideal.

The human duty is to feed them and protect them;

there's almost no communication between the parties. That last part is what surprises me. Yet it shouldn't. The Pitcairns know their tasks, and the Remarkables rarely find reason to comment or micromanage. Neither species worships the other. Their relationship is durable and unsophisticated. In some ways it's similar to another symbiosis—between us and our mitochondria. Mitochondria are tiny organelles inside almost every cell, descendants of ancient bacteria. They have their own genetics. They run our oxygen metabolism. And our billion-year-old relationship is so obvious and so essential that worship would be useless. Worship implies thanks, and why bow your head to thank your mitochondria?

And Pitcairns, without doubt, are pragmatic people. Every account makes that claim. They avoid pointless noise, and likewise they don't waste time contemplating the minds of Remarkables. There would be no purpose in it. They've lived with them long enough to learn that potent lesson.

"Contemplate them," they say, "and lose your sanity."

They would know.

We introduce ourselves while standing on the boat's bridge. Wrapped in scratchy blankets, we say our names and give brief sketches of ourselves: our homes, our professional colors. The Pitcairn man seems to listen, sometimes nodding, perhaps making mental notes to himself.

Goottich sent them files about us before we left New Albemarne, I recall. Introductions might be so much wasted breath, and maybe the Pitcairn's being patient with us. Maybe?

A girl is piloting the boat, taking us toward the spit.

When we're done speaking the man says, "I'm Service," and the pilot says, "Snow," an instant later. It's odd to speak and hear Pitcairn. We learned the language after coming out of cold-sleep, electrohypnosis capable of wonders. Yet speech feels contrived somehow. It's like some false language composed of random syllables mixed with archaic words, sharp-edged and clumsy.

I watch Service. He seems quite old, worn in the face and his uneven teeth stained from a diet of nectars. Even Lumiere feels young compared to him. Which is an illusion, I remind myself. Pitcairns—at least these, I think—

don't have youth-enhancing genes sewn into their chromosomes. Service is raw biology gazing out at us. He's probably not even sixty years old. A young man by my count. Yet he looks weathered and faltering, glands drying up and his blood feeling its decline.

Bedford is talking now. "Isn't this a beautiful, beautiful place?" he asks Effie. Then everyone. "Even with the rain . . . isn't it splendid?"

"I'm sick of this rain," Pachel responds. She shakes her head solemnly. "It's depressing as hell . . . !"

Service watches her, his expression unreadable.

Then Lumiere says, "We'll be dry when we get inland. Isn't that right? Sir?"

Service nods and says nothing.

I turn and look through the glass windshield, nothing visible but the wind-smeared waves. How does the girl—Snow—navigate? I step forward, noticing a liquid-filled compass glued to the dash. I watch her hand on the steering wheel, the straw-colored wood worn smooth, and I watch the other hand lying on the throttle. Then I look at Snow's face. She can't be older than twenty standard years, meaning less than fifteen by her calendar count. She is pretty in the face, resembling Service. But then again she and he probably share a good portion of their genes. I look ahead and she glances up at me. Or does she? I grip my blanket with one hand, the dash with the other, and the boat slams into a wave, spray flying over the cages and onto the bridge, the windshields rattling in their frames.

I say, "Quite a storm."

She says:

"This?"

I look at her again. She's wearing a thick sweater under a workshirt, and the sweater's collar only partly covers her neck. A strong pale horizontal scar lies on her throat. That's where her filter is implanted. Every Pitcairn has an operation at birth, the trachea opened and the homemade filter installed. Otherwise this air is too thick to be breathed: There's too much carbon dioxide. It's the same for us, but our filters are thin membranes painted directly on our lungs. Elegant and durable. Pitcairn filters fail every few years. Snow and Service have to suffer the knife repeatedly, and that's a chilling prospect to me.

Snow smiles, drawing my eyes to hers. Then she care-

fully says, "Look," and points forward. The gray of the
rain has thinned, and I see the different gray of the spit.
Sand and rock lie straight ahead, and buildings and floating piers and motion. My companions are talking among
themselves, wholly unaware. I squint and say nothing.
Those motions acquire color and form, resembling enormous balls of purple fluff. They roll back and forth on the
sandy ground, ignoring the wind. Hundreds of them, I
guess. And I say nothing.

They're juvenile Remarkables.

I take a breath and hold it, excited to the point of shaking. Then I turn—I make myself turn—and I tell Goottich
and the others, "We're almost there. Almost to the spit.
And we've got a greeting party down waiting for us . . .
in this weather . . . look . . . !"

5
EXPECTATIONS

We dock and Service pulls ponchos out from under a seat, handing them to us. Goottich looks ridiculous in his poncho. The hood is skintight to his head and it doesn't reach his knees. But he doesn't seem to notice, always smiling. He's the first onto the pier, the big hands pointing and the voice shouting for us to look at them. The Remarkables; the juveniles. "They look like—" he begins to say; and I watch the mouthing of the word—"tumbleweeds!" as a crack of thunder makes the air shiver and people bend at the knees.

Our shuttle, airborne and climbing, roars over the spit an instant later. It seems enormous, covering half of the sky, yet Service scarcely gives it a glance. Then it's up in the clouds and the engines diminish into a low hum, then into rain sounds; and I think all of us feel uneasy in some way. Marooned, I suppose. Even Goottich pauses, face up into the rain; and it's Service who breaks the spell, saying:

"Go on. Move. Did you come all this way to stand?"

The tide is out. The floating pier is connected to the shoreline with an articulating wooden ramp, rain slickened and steep. I keep one hand on the rope railing and use the steps cut into the planks. Pitcairn's gravity finds me halfway up and starts to pull. My thighs are sore and warm, and despite the chill I'm sweating, salt mixing with rain and making my eyes sting.

The Remarkables are on the slope above me. A decade ago, in an earlier lifestage, they were squidlike predators hunting on the open sea. They do resemble tumbleweeds from a distance. Up close they seem very purple, and I think of sea urchins, what with their roundness. I reach the top of the ramp, and some of them are bunched on the sand nearby, black eyes staring at me. At us. And I don't think of sea urchins anymore. I think of children. Little boys and little girls. Children keep at a distance in the same way, curious but cautious. They're very, very curious. "Look at them!"

Goottich is panting, and Pachel asks him, "Are you dying?"

"I'm fine," he moans. "Fine, fine . . ."

Bedford arrives, the pretty face smiling.

His wife comes after him, looks around, and says, "There are an awful lot of them, aren't there?"

"What a perfect sight!" he declares.

"You're going to fall apart on the trails," Pachel tells Goottich. "I thought you said you were in condition—"

"The best of my life," Goottich mutters. He tries to slow his breathing. "I've been training a lot longer than you, Pachel. I'm just excited. Off my stride."

Lumiere is the last one of us. I expect him to be worn out, and I'm worried; but he seems strong and happy. Excitement has a rejuvenating effect on him, it seems.

"They're so big!" says Effie.

The largest juveniles are as large as good-sized rooms, yet most of their volume is air. Their size is an illusion. Specialized tendrils form a stiff rounded cage inside which are their stinging tendrils and grasping tendrils, the precious organs and eyes and mouth. They roll on the rain-soaked sands, and I watch how their eyes roll without ever looking away from us. Like adult Remarkables, they possess fantastic vision. The lidless eyes seem to be built on different principles from our eyes, absorbing every photon and sorting the data through guessed-at mechanisms. They perceive their entire surroundings where we can focus on just a tiny patch, and everything to them appears close and clear.

They're lovely, rolling here and there with a strange light and graceful purpose. They're like children ready to bolt with the first warning. I notice the complicated tracks they leave in the sand, and I notice them talking among themselves. They seem to whisper, then they sing. Then Service says, "This way," with impatience, and we follow him. We form a ragged line, and the Remarkables make

two lines flanking us. Where's Snow? She was working on
our boat when we left, and I turn, thinking that maybe
she'll step off the ramp now. Probably not even winded.

"Did you hear that?" asks Lumiere.

"Hear what?" I say.

"One of them just said 'hello' to us." He nods with conviction, then adds, "In our language, it did."

"Which one?"

"I don't know."

"I didn't hear it," says Bedford. "I wish I had. . . ."

"This is the shittiest weather," says Pachel. "I really hate
it."

"Maybe I didn't hear anything," Lumiere offers.

Goottich stops and turns, telling us, "Juveniles can't
speak human tongues. They understand us, but they don't
have enough control over their mouths."

And Service, like some impatient father, turns and asks,
"Did you come here to chatter?" The word "chatter" feels
like an insult. "We have a schedule," he warns, walking
backward while glaring at us. "A schedule, and I expect
you to at least try keeping up with it."

And like children caught in the midst of wrong, we shut
our mouths and find ourselves walking faster, a blush of
blood under everyone's face.

A party was given on the eve of our embarking. New
Albemarne's government meant to honor us and parade
their most important souls in front of us, shaking our fortunate hands and wishing us well.

I remember one tall pale woman with an agenda.

"You know," she said, "we're so much more successful
than they. Don't you think so?"

"Than who?"

"The aliens, of course." She was a serious person, and
humorless. She seemed the picture of confidence, sipping
her colored liquor and assuring me, "It's obvious. Just look
at this grove you're visiting. It's the only one in the region
with people. With Pitcairns. No cretins—"

"There are a few cretins," I countered. "Small ones.
Doglike, according to what I've read."

"What I mean," she persisted, "is that this grove you'll
visit . . . it's the largest in the region. People have made
it that way. . . ."

The woman swayed from side to side, obviously drunk.

After a moment and in some confusion, she asked me, "What was I saying?"

"We're successful."

"The Mount Au grove . . . yes!" She sipped her drink, then told me, "The largest groves always have Pitcairns."

"So I've heard."

"But no more than a fraction have made the change. Most of these aliens . . . they prefer their cretins. Do you know why?"

"Tell me."

"They are stupid." She nodded with great satisfaction, then said, "I myself don't think they're special . . . just big cabbages with voices, that's all . . . !"

"I've heard that opinion, yes."

"Stupid, stupid, stupid. They're mimics and computers and dumb." She gestured with her glass, slopping liquor onto the floor. "How else can you explain everything? Tell me that."

"They're smarter than us."

She gazed at me, her face confused.

"Smarter," I said, "and how can we know their motives? Their reasons? Any of it?"

She breathed through her thin nose, then told me, "I don't believe you. I won't!"

"We don't even understand their psychology," I continued. "Their circumstances are so different from ours . . . well, it's really impossible to make any conclusions. That's what I think."

She glanced down at the floor, watching a tiny robot cleaning up her spill. Then with great caution she said, "This is interesting . . . us talking like this." She paused, then said, "If you want to talk some more, maybe hear my other ideas . . . come with me. Now." She blinked and squinted at me. "Which one are you? Ranier?" She said, "Come away with me, Ranier. For a little while. Please?"

Dinner waits inside a large wooden building. Dishes and big bowls are set on a long stout table, steam rising and a Pitcairn woman overseeing the proceedings. Half a dozen smaller houses stand around us; we saw them as we approached. Farther south, on the tip of the spit, stands the low gray fort. Stone slabs and concrete rise against the weather. It's the oldest structure on the bay, I recall. That fort, built long ago by Service's ancestors, is older than anything on Rye's World or New Albemarne. It is the most ancient structure that I've ever seen.

We pick and choose from a variety of nectars. There are different flavors and consistencies. Some are liquid, bubbling inside bone-white ceramic bowls; others are solid, resembling candies and soaps. None of us act tentative. We know about nectars, after all. The *Pitcairn II* brought home samples, and they were analyzed and replicated en masse. A few people became wealthy with the fad. These nectars are much the same—excepting their origin, of course—and that origin makes them all the more exotic. Nectar glands secreted these treasures into elaborate systems of tubes and glass buckets, the energies of inedible fishes and trilobites transformed into delicious molecules that we'll digest with joyful ease.

The six of us stay close to one another. We sit at one end of a long second table, Service eating at the opposite end. Between bites I study the building itself—the heavy timbers; the high ceiling; the tall simple glass windows on the bay's side—and I remember that this must be a common house. It's a place for meetings and meals, a standard fixture in any Pitcairn community. The woods are golden and glossy. The furnishings and general feel of the place are ascetic. Nothing is functionless. Every feature has some job. There are two tables but benches along only one of them, and set in one corner, in plain view, are a matching pair of toilets.

They have no sense of privacy, Pitcairns don't. Strange, strange people. Different from everyone in the Realm.

I watch Service while I chew on a pinkish slice of hard nectar, thinking how it tastes like steak and then fish and then nothing I know. Service glances at a timepiece strapped to his wrist, and an instant later the single door swings open, almost a dozen Pitcairns filing inside. They pull off their ponchos and hang them on high pegs to dry, and each of them glances at us without speaking or even nodding. We have traveled light-weeks, I think, and at no insignificant risk to ourselves. We represent the Realm— vast and powerful—yet the Pitcairns seem more interested in eating, filling their plates and bowls and not even speaking to one another.

Snow is with them. I watch her walking; and Pachel, sitting next to me, asks, "Can they see us now?"

She is gesturing at the windows.

I look into the rain, knowing who she means. The bay is rising fast with the incoming tide, and the dim sunlight grows dimmer. This kind of twilight will last for hours. We're in the near-Arctic, and this is summertime. Through the rain and gloom I can just make out the northern shore and the grove. The purplish grove has become black, utterly featureless, and I hear nothing but the storm beating at the roof.

Goottich answers Pachel. He describes several theoretical mechanisms for Remarkables' vision, then adds that all might be used in tandem. Who knows? But it is clear that they see enormously well. The testimonial evidence of other visitors . . . that's plenty of proof right there!

"So are they watching us?" Pachel acts angry. She has a golden nectar mustache and dark squinting eyes. "That's all I want to know. Are they studying us?"

"Oh, sure," I say.

She looks at me.

"What's more," adds Goottich, "they can read your lips. Even in these conditions. And if they're as talented as we think, they can probably decipher what invisible lips are saying. They'll watch the panes of glass vibrating, or maybe the motions of airborne dusts. . . ."

Bedford laughs nervously.

Pachel continues watching me. Finally she asks, "Is that true? Or is Goottich playing games?"

"There are some incredible stories," I admit. "This is lousy weather, but maybe . . ."

Pachel turns and glares at Service, but he doesn't seem to notice. He's talking to one of the young Pitcairns, the voice quiet but intense; we don't exist to him. No, that's not right. We exist, but our existence is narrowly defined. We're strangers in a world where strangers come from other groves, competitors until proved otherwise, and I can't take his indifference personally. And with that thought I lift my bowl and sip a brownish nectar, sweet and only warm now. I take a mouthful, then another, then I set the bowl on the plain wooden table and softly, beneath my hand, I belch.

* * *

We finish dinner. The Pitcairns are first, their dishes removed by the one woman. Then she sits with them, waiting for us. Sometimes they mutter among themselves, and it sounds like work-talk. They tell Service about what they've been doing, and he listens without comment. Then we start pushing our empty plates toward the center. The woman rises and stacks the plates and carries them into the little back room where she took the others. Nobody offers to help her. She returns and sits just as Service rises to his feet, and the room's quiet is magnified. It's as if everyone, Pitcairn and not, is anxious about what happens next.

The old face nods.

"Tintoil," says a young woman.

"Salo," says a man. The largest Pitcairn, I notice.

"Shurgar," says the woman in charge of dinner.

All but Service seem young. I'm listening, struggling to match faces to the names, but there are too many of them. Thirteen Pitcairns, including Service and Snow. I get muddled. I don't have a Remarkable's superior memory, and I start to lose track—

"Briar," says the young man closest to us. He could be Service's son, I think. Or his clone. All the faces are similar, but Briar's is a smooth youthful version of our leader's. They have the same wiry build and the same way of holding their heads, and their dark eyes seem to watch everything at once.

Now Service speaks with his deep, well-worn voice, outlining our schedule without embellishments. We know the plans, but he wants no misunderstandings. Each of us will claim a house tonight. The doctors will come soon. As it happens, the storm is going to break tomorrow morning, and we have to leave on the *passion* in the afternoon. No delays. We are everyone who is going, he says. Then he pauses before adding that he hopes it's an easy *passion*. But of course such things aren't up to him. It will be what it will be. And Pachel mumbles, "Fatalistic," while dipping her head.

Service stops and says nothing. The eyes narrow and his thin mouth draws closed.

Pachel shifts her weight, intimidated by the stare.

"When I'm talking," warns Service, "I've got a purpose. Don't ever doubt it. Understand?"

She rolls her eyes, and after a moment says, "Fine."

Service is wiry and not tall, but he has a way of domi-nating. Leading a *passion* is a great honor, I recall. He must have been chosen by the eldest Pitcairns. Isn't that how it works? A grove's future is determined in part by the success of its *passions*, and I start watching the young faces flanking Service. I expect to see confidence and a quiet pleasure with being included, but instead there's just a hardness to the eyes and a remoteness. I can't tell what they're thinking. I can't even guess.

Service is talking again, telling us that it's a small *pas-sion* this year. One hundred and three juveniles. He says that nearby groves are going to do their annual best to grind the *passion* down to nothing. They'll send cretins after us, as always, but don't lose sleep over it. The cretins will want to kill Remarkables, not people. Not unless the people get in their way, and we won't. He means me and Pachel and the rest of us. He nods at us, then says, "*We* will protect them. With our lives, if need be."

He glances to either side now. For an instant. He watches Briar and Salo and the others, saying nothing. Then he straightens and says, "Thank you for coming." The worn face nods and almost smiles.

We fidget for a moment, then Lumiere says, "And thank you for inviting us. To your homes, to this *passion*. . . ."

Goottich coughs and says, "Yes. Thank you."

Then Service dips his head, examining his timepiece. "It's late. You need to claim houses and rest . . . the doc-tors coming soon . . ."

The other Pitcairns are standing, all but Shurgar mak-ing for the doorway. Then Service says, "Briar. Help with cleaning up," and I can feel the mood shift. There's a ten-sion blossoming. I can practically see it in the air. Snow glances at Briar, and Briar stops and waits, then turns and says:

"All right."

Nothing in the voice is harsh.

I look at his young-Service face, and the smile seems genuine. No rancor. Glad to help. Just like a Pitcairn is supposed to act. Yet there's something under the surface here. I can feel a palpable tension, an aggressiveness, and it makes me uneasy.

Service and the other Pitcairns leave together.

We start putting on ponchos, and Lumiere stops and thinks to ask, "Would you like any help?"

Briar is pouring excess nectar into a plastic container. He seems focused, perhaps deaf, sealing the container with a flexible clear lid. Then Lumiere repeats his question.

"Can I help?"

Briar looks up at him, a fire behind the dark eyes.

After a moment he smiles, and he says, "No." He shakes his head and says, "Why did you come here?" and I can't tell what he means. Is he reminding us of our duties? Or is he angry about our presence?

Somehow this isn't what I expected.

I had a mental picture of Pitcairns, and Briar isn't quite it.

6
NIGHT

❖

Pitcairn II was in orbit, goes the story, before it heard and deciphered the weak radio signals. Mostly it was ship-to-shore noise. Groves don't usually communicate with one another. On-board telescopes peered at the surface and found the Remarkables with the human-style buildings among and around them. First contact was made with a random tropical grove. A team of government people and scientists landed on the warm blue sea, and the Pitcairns greeted them with characteristic coolness. Millennia of isolation were finished, yet there was little said beyond cursory greetings and clipped answers to a rush of questions.

The landing team was ushered into an abandoned factory several kilometers outside the grove, and for five days they were fed nectars and allowed to ask more questions. "Can we meet your symbiotic partners?" Everyone wanted the opportunity. Research from a distance was proving fascinating, and in improving Pitcairn the visitors admitted, "It would be an honor and wonder for us. To meet the Remarkables . . . maybe soon . . . ?"

Their hosts had to explain what is instinctive for Pitcairns. No strangers were allowed inside a grove. No strange people, nor cretins. Remarkables have a rigorous sense of *self*. Visitors beneath their canopy are as repulsive to consider as one human being letting another put a bare hand up his rectum.

No, it wasn't possible. Not at all.

"Then just to the edge of the grove," the voyagers persisted. "How about that compromise?"

"Perhaps," was the answer. "It's doubtful, but we'll wait and see. . . ."

More time passed. The team had been there for several weeks, and suddenly a group of elder Pitcairns came to the factory. No warnings were given. "Would you like to come with us?" they asked.

"Where? Come where?"

"They've agreed to let you walk close," said an ancient woman. "For a little while."

They. The Remarkables. It's perhaps the most famous moment in the collective memory of the Realm. Everyone in that landing party took at least one holo camera—letting them float overhead and absorb everything. I've watched the show many times, from various perspectives. It was a hard walk to the grove, but the old Pitcairns easily outmarched their guests. Tired and dirty, the voyagers climbed the last ridge and found themselves just a hundred meters from the grove. There they were told to stop. To wait. Stinging tendrils dropped reflexively, burning their way. A few people yelled greetings and waved their hands, and everyone was nervous. I remember the faces, excited and joyous but worried too. They listened to the grove's complicated singing, understanding none of it. (Nobody has deciphered their language. Even now.) Then all at once the Remarkables stopped making noise, and they became absolutely still for a long moment. And finally, with one titanic voice, perhaps ten thousand of them said the famous first words:

"We saw you coming!"

Nothing else comprehensible was said by the Remarkables. That the words were in the Realm's language was easily answered. The elders said that the Remarkables had watched them from a distance, eavesdropping on conversations and the visitors' practice sessions with the Pitcairn tongue. They had learned at least four words . . . but what did it mean? "We saw you coming!" What in hell were they saying?

The elders shrugged their shoulders and grinned, asking, "Don't you like puzzles?"

A trillion trillion citizens have experienced that moment in history, watching the holos and for an instant wearing the same dumbfounded expressions. Did the aliens see *Pitcairn II* in orbit? Or the glare of its engines making the

long braking burn? Maybe there wasn't any significance
to the words. Nobody in the Realm was certain. Heads
were shaken, and together people smiled nervously,
breathed deeply, and attempted to clear their muddled
brains.

"I know my attitude stinks," says Pachel, "and I must
be getting on your nerves."

We're walking together, sand and little twists of greenery underfoot, and the rain has slackened to a driving mist.
I say, "I don't mind," and sound painfully polite. Then I
add, "You're just out of your element, that's all."

"I don't want to be here."

I say nothing.

She stops and makes me stop, looking at my eyes. "No,
I mean it. I never wanted to come here. . . ."

"If you're worried about tonight—"

"You don't understand." Her tone is accusing. She waves
her hands in the air, saying, "The shitty weather and crazy
foods . . . I should have refused them harder. I should
have . . ."

I want to be out of the mist. Travel and nerves have
made me tired, my patience faltering. I grasp Pachel's
closest hand and squeeze, telling her, "It's minor surgery,
and painless. They have good doctors, and they do this
operation a lot." Because infertility is a Pitcairn problem.
Because if they can pull out eggs and treat them chemically, then maybe they'll accept a burrowing sperm.

"Ranier," she spits, "that's not what I mean!"

I don't say anything.

"I'm here because I told my superiors about Goottich's
invitation," she explains. "I told them and they thought it
would be good politics. I'm supposed to make diplomatic
contacts with the Pitcairns. If I can. New Albemarne is still
pissed that they don't get a share of this solar system—"

I've heard stories along those lines.

"—and they keep thinking that there's another avenue.
Groves that will deal with us. That sort of nonsense. That's
why they paid my bill."

Now I understand. I nod and say, "I've wondered," and
she pulls away from me. The unwilling diplomat—

"I'm taking this house," she says.

We're both tired, and I don't want to pursue this any-more. I tell her, "Fine."

In the fading light the little twists of silver barely show on her face, and her poncho is bulky, hiding most of her shape. She stiffly tells me, "Good night," and walks away. I don't know this woman, I'm thinking. But somehow I don't feel I should worry about her. Anger is a tool for Pachel. She copes with her fury, perhaps storing it for later.

I offer a watery little: "Night."

She waves without looking back at me.

I select the house beside her house. It's empty still, the front door left open, and I stomp on the wooden stairs and shut the door behind me, hanging my poncho on a peg. I hear the wind against the thick new walls, and I smell alien saps and pungent Pitcairn soaps. This is a smaller version of the common house. There's a single toilet and an oversized bed and a crude heater fed with natural gas. I find a box of chemically tipped sticks, remembering something I read in someone's written account of Pitcairn. Scraped against the heater's ceramic shell, one stick ex-plodes into a hot noisy fire. I light the gas and blow out the stick, then I toy with the simple valve until the room's chill begins to retreat.

I warm my hands. I remove my boots, sniffing them and setting their controls to *Clean/Dry*. Then I stand and walk to the tall window overlooking the bay.

The water has climbed even higher. It's too dark to see the grove, and for an instant it feels as if I might be any-where. This isn't an alien world; I am somewhere in the Realm. *No pain*, I'm thinking. *Not a trace*. Then the il-lusion of ordinariness is spoiled. A parade of a dozen young Remarkables rolls past me, tufts of wet sand thrown up in its wake and those lidless black eyes gazing at me. At ev-erything.

In the gloom they appear solid and imposing.

I hold my breath for a little while, the tips of my fingers against the cold glass and my heart pounding.

In the wind, for a half instant, I think I hear someone talking. "Hello, Ranier," says someone. Only maybe it's the wind, and maybe I'm too tired to trust my senses. I listen and listen, but all I hear now is the chatter between

Remarkables. They have moved past, almost out of sight, and the darkness seems to swallow them whole.

A researcher on New Emerald, using data from that first mission to Pitcairn, solved the We-saw-you-coming puzzle and secured her place in history. She managed the trick by analyzing the sonic probes of different groves, noticing how the adult Remarkables had interlocking root systems. She saw signs of limited but persistent neurological links. Each adult seemed to be a separate entity, but what if they could share electrical impulses? What about visual data? Spaceborne telescopes with thousands of mirrors, all tied together by computers, can see amazing distances. What if the aliens possessed the same tricks?

The researcher made estimates, then she assumed perfect weather on a moonless Pitcairn night. A large grove could look skyward with every eye, staring at the star-thick heavens, and the Remarkables would be able to perceive a greenish glow in the direction of Earth. Assuming her estimates were sound, of course. Assuming that.

"We saw you coming!"

The largest groves would have noticed the sky changing some hundred centuries ago. Pitcairns wouldn't have been as common, but the human symbionts would surely have pointed home from time to time, and the Remarkables would know which yellow star to watch. The researcher asked, "What if the aliens are intelligent? What if for centuries they've been watching that expanding volume of terraformed space, knowing it was approaching? What would they think? Would they feel frightened? Excited? Would they make plans for the fateful day when we would meet them? And what would they plan?"

One puzzle answered, and a larger one given to the Realm.

Who knows?

I have no answers, I realize. But if every clear night showed me a brightening green haze, I would wonder about my future prospects. I'd focus whatever brainpower I possessed on the problem, and some nights I'd never sleep, full of worry.

It would be only natural.

* * *

The doctors wear white clothes under their ponchos, and that's comforting. That symbol is the same here as in the Realm. And like some doctors, they carry black satchels full of medical tools. Two women, one man. The older woman has been in some kind of horrific accident, her face burned and left scarred. I can't help but stare for a moment. Then I blink and force my gaze sideways. Then the younger woman opens her satchel and hands me a heavy glass tube, clean and shiny.

"Do you need anything?" asks the man.

"Privacy," I reply. I have practiced this moment in my head, my voice dry and smooth. "Give me a little while, will you?"

"Of course."

They leave me. I hear them on my stairs, then I can't hear them. I climb onto my bed, on top of a thick blanket, and undress a minimal amount. This feels silly. There's no privacy with the huge window. And to make matters worse, I'm no lusty adolescent. Those doctors brought in a vacuous clinical air, and I can't relax. I know there's no point in trying to do my duty now.

I start to daydream.

I think about Pitcairn independence. Stubbornness. Whatever force keeps them from accepting our tools and tricks. Pachel's bosses tried and tried to give them wonders like advanced lasers and nanotechnologies, probably hoping to receive gifts in return. Mining rights to Pitcairn's huge moon, say. Or maybe just a portion of their expansive Oort cloud. But every grove shrugged its shoulders and said, "Thank you, no." They claimed happiness with their technologies and limitations. Even potential weapons didn't raise their interest. Projectile guns and crude chemical bombs were enough for them, thank you.

Pitcairns trade among themselves, and sometimes they fight. I suspect they're very good at both activities. Their fishing boats carry hidden guns big enough to shatter other boats, and a couple times visitors like us have seen shots exchanged over fishing grounds. No full-scale wars, but the fort on this spit implies such horrors are possible.

We don't have wars in the Realm. I wish I could believe in our innate decency and intelligence, but the truth is much less sweet. Wars are always catastrophes for terraformed worlds. Modern fusion weapons would butcher and leave nothing habitable, and neither side could dream of profiting. No government could even attempt to arm itself without bringing itself down; that's been proved countless times. And besides, there are other ways to fight and to gain in the end. In commerce; in court. In the endless expansion outward.

I turn my mind back to Pitcairn. People like Snow will help care for me in these next weeks, and for their help I need only give several million healthy sperm cells. I try imagining Snow pregnant with my child. Then the daydream expands to a hundred Snows, and my descendants thrive in the Mount Au grove. There's an egotistical charm here, and I smile. And with the smile I feel myself relaxing, breathing deeply and beginning with my eyes focused on the steep wooden V of the ceiling.

I picture women—my ex-wives and the few recent girlfriends—but for some reason I focus on Pachel. She's not my type, but I'm remembering her crawling out of coldsleep after our voyage. The woman has wide hips and mammoth breasts, and she reminds me of something I saw in a history text. She resembles the crude clay totems made on the primitive Earth: ancient figurines meant to represent an ultimate woman, fertile and milk-rich. The totems helped crops germinate and made the old king's fluids vital again . . . and I laugh to myself, making no sound, an imaginary Pachel hovering above me, naked and splendid. . . .

I nearly forget my purpose. I almost lose the glass tube at the critical instant, grabbing it and trying to maintain a little dignity. But again everything feels clinical. My semen makes a little white pond at the bottom, and I sit up and breathe, then stand and fasten my trousers, holding the tube and carefully walking to the doorway.

The older woman waits outside. I see white trousers under her poncho and the brutalized face nodding at me. A thin voice says, "Thank you," without an ounce of warmth. I stare at the ruined white skin, wondering how she was injured.

Sealing the tube, she says, "Good night."

I feel hollow and rather sad.

She turns and walks across the sand, and I say, "Good night," weakly, wishing I could think of something memorable to inject here. But I can't. I try to look past her, noticing Pachel inside her house. Two white forms flank her bed, and she lies on her back with one doctor preparing some kind of instrument. I can't see details. I watch, knowing I shouldn't, and I'm rewarded with a fleeting moment of faint pain.

I ignore the sensation, retreating back inside.

For a little while I look outside, wondering about the Remarkables. Then I realize that they must be in cover, probably inside the fort. Out of the wind and safe. *Sure.*

I climb under the blanket, feeling loneliness and a horrible sudden homesickness. It's all I can manage to watch the steady blue flame of the heater, thinking I should get up and turn it off. Then I shut my eyes and open them an instant later, finding the house darkened and the brief Arctic night in power. I hear a gust of wind, sand grains rattling against the window. I smell nothing familiar except my own sourness. Then I shut my eyes again and hold them shut, and I wrap my blanket tight around me.

TALKER

◆

I cling to the highest portion of the wall, watching. Each of the new-built houses possesses a little square window facing south, toward me and set high in its wall. I can peer inside, seeing a dim-lit square of floor or of bed or in one the blue glow of a tamed fire. None of the strange humans are awake. At least they do not move. Yet still I keep watch, hoping to see them for an instant. Just a piece of them. Not even their faces, and I would be happy.

Sometimes one of my siblings shouts at me, "Come down, Talker! Come bunch with us and sleep. You need to rest. Tomorrow—"

"I know," I interrupt. "We cross tomorrow, I know. And I wish I could sleep somehow. I do."

"Come and try," they beckon.

And it occurs to me that none of them are sleeping either. Now and again I hear the bunched bodies fidgeting, tendrils slipping against tendrils and everyone muttering quietly. Only the oldest juveniles are in this bunch. We are the ones beginning our *passion* in the afternoon, and how can we sleep? Besides, I think, if we do sleep, we will surely dream about the *passion*. We will see ourselves crossing the water and rolling through rainforests, climbing the coastal mountains and striking across the plains. Then come morning we will feel exhausted from all the dream-work. Just as we will be without sleep, and what difference does it make? Why not stay up on the wall and watch for the strange humans? We might die tomorrow. A freakish tide or some enormous air-breather could destroy all of us. I might have few other chances to study our guests. Goottich and his friends. His friends who do not like him. . . .

The wind gusts, and I grasp at the wall with every tendril. Rain pours through me and soaks the cold concrete beneath, robbing my heat, and I have to shrink and huddle with myself, only one eye now lifted over the rampart.

I do love this place. This ancient fort. I remember exploring its tunnels and little rooms and the huge keep at its center, guns and shells sealed and stored away. Several summers ago I made the journey here, and when I returned home, safe under the grove's canopy, I asked about the place. The adults began describing the fort's construction and its purpose and its triumphs too. It is more important than its walls and weapons, I learned. This fort is a symbol, a great warning to Pitcairns from any other grove. Any raiders coming here to assault the Mount Au grove will think again. Humans are not fools. They will see the gray walls looming at the bay's mouth, and maybe the raiders' leader will tell the others, "I don't like this weather." He will say, "I don't trust these fucking tides. Let's wait for some other day. We can hit them another day." And his followers will breathe and nod quietly, glad for the change in plans.

Our humans built this wondrous structure. We were a smaller grove in those times, poorer and weaker, and the work meant sacrifice for many generations. I have heard stories. Every juvenile knows about the raids coming from the south. They came long before the Old Ones were eggs, people killing and stealing. But eventually our people fought and won, saving us and themselves. And afterward they insisted on even higher walls and even bigger guns. The Old Ones of the time thought the fort was finished. It made no sense to them, and they said so.

"But we're not satisfied," said the humans. "You don't understand. We want something that's going to scare *everyone*. No exceptions."

We have tough and smart humans in our grove. They are a great pride for us.

I remember feeling pride when I heard the stories, and I am feeling it now. "We want to scare everyone," I say quietly, using the human words. Then the wind ebbs and I lift myself again, looking at the little darkened houses beneath me. Nothing moves. Nothing at all. Then I look past, my eyes together to concentrate the weak light. I study the little piers nearby. Service and his people are sleeping on a fishing boat tied there. Past them, across the rough water, I see the grove. It is partly illuminated by incandescent lamps. I can see the nearest piers and the freezer ship being unloaded by the night crews, and beyond and above that ship are the Old Ones themselves. I imagine myself being among them, standing beside them in the best soils and enjoying first pick of the day's catch. In my imagination it is daylight, unusually bright and clear, and the fort is a great human-made hill set on the end of the long spit, appearing ancient and solid and somehow angry too.

And I think: *Of course.*

Of course!

It occurs to me that the fort was not made to impress only other Pitcairns. Our humans kept working on it in order to impress another audience—a closer and more immediate audience—and I stare at the Old Ones, and I stare, and after a while I hear myself laughing.

"Talker!" shouts someone below me. "If you cannot sleep, shut up! Will you please?"

I cannot stop my laughing.

"Talker!" scream several juveniles. "Stop! Stop!"

And now I turn my eyes, gazing at the great fort itself. As if for the first time. As if I knew nothing about its builders, and of course I am impressed. I am.

7
THE STORM BREAKS

✛

A door closes—my door—and I sit upright and find myself alone. Yet there's a residual motion hanging in the room, a distinct sense of someone having just left.

I rise and shuffle to the toilet and sit, then I notice the big backpack propped against one wall and the new clothes folded beside it, heavy Pitcairn boots set on top of them. *For me.* I wipe myself with a square of rough paper. Flushing the toilet, I watch the swirling water vanish and new water flood the little bowl. Then I undress myself and dress again. I'm supposed to wear what they gave me. Even my fancy boots have to remain behind, probably to be burned or buried as trash. *Too bad*, I think. I struggle with the buttons and my new boots' laces, but everything fits perfectly. Did Goottich send our measurements ahead of us? Or did some Pitcairns stay awake all night, sewing and stitching, making this garb out of eyeball assumptions?

I spend a few minutes examining the backpack. Its frame is plastic and the thick fabric feels water-resistant, slick and tough. A mummy bag and bulky tent are strapped to the frame with elastic cords. Grabbing hold, I lift to gauge the weight. I expected a heavier load, and I mutter, "Not bad," and set it down with care. "Could be worse. Sure."

I put on my poncho and step outside. The wind is even stronger this morning, but the rain is scarce, fat drops coming in bursts and nothing between them. I walk into the wind, crossing loose rounded rock and then gray-white sand. Half a dozen young Remarkables are strung out in a line. They're at the spit's center, on the highest ground, and I reach them and look down at the raw ocean, waves crashing on a graveled beach and the wind making me bend at the knees.

I'm standing between two Remarkables. Neither moves. I glance sideways, feeling nervous. Their eyes look at me, unblinking and perfectly black, and I can't think of anything to say. I feel I should and can't, and I turn and look at the beach again. The wind rips my hood off, and an instant later the rain finds me, my face and long hair soaked in an instant.

I'm an honorary Pitcairn now. Isn't that right?

I tell myself I belong here. I watch the pseudogulls and smaller birds circling above the surf, and sometimes they light and run and poke between the rocks. The curling waves seem distant, the tide low for the moment. These local tides run ten meters or more. The high-tide line is marked with trash and whole trees stripped clean of limbs and bark, and I notice the spiraling grain of the wood. Sometimes I feel the waves through my toes. I keep my eyes forward, and the Remarkables start talking among themselves. Whistles, chirps. Many of their sounds are too high to hear, I recall. Plus there may be a visual component to their language. A kind of intricate sign language.

I feel alert and suddenly quite happy, enjoying the thrill of these circumstances. I start to smile, and one of the Remarkables says, "Ranier."

"Yes? What?" I sputter, turning toward the voice.

The Remarkable on my right comes closer, rolling with that peculiar grace of theirs. Its outer tendrils grasp at the sand, and there's a faint creaking noise that persists after it quits rolling. We're a couple meters apart. A single black eye is extended, pushing through the tendrils and stopping when I can smell my breath bouncing back at me. And I wait. I hear the other Remarkables chattering loudly, tendrils in motion. The surface of the eye is glossy and apparently smooth, no hint of structure and certainly no emotions betrayed.

Again its owner says, "Ranier."

The voice is precise and too-human, unnerving me. Juveniles shouldn't be able to speak like this. They aren't as coordinated as the adults, nor even a fraction as intelligent. The Pitcairns say as much. Juveniles can learn to understand the Pitcairn language, and sometimes say a few tattered words . . . but how can this thing manage to . . . ?

"You slept well, Ranier." The eye lifts higher, appraising me from a different angle. I can see into the core of the organism. The opened mouth is round and rimmed with countless white teeth, triangular and sharp, and from deep inside that mouth it tells me, "But you look rather dehydrated, Ranier. Drink water with your breakfast, will you? *My friend.*"

I am thirsty. I find myself licking at my dry lips, nodding. I say, "Okay . . ." weakly, and I manage a deep breath.

Then every Remarkable rolls back off the ridge, toward the bay, moving fast enough to throw up high gouts of sand and loose gravel. Our conversation is finished; I've spoken to an alien intelligence, earning membership in a most exclusive club. Quite the start to the day, I think. *My friend?* Then I laugh aloud and start after them, aiming for the common house with the rain and wind helping to carry me along.

Lumiere has already eaten. Nobody else has arrived yet. A large paper map is lying on the tabletop, and Lumiere examines it with a single finger, tracing our course with obvious zeal.

"Hello," I offer.

"Good morning," he says.

Breakfast is a hot liquid nectar and cold sweet slabs of a dried variety, blue and nearly transparent. I claim shares and a tall glass of water, and I sit beside the old man. He seems happy, red-eyed but alert. After a moment he says, "Mount Au," and makes a slow circle with his fingertip.

"Where?" I ask.

He says, "Here." The map is a crude topographic affair. The Mount Au grove has a little fleet of airplanes, and I suppose they used airborne cameras to get the data. I look at the curling ink lines and ask where he found the map. It and others were in his pack, between his first-aid kit and the extra socks. Probably everyone has copies. Then he says, "You know, Mount Au is awesome. A true wonder." He pauses, leaning back as if to see it better. "Did you study that portion of the files?"

"Some. Not enough," I admit.

A thick red line encircles the mountain. An extensive plain stretches toward its north. The huge bay in front of me is just a little finger buried in a rugged coastline, almost invisible. And Au is huge, yes. I see its boundaries and the flat white top, only that's not its summit. That's just the highest altitude reached by the planes. I remember how it's the tallest mountain on Pitcairn. Radar soundings from orbit made that clear. The summit itself is rarely seen. Even on sunny days there are shrouding clouds, the mountain making its own weather. . . .

"This belongs to them," says Lumiere. He means the plain within the red line. "It's the holy ground for this grove. Dry and bright. Perfect to initiate maturity in the juveniles, and their chance to commune with their All-Answer."

I say nothing.

"The All-Answer lives in places like Au."

"I would too," I say. "If I were a god."

Lumiere nods, scratching his puffy face. I notice how the old skin creases under his fingertips, smoothing again but slowly. "If that mountain were on Earth," he tells me, "we would have worshiped it. Our ancestors would have built temples on its slopes, and devoted souls would have dragged wooden crosses and crystal einsteins to its summit. Nine kilometers above the sea—"

"Probably so," I offer.

He doesn't seem to hear me. His hands drop into his lap, and he remarks, "Today we'd have skimmers and trams for the tourists. On Earth's Mount Au, I mean. Millions of tourists with robots to help guide whoever wanted to climb it. And there would be hotels buried in the glaciers and just beneath the summit too. Not on top, however. That would destroy the mountain's charm."

There is life and a certain heat to the voice. I look at Lumiere, surprised by his intensity.

"You're probably right," I allow. "That's how it would be."

He says, "People," and tries to smile while shaking his head.

I watch him.

"Remarkables," he says, "have it right."

"Do they?"

He touches the blank area in the middle of that great

mountain, telling me, "It's the symbol of their god. Every grove has its holy ground. Usually it's a mountain, always unapproachable. Some feature that they can reach when they're juveniles. But not climb. They could never climb such a huge lump of rock."

"They aren't tough enough," I agree. "They don't have the strength and coordination—"

"Which means Mount Au and the other places . . . they're remote. Their holy ground can't be trivialized."

I nod.

He's aware of his intensity, and he shrugs and laughs. Suddenly he's embarrassed with himself.

"You're right," I tell him.

"A good lesson for people, don't you think?"

"Probably so."

Then he gazes outside and says, "The rain's dropping off, isn't it? And those clouds don't seem so ominous anymore."

I say nothing.

"As promised," he says.

I look outside too.

Goottich is the last of us to arrive. He wears a new poncho, large enough for him and nearly large enough to serve as my tent. He's smiling and muttering quietly, ignoring us, dishing up a substantial breakfast and sitting at our end of the long table. Between mouthfuls of chewy nectar, he gazes down at the table's far end, no Pitcairns here. "I talked to Service," he says eventually. "He told me what he wants us to do this morning."

I'm beside Lumiere. Pachel is farthest from Goottich, having said nothing but a few throaty *good mornings*. Bedford and Effie are across from me, their prayers finished. Effie's nut-colored skin is translucent in the brightening light. Bedford, as always, smiles as if nothing were more important to the world. He has an effortless and radiant smile.

Goottich waits, wanting someone to prompt him.

"So," I say, "what's our guide and protector want?"

"We should practice wearing our packs. Get accustomed to them." He sips from a wooden bowl and belches with authority. "And go through them. We should be familiar with our equipment."

"I'd like to explore first," says Bedford. He gestures toward the fort, asking, "How many people get the chance to see a military fortification? Outside of history holos, I mean."

"What else?" I ask Goottich.

"Practice carrying the canoes," he says. "Some extra ones are waiting for us above the pier. We need to get accustomed to making portages."

"We should," Lumiere agrees.

"Effie and I are going to explore first," says Bedford.

The doll-like face frowns briefly, and Effie nearly speaks. Then she doesn't. Bedford clasps her hand with both of his hands, and she stares down at them for a moment.

I look at all of us. Such variety, I'm thinking. In every possible way. Shapewise and sizewise and in temperament too . . . a fine collection of novel genes for our hosts. I hope they do better with them than we have—every parent's heartfelt wish—and with that little prayer I look outside. Remarkables started gathering below us a little while ago. There are several dozen of them now. Juveniles and big ones, I realize. They've formed a line near the high-tide mark.

"One of them talked to me," I mention.

Goottich blinks and says, "Not possible," and shakes his head.

Lumiere says, "Talked to you? Really?"

I gesture at the rounded shapes, and I watch the idea register on the others' faces. Then I tell them, "One knows how. It told me to drink water."

"That's what it said?" Pachel responds. " 'Drink water'?"

It sounds trivial, yes. I shake my head and laugh, then I tell them, "That and we're supposed to kiss each other's hands. Now. They want to see our solidarity."

"Juveniles don't have the right mouths for our language," Goottich repeats. "They just don't."

"Kiss hands?" Effie moans. "You're sure?"

"Absolutely!"

And they amaze me. Everyone does the deed, even Goottich. It's all I can do to keep from laughing. The taste of skin, salty and familiar, mixes with the flavors of the nectars; and afterward I hide my grinning mouth with my hands, staring out the window, seeing eyes and wondering once again what those aliens could possibly be thinking.

8
THE CROSSING

✦

I am a person stripped down, made simple, no overt symptoms of my civilization showing on me. That's what I tell myself. I smile as I work, doing what Service wants. I've completely unpacked my belongings, identifying everything to my satisfaction, and now I start to repack socks and the paper maps, extra trousers and the various kits and tools and hard, plastic-wrapped bricks of concentrated nectars. The trouble is that repacking is the harder chore. I'm not very good at this business. There was room to spare in my pack, at least when I found it this morning. Now the pockets bulge, fabric straining, and the cords and nylon zippers fight me, refusing to do their jobs.

Modern campers would have floating packs and maybe a hundred kilograms of important equipment. Holo cameras would hover about like flies, absorbing everything. The food would be varied and sealed inside shaped vacuums, and it would be prepared by automated stoves, battery powered and fire safe. Cushioned earphones would supply music, every piece selected to match the mood and scenery. The tent would be spacious and well padded and capable of deploying itself on any ground, at any time. The bed itself would be self-heating and self-cooling, equipped with twin pillows and a sonic scrubber for removing grime and perspiration.

But I'm not modern anymore. I think that with some satisfaction, nodding and smiling to myself.

I think of Lumiere and those tourists of whom he spoke. I am not like them. I won't trivialize any ground. My own muscles and bones will carry myself and my possessions, and there's a purity in that fact. Isn't there? An ascetic sense that, once I see my fate, seems proper. Even splendid.

The truth told, I would like just one holo camera. Just to record the scenery, on the sly.

But cameras are against the rules, of course.

Against the rules, and besides, there are things no holo can capture. No technology can replicate the sense of being somewhere, not without flaws. That's what I'm telling myself when I discover one last pair of heavy socks hiding under my pack. Where do they belong? I wonder. I laugh aloud, folding them and crushing them as flat as possible, then stuffing them up under the top flap and trying to smooth everything to make it appear neat. To fake tidiness. To lend to the illusion of order.

The tide rises and crests, then it falls fast with a strong current roaring out of the bay. I watch while an empty freezer ship approaches, using the current. It rides high on the jade-colored water and leaves a brief white wake. I can make out tiny figures working on its deck, using hoses and brooms while the gull-like birds circle above or perch on the superstructure, ready to help with the cleaning.

I'm up on the sandy ridge, alone, carrying my pack back and forth with the straps cutting into my shoulders and my legs aching. Eventually the great ship vanishes behind the fort, and I notice a figure standing on the nearest wall. No, two figures. Bedford and his wife, I realize. And I watch them watching the ship until it passes into view again, its engines audible now. They make a deep throbbing sound, and the wake begins to splash against the spit.

Goottich sees me and climbs to me, his pack riding high on his back. His face is damp, and he wipes at his forehead. "They're loading our boat now . . . for the crossing. I'm supposed to get you."

"Where's Lumiere? And Pachel?"

"Where's our married couple?" he counters.

I show him, and he grunts. Then he says, "The old man and bitch are practicing their portages. Down below . . ."

"So why'd you invite her?" I ask him.

"I don't know. She was someone I remembered." He shrugs his shoulders, the pack frame groaning. "Pachel's got some kind of grudge against me. You notice?"

"I know she doesn't want to be here," I mention.

He says, "Then why did she come?" He grunts and looks at the fort, then he lifts one arm and waves hard. Bedford and Effie don't notice us. Goottich says, "Shit." He waits for a moment, then says, "Do me a favor? Go get them, will you?"

"Service told you to get them. Right?"

He frowns and says nothing.

"You know Pitcairns," I remind him. "They obey commands. For the common good and all that."

He says, "Shit," but starts walking again. His pack creaks as it bounces, the sound almost pleasant. And I start for the pier, my straps cutting into me but the meat not feeling them as much now. Maybe I'm getting accustomed already. Or maybe my circulation has quit.

The pier is dropping quickly. I notice that yesterday's boat is gone, replaced with a larger boat full of figures in motion. Packs and canoes are being lifted to the deck and secured. There's an antlike intensity to the scene, and I remember accounts of Pitcairns working. They are tireless and well organized. Strong and efficient. Up flies a canoe, then another one. After the canoes come wooden boxes, heavy-built and filled with cargo, and those aren't for us. I notice fishing nets neatly folded and too many Pitcairns. These others must be fishermen, I realize. After taking us to the bay's south shore, this boat will head out to sea. Maybe it's going to join that freezer ship. The Remarkables need their food, after all. No sense making two trips. The Pitcairns know what they're doing, all right.

"Heel," says someone. "Heel."

I turn and see Snow approaching. I'm sure it's Snow, but the brighter light changes her face a little bit. She walks with half a dozen cretins. Each cretin is about my size, maybe larger, black feathery plumage with bright red eye patches and orange throat patches and a golden underplumage that shows when they start to growl, eyes focused on me.

I step back instinctively.

She says, "Go," and touches the last cretin. I notice its odd front leg. Starting at the elbow joint and going down to the paw, the plumage is gray and long and soft to the eye. "Go," she tells them. Except she touches the last cretin and stops, and it stops too. The other five trot onto the articulating ramp and down to the pier, and I notice Lumiere and Pachel shying away from them. Then Service shouts, "Come!" and the cretins break into a lazy run.

Snow watches me. The gray-legged cretin is male—a penis but no visible testicles—and its jaws open, showing me long white teeth and a brilliant red tongue that curls, dripping saliva onto the packed sand. I look at the bright yellow eyes and the dead stare. It's alert and not stupid, I remind myself. These pseudomammals don't have large brains, but millions of years of selection forces have produced creatures easily trained. In some ways they're quicker to learn than people, and I shouldn't feel superior.

The first two missions studied cretin tissues. They possess enormous amounts of genetic material. Huge ranges of traits. That helps explain how they can come in so many sizes, filling all kinds of valuable niches. All kinds of biological professions.

I tell Snow, "He looks impressive."

She says, "Does he?" and seems amused.

"What happened to the leg?"

"It was cut off. Somehow."

"And grew back?"

"Oh, sure."

"Tough critter."

She doesn't say anything. Her face is pretty and sober, and her gaze is directed toward the southern coastline.

Bedford and Effie arrive, followed by Goottich.

"Can I touch it?" asks Bedford.

Snow blinks, some kind of spell broken. "Touch him? Oh, sure."

He says, "Nice," with that constant smile beaming at us. His hand is buried in the deep plumage, feathers in place of hair—as with all the pseudomammals. Now everyone wants to touch. The creature feels warm and vividly alive. I remember a story told by Pitcairns and retold by visitors like ourselves. Newborn cretins are examined by their Remarkables. Yelps are deciphered. Colors and strengths are measured. And according to Pitcairns, the Remarkables can actually *see* how the cretins will look and how they'll act when they're adults. It's as if the aliens can peer inside their symbionts' flesh, into the cells themselves, and decipher every last gene.

Goottich is scratching the creature's head, and it rolls its yellow eyes and emits a thin growl.

"Don't show your teeth," warns Snow. "It makes them nervous."

The big man pulls back his hand, saying, "I know that!"

Snow says, "Come," and starts walking. The cretin shadows her, paws kicking back the sand.

"The fort's empty," Bedford reports.

"You sound disappointed," I add.

He doesn't seem to hear me. "They must have cannons somewhere. Maybe they're stored away. This weather must be awful on equipment."

"Let's go down," says Effie. "I'm tired of carrying this thing." She means her backpack.

The four of us begin picking our way down the ramp. Snow is far ahead, taking long fast strides. I'm concentrating on my footing and the hand on the rope railing, thinking how easy it would be to fall. For an instant I see myself sprawled out on the pier, limbs shattered, bones jutting from my meat . . . and I shiver, moving slower now. I don't want any last-minute disasters. . . .

Bedford says, "It's a beautiful structure, however."

The fort. He can't stop talking about it.

"Elegant and stately—"

"Built in order to butcher people," I remind him. Someone has to make the point. "Cannons and walls aren't there to be amusing."

He's behind and above me. The smiling voice tells me, "It's part of nature's perfect plan. In the Realm we have order and eternal peace, and that's our slice of perfection."

I say, "Never mind."

"Maybe the Pitcairns will become civilized," adds Bedford. "With visits like ours, we can teach them how—"

"To be perfect?"

He waits for a moment, then says, "Sometimes, Ranier . . . sometimes I think you must be quite a cynic. I really do."

I say nothing.

He says, "You seem like a very confused man, at least."

Which in some ways is absolutely true. And I would have it no other way. Confusion is honest. I don't trust people who aren't in some magnificent way confused.

I stand on the boat's wide bow as we pull free of the pier, a thick bluish cloud sweeping over us. Half-burned hydrocarbons leak from an engine. Bedford prays, drawing circles; we're starting across the bay, the sky white and high and almost bright, the thick air drying and nearly calm.

I don't like the Unity Faith. I don't like its vision of

humanity reigning supreme over nature, nor can I convince myself that remaking worlds is part of some grand design. Maybe I am a cynic, yes. And I suppose that if I were more tolerant and self-secure, I wouldn't take offense so easily. People like Bedford are eternal, I'm thinking. They are shallow and happy in the worst ways, ignoring what displeases them. I am not like them. It's my great pride—my cold white knowledge that life is not perfect or infinitely sweet—and when I'm around Bedfords I find myself feeling smug and self-assured.

Just like them, I'm thinking. Which might be another reason why I dislike the smiling, pretty-faced man.

The *passion* has begun without ceremony. No fireworks; no choirs. No important citizens dissolving ribbons or releasing a thousand perfumed doves. I feel disappointment with the scene, then I reprimand myself for expecting human-style pageantry. Would that be reasonable? Should the Remarkables and the Pitcairns behave as I expect?

I laugh at myself. For a moment.

The spit looks like a long gray wall beside us, and the largest of the juveniles are rolling down to the water. Air sacs inside their tendrils and bodies inflate. They partway sink and then stabilize, then they start rolling with a waterwheel motion. This is a sprint for them. We start at low tide, and there's less than seven hours to cross ten kilometers of open water. That's when the current reverses and the bay is flushed clean.

Our boat slows and the Remarkables ride over our wake, turning faster and spreading apart as they move.

The bay looks very green against their purple tendrils, and it looks cold. Pitcairn has sharklike fishes and whalelike air-breathers, plus there's the constant risk that neighboring groves have sent swimming cretins to make attacks. There might not be any human wars at present, but there's no shortage of enemies either.

A sobering notion, and the absence of celebration makes more sense all at once.

Service appears. He's in a little boat filled with Pitcairns. They come past us, showing sharp profiles, and each of them holds a long rifle with a curling ammunition clip. Service is the one waving his free hand, giving directions to the Pitcairn who steers.

Our boat pauses, its engines falling back into an idle.

Lumiere says, "Listen," and cocks his head.

I look at him and listen, hearing Service's voice and then something softer. Remote and diffuse. What is it?

"The grove?" says Effie. She turns to Goottich, asking, "Those are the adults, aren't they?"

He says, "Absolutely."

The sounds are different from yesterday. I can't tell how, but there is something new.

Pachel asks, "What do you suppose they're saying?"

I tell her, "Shush."

She shakes her head, unhappy but complying. Only I can't hear the singing, whatever it was. The engines flare to life, pushing us ahead again. The next time we pause we're too far away, or maybe the winds have turned. I'm a little angry. I was hoping to be baffled by their noise for a while longer.

We drift again, then move.

I turn and watch the long, long purple shoreline in the distance. The air is clear enough for me to see the general waving of the adults, tendrils like shaggy grass twisting in the wind; but after a while we're too far away even for that detail, nothing showing but the purple color itself, smooth and dark and deceptively simple.

Pitcairns aren't cretins, and saying they are is an insult. And more to the point, Pitcairns are not slaves.

The human symbionts are free to choose where to build homes, mostly, and with whom they will reproduce, and how their children will be raised. Hard times and the rigorous environment have given them a stiff authoritarian hierarchy, elders on top and everyone quite sure of his or her place. But Remarkables don't rule human affairs. They can suggest and coax, beg and moan . . . but that's only in the rarest of unusual times, I understand. Only under exceptional circumstances.

If a deformed cretin is born, its mother kills it and consumes it without hesitation. But deformed children are made comfortable and given every benefit of being Pitcairn. Which is the same for people crippled in accidents. And for the senile and the terminally ill.

Certain human norms have held constant through the long isolation.

I take comfort in their charity, and I won't let myself think of them as slaves. Which they aren't. Not at all.

And they aren't cretins either.

Say otherwise, I have read, and someone will knock you onto your back, sit on your chest, and use fists, educating you in the finer points of Pitcairn etiquette.

We cross the bay through the afternoon, eating snacks and watching the tide lifting us, the current pushing us and the rolling juveniles back away from the sea. The weather remains calm, overcast but never gloomy. Colored birds work the water nearby. I find myself watching them more than anything. I watch them dipping their heads and sometimes diving out of view, their fishing done with the quiet intensity of any bird anywhere.

Nothing attacks the juveniles, and they don't seem to tire.

"Because they're ready," Goottich decides. "They're fattened and rested, and it's later where the troubles begin."

He launches into one of his impromptu lectures. There's an enormous attrition rate in young Remarkables, he assures us. Thousands of eggs might yield a few dozen babies swimming on the open seas, and maybe only one or two juveniles make it home again. Maybe none. And those lucky juveniles still have to undergo their *passion*. "Which seems peculiar," says Goottich. "Theoreticians always claimed that other intelligent species would be like us or like whales. A very few children cared for from birth to maturity . . ."

I can't quite imagine Goottich as a parent, patiently wiping up a child's mess or teaching it how to count.

Effie says, "It's something to think about, the carnage they've gone through—"

"Death brings life," says Bedford knowingly.

Effie quits speaking, dropping her head.

And I cough into my hand. The day's best news, as far as I'm concerned, is the utter absence of pain around me. I feel nothing. I can't sense the fishes being captured by the birds, then eaten. I don't feel the Remarkables aching with their exertions. Yet I don't dare dwell on my miraculous recovery. Like anyone sick for a long time, I'm superstitious about bringing on relapses. I don't trust my health or my confidence, and I work hard to hold rein on my thoughts.

9
FIRST CAMP

—◉—

The wrecked boat sits high on a rocky beach, broken under its waterline and stripped bare, the wood bleached and dried and tired. Snow comes up behind us while we stare, the six cretins padding behind her. Pachel asks about the wreck. "A bad storm," says the girl. "Two winters ago." Winter storms are much worse than summer ones, she assures us. The boat lost its engines and was thrown onto the rocks. She gestures at a mostly drowned island farther out, a single tree peacefully anchored on its crest. Effie asks about the people on board, and Snow tells the cretins to sit; they drop their haunches, tails straight out behind them and motionless. Then Snow says, "The ones who didn't drown made it there, to the beach, and died of hypothermia."

Nobody speaks. I look at Snow's profile, her mouth clamped shut and her eyes narrowed. She must have known someone who died. I see pain and then a trace of fear . . . and Pachel says, "Why were they out in a storm?"

"To fish," Snow responds.

"But in that weather—?"

"It's got to be done," the girl snaps. Then she laughs at stupid us, saying, "The grove has to be fed!"

Anger makes her prettier, I notice. Snow wears her hair long, tied in a ponytail. It's brown mixed with blond, and she plays with it when anxious or upset, one hand tugging hard.

Effie sighs and says, "They look like dogs." She means the cretins. "Don't you think they sort of do? In ways?"

We nod as a group, glad to change the subject. But cretins are different. They have the patient stillness of lizards, and even their black plumage is too bright for a dog. Only the very tips of their tails move—a very undoglike motion—and something about them is friendless and nonsocial.

Snow moves to the railing, looking ahead. The rainforest before us is dense and green in every shade, and the strange Pitcairn trees have inflated their leaves. Leaves hang like titanic sponges on the heavy black branches. Birds and swarms of insects weave through the canopy; long-legged shorebirds trot along the high-water marks. We're past the wreck now, pushing into a deep little bay. The forest rises on the mountain slopes, resembling someone's overgrown wall. Our engines cut back and die. Stone anchors fall, finding the bottom and stopping us when they bite. Then Snow says, "Hunt," with a sharp clear voice. And the cretins leap together, their hind legs driving them over the railing and their front legs tucked to their chests, tails erect.

They seem to vanish completely and forever. I'm almost surprised to hear them hit the water, and I step forward and watch them swimming for shore. They emerge running—*hunting*—bolting into the greenery at six different places. Gone.

Canoes start hitting the water, making distinct hollow booms. I walk toward the stern, thinking I should help. But there's no place for me. The Pitcairns move swiftly, something frantic about them. They don't have a robot's strength, nor its mechanical grace, and sometimes someone makes a mistake. There's a pause, a curse, then a resumption of the frantic unloading.

A large man—Salo, I recall—stands among the boat's crew and our Pitcairns. He sees me and shouts, "Pick a place and go! Come on!" He sounds angry with me for dawdling.

I'm first down the rope ladder, Goottich following. The canoes bob beneath us. Goottich settles in front of me, in my canoe. Then Salo unties us and sets us loose on the quiet water.

Our paddles are wooden, lightweight and white and varnished.

Goottich seems nervous, stroking hard but clumsily, sending salty fountains back at me.

"Watch it!" I warn.

He stops and turns and says, "What?"

"Do you know how to paddle?"

"What was I doing?"

I show him how I learned to do it on one of the muddy rivers on Rye's World, and he claims, "That's what I was doing!" The first Remarkables are passing us now. Goottich turns and tries again, but this time he's more in control. We pick up speed and slip between the leading Remarkables. They are breathing hard—a ceaseless whistling wheeze—and I watch the outer tendrils pressing at the water. They have a way of flattening sideways while pressing hard against the cool seawater, then straightening on the upstroke with water dripping free. They must be exhausted, I realize. So close to land but they're rolling slowly—big purple tumbleweeds covering the little bay— and I look backward, watching them and letting Goottich pull us along.

Our canoe bites into the graveled shoreline, and we climb out. The lead Remarkables come up beside us and talk in clicks and pops. Maybe they're congratulating each other; maybe they're praising the All-Answer. I help Goottich drag the canoe past the highest watermarks. Then a Pitcairn boy says something about finding your packs. Every pack is green, I notice, and the canoes are the same woody brown. The Pitcairns look like brothers and sisters, and the Remarkables are indistinguishable from one another. This place seems built from simple pieces. That's what I'm thinking when Goottich touches me, telling me, "Come on! You have to find your pack, okay?"

Service and Briar step off the little motorboat together. Side by side, they look like odd mirror images. They even hold their rifles the same way, the wooden butts to their hips and the ceramic barrels toward the sky. I notice them talking, and I catch a little of the tension. Briar says something, then Service responds. Then Briar starts to talk, and Service says, "Quit," and comes up from the beach alone.

Bedford spots Service and approaches him. The old Pitcairn is shouldering his pack, and Bedford asks, "Where should we camp?"

Service blinks and says nothing.

"Any suggestions?"

"Camp where you want," he tells Bedford. All of us. We've moved toward him, everyone eager for advice.

"Are there any guidelines?" Bedford persists.

Service swallows and glances back at Briar. Then he asks, "What do you mean?"

"Stay close? Keep alert? Don't, I don't know . . . don't take risks?"

"Those sound good." He shuts his mouth, and the jaw muscles bulge. Then he looks for Briar again—

"What about tomorrow?" asks Pachel.

A reasonable question. What about the future?

Service turns back toward us. He shifts his pack, breathing hard through his nose. He's furious about something. His face is taut and the voice is slow. Almost quiet. "You'll get partners," he tells us. "They've been told who goes with each of you, and they'll find you."

The six of us nod.

Then Service walks past us. Nothing else needs to be said, it seems. Somehow I imagined that our guide would be a mentor, fatherly and caring. Another example of my guessing wrong about the future.

"This old body needs rest," jokes Lumiere.

I shoulder my pack, feeling its weight in the legs and back. Lumiere is marching toward the trees. I decide to stay near the shoreline, finding a narrow trail that climbs onto some cliffs. Pachel is behind me, telling everyone, "Did you notice? He's pissed at something."

"Who is?" asks Effie.

"Service! Didn't you see it?"

Bedford says, "I think he's tense. What with his responsibilities and all—"

"Shit. The man's *furious*."

"What about?" asks Goottich.

"How should I know?" Pachel responds.

"He seemed all right to me," Effie says.

"Never mind," says Pachel. "Never the fuck mind."

I find flat ground where there aren't any trees between me and the bays, and I drop my pack and mat down the lush green vegetation before unrolling my tent. Stakes and ropes give me problems. My first attempt collapses. The second one at least stays upright, sagging in the middle but not badly. Not really. I stand and feel satisfied, then

I climb inside, sprawling out on the slick, chemical-stinking floor.

Goottich comes past. I know him by his grunts and the ragged wet breaths between. He pauses, probably judging if there's room here for two tents. Then he continues climbing. When he's gone, I climb out and open my mummy bag, tossing it in through the flap. Then I pull out a flask of clean water and a brick of butter-colored nectar. Where's that knife? I can't remember where I put it. Finally I find it in the last little pocket, and I open the ceramic blade and shave off a long piece of dinner.

I eat and study my maps. One map shows these bays and others to the south, plus the coastal mountains and the beginning of the interior plains. Someone has marked different places with red Xs. We're camping on one X now. These must be our scheduled campsites, I decide, and I try to measure distances and eyeball our courses. Then I pause and look at the white knife blade, thinking how the Pitcairns are living in a fancy Stone Age. Amazing people, I think. Several thousands of people in one grove, and they can build everything they need. Could the Realm produce such resilience? Such adaptability? "Not often," I mutter. Then I slice off another piece of nectar and look up.

A long, long freezer ship is coming into the bay. It rides low, more cargo there than ship, and I watch its wake rolling toward shore and breaking on the rocks below. The tide is dropping fast. The exposed shoreline is banded. Different species of algae; different species of shellfish. It's too bad I can't do research. Next to nothing is known about Pitcairn lifeforms, much less the various communities. But I'm just a terraformer, not a field biologist. My specialty is the tailoring of slightly novel species, plugging them into established niches. I wouldn't know where to begin if somehow I could do research here. The truth told, I'd probably screw up the job a thousand ways.

But who would do better?

The Realm has zero experience with active, complicated alien biospheres. Multicellular life is enormously rare, at least in our galaxy, and that's why Pitcairn is priceless. It's a fluke, much like Earth, and there's probably enough here to fuel a hundred thousand science careers. In biology and ecology, meteorology and biochemistry.

Terraformers are not scientists. We're architects and so-

phisticated construction workers, and some of us can boast
of being artists and not sound too silly or self-important.
But our purpose is rigorously simple: we replicate Earth
on and inside raw worlds. Our clients are settlers and their
descendants, and they want familiar settings. Enough
novelty to create individual settings, yes. But no more.

We are conservative creatures trained by time-honored
methods, and our basic technologies haven't changed in
millennia. When I was young and in school, full of my
youth, I angered my teachers with plans of changing the
hemoglobin molecule. I'd found a smaller molecule that
did a better job of carrying oxygen, and wouldn't that be
wondrous? Stronger and healthier people; more efficient
animals everywhere. It was just talk, of course. The ma-
nipulation of genes would have been tough work for experts inside well-stocked labs. But the teachers had larger
rebuttals. "What good would it do?" they asked me. "Suppose we do throw aside one billion years of pragmatic
biology. Rich worlds and enworlds pay for the gene-
tailoring, and the poor ones would be left behind. Or
maybe only the new-made worlds would be in a position
to benefit. Do you understand, Ranier? What if the Realm
was divided into an outer Realm of radically altered people—the descendants of wealthy settlers who could afford
the changes—and an interior Realm forced to keep pace
as well as possible. Is that a reasonable future, Ranier?"

"Over blood?" I responded. "Because of the stuff in our
veins?"

"This isn't about blood," they told me. "Admit it, son. You're
conjuring up profound changes. You want to break our ancient taboos. The Realm thrives partly because everyone is
essentially the same. Our environments are interchangeable,
and we don't waste time and resources on trying to outperform
our neighbors. There is a status quo—"

"Boredom, you mean."

"Blood would lead to other changes," they assured me.
"Our minds and our basic human qualities. We'd change
ourselves and divide ourselves and then there wouldn't be
any more boredom. That's true."

"I'm talking about efficiency," I whined.

"No," they countered. "No, you're talking about your
own ego. You're talking about wanting to rebuild worlds

to suit your own dreams of power and success, and don't say it's not so, Ranier. Don't."

The truth told, I couldn't deny that ego had its role.

And remembering the moment now, nearly eighty years afterward, I feel an intense embarrassment. I must be getting older, I reason. Old and conservative, only it's not being conservative anymore. I've learned about people and about myself, and my teachers weren't just cobwebs and old air. Their logic has acquired a force of its own, and I don't feel like wrestling with it anymore. I just don't care enough.

Putting away the last of the buttery brick, I rise and enjoy a lazy stretch. Diesel smoke drifts from the freezer ship. I smell it. For a long moment I look across the open water, the violet-black grove covering the soft mountain slopes and the world beginning its infinite curve. There is a sound. A voice; a sudden motion. The motion becomes a galloping noise, sudden and close, and I turn and see one of the black cretins roaring past me. It charges down the slope, and Snow's voice is calling from below, saying: "Dinner dinner dinner . . . *dinner* . . . !"

TALKER

You can never know another creature's thoughts, claim the Old Ones. Time and again I have heard them counsel against feeling too certain about any animal more substantial than a flatworm in the tidal muds. You can never see inside a cretin's skull, for instance. Not even a cretin's. "They-In-Whom-We-Trust." (That is what the adults call them, in part.) We trust them and certainly understand them better than any other animal—our priceless symbionts since the beginning of time—but not even the wisest Old One can guess precisely how any cretin will respond to a simple circumstance. A ribbon fish trapped in a shallow pool, for instance. Or just a downed tree across a trail. Not even if this Old One has watched the one cretin throughout its life, studying its strengths and its tendencies . . . not even then can it predict just how the cretin will catch and kill that fish, then bring it home to the grove . . . nor how it will approach the downed tree, sniffing at it and then leaping across . . . when . . . ?

(Only the All-Answer knows such mysteries. I repeat this to myself again and again, particularly now that the *passion* has begun.)

And if cretins are impossible to understand fully, then what of the humans? "They-In-Whom-We-*Must*-Trust." They are such complicated beasts. Not nearly so complicated as adult Remarkables, but at least as intelligent and convoluted as most juveniles. Almost as intelligent as me, I think. And humans are skilled at deception too. It is in their heritage—a symptom of their competitiveness—and it can frustrate us. Humans deceive to win status and create uncertainties. They even deceive themselves, their own true natures forever out of reach. Thoughts can run through their minds for years, never detected, sometimes gaining mass and speed until some minuscule event triggers an eruption. A cataclysmic detonation. No Remarkable could see it coming. Perhaps the possibility, but certainly not the moment. Nor the subtle trigger.

I think on these difficult matters, fresh out of the seawater and thankful to be alive. I think about Service and Briar having their sudden little fight while riding together. I saw the entire exchange. I read lips and sometimes heard the hard angry voices chewing at one another. It is not unexpected, but no one had guessed it would begin this soon. I never guessed it would. And now in the aftermath, in the near-silence of the campsite, I see tension everywhere. Every Pitcairn has learned what transpired, at least in part. Even some of our visitors seem aware of the bitter mood and the knotted jaws. Pachel noticed, as did Ranier. Ranier with his strange green eyes, and Pachel with her silver freckles . . . and I watch who I can watch. Every face in view. I stare and stare, as do my siblings.

"This is how it begins," says one. "A fight about an assignment."

Another says, "Maybe it means nothing. Briar has his temper and we knew this . . . maybe it has passed. . . ."

"No," I say.

My voice is loud and sharp, in sound more than motion.

The bunched juveniles are silent for an instant, considering my pronouncement. Then they speak as one. "But our *passion* will come home again!" they shout. "The Old Ones told us—!"

"Many things," I interrupt. "And it has begun, as promised. And we will have to do our best, as we promised. Am I right?"

I am right.

They cannot argue with me.

And after another pause we begin talking about new matters. Little ones. None of us wish to stare hard at what matters. Instead we speak about the weather and our long trip over the bay—what an adventure!—and the sounds of this wild forest and how it seems so strange to be this far from the grove. We see the grove's high slopes in the distance, and we can scarcely make out individual adults. "So far from home," we moan. "So far."

I watch the Pitcairns all the while. They pretend that everything is normal—this is any small *passion* in any typical summer—and the visitors seem completely unaware. I watch faces and study the attitudes of the variable bodies, and I listen to the visitors as they move and clumsily do their work.

They are not too different from the Pitcairns.

Somehow I anticipated them to be very strange and difficult to interpret, but if anything they are easier than Pitcairns. There is an openness to the faces, expressions easy to decipher. Smiles are smiles, frowns are like any frowns. Moods translate into the curl of the lips and the flavor of the eyes. Humans must be the same everywhere, at least in these respects.

Goottich, I notice, is tired but thoroughly happy, indifferent to anything that might intrude on his important fun.

Pachel is angry to be here, as always, and sometimes she glowers at her one-time schoolmate. Why does she dislike him so? And distrust him? None of us know, and I myself am curious and intrigued.

Bedford and Effie are quietly squabbling among themselves, as always. We have never before seen married people, and they seem singularly unhappy. It appears that Bedford impoverished them by using her family fortune in order to pay Goottich's fee. At least Pitcairns are better at sharing, I tell myself. That is one ringing difference between the two groups.

Lumiere, as always, is thinking his private thoughts, the eyes red and calm, tired but buoyed up by a weathered hope.

And Ranier is elsewhere. He put his tent on high ground, virtually invisible from here; and for a long while he has had no urge to come join the rest of us. He seems suited to being alone, I think. I have never known a person so solitary, so strikingly vulnerable, and he intrigues me. More than any of the others, and I cannot say why.

I think and think, and sometimes I chat with my siblings.

Then the wind shifts, soft and from the north, and we start to taste some expected words:

"It has begun!"
"A *passion* for the ages!"
"A *passion* for the world and the stars!"

I am afraid.

I am surprised, very surprised, by how much I am afraid.

10
VENGEANCE

Most of the juveniles are ready for night, their tendrils laced together and their central cores touching. They are in the open, and the outer juveniles have deployed their stinging tendrils—finger-sized needles fat with alien toxins. They cover the barren ground above the beach. Except for one Remarkable, that is.

I walk toward the camp fire, noticing the purple form, and I hear it speaking Pitcairn. I recognize its voice. It must be the one who talked to me this morning. "My friend," it had called me. Now it's telling some kind of story, that voice human. Genderless but otherwise ordinary. It says, "I felt such a consuming urge and had no choice. I recall that much. I remember swimming hard with my school and how we found other schools along the way, knowing them to be siblings by the taste of their skin—"

"You ate each other?" asks Effie.

The laugh is instantaneous, and it's less convincing then the words. Brittle; learned. Then the Remarkable says, "No no no. We just touched mouths, in recognition . . . that's all!"

Pachel notices me and says, "Hey! We were just getting introduced. This is Talker—"

"I know Ranier," says the alien. "We conversed this morning, in fact."

"You should have come down sooner," Bedford tells me. "It's such a lovely evening. A perfect one, in fact."

"Go on with your story," says Effie.

"What story?" I ask, finding a place to sit.

"About how Talker came home to the grove," says Goottich, never mentioning his doubts about the articulate juvenile. He looks at the alien, telling it, "You were talking about your siblings."

"Filled with the same urge. My school and every school. We were as big and old as Remarkables can grow at sea, and we dreamed of this bay. This water. We could taste it in dreams and awake, and that's what drove us to the coast. Past those damned air-breathers and sharks. Shitholes all. Past them and a lot of us gone. A lot of shitholes fat because of us, and they're too stupid even to thank us. 'Thank you!' "

Again the laugh, and this time it's louder. Almost mocking, I think.

"More of us died in the surf," says Talker. "And many others sickened and died in the next months. During our metamorphosis. The parents of these fine people"—the Pitcairns—"carried us into the grove, and the adult Remarkables took us into their canopies and cared for us, lovingly and endlessly, while our lungs grew stronger and our gills faded away. Our metamorphosis. A good spring for diseases, sad to say. Scarcely two hundred of us lived until winter, and now look at us! Just a few of us. Hardly any left whatsoever."

Is the creature sad? Indifferent? What?

I don't know. I listen, expecting more, but Talker offers nothing else. The young Pitcairns start muttering among themselves; they must know that the story is finished. I look across the fire at them. It still feels like dusk, still near daylight, and after a moment I realize who is missing.

"Where's Service?" I whisper to Pachel

"On watch," she answers. "They were explaining . . . it's some kind of tradition. Something for luck. The leader helps with the first watch."

"For good luck," says Briar.

The Pitcairns seem terribly young tonight. I stare at them for a long moment, particularly Snow.

Then Briar says, "The first watch is easiest too. That's another reason." He sits straighter and frowns, shaking his head for a moment. "What's hard is pulling yourself awake in the middle of a night, getting up and going out and then working hard again the next day."

The Pitcairns don't look at Briar, and they say nothing.

I feel uncomfortable. It's as if I have walked into some family squabble and that maybe I should leave again. I feel like picking myself up and slipping off to bed. . . .

Then Talker says, "You are fortunate, Ranier."

Am I?

"To have Service in the lead . . . the great Service . . . !"

Briar folds his legs against his body, saying nothing, but his expression bitter.

Another girl—Shurgar?—touches Briar, whispering with a scolding tone.

"Do you know how Service was named?" asks Talker. It seems to have no interest in Briar's pouting. "Would you like to hear that story? It's quite good, I think you'll see—"

"Yeah," Briar interrupts. "Tell them who's got their hearts in his hands. Someone should. Snow? What about you?"

The Pitcairns turned toward Snow.

"Yes, yes! Tell about Service," says Talker. "Will you, Snow?"

The girl says, "Okay," with resignation. Then she says nothing. We watch while she stares at the burning driftwood, and the wind changes, the ashes and smoke blowing toward me. It's a chemical smell, alien molecules carried into my lungs, and I cough once and fidget, and Snow suddenly begins talking. Her voice is calm and practiced. It seems to go nowhere, but somehow it puts us in the middle of something. I find myself listening. I absorb every word as well as the silences between.

There are two flavors of luck, Snow maintains. Sweet and ill. But hard work sweetens and clear thinking can heal most ills. Every Pitcairn believes these things. She tells how people with the sweetest good luck become elders. She tells how elders live in ordinary houses beneath the Old Ones, and most of the time the Remarkables say nothing memorable. They sing and gossip among themselves, and there's no need to converse with Pitcairns. But there are times when the Old Ones start to babble in the human language. It's one of the elders' most sacred duties, listening to the babble and learning, gathering up anything that might help sweeten and heal.

Snow repeats what we should know by now. She's no

slave and no cretin, and with a sharp tone she warns us
not to suggest otherwise. All right? Then she says that the
elders decide who goes on a *passion*, and the Pitcairns fidget and glance at one another. Then she says, "But there's
one famous summer," and she pauses again.

I watch Snow's face and her hands. One hand tugs at
her ponytail, and she tells how there was one summer
when the Remarkables started chattering about everything. They'd been silent for months, but suddenly they
were telling stories from ages ago—remembering dead
people and their own ancestors, adventures and jokes—
and in the midst of everything, without warning, they told
the elders, "Don't let Lyetle into this year's *passion*," and
the elders said, "What? What was that?" But Remarkables
don't repeat themselves. And they rarely explain their
wishes. Don't let Lyetle go on the *passion*. A strange re-
quest. Practically unheard of, in fact. But it was still the
elders' decision to make, their responsibility. Not the Old
Ones'. They argued the relative merits for a long, long
time, the responsibility heavy upon them.

Lyetle was the famous son of a famous Pitcairn. Snow
tells us how Pitcairn fathers aren't normally close to their
children. But Lyetle's mother was captain to a freezer
ship, absent most of the time, and that's why the father
raised him. Lyetle was famous for being strong and smart,
perhaps small but very tough and full of heart. He was
also old enough to go on the summer's *passion*, and it
would be a large one. A thousand Remarkables were to
travel to Mount Au. Every worthy person would accompany them. Not Lyetle? It seemed ridiculous, but the elders could do as they wished. The Old Ones saw and knew
things humans couldn't imagine, they realized, and that's
why the boy was taken aside and quietly told, "You have
to stay home this summer. We need you at the grove.
That's our decision, Lyetle. It's entirely our own. We're
sorry. Sorry."

He was headstrong. Proud, says Snow. Lyetle went into
a rage, screaming and racing through the grove. He had
heard what the Old Ones had said, and he actually tried
to kick one of them—a terrible, immeasurable crime. But
another Remarkable caught him first, grasping him with
its tendrils and lifting him through the canopy, holding
him high in the bright warm air. A cretin guilty of such a

deed would be dropped in an instant. But humans receive human justice; it's part of the sacred covenant. The boy was brought back down to the black earth, wiser and compliant. The elders met and decided on a punishment, and Lyetle was put to work on the piers, helping unload the greasy frozen cargoes onto the great mechanized belts.

The *passion* left the grove when the weather was clear— the adults have an innate sense about the coming and passing of storm fronts—and Lyetle pretended not to notice. He did his dirty work, sometimes pulling double ten-hour shifts, and he never complained. Every few days the planes would lift off and carry nectars and other supplies inland, but nobody caught the boy watching them. He rarely spoke to anyone. People said, "He'll get over it next year," and sometimes they made sure he could hear them. They said, "He's sure to be chosen next year. And besides, this seasoning will do him good."

Then some planes returned with horrible news. The Two Sisters grove—their worst enemy on the northern coast— had sent hunting cretins after the *passion*. Snow describes the cretins, and I imagine long-legged bears. They attacked at night, trying to kill as many juveniles as possible. And the Pitcairns fought the cretins, using guns and grenades. Several died in the fight. Lyetle's father was disemboweled and partly eaten, and Snow pauses. Then she says, "A hero's death," and everyone sit motionless for a long moment.

An elder told the boy the tragic news.

"I want revenge," Lyetle told her. "It's my right!"

She told him it was impossible.

Lyetle didn't care. He went to every elder, asking permission to lead some kind of raid. And he was refused by everyone. The Two Sisters grove was a long distance south, and there were too many dangers. What if another grove caught word of a raid? What if other Pitcairns decided to attack the Mount Au grove, knowing the best fighters had left and the big fort would be mostly empty? Did the boy really believe one person's death was worth such a terrible risk?

Lyetle had only one recourse. He went to the same Remarkable that he had tried to kick, walking up to the blackened trunk and asking it for help. He showed no fear. Arguing his case, he kept his voice even and firm. Then he sat on the black ground and waited, eating nothing and never drinking and spending two days and a night there. He refused to leave. And finally, after who-knows-what thoughts, the Old One broke into voice, bringing the elders out from their houses to listen and to write down any gems of wisdom.

"Let him take a small boat and himself," said the Old One, "and whatever trickery he wants. He can make a raid. Just himself. Give him his chance of revenge, will you?" Then it spoke about times past and the Two Sisters grove, recounting other *passions* where there were fights and other tragedies . . . the stories, like so many Remarkable stories, going no clear direction and ending in a gray muddle of noise and swaying tendrils.

Lyetle was given a leaky old boat, and he made an elaborate bomb from petroleum and high explosives. Then he set out alone, and every Pitcairn muttered, "Sure death, and a waste. Letting his temper rule that way."

Lyetle hugged the coastline. He worked his way south and reached the bay beside the Two Sisters bay, a great raw wall of rock between him and the grove. He hid his boat in a sea cave and strapped his homemade bomb to his back, then he began climbing during the brief night. A hard mist was falling, making every surface slick. With morning he climbed into a crevice halfway up, sleeping and eating the rich *passion* nectars. "Like ours," adds Snow. Then he awoke to find it raining, a little storm coming off the sea, and he climbed in the darkness, hand over hand, reaching the flat ridge on top just before dawn and then dropping to his knees, exhausted, carefully beating his cramping hands against stone to make them open and close again.

Lyetle had no gun with him, and there were sure to be cretins nearby. But not many, he reasoned. The terrain was too formidable; no sane attacker would come in such weather. And sure enough he wasn't discovered. The sharp winds blew the storm to its death, and the sun rose over the coastal mountains. "Sweet perfect luck," says Snow. Then with a clear, matter-of-fact voice she tells what happened next.

Lyetle set the bomb's controls and carried it to the ridge's lip, and as soon as his face appeared, he was seen. The

Remarkables of the Two Sisters grove were shocked to see an enemy—a hated human animal—just above them. They moaned and sang, lashing at the air with every tendril. The boy lifted his bomb by its straps and disappeared. He stepped back and turned fast, gaining velocity before he flung it over the edge with a solid grunt. The entire grove watched the plastic box tumbling, growing larger, and Snow tells how time moves slowly for Remarkables. They think fast, and the terror must have made time slow even further. Some of them tried to reach high and catch the bomb, then fling it into the water. Only it detonated too soon, out of reach, the blast followed by a ring of scalding red-white fire as the napalm flowed across the grove, tendrils and the trunks burning and shriveling and the maimed Remarkables screaming until the air itself seemed to rip open, the heart of the grove being killed.

The Pitcairns are smiling. The fading light and our camp fire make their faces seem close and clearly drawn, and they are scaring me. I feel an instinctive empathy for the wounded grove, somehow expecting to sense its pain across time and distance. I shut my eyes and breathe, waiting for a long moment. Snow pauses again. I open my eyes, noticing Salo staring at her pretty face. There's anticipation in his. The story is not finished.

Effie stares at the fire, her big eyes empty, and her husband seems puzzled. Goottich has lifted his head and cocked it as if trying to hear something soft and distant. Lumiere looks at me for a moment, then he shakes his head sadly. And Pachel, lone among us, seems almost understanding. Her speckled face glitters in the flickering light, and one of her hands combs her black hair over and over again.

"Lyetle watched the bomb explode," says Snow, "and he waited until the fire began to burn low. Then he stood on the edge, toes in the air, and he opened his trousers and pulled out his prick and peed. He peed off the cliff, right onto the grove, and he screamed at the Two Sisters, 'Does this help? Does it? Tell me if it helps!' "

Salo and some others laugh quietly, enjoying the moment.

I lean back and stare at the toes of my boots, embarrassed and not sure why. What kinds of people did I expect to find? Plucky survivors full of native wit and compassion? I feel angry with myself, listening to Snow tell how

the boy returned home after several more adventures. How
he returned as a great hero—"Telling the story just once,
to one person"—and how the Remarkables, Old Ones and
not, told Lyetle that he had done the grove a great service.
That was when his name changed.

By the next day every person was calling him Service, she
claims, and we should feel honored. No other citizen of the
Au grove is half as famous as Service. I watch the other Pitcairn faces, thinking how they should seem proud and honored, full of respect for the man. But there's none of that. None
that I can see, at least. There is a kind of collective gloominess
pervading here. A stiff iron tension. Then I notice how Salo
and Shurgar and the others look everywhere but at Briar, and
Briar finally says, "You know what it means?"

He is staring at me. Me.

"What the story means?" he repeats.

I manage to say, "What? That Service has done heroic
deeds?"

Briar laughs. It is a harsh noise, and bitter. Then after a
moment he tells us, "The Old Ones didn't like him. They
thought his temper would endanger the *passion*, and that's
why they didn't want him going. Then they decided to let him
attack the Two Sisters, knowing that he'd die first. They were
as surprised as anyone that he succeeded. I bet they were!"

Nobody else speaks.

Something moves. Talker is rolling backward, making for
the other juveniles, and I can't count all the eyes poking up
out of that tangle. None of them are asleep, it seems.

Then Briar says, "He really fooled them, Service did.
And Snow's right. You should feel honored."

Salo says, "Briar?"

Snow says, "Maybe you should—"

"All these years," says Briar, "and the Old Ones remember. They've been planning and planning. And now that
Service is getting old, wearing out—"

"Stop," warns Salo, one large arm reaching for Briar.

"—now they've finally come up with a way to punish
him!"

"Don't," says Snow.

"Briar," says Shurgar.

And Salo pulls back his arm, looking at us with embarrassed eyes, saying, "That's not true. Not true. Briar's just
teasing you. That's what he's famous for, believe me. . . ."

11
FIRST DAY

✛

"Higher."

"There?" I ask.

"Center me."

"What?"

But Snow finds the center herself, saying, "Okay, pull down. On the bow. Steady hard." The canoe's stern is rammed into the rocky ground, a knotted rope dangling from the bow, and I grasp the rope and grunt and she says, "There," the instant everything is level. Then she says, "My gun, give it," and I kneel and lift the rifle as if it might explode. It weighs almost nothing. She can walk and hold it in one hand, moving surprisingly fast over the uneven ground. The plastic canoe is an enormous clumsy hat fitted on the brackets built into her pack's frame, and she moves smoothly, her back straightened, the free hand sometimes rising to make an adjustment, always minor, then dropping to swing at her side.

Snow is my partner. She came to my tent this morning and told me. I felt a surge of pleasure and relief, glad to have this chance to accompany her. *Sweet luck*, I remembered. *Sweet luck*.

It's a short walk to the next bay—a modest bay on my map—and the path resembles a dried riverbed. Winter storms drive the high tides even higher, salt water flowing between the bays and leaving gravel beds and stacks of driftwood. This is a natural highway. I follow Snow, passing her when the channel widens and spills into the open. I follow her instructions, grabbing the gunwales with my arms extended, driving the stern into the ground and her

kneeling and slipping out from under the canoe. She says,
"Easy," when I drop the canoe. It booms, and she says,
"Easy," once again.

The tide is out. We load our packs between the seats
and untie the paddles, and she shows me how to secure
my pack to the crossbeams. "You don't know knots, do
you?" She begins to laugh.

"Things should be able to fasten themselves," I argue.

She keeps laughing. Together we shove the canoe over
the dampened ground, shellfish breaking under our boots.
I tense up with the crunching, waiting for any sensation.
But there's nothing. What I need to do, I tell myself, is
quit worrying. I'm healed. And when I get home, first
thing, I'll thank my wonderful physician. That's a promise.

Our canoe sticks out into the water. Snow says, "In
front," and nods, her dark misaligned teeth showing. "Go
on."

We slip onto the bay. The Remarkables come up behind
us, never pausing, and I notice how their voices change as
they hit the cool water. Snow tells me to paddle. Already
my butt hates the plastic seat. I work to make my motions
unconscious, paddling on both sides and trying for efficiency. Snow seems able to keep us in a straight line re-
gardless what I do or forget to do. Service is ahead of us,
a pair of the black cretins sprawled out on his canoe. The
Remarkables are everywhere, and the other people are
mixed in with them. The *passion* is a living chain trailing
back into the tall rainforest.

There's purpose in this scene. I feel it and feel part of
it, and I feel quite happy. I haven't been this way in a
long time.

I notice big graceful butterflylike insects with silvery
wings flying inside the Remarkables, in the spaces between
the tendrils. The Remarkables seem to ignore them. Why?
Snow gives me a strange look, surprised anyone would
waste breath on such a question. She's alert, her rifle on
top of her pack and two ceramic grenades beside the rifle.
They're probably for discouraging sharks and whatnot. But
can't Remarkables keep better track of possible foes? I ask
her that too. Then she says, "Wait," and we coast for a
few minutes. We allow some of the Remarkables to pass
us, plus a canoe manned by two Pitcairns—I don't remem-

ber their names—and I hold my paddle in both hands, on my lap, the cool water dripping down the handle and onto my trousers and soaking through, feeling good against my skin.

I watch the Remarkables. They keep at least one eye underwater at all times. Sometimes the flexible inner tendrils reach down and catch a fish, lifting it into the air and clumsily shoving it into its mouth. They eat their fish whole. Some of the silver butterflies land on the fishes, just for an instant, then they flutter up and avoid the tendrils. It is a bright overcast day, and I can see clear through the Remarkables. They're more air then flesh, I'm thinking . . . and Snow says, "Paddle," with a crisp quick voice.

"Sorry," I offer, digging at the water.

She says, "Easy," and brakes with her paddle. Then she asks, "What was your question?"

I remember one question. "Why are you so alert?"

"Being ready means I can react faster."

I nod, thinking that makes sense. Then a voice beside me says, "We call them—" and I can't follow what I hear. There are knots of sound, almost musical, and Talker says, "Quite pretty in the light, aren't they? 'Butterflies' is your name? A lovely name. We let them fly among our tendrils because they are pretty. And because they taste horrible. Full of bitter trash . . ."

I remember my question now.

"Thanks," I offer.

Then Snow says, "Work," with an almost-harsh voice. "Why don't you try work for a while?"

I say, "Sorry," to myself, digging at the water, noticing how my hands are growing accustomed to the feel of the wood and the paddle's balance and the way seawater swirls around it. It's as if I've been doing this forever, I think. At least that's how it seems.

I carry at the next portage. Like before, the path is waterworn stone on a dry channel, rising and then dropping to the next bay. Snow helps me get centered. Balance is the most important trick, she claims. Did I practice yesterday? I avoid the question. Strength isn't half of what I'm doing, she claims. But the weight of the canoe and my pack make every muscle ache, and my strength wavers. I feel awful. I remember all of my hard training, and it seems like paradise now. It was nothing by comparison, and I'm not prepared for this shit. Not at all.

I rediscover something every laborer must learn. Anger builds strength. Cursing inside my head, I focus my fury and make the load lighter. Fuck this canoe. Fuck its mothers and fathers. Fuck its hollowed-log ancestors and the idiot who invented the first one. The ground is tilting under me, and I start fighting for balance. I pull with both arms, Snow saying, "You don't need to!" *Fuck Pitcairn*, I think. Why the hell don't they build airplanes big enough to fly these damned aliens inland? Take them to their fucking holy mountain and push them out with parachutes attached . . . and that hurts me. The image breaks my concentration. I'm imagining more than a hundred purple tumbleweeds dropping from the sky, suspended on colored parachutes, and I nearly laugh. I gulp at the air and stagger, and Snow says, "We're close," as I push ahead faster, trying to regain my fury.

Something comes up beside me. And it snorts. I force my tired head to pivot. A velvety black cretin looks at me and takes a hoarse wet breath. A little tear of fluid dangles from its black nose, glittering for an instant and then falling away. I tell it, "Hunt." It blinks and does nothing. It's certainly not hunting. Then it starts trotting faster, and I say, "Heel." Only it won't. It goes down to the water's edge and dips its head, greedily drinking from the salty bay.

Snow comes around me and helps me climb free of the canoe. Then we load it and secure the loads, and she says, "We can wait. A minute." A little knot of Pitcairns are sitting on some dry rocks. I'm the first visitor to make his portage, and I sit with them and wait. Bedford is next, accompanied by one of the young almost-boys. Pachel follows. Briar is her partner, and he looks calm and indifferent today. Thank God. Then comes Effie, of all people. She looks like a sketch of a person beneath the big canoe, Salo loping beside her. Just like Snow promised, it's a matter of balance, not strength. That's Effie's secret. Salo takes her canoe and sets it down gingerly, and Bedford tells her, "You did it! I told you you would!"

She ignores him, gasping hard.

I look around, then ask, "Where's Service?"

"Guarding us," says one of them.

"Thank goodness," says Briar.

Snow looks down and says nothing, her mouth clamped shut.

The Remarkables are moving along the dried channel, rolling in close masses. Another cretin moves among them, its long pink tongue curling between thumb-sized incisors. Dust and bits of dead deflated leaves cling to its plumage and to the Remarkables. The aliens don't appear so purple, I notice. But when they're dirty they seem more substantial somehow.

Goottich is among them, big and slow and wet in the face. "Who's his partner?" I ask Snow. It's Tintoil, the largest girl, plainer than Snow and quiet. I watch her take the canoe from him and he halfheartedly helps get it ready for the water. The big man is unaccustomed to any physical work. The more I watch him, the more I think it. The simplest rules of conduct haven't impinged on his brain. He is more in the way than helping, and to her credit Tintoil seems endlessly patient with him.

Lumiere finally arrives, sweaty and pale but otherwise in good shape. Shurgar is helping him, easing the canoe down without effort. He blows hard and sees me, then he lifts a hand, waving until I wave back down at him.

Remarkables roll onto the bay, eyes submerging and their chatter quiet. Another cretin laps up salt water. They must have wonderful kidneys. I start to admire the mountains that flank the new bay, and the endless trees, and how the dirt washes free of the aliens as they spin in the greenish water, transforming themselves back to the vibrant clean purple.

Suddenly the Pitcairns around me stand together, as a body.

I blink and turn. A moment later Service emerges from the rainforest, his rifle held high and a pair of cretins bolting for the delicious sea.

Service pauses, staring at everyone.

I climb to my feet, feeling strange. He's angry with us for just sitting. I wouldn't know what else to do, but the accusing glare makes me feel guilty. I'm a little boy caught doing evil by my father. Then the old Pitcairn moves between us, goat-walking down the rocks and setting the rifle into his canoe—smaller than the others, probably lighter—and he pushes out among the Remarkables and orders one cretin on board. It leaps from the shore to his pack, landing deftly. Then Service takes a few smooth quick strokes, pulling away. and finally he turns and shouts back at us, "Come on, come on! You're growing roots standing still like that! We need to move!"

"It didn't obey me."

Snow doesn't speak. We're working against the outgoing tide, and even the tail wind doesn't help. It just roughens the water, cold spray coming over me, and I keep noticing how the shoreline barely moves. We're making the sketchiest progress just now.

Finally Snow asks, "Who didn't?" and strokes. "What are you talking about?"

"The cretin. I told it to hunt, then heel, and it didn't pay attention to me."

She says, "Oh," and nothing else. I'd turn and look at her but I've got to concentrate on the paddling. I'm out of my element here, scared and wondering how long I would last if we dumped. Then Snow says, "Because," and grunts hard, straightening us in the choppy green water. "Because you aren't . . . aren't human." Then she grunts again.

"Who's not human?"

She says, "To them," and doesn't stroke. She tells me, "You smell wrong and you look very strange."

Naturally, I think. *Sure.*

An old tarball is straight ahead, big and covered with a pinkish fungus, and it looks almost pretty as we drift past. I stare at it, turning my head and no longer paddling. Neither is Snow. We find ourselves looking at each other, saying nothing for a long moment; then I have to ask, "What did Briar mean last night? That noise about this being Service's punishment—"

"He was teasing. Like we told you."

We start drifting sideways and rocking a little too much.

"Teasing?" I repeat.

"Yes," she says stiffly. Then she says, "Yes," again, louder this time. It's as if she's trying to convince both of us and maybe the wind too. Maybe the whole world . . .

12
MOONRISE

❖

Our campsite is an island at high tide, a long peninsula when the water drops; it has trees and open ground beneath them, plus a single log structure built out on the tip.

"A sauna," Service explains to us. "There's a stove inside and benches. It's a party place for the kids."

The six of us are sitting with him. The other Pitcairns are on watch or chopping firewood for the sauna. I hear the axes and sometimes voices, and they sound more nervous than festive. Service is building our fire, kneeling and coaxing the tinder to ignite under a tepee of damp sticks. And Bedford, feigning innocence, asks, "What kinds of parties, sir?"

The weathered face lifts, and he says, "The screwing kind."

Pitcairns have a reputation. Maybe it's because they have nothing like marriage. Their couplings can be frequent and varied and sometimes wild. Certain holos were brought back by the first two missions—tropical groves and sunbaked naked bodies involved in orgies—and for a lot of people, particularly deep in the Realm, those are their first images of this place. Ancient taboos have been strained to breaking here. Couples from opposite ends of the grove, practically strangers to each other, nonetheless are genetically like brother and sister. And that's pornographic on almost any other world. That's worth the exorbitant prices those holos command.

Lumiere asks Service, "Why don't you join them?"

There's a glimmer behind the eyes. Service nods and tells us, "Youngsters can embarrass old men."

There are various scholarly explanations for the Pit-cairns' sexual ways. They've got no other release. It's a social mechanism and a good way to build community intimacy. And maybe it's a holdover from the desperate times when populations were tiny and any reproduction was welcomed.

Service stands over the growing fire, then starts breaking a long stick under his boot. Lumiere is saying that it's true, he understands about the failures of age, and he gently laughs and starts to help. He breaks up a larger stick and lowers the pieces onto the burning tepee. Then Snow's voice is audible, almost close, and Service catches me looking for her. I'm craning my neck, not even aware of it, and he halfway smiles at me. Just for an instant. Then he turns and starts to chase down some more sticks.

The Remarkables are bunched at the island's center, on a clear high place. We can see them from where we sit. Lumiere asks, "How did you come to live here?" and I notice a few of the alien eyes swinging our way. Then Lumiere persists, asking, "Didn't your ancestors come from the south?"

"Escaping wars," Service tells us.

"It was in the files," Goottich remarks. Haven't we been paying attention? he implies.

"There were several dozen in fishing boats," Service continues. He wipes his hands on his trousers and backs away from the fire. "We went from grove to grove until one of them took us."

"Did it take long?" asks Pachel.

He says, "Almost too long."

"Why?"

"There were no people on this coast. The Remarkables knew about us, but they were happy without us." Service nods appreciatively. "They can be stubborn. Big brains full of inertia, and you have to work hard to change what they think."

Pachel glances at me. It's late enough for the first traces of night to gather under these trees. Her silver flecks catch the firelight, and she turns back toward Service. "But why wouldn't they accept you? I mean, isn't it obvious that they'd prosper?"

Service starts to chew on a pinkish slice of hard nectar.

It's the color of his tongue, and sometimes it looks as if he's got two tongues in his mouth. He isn't in any hurry. He swallows and looks at us, then says, "The grove that took us was tiny. Young. Hungry." He waits for a moment, then says, "Desperate."

"Is that so?" says Bedford.

Pachel asks, "How about yourselves? You came a long way . . . you must have been running out of supplies. Nectars. Is that right?"

"Oh, sure," he says. He nods and takes another pink slice, then explains, "Some of us were hungry enough to eat ribbon fish. You know what that means? We were too hungry to think, and we poisoned ourselves. A couple of us died from the meat."

Pitcairn amino acids and lipids—biochemically useless and oftentimes toxic. Two hundred centuries hadn't brought people any closer to losing their status as aliens on this world.

"It still puzzles me," says Pachel. "Why doesn't every grove have Pitcairns? Why aren't people more in demand?"

Service is puzzled by the question.

"If you do them so much good," she persists, "why not?"

A brittle energy runs through her. The woman has a definite point to make, and I'm the one who blurts out, "It's not that simple."

"Why not?"

"Because." I say the word, then pause to consider what comes next. "Because," I say, "they're throwing aside millions of years of success when they take us. Replacing symbionts . . . it's not an easy decision. That any groves agree to do it . . . that's almost miraculous, I think."

Pachel watches me, maybe surprised by my intensity.

I know I'm surprised by it.

Then she looks at the fire, saying, "I don't doubt that they've got good memories and they can mimic us. That they see wonderfully well. But intelligence, true intelligence, is more than a summation of neurons."

Service studies her.

She tells him, "We used to believe that whales and porpoises—our air-breathers—were intelligent. Thousands of years ago people almost worshiped them. Then we learned that their big brains concentrate on one task. They inter-

pret sonar signals, sorting and measuring the echoes.
There's no room left for rational, calculating thought."

Goottich seems amused. "I know that argument," he
says. "Remarkables have their all-seeing eyes. Their ability to synthesize organic wonders." He holds up a black
brick of nectar, illustrating his point. "They've got many
talents, but they're really nothing more, or less, than vast
organic computers."

"I hope you're not offended," Pachel tells Service. "I'm
just giving my opinions. That's all."

The old Pitcairn narrows his eyes; otherwise he doesn't
respond.

"It's all quite speculative," says Goottich. "Answers take
research, and research requires opportunity. We haven't
had that opportunity yet." The big man smiles at everyone, the expression superior and grating.

"I believe that the Remarkables are intelligent," says
Lumiere. His smile is disarming, in contrast. "Perhaps
they're even brilliant. But any opinion comes out of hopefulness. A certain aesthetic desire. I can't claim to being
rational here."

People fidget for a moment, unsure of themselves.

Then Effie asks, "What about tools?"

"Let's stay out of this," Bedford suggests. "I don't see
the good—"

"They never use tools," the tiny woman continues.
"Those tendrils . . . couldn't they grasp like hands do?"

"Well—" I begin.

"No, no, no," Goottich interrupts. "Their tendrils don't
have the coordination. They're more like tongues than fingers. Good at picking up dead fish and herding birds to
their mouths. But they couldn't manipulate the simplest
screwdriver, much less build fusion reactors and torchships."

It becomes quiet. Service closes his eyes, scratching his
throat above the fat horizontal scar; and after a moment
he starts to shake his head and run the same hand through
the graying hair.

"I'm sorry," Effie says stiffly. "I shouldn't have said anything. It was my mistake."

Goottich is oblivious to her anger. He grins and shrugs
his shoulders, happy to be able to correct wrong and
shoddy thinking.

"I thought it was a reasonable point," says Bedford.

Effie says, "Leave me alone."

"Completely reasonable," he mutters.

She says nothing, hugging herself and looking exhausted.

Then Service spits, a spinning gob of fluid vanishing into the fire, sizzling and boiling and everyone listening. He watches us, showing nothing with his expression. Skin laid over carved stone . . . that's how his face looks. Skin and stone with polished stone eyes glittering in the firelight.

"What do you think about them? Really."

"The Remarkables?"

Pachel says, "Sure."

"I'm in Lumiere's court, I guess. I want them to be intelligent. Brilliant. Beyond our simple means."

We're standing beside my tent, and I'm watching Pachel. She's a handsome woman, strong-faced but in an appealing way. And this is an exotic locale, like in any good romance holo—

"They don't like us," says Pachel.

I blink and ask, "Who? The Remarkables?"

"No, not them." She's disappointed in me. "The Pitcairns, I mean. Particularly Service."

"What? Did your partner tell you something?"

"Briar didn't talk all day." She shakes her head. "No, it's something I can feel. Can't you? He's got very little respect for us. We're strange and weak—"

"Who's *he*?"

"Service," she snaps. "Aren't you listening?"

I'm too tired to listen. It's all I can manage to stand upright, and suddenly I've lost my interest in the woman. I want to go to bed and sleep hard. Service was right about the young embarrassing the old. My younger self would have pursued Pachel. Liking her wouldn't be a factor. I just don't have the drive anymore, and with that sober assessment I offer a smile, telling her, "Thanks for walking up with me. . . ."

And she says, "Good night," turns, and starts for her tent.

I climb into the mummy bag and build a pillow from my clothes, and for a little while I listen to the night wind in the trees. Then I hear voices, distant but clear, and I realize that the Pitcairns are coming out of their sauna. I imagine them naked, pale asses infinitely young. I actually think of climbing outside and eavesdropping on their orgy. But then some superior part of me says, "That's childish," and I think again. I roll onto my belly and shut my eyes, concentrating on nothing, and after a few minutes I fall deep into sleep.

And I awaken.

It's later, only I don't know how much later. Did I hear something? Then comes the familiar chill working through me. It's happening again. The physicians are shits. More promises broken, I'm thinking. My illness has reclaimed me, not full-blown but still awful. I touch my face, sweat drenching me, and I remember to keep still and breathe calmly and distract myself as well as I can manage.

Something outside is in agony.

It's in the bay, I decide. It's huge and nearby . . . probably one of the big air-breathers. Air-breathers have modest nervous systems, don't they? What is it? Harpooned? Partly consumed by sharks? I curl into a ball and shiver, and I breathe like a sprinter, hoping the new tricks can readapt somehow. Make this bearable somehow—

—and I'm crying, almost sobbing. FUCK THIS. . . . FUCK . . . ! And in an instant it is finished. Suddenly gone. Either the creature died abruptly—not likely—or the countermeasures took hold again. *I hope.*

I try to sleep again, and I fail. I lie on my back with the tent flap partway open, eyes looking outside. I notice that the Pitcairn moon has risen, and somewhere the clouds have thinned to nothing. A cool silver light pours through the deflated canopy and into my little house. I can't see the moon itself, but I can see my own shadow. Lifting a hand, I spend time making shapes against the tent wall. Long-necked birds; strange toads. A simple game from my boyhood, and I'm surprised how long I stick with it.

TALKER

❖

Then the hand shadows drop, Ranier asleep. I watch his body inflate and freeze, then the breath flowing out of him. Then a sibling says, "Look there." It speaks with motion, and very little motion at that. I pull my eyes together, collecting the thin light and the heat and refocusing, watching two figures become Salo and Snow. Nude. Side by side on the forest floor, their faces toward the bay and away from us. They have just made love. I can see the heat bleeding from their skin, much as I watched Ranier's brief fever. Peering down between trees, I watch the backs of their heads and listen, concentrating, letting the quiet night air bring me their voices—

"Got to go on watch," Salo says.

"So go," Snow tells him.

"In a minute." He eases away from the girl, then he touches the back of her neck and asks, "Did you ever see the boat? The one that came in last winter—?"

Snow moves, slipping from his grip.

"—after the big storm? You know which one. The banished—"

"Quiet," she tells him.

"Why?"

"Shush."

Salo says, "You did see it, didn't you?"

The two of them met not long before the *passion*. Salo was working on the piers, and Snow was learning to pilot the airplanes. They do not know each other. Humans, even humans from the same grove, take forever to feel at ease with one another.

Again Snow says, "Shush."

"Why?" he responds.

She has no good reason. They can talk about whatever they wish, of course. Why not?

"All right," she says. "What if I saw that boat?"

"I *really* saw them," Salo tells her. "Did you know? I was in the tug that went out to meet them first."

"Were you?"

"Where were you?" he asks.

"Way up above. On the ridge." Above the grove, she means. Higher than the frost line. Then she says, "Tell me later. If you're late for watch, Service will start hunting you—"

"They were a mess," Salo says. "In the boat? Starving. Sick. Do you know how far they came? Did you hear?"

"Yes," she says.

"From the tropics. In that little boat."

"I know."

"Banished from their grove—"

"*I know,*" she whispers.

"Months wandering at sea. No weapons and their nectars running down and down—"

"It happens. So?"

And for a moment Salo is silent. For a moment I am remembering the incident. It was the darkest time in winter, and during a hard storm a strange boat was blown into the bay, blown from the open sea. It had a makeshift sail, no fuel in its engines. Seven Pitcairns were left alive, the others stacked below to serve as food. To stretch out their nectars for a little while longer . . . the banished always given supplies, always given an opportunity to find some willing grove . . .

"I never got on board," Salo tells her.

Snow says nothing, but she stares at him. At this angle, for just an instant, I can make out the darkness about her eyes.

"I wanted to climb over. But it was a different boat, a later one, that got the job. It wasn't our business."

"I know."

"Service was the one in charge. Of that next boat."

"I know."

I watched the drama. Service and his boarding party had had to wear masks, the stink was that terrible. The rot and sick wet human shit. The malnourished crew was brought up on deck. I remember watching the scene with my hearts squeezing fast. I could just make out the strangers' faces, knowing by looking that they were not from our grove. And Service did as Pitcairns always do with banished people. He warned them that there was no staying here. They were not welcome. They were criminals—he didn't want to know for what crimes—and the most he could offer them was to tow them out past the spit.

They could scarcely stand upright, those criminal humans. And the dim glow of the winter day washed over their faces, making them look waxy to me. Cold to me, the same as dead.

"We watched Service tie on the line and cross back over again," Salo says. "We even caught a whiff of them. We were that close. And it was some stink too. They didn't smell like people anymore."

Snow says nothing.

"If I'd been in charge," he says, "I wouldn't have towed them."

"No?"

He shakes his head and says, "I'd have put them out of their misery. In an instant."

"You'd have shot them?"

"The cleanest way," he says. "Unlike towing them back out to sea. In that boat? Can you think of anything crueler? Service could have shown pity and he didn't, and that's bothered me. Ever since."

Snow is quiet.

"Letting the sea do his work." Salo groans and finally stands, his trousers gathered up in one hand. "The man's not perfect. All that talk about Service being fearless, the ideal Pitcairn . . . it's just that. Talk."

Snow says something too soft to understand.

And Salo laughs, saying, "All right, I will. But why don't you sometime listen to Briar? He's full of opinions. About everything. Why don't you give him a chance sometime?"

"Go on watch," Snow says.

"I'm gone." The muscled Pitcairn finds the rest of his clothes and leaves her, not another word said. I study Snow's back and how she sits motionless, inflating herself with long breaths and thinking about many things. I can guess what things. And all the while I remember the story told by the adult Remarkables closest to the sea, at the westmost edge of our grove.

Service did tow the leaky boat past the spit.

As tradition dictates, he set them adrift and warned them not to come inshore again. Not near the Au grove, at least.

But before he climbed back over to his own boat, something happened. Distance and the growing night made it impossible to be certain, but he seemed to hand something to the banished crew. The adult Remarkables thought he was handing over bricks of nectar. He was pulling them from beneath his bulky poncho, giving several bricks to each person.

Nobody on his ship could see him.

To my knowledge, Service never told anyone about the deed.

Most humans would not approve. But it was Service's nectar, earned by his own hard work, and he could give it to the fishes for all they cared. Or to the dead, as he did then.

Then he came home again, piloting his boat around the fort and the spit, its engines roaring and his eyes ahead and his face almost unreadable. And behind him, after much frantic effort, the banished humans raised their worn sail and coasted off, a new rain beginning to fall.

Snow cannot know that part of the story.

Only the Remarkables know it. And Service himself.

And if he wishes to tell it, he can tell it. We will not intrude. If asked, we will verify. We will elaborate. If this *passion* survives, Snow can hear the whole tale from the Old Ones themselves.

But Service won't tell; I sense it.

"I gave them the stuff because you never know. You never know who might get sweet luck."

That is what he might say if he was asked.

If he had to explain himself.

13
SECOND DAY

✦

The Pitcairn leaves begin inflating with the first tentative bites of sunlight. The intake of cool damp air makes a peculiar sound, gentle and oddly reassuring, and this is the first time I've noticed it. I'm sitting outside my tent, staring up at the baggy leaves and noticing how their greenness weakens with the influx of air, and how the dead leaves hang tight, drying into hard brownish husks that slowly crumble away. Then I hear someone walking in the leaf litter, and I look at the sound. The girl is carrying her clothes across her shoulder, immune to the morning chill. She stops in the distance, just before I'm sure it's Snow, and she steps into her trousers and slips on her shirt. Then she comes closer, amused to see me staring. "Partner," she says. "You're awake."

"An illusion."

She doesn't stop to talk, not to tease me about my ragged appearance or make neutral noise about the weather. Cloudy again, I notice. Rains coming? Snow walks past me, some destination in mind, and I watch her broad back and the feminine rump and the pale soles of her bare feet kicking up the brown litter, her boots laced together and carried in her left hand. Somehow I decide that she's not smiling anymore. It's something about her posture, her pace. I feel a pang of jealousy, wondering with whom she spent her night. But it passes. I'm too old for that crap, I remind myself. Then I rise to my feet and pack my belongings, making ready for today.

The passenger lounges across our packs. His gray leg is crossed over his older leg. He climbed on board before

Snow pushed us away from shore, and sometimes she says, "Heel." To the cretin. At least I think she's talking to the cretin.

Sometimes I'm nervous, glancing back at the glossy black head with the bright red eye patches, the yellow eyes seemingly cut from glass. It sniffs me occasionally, the tiny brain absorbing every portion of my scent. Goottich and Tintoil are ahead of us. They're also carrying a cretin. We're moving between the shoreline and the Remarkables, and Snow says that the cretins are here to sniff at the trees and crevices. Nothing else alive has such a fine nose. A special breed; the best of the best. They're our radar, our sonar. Our means of looking around dark corners.

The coastal mountains grow rougher and taller. In places the sponge green of the rainforests show breaks, old avalanches fenced in with tilting trees and undergrowth. The sky is gray and smooth, cutting off the peaks, and sometimes there's mist or a light rain. I have to wear my poncho periodically, but the rain never lasts. I feel hot and remove it, folding it and sticking it under the seat, and in another few minutes it starts raining again.

A cliff drops into the sea, blackened with oils. Mats of oil-eating fungi and microbes surround the slick on the water. The fungi resemble colorful furs, long and luxurious. Petroleum is everywhere on Pitcairn; its carbon cycle is skewed from earthly norms. We swing wide to pass the mess, and a pair of stout gooselike birds fly low in front of us, landing where the water is its blackest.

They splash and dip their black heads, drinking and then cackling with wild high-pitched voices.

"What are they?"I ask.

"Gleaters."

Oileaters. Gas-geese. Different groves have different names for the related birds. They've got specialized guts full of oil-adoring bacteria—a useful symbiosis—and they're typically large and slow, ample layers of fat keeping them buoyant and warm. Natural selection, rigorously adaptable, has fit two species to suit this world. Novel enzymes; a reliable energy source. I salute the birds, and they cackle once again.

We work our way into the bay, and I ask the names of trees. Snow's responses are brief. Efficient. A stand of tweedtrees; a single old rumplerundle; a small knot of steelwoods. Too young to cut, she complains; steelwood takes forever to grow. . . .

There's a distinct line on the mountains, and above that line the greenness changes, becoming lighter-colored and rougher to the eye.

"The frost line," she tells me.

We're going to have to climb a lot higher to cross these mountains, and the magnitude of this business both excites and worries me.

The tide is dropping. The Remarkables breathe in wheezes, their lines stretching apart. Through the gaps I see the bay's open water, gulls circling and their bright musical voices wrong sounding. A closer bird is huge, resembling a pelican. "A baleen bird?" I say.

"A hungry one," she adds. "No sweet clouds in weeks."

Sweet clouds. Airborne planktons are mixed with flying insects, some of the clouds low to the water and others mixed with water clouds. They're born in the broad tropics, blown to the higher latitudes, and usually diluted along the way. Their absence must affect the local groves. There are few swarms of fat bugs to be lured with nectar baits, and the Remarkables are even more dependent on game and fish.

The cretin behind me sits up and stretches, then gives a huge hot snort. I smell its vivid breath and I turn, yellow-white eyes gazing straight into me.

"Heel," warns Snow.

The cretin stretches again, pretending not to hear.

Snow cracks it with her paddle, the blade in the back, then says, "Down!"

I feel its pain, a quick chill running along my spine.

Then it hunkers down again, returning to its olfactory duties. Snow's pretty face is framed by the greens of the water and the sloping land. Sitting in the stern of our bulky canoe, she seems remote and extraordinarily attractive. All I can think to say is, "He's awfully stubborn, isn't he?"

"We want them that way."

"That surprises me."

And she almost laughs, shaking her head and telling me, "Stubborn is a good thing, Ranier. Sometimes." Then she says, "You don't know much at all, do you? Do you?"

* * *

We eat on the water, one person constantly paddling. I learn to pee off the bow with a modicum of dignity, and I ignore Snow's indifferent version of the same. And she warns me to eat more. Don't hoard the nectars. We'll have plenty airlifted to us, very soon, and I choke down a double portion and find myself getting stronger. Stimulants sewn into the sugars and proteins? *Some sweet luck*, I'm thinking. *Aliens who can cook on a world where nothing else is edible.* I finish with a long drink of filtered water, belching twice and feeling like a superman.

Eventually we catch Tintoil and Goottich, the big man tired and their canoe overloaded with his meat and their cretin. Tintoil signals for us to pass them, and Goottich seems to take it personally. His round face is sweaty and pained; rainwater drips over the brim of his hood, resembling an anemic waterfall.

"Keep digging," I tell him.

"Dig yourself," he groans.

Ass.

This bay is deep in two ways, reaching into the mountains before curling south with a large island on the seaward side. Our passageway narrows until the forests form walls on both sides of us. I'm aware of their weight and latent energy, and I can smell them as well as the seawater and the exposed seafloor. There are stretches of rock and shellfish, green beds of algae resembling fancy lettuce, and big varnished trilobites scrambling toward holes. The canoes and Remarkables have closed into single file. Remarkables are ahead and behind us, and we can't see people. Our cretin sniffs; I think of ambushes. I find myself wishing that I could hold a gun, even just a little one. Something to help me feel as if I belong a little more.

There aren't any attacks, and the passageway widens into a new bay, large and protected seaward by a long low spit of sand. The sand is white against the darkening skies, barren in a clean way, and the bay itself is nearly smooth under a fitful wind. We spread out and head across the open water, leaving even the pretense of land, and I try relaxing. I try to work steadily. Sometimes I splash myself to feel the cold stings of the water, then the healing rush of blood. We pass the lead Remarkables, and only Service is ahead of us now. I watch his steady, almost effortless paddling, and after a little while I notice how I'm trying to mimic his style. The student following the teacher . . .

Service has a cretin. It starts whining, the sound more birdlike than doglike. Ours sits up and makes the same sound.

"What is it?"I blurt.

The Remarkables are rolling faster too. "Look ahead," says Snow. An island stands at the precise center of the bay—I remember the maps—rocks on rocks and every surface frosted with brilliant white guano. Birds circle and others perch above the high-tide lines. I hear them squawking. The shifting wind brings their stink to us, rich and wrong smelling. Not part of nature, as I remember it.

"Move," says Snow. "Keep digging."

We pass the island rookery, close enough for me to notice different species and the shapeless youngsters with their colorless, incomplete coats, stubby wings, and the always-gaping mouths pointed skyward. Every adult is flying, staying low but never lighting. They cry and wheel and come low over us, and the water is peppered with little shit bombs.

Goottich comes up beside me. "Caught you!" he announces with winded satisfaction, his face full of blood and the big teeth shining.

"Congratulations," I offer.

Snow says to stop now, to wait, and I watch some of the stubby, candy-colored birds called goofies. They race past us, not an arm's length above the surface, their faces in a perpetual panic. Something's happening. It occurs to me slowly, intruding on my tiredness. The other people catch us, canoes making hollow thuds as they bump together. We're drifting away from the island and the Remarkables. The aliens, a few more than a hundred of them, are gathering into mass, preparing for their assault.

The adult birds wail and howl and cackle, circling faster, and the Remarkables climb onto the island in a solid wall of clinging, scrambling tendrils. Sometimes a gull or goofy dives as if to attack, pulling out too soon and just avoiding being grabbed. The Remarkables are bunched together and feasting. I think of a purple-stained cloud clinging to a white-capped mountain, the cloud moving furiously within itself. The physical pain comes to

me in spurts and little dribbles. The squabs, the chicks
. . . whatever. They're being consumed now. This must
happen every year that the *passion* comes this way—a dose
of easy proteins—and every year the nesters have to begin
again. The poor goofies. I think of their faces and their
pretty colors, and isn't that silly? The Remarkables start
climbing back down to the water, and I find myself wishing that some big air-breather would grab one of them
now. I want justice of some kind. Stupid as that seems . . .

This is a biosphere, after all. I'm watching the endless
transfer of living energies—a thing of beauty and purpose—and there's no crime here. No crime and no need
for justice. An air-breather would be meaningless . . . just
another energy mover, I tell myself.

"What's the matter, Ranier?"

I think it's Snow talking, but I turn and find Pachel
drifting nearby, the only concerned face to be seen.

"Nothing's the matter," I promise.

"You look pale," Pachel explains. "Is the nectar turning
on you?"

"No. I'm just tired, that's all."

The birds are still circling the island. The Remarkables
have gone, but they seem unwilling to land and survey the
damage.

"If you're tired," says Snow, "you should work harder."

I look at her, noticing a thin smile.

"Work cures," she tells me.

And our cretin snorts, seemingly agreeing with her.

14
TERRAFORMERS

◆

The camp fire is big and hot, everyone sitting back away from it. Bedford's talking. Somehow he's launched into a description of their home. They live in a Unity community, in a private enworld out among the comets, and they've got a little park amid the buildings and many-tiered farms. The park is stocked with game animals—roodeer, for instance, and rainbow quail. Sometimes there are little hunts, formalized and ceremonial. Hunting shows how humankind has dominion over nature. Pausing for a moment, Bedford shows a thin dreamy smile. Then he tells how he's hunted and even eaten what he has killed. The guns are sophisticated, true. Laser sights make certain that the prey will die immediately. No suffering, no wastes. But otherwise they're like Pitcairn rifles, basically—

—and I know what he wants.

"I was curious," says Bedford, "if perhaps you'd let us carry some extra weapons. I can help you. So can Effie. We could even stand watch some night . . . give you a little vacation. . . ."

Faces turn toward Service, Pitcairn and ours. He is sitting on a lump of chipped limestone, eyes down and his expression unreadable. He says nothing. He seems not to have heard anything.

"I'm not carrying anything else," says Effie. "And I'm not standing guard. I won't."

Her husband frowns and says, "But it would be a good gesture. And we'd get a better appreciation of things—"

"We won't let you," says someone.

Briar, I realize. He sits forward and repeats himself, the

sour voice telling us, "You're not carrying guns, and we're sure as hell not trusting you on our perimeter."

Bedford seems more puzzled than insulted.

Effie says, "See? They don't want us helping!"

Service coughs to get our attention. "It's a generous offer, but no thank you."

"Them standing watch," Briar snorts. "Imagine it!"

A few Pitcairns laugh quietly. Service glares at Briar, making no response. Snow seems embarrassed and tense. She glances at me, then her eyes drop.

"My family built your enworld," Goottich mentions. "A standard twenty-klick cylinder, isn't it?"

"It is. Yes."

"There's enough forest for roodeer?"

"They're a little species," Bedford replies. "Our own, actually. And we augment their feed."

The Pitcairns watch him and Goottich.

Briar asks, "How many people live there? Inside this big cylinder of yours . . . how many thousands?"

"One hundred thousand," Bedford reports.

"That's crazy. Insane." Briar laughs with contempt. "People packed that close together. You wonder how they keep their sanity." He shakes his head, every motion overdone. Theatrical.

Service watches him, saying nothing.

"But that's the Realm," Briar continues. "No self-control. People everywhere. Homes built on top of homes, nobody ever alone—"

Pachel snarls, "What the hell do you know? We build buildings for maximum privacy. We don't overtax the land. And even our most crowded cities, the ones deep inside the Realm . . . they've got trees and flowering shrubs and a wide, wide variety of creatures."

"It sounds lovely," says Briar, his tone sharp and satirical. "All those worlds, and they keep filling them up. They keep moving out and out, always needing more worlds." He seems to be talking to the fire, telling it, "They're insane people. Just like everyone says, they've got no sense. No self-discipline. Long lazy lives and too many children to count."

Pachel looks angry, but she won't let herself say more.

Then a familiar voice cuts into the tension, almost loud. "Can I hear about these enworlds?" asks Talker. It has rolled up behind me, confessing, "I am curious. Tell me how you build them, how you make them live . . . tell how you remake whole worlds. I want to hear. Enough to get the flavor of it, please. Please? Please?"

"Talker is strange," Snow confided today.

"Because it's a juvenile and talks?" I asked.

"Partly." She paused for an instant, then said, "But it's more. Talker thinks in straight lines."

"Straight lines?"

"Not like the others. Juveniles and adults . . . even the Old Ones sound confused when they talk. Too many thoughts, and they come busting out at once. You have to listen carefully. Sometimes they'll say one thing and then its opposite—it'll rain in two days; it'll be clear in two days—and if you ask which it believes, it will say, 'Both. Both at once and equally.' "

I have heard similar stories. Remarkables act as if their minds have subminds, and they don't speak as much as they debate aloud. Maybe it's a consequence of being truly brilliant.

"And Talker?" I asked.

"Talker's organized. Almost human, sometimes." She waited a moment, then added, "Talker will keep that power when it's grown up. At least it should be an improvement over most adults."

"An improvement?"

"No," she decided. "But more human. In that one way, at least."

I watch the Remarkable now, remembering the conversation. Goottich is busily explaining enworlds, thrilled with the opportunity. True to his nature, he lumps too many details on top of his overdressed words. What can the alien understand? Or does comprehension matter to it? "We build our hulls from plastics and hyperfibers, using force-molds and standard zero-gee robots. Synthetic rocks coat the interior walls, then people like myself elaborate tightly coiled biospheres—"

"Fascinating," says Talker. "It truly is!"

I find myself looking into those tendrils, hunting for normal eyes and a human face.

"Biospheres based on a dozen basic models," Goottich continues. "I prefer semitropical ocean climates in my own work. In order to keep up with our production levels—we make nearly a hundred new enworlds every year—I have developed three basic packages. Collections of proved species, in other words. A little tinkering, a little random reshuffling, and that's how I can keep up with my work load. And still have time for my private projects."

Goottich pauses and blinks, and he beams his smile at everyone.

"You must be gods," Talker responds. "All of you . . . gods!"

I say nothing, aware of my own breathing.

"And you rebuild whole worlds too!"

Goottich enjoys being called godlike. "It's not difficult work," he states, giving an offhanded wave and a cocky grin. "Take New Albemarne, for instance. Its terraforming began with sunlight. There are five standard models for orbiting fusion reactors, proved and durable and mass-produced by older worlds. By New Emerald and others. The B model was chosen for its compact size, and it was placed in a suitable orbit. Its light emissions were tuned for maximum heat output, melting the ancient ices. Then later the reactor was retuned, giving off the best frequencies of light for photosynthetic systems—"

"Plants," I interrupt.

"—and the landscapes chemistry was changed." The big man nods with a god's easy authority. "Millimeter-class robots were injected into the raw atmosphere, each acting like a chemical factory. That's routine. Toxins are destroyed, free oxygen is created, and the first formation of soil begins—"

"Holy work," Bedford interrupts. He doesn't like being excluded, and his voice is shrill and self-important. "We're vital to the Realm. Terraformers, I mean. We've got enormous duties and responsibilities. We're the ones who make the Realm possible."

Lumiere smiles at me, shrugging his shoulders as if embarrassed by this endless praise.

"New lifeforms were introduced later," says Goottich. "New Albemarne, like anywhere, was built up with simpler lifeforms first. Bacteria, then algae. Fungi and vegetation, then the trophic levels of animal life. That's the pattern."

"Inventing species!" says Talker. "You actually fashion such wonders with your fancy tools?"

Goottich nods and says, "New species. New genuses. Sometimes even new families. But the higher organizations, kingdoms and phyla and the classes . . . they're unchanging, for the most part—"

"Sparrows," I inject.

Faces turn.

"We've excelled at making new sparrows. A small, dull little bird. I've never been able to tell any two apart, but there might be more than a hundred billion species of them throughout the Realm—"

"Sparrows," Talker repeats. A dutiful student.

"And nobody even guesses how many kinds of beetles you'd count," I add. "If you could count them, that is."

Goottich tolerates me, silently shaking his head. Then he says, "An entire world, New Albemarne or Rye's World . . . each one involves thousands of terraformers. Maybe a hundred thousand in the first critical centuries." Another pause. "Even with the tiniest enworlds there are many participants, many specialties. I'm in charge of my own, yes, and robots do most of the actual work. But I have staffs. Detail people. In all cases but one . . ."

It is bait, and Talker can't resist.

"What's the exception?" it asks.

But Briar interrupts. "How many people are crammed into the Realm? Do any of you know?"

Goottich blinks and looks at the Pitcairn. "There is no agency nor any pseudogovernment capable of even pretending a census. But the estimates are in excess of a trillion trillion. Perhaps as many as ten trillion trillion. Deep in the Realm, in areas with ample industrial capacity, huge factories spit out new enworlds at a prodigious rate. You can't count them, much less the people inhabiting them."

There is a long pause, and the Pitcairns seem to work on those numbers. It's like contemplating the numbers of atoms making up their own bodies. It's entirely beyond their reach, and it's beyond ours too. The Realm is a vast round ocean filled with humans and sparrows, beetles and spinning enworlds.

"Such important work," Bedford has to proclaim. He sounds like Talker's praising, except he's praising himself. "Bringing life to the cosmos . . . !"

Goottich gives a vague smile.

"I feel fortunate in working with so many talented colleagues," Bedford continues. "As the Unity Faith teaches, through such work we learn the values of cooperation and trust."

The Pitcairns become very still, every face stony. Cold.

Then Talker says, "What's that exception of yours, Goottich? You were going to tell us."

The round face glistens. "I have a very special home. An enworld of my own. A giant hundred-klick cylinder built for me as a graduation gift." He continues with a lengthy description of the world's little sea and its rivers, small mountains, and forests almost mature now. "All of it designed and overseen by me. No colleagues, talented or otherwise. Every facet of the work is mine."

A long silence is broken by Tintoil. "How many people live with you?"

Her voice is quiet, almost respectful.

"Nobody. I live alone."

"How do you manage that trick?" Briar asks him. "If everyone else is packed in like fish in a cargo hold—?"

"I'm wealthy," snaps Goottich. "I'm extremely wealthy."

Lumiere leans close to me, whispering, "What do you think they make of wealth?" He means the Pitcairns. Societies where nobody owns property but for identical houses; people without currency beyond records of bravery and selfless duties fulfilled.

"They understand more than we think," Lumiere says, answering his own question. He has an old man's surety. Or wisdom. Or maybe enlightenment.

I say, "Perhaps," with a soft, neutral tone.

"I envy you."

Effie says that to Goottich. Then Bedford turns, saying, "What do you mean—?"

"Solitude sounds wonderful," she adds with defiance. And with a harsh chuckle, "I envy the wealth too. That sounds doubly wonderful!"

Bedford makes a frustrated sound and sits back.

And Goottich continues describing his giant home. The godly role does suit him, I decide. The gestures of his hands and the occasional low cough are done with ceremony and a tireless confidence. Effie is always watching him, genuinely enthralled. Her delicate face is such a contrast to his titanic round one. All eyes and his face with such tiny eyes. When did she start looking at him this way? That unrestrained dreamy gaze—?

"My circumstances are almost unheard of in the Realm," Goottich explains to everyone. "Not even the wealthiest of the wealthy can have their own world inside the Realm. Living space is just too precious. But on the frontier, in special cases . . . well, a few of us are blessed. With skills as well as money. With the training and vision."

"You can do anything you wish?" asks Talker.

"Virtually," Goottich replies.

Tendrils move in the air, curling and uncurling while swaying back and forth. Then the almost-human voice asks, "Could you, if you wish, remake your enworld?"

"Of course."

"Could you make it like Pitcairn?"

"Pitcairn?" He shrugs and says, "Yes, I suppose so."

"This gravity? This air?"

Goottich draws into himself all at once. He says nothing, shows nothing.

Could it be done? I wonder. Assuming every legal problem could be solved, of course.

Then Effie says, "It sounds splendid just like it is."

Bedford nods and says, "A perfect home for a lot of deserving people."

Goottich smiles, his gaze distant. Indifferent.

Talker abruptly says, "Such a long day. Good night now," and begins to roll toward its siblings, seemingly forgetting its questions. "Good night to everyone!"

"Good night," Lumiere echoes.

Effie says, "I'd love to see it someday."

Bedford asks, "Why?"

"What are you looking at?" says Briar. "What did I do now?"

He's growling at Service, and Service says nothing in response. He merely blinks and sighs, then rises to his feet and stares at everyone. I start watching his eyes. They don't absorb everything like a Remarkable's cold black disks, but they have their own kind of power. A certain unmistakable force. That familiar landscape of pupils and irises and clumsy wet lenses cuts through everyone here. Nobody is spared.

15
INLAND

✦

The trail lifts in front of me, and I drive the canoe into
the ground at eye level, the impact caught by my shoulders and back. I don't have enough breath to curse. I stop
and use my arms, tilting my load out of balance, and the
world under me tries flinging me backward while I move
aching legs. I can't see the top of the slope. The universe
comprises a tilted strip of stony ground, the pale earth
slickened by rains. I hate this place. I vow to return someday with construction lasers and robots, flattening the
whole fucking planet and paving it under spongy asphalts
. . . graceless conquest, a human tradition . . . and again
I misjudge—*thud*—feeling the impact and then my own
rage, blaming the ground and the canoe and the gravity
too . . . everything but the idiot in charge. . . .

The trail flattens suddenly, and Snow tells me, "Stop."
She trots out ahead of me with her pack bobbing and
creaking, and I tell her:

"Let me finish. . . . I can—"

"Too far, Ranier." Up come her arms, and she takes the
canoe off me. Then she waits, the pretty face smiling—
amused with my attitude, I suppose—and I breathe in
gulps and take her place. I hold up the canoe until she's
positioned, and she is up and everything is in balance, her
smile hardly wavering.

There's one last upslope, and she attacks it and then goes
downhill again. She seems to know the precise location of
her cargo, never clipping the ground or the tree trunks.
She does slip once on mud, but even slipping is nothing.
It's a game. She skis for a few meters, then her boots find

purchase again; and she starts walking, calling back to me with a soft teasing voice:

"Careful. Watch your step."

The next bay is visible between the trees. It looks odd. Dark, almost black. Then the trail dips at the end, my knees aching as I descend, and we burst from the forest onto a wide shelf of barren stone.

The bay is shallow and choked with sediments exposed by low tide. Black-brown and littered with debris, the sediments exhale a thick rich stink that must help bring the hundreds and thousands of birds. Flocks dabble in shallow pools. Long-legged waders scurry back and forth, probing the salty muds for nameless sweet worms. A solitary eaglelike something squats on a carcass, watching us between bites. Are we a threat? Or food? Neither, it decides, and it stabs at the shapeless meat, then chews like a dutiful child before swallowing.

I start sensing little pains around me. From the bay; from the nearby people. But it's not bad. It's no relapse, and I tell myself to be optimistic. It won't get worse. And if it does, I decide, it'll just be a distraction. And if it's worse than a distraction, then I'll just concentrate on my own agonies. I have enough of them to be preoccupied.

The Remarkables emerge from the trail. I scarcely give them a second look, already accustomed to their shapes and gaits and the sounds of tendrils brushing against foliage. They're talking with whistles and clicks, and I refuse to listen. Listening is useless, I've learned. Try and try, but it'll never sound like a real language. Just a mess of random pointless noise.

Snow pulls a map from her shirt pocket, and she shows me our course. "We'll follow this river inland. To the lake district, then up into the mountains. Then down and over another river and out onto the Au plain. You see?"

I've pored over the maps myself. Each future campsite marked with the red X; our schedule designed to balance the Remarkables' limits with ours. I look at the weak ribbon of clear water curling along on the mud, and I ask Snow, "That's the river?"

She turns once, maybe hearing something. Then she says, "Yes," and stuffs the map back out of sight.

A thin mist becomes rain, and winds drive raindrops into my face. We load our packs in the canoe and find our ponchos. I manage to put my head into my sleeve, and she tugs on my hair and says, "Try again."

Service comes out of the trees, not on the trail, carrying his rifle with its white ceramic barrel up. He walks past us without a word or a glance, and he sets the rifle into his canoe and starts pushing, fighting his way across the soft stinking muds.

I help Snow, or at least I try to help her. But the mud clings to my boots, caking them, and they slip sideways with every push. It's fifty or sixty meters to the little river, and it takes an age. Twice I drop to my knees, then stand and scrape myself partway clean. Finally we're climbing on board, Snow straddling the stern to steady the way for me. Gobs of mud stain our packs, and more gobs fall from the underside of the canoe, the water full of smoky black clouds that tumble as they move.

I feel an instinctive regret. We're making a mess.

The Remarkables remain on the mud, their tendrils coated. They resemble overly elaborate wheels, shiny and slow, moving in lines so the trailing wheels don't have to navigate through as much goo.

The little river works against us, then it pauses. The slight current vanishes for a few moments, then it decides to run backward. Suddenly we don't have to paddle to keep close to the Remarkables. We just steer and the river lifts, eventually spilling from its channel and across the mud.

I don't talk. I'm resting and watching my surroundings. There are fishes in the water and sometimes strange-colored bits of living gelatin, and the forest around this bay looks different. More steelwood trees, I realize. Massive ones, ancient and safe from logging. The water's too shallow to bring in the logging boats. A happenstance sanctuary. I dig out my own map and look ahead, trying to visualize our route. The mountains are shrouded by clouds. Straight ahead is a V-shaped gash—the river's source—and the steep walls are covered with ancient timber, vividly green and hopelessly impenetrable. And it occurs to me that everything ahead of us that isn't air and water has been built from air and water, and from sunlight too. The steelwood trees and the circling birds. And the Remarkables. And me.

The Pitcairns work above us, unburying and assembling some kind of winch. The trail begins far above the river, and the six of us have to stand together and wait, nowhere to sit.

There's a noisy rapids beside us, waterworn stones littered with smashed trunks and smaller forest trash. Maybe a dozen Remarkables are clustered where the water deepens, fishing with their longest tendrils. The tide is peaking. I can just see the open bay when I crane my neck, and I'm glad to be here now. The open water is rough. Service was right to hurry us. I remind myself never to doubt the man again.

"Think what they could do with tidal dams," says Pachel. "Strings of them up and down this coast."

"I don't think they want dams," Lumiere replies.

"Simple technologies, minimal maintenance." She shrugs her shoulders. "Why not?"

"They don't need the power," I offer.

"So far," she adds ominously. "One of these days, however . . ."

Then comes a sound—a single tone that makes our heads jerk—and the Remarkables on the water start rolling. They roll faster than I'd have thought possible. Tendrils slap the water. Someone says, "Shark!" The Remarkables seem to fly off the water, and their Pitcairn guards start lobbing grenades into the current. The blasts are sudden and muted, fountains of water white and rising high, and the fountains collapse while the aliens chatter among themselves. They don't sound excited. Or anything. It's just more random noise mixed in with the cackling chatter of gulls, the Remarkables on shore now. Safe.

Dozens of dead and stunned fish rise to the surface, muscular and aluminum-colored. Sea pike? I feel them for a moment, their pains feeble. Then gone. Then the gulls descend from everywhere. Up close they look more like feathered lizards than birds, but they've got a gull's mentality. They fight for treasures, grabbing and tugging, and the losers stay close and pretend not to notice too much. To have no motives; to be enjoying the day. Then a winner is distracted or lazy, and its meal is stolen in a blink.

"Fuck you!" the gulls shout at each other. Or words of similar intent. "Fuck you! Fuck you! Fuck you!"

Snow lies to me. "It's not far," she says, then remembers to smile. To give the lie more life.

I appreciate the gesture. She thinks she can help my spirits, and I look into her eyes and nod and say, "Okay." She grabs the bowline and tugs hard, and I absorb the new mass, expecting agony and not finding it. It's not as bad as before. Or at least I've redefined *bad*, and this chore is merely awfully uncomfortable.

We are far above the river, walking a trail seldom used by people. It was a hard sloppy climb to get here, on hands and knees. The soaked earth is crushed into my clothes and under my nails. I stink. Under the canoe, sheltered from rain and the wind, I can't help but smell myself. What a mess! I feel guilt mixed with disgust, twisting my head sideways. Lush vegetation lines the trail, chest-tall and sometimes adorned with long spines. *Keep on the trail.* Every tree is a steelwood, broad and massive and the bark slick and smooth, and I tell myself to borrow the strength around me. To will it inside myself.

Snow is behind me.

Goottich is straight ahead, legs and his oversized boots visible beneath his poncho. I ask him how he's feeling.

He waits a moment, collecting himself. Then he says, "Fine," without sounding like a man on the brink of collapse. But I know better. I know it by watching how he slows on the upgrades and how he tries to stop and kick away some of the caked-on mud. And sometimes I feel his misery. It's a cold blotch, prideful and stubborn. Goottich doesn't want to break first. Like everyone else, he doesn't want to be the first to collapse.

The trail tilts upward, my universe narrowing again.

"How far . . . have we gone?" asks Goottich.

"A long ways," lies Tintoil, turning around and walking backward. She shows him a quick vague smile.

I drive with my sorry old legs, breathing fast now. The air under the inverted canoe is hot and close. I surprise myself with a fart, loud and harsh; and Snow laughs, saying, "Quiet. Shush."

I watch the ground. I step with care, only vaguely aware of the Remarkables nearby and the distant heavy roar of the river. Time contracts. My goals contract. I want to survive my next step, and the next . . . and after a while the discomfort blossoms into something almost familiar, nuzzling close to me and becoming routine.

* * *

Effie is first to crumble. Dissolve. *Fail.*

I hear the crash, and the line abruptly stops. Then Tintoil is shouting, "Trade!" back at us. Snow appears, and I'm out from under the damned thing. I feel buoyant, like smoke. Someone, I think Salo, says, "She's all right," and I feel guilty for being happy. For thinking, it's not me. I'm saved the embarrassment, thank god.

Again we move, and I walk behind Snow. Rain is seeping through the canopy, bringing a gloom and chill to the scene. Plants like ferns and plants like soft green hairs cover the ground, shining with the dampness. The Remarkables are everywhere. On the trail and not. Snow is singing to herself, almost silently. She carries and carries, not minding anything. We go down a little slope and up a long monster slope . . . and people shout, "Trade!" A joke, I think. But it's not.

Again I'm under the preposterous canoe-shaped hat. Again every stride takes an hour, my breathing quickening, yet my tissues can't pull enough oxygen from this air. The saving grace is the mild slope. Uphill, always uphill, and Snow decides to give me another dose of encouragement. "Almost there," she promises. "We're close now."

Maybe. But Goottich stops abruptly, my bow ramming his stern. We curse each other and the delay, and Tintoil walks ahead and returns with the news. The trail has collapsed. Hard rains ate out the slope, and we'll take the gully one at a time.

Gradually, too gradually, we work our way forward.

Eventually Tintoil takes the canoe from Goottich, and she walks it through the raw gully. The brown hull twists, almost vanishing, then rises on the far side, her feet making a string of quick, dancerlike moves. Then she's up and Goottich follows, and Snow says, "Let me."

I don't argue. Standing at a safe distance, I stare into the gouged earth, watching Snow follow the bootprints down into a thin brown stream, then rising again. I worry about her. She's climbing the far wall and a wedge of soaked ground begins to sag, roots breaking with a muffled sound, and I feel a thick cold lump in the back of my mouth. What if she falls? She'd fly down the chute and over the brink, tumbling into the river's gorge . . . only she doesn't pause or seem the least bit concerned, over the far lip now . . . Goottich beckoning to me, telling me, "Come on, Ranier. Your turn, Ranier!"

Heroism is riding the bubble of fear.

I feel light and maybe too strong, adrenaline trying to make me run. I hear the steady white roar of the river and smell the mud and slip once, sliding to the bottom with my pack driving into my kidneys. The mountainside tilts, threatening to spill into the river. Then I leap and dig with my boots, climbing fast, practically flying up to the solid safe ground.

Not so awful, I think. Then I realize that I'm breathing in gulps and shaking, and I start laughing. I look at Snow, wanting congratulations, but she's staring back across the gully, oblivious of me.

Pachel stands under her canoe, talking to Briar. The river and rain cover her voice, but she wants something. And Briar doesn't answer. He merely waves a hand and steps back out of her way, and I can't believe what she's doing. She turns the canoe sideways and deftly slip-steps to the bottom. I should shout encouragement, only I'm afraid to distract her. She twists into a new position and starts climbing, then slips and slams the canoe against the mud-and-root wall. But she keeps her balance. She grunts and comes up over the edge, her expression fierce. Triumphant.

Briar climbs up after her and grins.

"Not so hard," she mutters. "Not bad at all."

The Remarkables are crossing farther up the slope, their airy bodies filling the gully and their tendrils grasping at every stalk. The ones not crossing are watching us. Almost every black eye is fixed on our little drama.

"Good job," Briar tells Pachel. "Too bad you're not a criminal. You could become one of us, if you were."

I hear him, and I don't. I understand the words, but they're too surprising and odd to be digested. What did Briar just imply? That he's a criminal? That all of them are . . . ? Or is he just teasing again, like with that business about this being Service's punishment, this *passion* . . . ?

Then I decide that I misunderstood him. Or maybe the Pitcairn word for criminal sounds like something else. Something I haven't learned. That's got to be it. Sure.

"Ranier," calls Snow. "Are you coming?"

And I turn, glancing up at the Remarkables now. All those eyes, and my skin feels like glass, their gazes cutting through me. I suddenly feel very simple, like a little aquarium fish, a fragile twist of cold brain visible inside my fragile wisp of skull.

16
ATTACK

◆

The fire smolders in the steady rain, producing more smoke than heat and stinking because of the steelwood. Steelwood makes superior ship hulls, but it burns poorly. Service asked the six of us to collect tonight's firewood, and now we're wiser. Cold but better for it.

Service pokes at the fire with a stick, and Pachel approaches him. She gets his attention, then says, "This is lovely country," with a slow, grudging voice. "I never guessed it would be this way."

The old Pitcairn gives a little nod and the barest smile.

"I'm really surprised," she confesses, coming back toward us.

People stand between the fire and gorge, letting the wind blow the smoke away from us. Craning my neck, I peer over the edge—waterfalls and swirling mist clouds and the little river white—then I look at Snow sitting on the edge, her feet dangling. The girl has no fear. I keep asking myself how she could be any kind of criminal. Briar's words stick at me. I wish I could ask someone. Her, maybe. Or Service. Or Talker. Probably Talker, I decide. When I get the chance—

"I thought you hated the rain," Effie says. "Don't you, Pachel?"

Bedford's wife looks beaten in some deep way. It's more than exhaustion. She's brittle and weak to the bone, and her voice matches her appearance, squeaky and uneven. "How could you like . . . this place . . . ?"

"Now, now," says Bedford.

Effie stiffens while her husband pats her shoulder.

"I still hate the rain," says Pachel, grinning and shrugging. "But these mountains, the trees . . . why don't you make these kinds of trees, Ranier? This kind of forest . . . ?"

"Give me money and room," I joke.

Bedford nods and announces, "Life is certainly vibrant here."

Only it's more than life. There's the huge effect of water erosion—river-made gorges don't exist on most terraformed worlds—and there's the age and the history of life here. This isn't some veneer laid down for cosmetic purposes. Each native organism stands at the summation of endless raw biologies, survivors buoyed up by sweet good fortune.

"Pitcairn is a great resource," says Bedford. He sounds as if he's given the issue constant attention, his manner cool and professional. A finger draws a smug little circle in the air. "I'm sure Pitcairn can be an inspiration to *everyone*."

Lumiere is beside me. Like Effie, he looks beaten down by the day's work. But he winks at me and smiles, then asks Bedford, "Do you believe this world should become part of the Realm?"

Bedford considers the question, and he doesn't. I sense that he's pretending to deliberate. Then he rolls his eyes. "I think not. No. Pitcairn should be preserved as it is. Untouched and innocent. As a laboratory, perhaps."

Effie hugs herself. Her arms move under her poncho, and she sighs.

Bedford turns to Snow and the other Pitcairns. "You see, I believe in the human species. Its natural perfection. You and I are part of that perfection. Humans are in a titanic struggle with entropy—disorder and heat death—and by doing what we've been doing, by terraforming and expanding, we've helped spread human perfection. The human dominion. We're making the galaxy live!"

"Shit," I mutter.

Bedford turns and says, "Pardon?"

"Proselytizing to our hosts," I respond. "That's tacky."

The pretty face seems wounded.

I look at Snow. Salo sits next to her; Briar is out on watch. "My associate belongs to a popular religion," I explain. "The Unity Faith believes the *everything* in the universe was created to serve life, and particularly human life. That terraforming is God's plan."

"We don't have a deity," says Bedford.

"Unity," Effie says. Her tiny mouth is fused shut, and she seems full of a sudden conviction. "People rule by design."

"But you don't have a deity either. Do you?" Bedford asks the Pitcairns, then answers for them. "You don't. Remarkables have their All-Answer, but you believe in yourselves. You work hard and make your own good luck, and you're making this world serve you. And you'll succeed, I'm sure. Just as we make the Realm serve us. It's all the same."

I'm surprised by my own anger here. "Listen," I say, "I've never liked this Unity shit. It's just wind. Humanity is nothing perfect, and the creed is just so much wishful thinking—"

"And I disagree," says the pretty man. "Completely."

I look at Snow. "Life . . . it's the product of complex self-replicating molecules and selection pressures. Nothing perfect there. The system that made us is amoral. Pragmatic and amoral." I pause, then add, "And oftentimes cruel too."

Bedford asks, "Who's proselytizing now?"

I say nothing.

Goottich is chewing on a brick of nectar. It's like a little honey pear in his hand. "I agree with you, Ranier. I've seen it a million times in my home. My enworld." He pauses to smile and swallow. "Animals cheat each other. Even the peaceful species try to dominate their herd. Their flock. Their school. It's just natural. And predators always attack the unlucky ones—"

"Death means life," Bedford proclaims.

The Pitcairns watch us. This must be the strangest conversation they have ever heard. At least among humans. I turn and glance at Service, still poking at the worthless fire. He doesn't seem to listen, and I wish he would. I have the irrational desire for him to break in and tell us to shut up. To act like a parent and prevent a fight.

"Death balances life," says Bedford, "making it perfect."

Pachel says, "I agree with Bedford, but for none of his

reasons. I want us to leave this place alone. To keep it safe from ourselves."

Effie says, "I don't care. One way or the other."

Her shrill voice gets everyone's attention.

"But the rest of this solar system . . . I hope we terraform everything. Mine the Pitcairn moon and fill up the sky with enworlds. Millions and millions of enworlds."

"Now, now," says Bedford.

Effie says, "Don't touch me!"

He lifts his hand, saying, "There are laws. I mean, the Pitcairns do own their solar system. They've got legal rights and haven't shown any interest in selling—"

"So we take it," she growls. "Who's to stop us?"

There's a tension, thick and sharp. Effie is angry about today—about collapsing—and maybe this is her revenge. Or maybe she believes what she says. Turning to Goottich, she reports, "I agree with you. There are predators, and there are prey. Everything is out for itself. And we're the same as the rest of it."

"But you want to preserve this biosphere, don't you?" Bedford asks the question, his expression concerned. Dumbfounded. "Love? You do recognize the uniqueness of this world, don't you?"

She shrugs and says, "We'll study it, sure. Then we can terraform Pitcairn too. Cut the air down and plant edible crops . . . and everything. . . ."

Pachel turns away, tired of the noise. She joins Service at the fire, and the old Pitcairn throws in more wood, orange sparks flying out in neat arcs. "I feel stronger," she tells him. "This diet and the exercise . . . it's making a difference."

Service glances back at us, saying, "Good."

"It's beautiful here."

He says, "Yeah," while glaring at Effie.

"If we have to," Effie says, "we can store Pitcairn in tubes. Cells frozen in tubes. Then we can do worthwhile things here—"

"But, dear?"

She snaps at her husband. "What?"

"Do you have any idea how you sound?"

Effie begins to cry, curling up into a ball and Goottich sitting beside her now. He watches her cry, mildly interested, and he pops the last of the nectar into his mouth.

Effie looks minuscule beside him. She whispers something, and Bedford says, "So go to bed. Go on."

The Pitcairns are huddled at the gorge's edge. They aren't watching Effie anymore. They stare down into the mists, saying nothing, something in their posture implying nervousness barely restrained.

"How soon do we reach the lakes tomorrow?"

Pachel is asking Service for the timetable.

"Early?" she asks.

He looks at her, nods and says, "Early." Then he gives the fire one last hard poke.

I'm awake.

There's blackness and the waking sense of being lost. Where is this? Then I remember sounds without dimensions or volume. I listen for them. I hold my breath and keep still, waiting and waiting and wondering if what I heard was a dream.

Then there's a huge roaring shriek from nearby. I jerk upright and gulp a breath. The shriek fragments into voices, then a burst of gunfire. "There, there!" A man shouts. More shouts, then something roars . . . and an icy sensation races through me, my knees to my mouth and my own voice moaning.

Something's in agony. I feel it and hear the Remarkables crying out. It's not them I feel. I sit motionless and wait, and something massive bolts past my tent, the fabric walls shaking and a single bullet glancing off a steelwood trunk. *Ping.* I hear its passage and drop flat an instant later. Then a woman says, "Down there!" and the fusillade moves toward the gorge, the shots quickening, ending with a last hard flurry.

Strange quivering sounds come from uphill, but otherwise there's nothing. I make myself dress and climb outside. It's night, the seamless black mixed with fog. Where's my flashlight? I find it and decipher the switch, a modest yellow beam swallowed by the fog. What's happened? Snow happens past, her rifle in both hands, and I ask her. "Is it serious?"

"Come see," she tells me.

The dead cretin is enormous, larger than any New Albemarne bear and thickest through its shoulders and forelegs. The saberlike teeth are as long as my hands. Its plumage is brown and golden under the brown, and the blood is an intense crimson.

Goottich is touching its head. He looks thoroughly impressed.

The Remarkables are above us. They're talking and moving, tendrils in the foliage. I notice a severed chunk of tendril dangling from the cretin's mouth, Goottich removing it and examining it in my light.

Snow kneels, inserting a finger into a bullet hole. "It's from the Black Mountain grove."

"You can tell by the feel?" asks Bedford.

"By its plumage," snaps Goottich.

Snow retrieves her finger and wipes it clean on her trousers. "One trouble done. One to go."

What does she mean?

Then I hear Service calling for us. He says, "Get over here," from somewhere near the camp fire. "Everyone!"

People seem to be fastened to their flashlight beams, the beams pivoting fast and focusing on the Remarkables. Several dozen of the aliens are descending on us. In the darkness they seem substantial, forming a wall that rolls between the great trees.

I move out of their way, plant spines piercing my trousers.

The Remarkables reach the carcass and begin to eat. I might be seeing what I expect to see, but there's relish in the sounds and the motions. Teeth cut into the meat, slicing tendons and heavy ligaments. Suddenly I remember when I was eight years old and killed a desert squirrel with a blowgun. Then I cooked it over an open fire, eating half of it before the strong creosote flavor made me sick.

Service calls again. "Now, now!"

Snow says something, and I turn and ask, "What was that?"

"I think's it's Salo."

I see her face in the reflected glare of my light. At first I think she's crying, then I'm not sure. Maybe she's angry, only at whom?

She turns and starts to trot.

I take one last look at the Remarkables. I can't see the carcass amid the tendrils, and I remember the cretin's pain. I feel sorry for the dead cretin. It's nothing I intend to feel. It's just something that is.

* * *

Eleven of our Remarkables have been seriously injured. The cretin slipped past Salo, then at the last possible instant charged them and started bashing them with its forepaws. This is a disaster. It's too early in the *passion* for this kind of attack. And there's no doubt about where to place the blame.

"My cretins kept fucking up," Salo tells us. He shakes his head and says, "It's not my fault. They kept smelling false smells in the fog . . . sending me to the wrong places—"

"No excuse," Service replies. "You know how an attacker can work. It lays its scent everywhere, then it waits for us."

The big Pitcairn glares at Service.

Pachel comes up beside and asks, "What do you think?"

"About what?" I whisper.

"What Briar said . . . criminals. . . ."

"*Quiet*," Service warns us.

Salo repeats himself. "It's not my fault—"

"You stay quiet too," warns the old Pitcairn. "No more excuses."

This is a trial, Service both judge and jury. We're surrounded by an audience of Remarkables. The wounded ones are bunched together, tendrils ripped loose and the thick purple blood oozing onto the forest floor. The air stinks like old fish. I hate the smell and this entire show. I'm lucky that I can't feel any of the Remarkables' suffering. Their neurons must be too different. Out of reach, thank goodness.

"Eleven injured juveniles," says Service, "and the negligence is obvious." He is holding a canoe paddle and some kind of drill. He kneels and starts working on the white wood, boring holes while saying, "You serve this grove, Salo. You don't serve yourself. That's our covenant with each other. Humans to humans. To Remarkables. To their groves." The words have a practiced force, a sense of being prayer, some kind of holy chant. "I don't know if it's because you've always been a lazy one, Salo . . . or if it's the influence of these strangers. Their laziness and weakness. Their ceaseless selfishness—"

He means us. It dawns on me all at once.

"—from this Realm. Worlds upon worlds, all green and

the same. Crowded and everyone for no one but themselves. Is that where you got the idea that it's all right to
slough off? Salo?"

Salo says, "No. It's all my fault, old man."

Service's voice turns icy. "Show me respect, young man.
Now!"

Briar stands nearby, the faintest trace of a grin in the
corners of his eyes. I see the grin, then I can't.

Salo says, "I apologize. I've done wrong and I'm to
blame, and you are right to punish me." His face is impassive. Almost cold. He begins to unfasten his trousers,
and when they drop, he leans across a thick log, the bare
ass showing in the flashlights' glare. Rain is falling again.
It must be miserably cold, but Salo doesn't move or act
the least bit uncomfortable.

Service is done with the paddle. Those holes are for
speed, lessening the air resistance. He approaches Salo and
grasps the long handle, then lifts with both arms and drives
hard, the sudden slap loud and brief and me feeling it
against my face. Then Salo's pain washes over me, raw
and massive, and I can't help but moan under my breath.

Everyone has to take one swing. No exceptions.

The Pitcairns take their turns, and Salo's agony mounts.
The blows have a practiced intensity, a sameness born of
repetition. Salo grips the log's smooth bark, holding himself stiller by the moment. I breathe deeply, again and
again, hoping oxygen will cure me—

—and Snow hands the paddle to Effie.

"Not me! Why should I . . . ?"

"You're on this *passion*," Service responds. "Now do it."

She swings badly and not hard, the impact almost gentle. Then she hands the awful tool to Bedford, and he gives
a little Unity prayer. "Nature makes all bearable," he says,
swinging hard. *Slap*.

I flinch, my own guts recoiling.

Lumiere has no heart for the task, and he swings like a
tired old man.

Pachel glances at me knowingly, then she tells Salo,
"You should have done your job," and she swings. Salo
stiffens and nearly moans aloud, his teeth clenched and his
face soaked with perspiration.

The paddle looks like a toy in Goottich's hands, and he

swings with a boy's clumsiness. He only clips the ass, then turns and asks Service, "Do I try again?"

"Next!"

Me. I start wishing that I could feel the Remarkables' misery, believing that would give me the will. I feel their stares as I grip the paddle. The wood is warm where people held it. The rain falls harder now. I watch the Pitcairn shifting his weight, his pain beginning to ebb.

"Hurry up!"

Salo is the one who snaps at me, turning his head and glaring. "I want to get to bed tonight," he tells me. Then he says, "Service is right. Everyone is. Just a bunch of spoiled soft crazy assholes . . . that's you . . . !"

His face is hard and furious as I've never seen before.

Not in any person.

I lift the paddle and swing hard, the pain worse for me than for him. That's what occurs to me with the impact. It's a lot worse for me than for him.

TALKER

❖

Calling our visitors lazy and spoiled is not fair. We discuss this among ourselves and decide, "No, it is not." Remembering that we must see past surface concerns and qualities, we try to build a more complete portrait. Service is only partially right. And since he is a wise human, perhaps he is aware of the unfairness of his noise. Almost certainly. But this is Service's *passion*, threatened from without and within, and we can appreciate his motives. He wants to retain control. He chastises in hopes of engaging some buried core of pride, some sense of Pitcairn self. Plus the insults might challenge the visitors, helping them do better and accept more, angrily trying to prove him wrong with their good deeds.

And he is wrong about them. We watch the visitors; we know. Pachel has a fire and superior genetics. By now several dozen Pitcairn women are impregnated with her muscular eggs, the entire grove growing stronger by the instant. And most of the others—even the wispy and scared Effie—possess talents better suited for Pitcairns then for them. We can see these qualities at every glance. Balance and the mental toughness. The clear and potent little minds. Plus a fierce, half-submerged desire in most of them to belong to some group, any group, and contribute to a greater good.

These are human qualities, and we are fortunate. Remarkables are. The Old Ones claim that luck is an illusion, a series of bloodless coincidences reaching everywhere; yet I cannot help but think of us as being sweetly blessed. What if different aliens had come from the stars? Different from humans in temperament. Different in their strict biological needs. Inflexible. What if they were aliens unable to marry into our symbiosis? How would the Future appear now? I ask myself. Time and again.

What if the first humans—Service's ancient ancestors—had died out when their numbers were so tiny, so weak?

I imagine possibilities, and I am not even a young adult. My mind is tiny and bland, yet I can perceive countless horrors. How would Goottich and the Realm look upon us? Without human symbionts and human legalities, what would be the Remarkables' fate?

Everything that has happened was seen by the All-Answer.

The All-Answer—vast past vast; great past every other greatness—knew that Salo would fail at his post. It was aware which eleven of us would be injured by that Black Mountain cretin. Which eleven would die. And while I feel sorrow for them, I am happy too. I make no secret of my feelings, nor do the other juveniles. We sing happily amongst ourselves, even as the campsite becomes quiet again. Still. People back to bed. New guards posted. Forest worms climbing onto the fresh cretin bones. We sing in whispers and in motion and in touch, discussing all that has transpired in these last days. And meanwhile the injured ones keep bunched to themselves, their blood coagulating and their flesh dying, knowing it is death coming for them. Sad, yes. But just death, and them left with time and energy, making ready to meet the All-Answer at long last.

The All-Answer beckons to everyone.

I am not childishly spellbound in the All-Answer; but I do feel its presence now. Even here. Even this early in our *passion*. Even with mountains between us and the endless Au plains. Even with the considerable possibility that somehow I too will die soon.

To live in any sense is a grand honor.

I remind myself of this salient fact. Time and again.

Just to be an egg, tiny and sickly, then to be gobbled down by a sea pike an instant after being set into your home bay . . . even that mere taste of life is precious.

Every Remarkable old enough to comprehend is mature enough to appreciate this truth.

To live—to be pulled from the realm of the mere possible—is an extraordinary gift.

With the sun's warm rise, first light feeding the flesh, every Remarkable proclaims its thanks in being allowed this honor. Because it knows as surely as it knows the sun's touch that the great bulk of possible Remarkables—every possible egg's pairing with every possible sperm—shall never occur. No span of reasonable time will allow it. Not a trillion summers are enough to see more than a slender fraction of us made real.

Just to be drawn from the infinite is miraculous.

And it is true for every species. All the possible baleen birds; every conceivable steelwood tree. Cretins and algae and even the hugely successful human beings.

Even with the Realm, I think. A trillion trillion people, yet there remain infinitely more whom the All-Answer has never seen. Not in the Past or the Now. Or even in the furthest reach of the Future.

It is sobering to consider such things.

Some of us are dying, and what better time to celebrate life?

Dawn is beginning. The long lazy dawn of high summer, and the weak light is weakened further by the canopy above us. For a little while we grow silent, contemplating our circumstances. Thanking the All-Answer for seeing us here. And then speaking again. Me speaking again. Me asking my bunched-together companions, "How do you think *they* are thinking now? Each of them. Pitcairn and not. Give your impressions, will you?"

My healthy siblings respond, one by one. They guess about Service's mind, and Salo's, and of course Briar's. Each ends with long assessments about Goottich's state of mind and his plans. How far along are his plans, and are they as anticipated?

Ninety-one juveniles. Nineteen impressions each.

The process takes a little more than eight human minutes.

And afterward I say, "No, no. No, no." I tell each of them where I think they have gone wrong. "And you need to watch different people more closely," I add. "The ones who will matter most at the end. We know how Service and Briar will act, we hope . . . but the ones that count are on the periphery. Pachel and Ranier. And Snow, I think. They will end up at the hub of things. Whatever happens. Whatever it is that the All-Answer, blessed with its perfect vision, has always seen in the Future. . . ."

17

THE LAKES

◈

"It must be an honor."

"What is?"

"Being here," I tell her. "Isn't it?"

Snow continues paddling with the same sure rhythm. I don't have to turn my head to know her posture and the stroke. I feel everything through the canoe itself.

"Of course it's an honor," she says.

"I bet."

"A great one."

But she doesn't sound as if she's smiling. I hear it in her voice.

"I assume the elders picked you. . . ."

She is quiet. I turn and see her face framed by the unsmooth oval of her hood. She looks serious, conjuring up a smile that's devoid of amusement. Of life. I've struck a nerve, just as I suspected.

"I'm just curious," I confess. "I want to know things. I've always heard that elders choose who goes, and it's a big honor. I think all of us assume that you're the best of the best. But just in case, I'm asking. Now. Did the elders choose you?"

She says, "Of course," and shrugs her shoulders.

I turn forward and ask, "So why you?"

"I deserved this," she replies.

"You've been on other *passions*?"

"Last summer's."

"Well then." I nod vigorously. "And how about the others? Can you tell me—?"

"Service has been a dozen times," she blurts. "Maybe more. And he's led the last three *passions* too."

"Eminently qualified."

She pauses for a long moment, then says, "This is a silly topic. Let's talk about other things."

Her laugh is forced. Brittle.

"What about Salo?" I persist. "How many of these has he been on?"

She waits a moment before saying, "One."

"Last summer's?"

She says, "No. Three ago. I think."

I keep silent for a little while, hoping to lure her into a false confidence. Then I ask, "And the others?"

"Like who?"

"I don't know."

Her stroke changes. It becomes stronger for no reason. At least no nautical reason.

I say, "Okay. Briar?"

"I don't think so."

I turn and look at her again. "You aren't sure?"

"Why should I be?" she counters.

"Who else has been on a *passion*?" I stare at her for a long moment, then I turn forward again and tell her, "Name one."

She says nothing.

"Not a very experienced group," I mention.

And she says, "A three-year-old knows more about canoeing and camping than you do, Ranier. Any three-year-old Pitcairn."

True. She is right. But that has nothing to do with our subject, I want to say.

Turning again, I see her razored smile. Before I can speak, she says, "No more talk. Let's work for a while."

I try my ignorant best, my arms comfortably sore but stronger. I paddle steadily and look ahead at the nearest Remarkable. Talker? I know Talker is uninjured; I heard it speaking to Service this morning. But I can't tell which one is which. I watch this Remarkable rolling, the water falling from its purple tendrils, the sound not like rain or anything else familiar.

What is a criminal? To a Pitcairn, I mean.

I keep wondering. I barely slept last night, after the attack and the punishment, and I promise myself to ask more questions. I'm tired of being passive. Somehow I need to pry open some Pitcairn head and take a long hard look at things. . . .

. . . but for now I settle on telling Snow, "You are right. I'm very ignorant. I don't know much at all," and I nod so that she can't help but notice. "Thanks very much for your patience."

She doesn't answer.

I wait, listening to the Remarkables rolling and the patter of rain on plastic and the swirling of lake water around my paddle; and for a moment I can even hear the muscle-driven roar of the blood moving inside my ears.

These lakes are deep and cold. Their clear water implies an impoverishment: few nutrients, fewer algae, minimal energy. A clean and lovely poverty. Eventually I ask about the fishing—a safe subject—and Snow says it's poor here. Not even ribbon fish can make it up the gorge. Too bad, I reply. Then she says there are plenty of them on other rivers, the runs thick enough to walk across in places. The Au grove is the only local grove, and they have the monopoly. She tells me that with pride edging on cockiness.

All those Remarkables, I'm thinking. One of the largest groves on Pitcairn, and I wonder aloud if even this sea can sustain so much life. I'm estimating the calories required. For Remarkables and for Pitcairns too. "Doesn't overfishing concern you?"

She says, "No."

"But your grove still is growing, isn't it?"

"Every summer," she says. Again there's the pride, instinctive and effortless. "More and more."

"So what will you do when the nets come up empty?"

"Fish the Arctic waters too. Right up to the great glaciers."

I glance over a shoulder. No other grove has easy access to those waters. It's too far away for the cretins, and more southerly humans would be in competition with the Au grove. They'd be out of their element. Exposed and perhaps vulnerable.

"How is the fishing up there?" I ask.

"Rich." She nods and says, "One day? Someday? The Au grove will cover both sides of the bay. More than a million Remarkables, and the largest grove anywhere . . . !"

"Well," I say, "that'll be something to see."

She agrees with me.

"Sweet luck," I offer.

"And to you."

* * *

Low mountains surround the lakes, these rainforests lush
and ancient, and the lakes themselves are linked with brief
little rivers. The clouds feel lower today. Maybe it's our
altitude, or maybe it's the next storm coming. The wind
is gusting at our backs. I keep forgetting that this air is
thick, then the wind starts pushing me. Us. It feels like
some thin species of water, curling hard around me.

Greatnests live in the trees, keeping at a distance. They
look like eagles with bright red crowns of feathers. Snow
told me their name, and I told her about eagles. Greatnests were better, she maintained. Bigger and faster, she
was certain. I'm watching one of them now. It's perched
on the high point of some tremendous dead tree, the
stripped wood white as bone, and it is a tremendous creature. No world in the Realm has enough atmosphere to
support those wings. Even if I could design such a creature, I decide, I wouldn't. Too many people would be
afraid that it would carry off their babies. Its habits would
have to be tamed down, diminished into an acceptable
blandness. Made into a kind of pet, in truth.

Over the greatness are little clouds, white-gray and holding
their shapes as they move beneath the main clouds. They resemble masted ships and bat-winged monsters. Taller mountains stand to the east, almost obscured, and the low clouds
break against them, pushing into the gaps and the high passes.
Our pass is straight ahead. High but not too high, say the
Pitcairns. Not to where we have to worry about summer blizzards, at least. The juveniles would die in any cold storm;
that's one of every *passion*'s worst fears.

The Remarkables study the mountains too. Sometimes
one of them pauses, holding several eyes together. That's
how they squint. The distant green mountains are beckoning to them; they're anticipating the coming days.

I turn and look behind us. There's a long empty stretch
of open water, whitecaps under the gusting wind. I can
just make out the injured Remarkables. They've been following us since early morning, struggling to keep up. They
seem tiny and already half-dead, their color fading to a
ruddy gray. They're pitiful. I want to help them, but
there's nothing to do. We don't have time or the resources,
and I can't dwell on them.

This is a *passion*, after all.

Like a run of ribbon fish or sockeye salmon, the carnage is natural. Expected. And besides, every death makes every success more important. And the dead, in their timeless fashion, will help feed generations passing into the green future.

Sometimes we portage between the lakes, the connecting rivers too shallow or swift. Each lake is higher than the last one, and each of them has the same clear water and the same tiny silvery fish hovering near us, using our canoes to hide beneath.

We eat as we move, and the injured Remarkables fall farther behind. There's a point, I notice, when they're too distant and compassion begins to fade. I feel indifference and a momentary guilt because of it. Then we're out on an exposed lake, the skies low and the wind lashing at us. I forget about the Remarkables. I have to concentrate on the white water, helping Snow move us in a straight line. What if it gets worse? A gale could pitch us over in an instant. Glancing back, I look at Snow's calm face and feel reassured. "Sit low," she screams. "Paddle!" The spray comes over me as the waves catch us, lifting us and dropping us, again and again. Two fingers blister. My cold legs tighten and cramp, and a hot blade has been driven into my back. I try retreating into comfortable memories. My home on Rye's World; the peaceful lake just below it. And women. I think of my long-ago wives and my most recent failures, every memory full of a sudden fondness . . . and I hear Snow shouting at me, probably for a long while. Straight ahead of us is a stony beach, the land rising sharply and her telling me, "Right right right right . . . hard . . . !"

I drive with my paddle, my right hand high, and she deftly turns us at the last instant, balancing momentum and the waves and leaving us on the beach, mostly dry and quite safe.

Snow climbs out and grabs the bowline, pulling us higher, dragging the canoe and both packs and me even higher—

—and I fall a little in love.

My savior, I think. *My lovely angel.*

Young and strong, yet blessed with the competence of a parent. The best mate imaginable, I tell myself. And maybe she hears my thinking, giving me a quick smile now. Letting me climb out and go through the clumsy motions of being helpful.

18
RYE'S WORLD

❖

"Mind a neighbor?"

I lift my head, adjusting my hood and discovering Lumiere beside me. He smiles, looking pale and quite tired. I welcome him, glad for his company. "Let me shift my stuff," I tell him. "I'll give you more of the good ground."

He's exhausted, too old for this work and admitting it. "Entropy," he moans, then he drops his pack and unfastens the tent and assembles it in slow spurts, and I help when I can. As always, he dresses his complaints in humor. He moves stiffly, and I watch the puffy face and the too-pink tongue.

"That's that," he says, wiping his hands on his shirt.

We offer each other hard pieces of nectar. Then Lumiere produces a flask of water mixed with dark nectar, and he opens it and sniffs, pinching his features and deciding, "It's a little fermented."

"Whose bugs?"

He sips and says, "They have to be ours," then sips again. Then he passes the flask to me. It has a sharp taste, almost bitter, and he tells me that Shurgar showed him how to dissolve nectar in water. Then he pauses, both of us listening to distant voices. I recognize Bedford's and admit, "I have trouble enduring that man."

Lumiere nods and gives a wise grin, then takes a long sip. "A difficult fellow, yes. But he means well, I think. In his fashion."

I say nothing. I'm sitting with my poncho pulled up under my butt, the vegetation mashed and stinking beneath me.

"But you yourself," he continues. "You seem like some-one who might be interested in spiritual concerns. Some-one to ask the big questions. Our place in the cosmos, and so on . . ."

"Maybe once. A long time ago."

Lumiere watches me.

I shake my head, forcing a laugh. "I've tried a few things. Made my mistakes. It's history now."

"You came here—?"

"On vacation. Like I said before." I make myself laugh, shrugging my shoulders. "So let's talk about something else. Okay?"

"Fine."

I am sober. Calm. "What do you think about our Pit-cairns?"

Lumiere seems to understand the question. Not how it is on its surface, but its implications too. "They seem rather . . . well, rather young." He looks across the lake and tells me, "Shurgar has mentioned things. Now and again, noth-ing too obvious. But my impression's that we've been given less than the best—"

"They're criminals," I inject.

"Briar and his teasing about Service." The old man nods. "What was it? That Service is being punished here? For ancient crimes?"

I look across the lake. The wounded Remarkables never crossed the big round lake—the one that nearly dumped Snow and me—but I keep watching for them to appear on the far bank. We're two lakes higher here. The surround-ing forests help block the ceaseless winds and keep the wa-ter half-smooth.

"What I think," Lumiere explains, "is that they've given us competent people. Service is one of their best, but the others . . . well, they're considered expendable. I mean that in the most charitable sense. Maybe the elders de-cided not to risk anyone too valuable."

"Risk?" I echo.

"Maybe this *passion* will be killed by the cretins. Or maybe . . ." He pauses for an instant, then says, "Maybe we'll contaminate the Pitcairns in some way."

"Socially?"

"Well," he says, "I meant physically. These people are

biologically isolated, perhaps subject to odd infections. Without modern medicines—"

"We're clean," I remind him. "Before and after cold-sleep we were thoroughly treated—"

"Leaving gut bacteria. And old viruses laced into our DNA."

Nothing dangerous, I think to myself.

"An unlikely contamination," he admits, "but they're cautious people. They have no choice, what with their limited genetics. The effects wrought by any tough pathogen could be catastrophic."

"What about social contamination?"

"Oh, I don't think that's possible. Not with Pitcairns." He shakes his head and squints into the wind. "For instance, there's my partner. Shurgar. We've talked when I have the breath in me, but I'm the one who asks questions. About her. About the grove. Remarkables. Their All-Answer. And do you know what one question she's asked me? The only subject that's interested her enough to bother with?"

I say, "Tell me."

"My age." The answer brings a smile. But the red eyes are sad and distant, a puffy hand wiping at the puffy face. "One time she's asked me about my age."

"And you told her?"

"No," he says. "No, I told the usual lie, Ranier."

"What lie?"

"I'm not from New Emerald," he admits. "I said so, but I'm not. And I'm really much older than anyone knows. Free-radical scrubs are blessings, let me tell you. I've got painkillers and a dozen potent medicines implanted in me, that release as needed." His hands float before him, curling into soft fists and then relaxing again. His face is shot full of blood and a strange gravity. Oftentimes Lumiere appears distracted. Distant. I notice a nest of broken vessels in the tip of his nose and the paled flesh left soft by exotic compounds. He looks very much like someone partially boiled.

"Where were you born?" I ask him.

"Our secret?"

"Of course."

He pulls up a gob of mud and fashions a simple ball, then he flings it overhand into the cold lake water; and with the grunt of exertion he says one incredible, impossible word:

"Earth."

"Pardon me?"

He smiles and says, "You heard me." Then he rises, saying, "Really, I need my sleep."

"Good night," is all I can think to say.

"And to you, Ranier. And to you."

I dream that I'm home again, walking on the highlands with the red rocky ground sprinkled with hardy weeds, dark green and frosted with dust. I can hear my boots in the dream, and I feel the ground under me. It's dusk or dawn; I can't decide which. The skies are clear with a thin chill wind blowing through me, and I look north at the local jupiter and New Albemarne. A black wafer and a tiny speck of jade. Then I turn and walk along a sketchy path, finding my lake waiting for me, nestled at the bottom of an eroded impact crater.

A transparent canoe waits for me, a giant black dog on board and wagging its tail. I climb in and push off, looking into the clear water. I see every rock on the bottom, sharp-edged and glittering, and hovering over the rocks is a single thick trout. Patches of a cream-colored fungus are eating at its gills and fins. I reach for it, and it kicks feebly, evading me. And I start to feel its suffering. Its constant blunt agony. The sensation worsens every time I try to grab hold of it. Kindness is a swift death, and I'm trying to be kind. But I'm too slow, too old, and finally I quit out of frustration, cursing and looking at the black dog.

"I miss you," says the dog.

The second time I see its mouth moving.

"I miss you," it tells me.

I awaken, opening my eyes while remaining motionless. I hear rain against the tent, then there's a familiar voice. Quiet, yet forceful.

"I miss you," says Lumiere.

The old man is talking in his sleep. Babbling. For a moment our dreams had been linked together, after a fashion. . . .

Lumiere moves and then farts. Then he's quiet, and I keep still, listening to night sounds, knowing from experience that I won't fall straight back to sleep. All I can do is relax and wait and hope that my nervous energies fade before too long.

I miss my home. I miss the familiarity of its rooms and the worn furniture. My last wife lived there with me. For a little while. It was decades ago and she fancied herself as being adventurous. Living on a half-terraformed world? Toward its southern pole? She felt she could adapt to my life. Besides, she told me, we'd travel quite a bit for our work. She was a gene-tailor like myself. It wasn't as if we were *always* going to be isolated, was it? It wasn't as if she was *trapped* out in the middle of nothingness.

I don't often think about my former wives. Today was unusual, and even today they were little more than half-seen faces. The qualities of each blended with those of the others, creating an ultimate wife in my harried mind.

Who does Lumiere miss?

I suppose it's someone from Earth. From long ago. I can't say why, but that's my intuitive feeling.

Tonight Lumiere called me a spiritual person. But there's more of the loner in me than any spiritual element. With my "illness, for instance." I remember the first doctor who examined me. "You let them do what?" she screamed. "You willingly allowed them . . . with nanots . . . and you're a responsible adult person . . . !"

"Is it bad?" I asked. The eternal first question of a patient. "I mean, can you help me?"

"By referring you elsewhere. If I can find someone with credentials." A head-shaking pause, then she asked again, "How could you agree to this . . . this madness?"

The truth told, I've never been sure.

Emptiness. Loneliness. A group of people who seemed to be my genuine friends. A single lover. What can I say? I've always been preyed upon by longings, by persistent darknesses and feelings of emptiness. And in the Realm, where comfort and contentment rule, one has a hard time finding souls who know that same bilious darkness.

My second doctor listened to my partial story, showing more restraint. He nodded while looking down the front of his clean white coat, the face a portrait of professional calm. Finally he cleared his throat, telling me, "We can try things. But I'm afraid the chances are poor. These agents inside you are only glancingly legal, and honestly I don't know what will be useful."

I nodded and shivered. We were near Rye's only sea, and it felt as if the entire basin was in misery. Mud sharks gnawing on fish; fur seals tormenting Rye's penguins. Millions of neural systems were in turmoil, and sometimes that meant people too. A nearly empty world, but it was all I could manage just to say, "Thank you . . . for everything. . . ."

"Your best hope," he added, "might be to emigrate."

"To where?"

"A comet. Perhaps a little one not associated with any Oort cloud." He watched my shivering with a measured concern, then said, "No lifeforms but yourself. A home and reactor and nothing else—"

"No. Not that."

He gave a slight nod, then said, "Well . . . keep the possibility in mind."

Better death, I felt, than living alone on some frigid chunk of ice and organics, nothing surrounding me but vacuum and the perpetual silence. *It won't come to it!* I vowed to myself.

Never!

I breathed deeply and thought those words until I believed them. *I won't. I won't let it happen. Something . . . there is always some better answer . . . always . . . !*

I unfasten my tent flap and emerge, needing to pee. Rain falls hard with a gusting wind coming through the trees, and I shuffle to a likely place and put my back to the wind, lifting my poncho and half aiming. I feel the pleasant warm rush and the diminishing pressure, my eyes focused on the wall of vegetation before me. It takes me a long moment to notice the eyes, wide-spaced and infinitely calm. I recognize their color and the red eye patches and the deep black plumage. The tongue lolls amid the curling teeth, the cretin sitting on its haunches. Then Snow moves, her camouflage defeated. She smiles, watching me without shame, and I say, "Yes?" with a flick of the penis. I tuck and button, and she tells me:

"I thought you'd look different."

"Different how?"

"Improved. All those fancy genetics, and the equipment stays the same."

"Sorry."

Either it's early morning or the last water-strained trace
of dusk, the light minimal and every surface left gray and
simple. I hear the crinkling of her poncho. Her rifle is
inside a bulky sleeve. She tells me, "When I saw all of you?
The first time? You came on board, and I thought you
were the ugliest people. . . ."

"Did you?"

"Not you so much." She smiles and shakes her head. But
the eyes don't smile, I notice. Just her mouth. "Goottich
is really ugly."

"What about Bedford?"

She says, "He's got a girl's face."

I stare at Snow, almost ready to tell her how I thought
she was pretty. The first time I saw her, and now. Only
she interrupts, saying, "I've got to move. Walk my watch
some more."

"So you don't get paddled," I remark. Stupidly.

She blinks and presses her mouth closed, thinking carefully. Then she tells me, "Lucky dreams."

"And to you."

She vanishes into the tangled foliage, making noise but
not much and the rain and wind obscuring her move-
ments, the cretin snorting once and turning, then trotting
after her.

TALKER

❖

Humans are They-Whom-We-Must-Trust. They-Who-We-Must-Understand. Who-Make-The-Sky-Anew. Who-Twist-Nature-Into-Knots. (With their countless tools. With their forts and factories, their ships of the sea and the stars.) Humans. Our new symbionts. Strangers-Walking-Our-Groves, some adults call them, with resentment and with respect at the same time and with several voices.

Adult Remarkables think of the human species in every way—as heroes and saviors; as hazards and puzzles—and being magnificent, the adults can believe each contradictory assessment equally. More than any juveniles, even talented juveniles like me, adult Remarkables can embrace countless opinions on every subject, minor or major. It is their talent and curse. It comes from their vast minds dividing themselves. It's a trick of biology, of evolutionary history.

Adults do not have to have mobile brains. They do not have any need to pick up and move themselves. That is why they can afford giant nervous systems. (I am borrowing from human explanations here.) What do their minds cost? A few more fish; a greater risk of boredom. But maybe their wishy-washiness helps fight their boredom. Division. Debate. Internal dialogues, dozens of separate voices . . . each choosing a different side on an issue. Unlike humans, for instance. Completely unlike them.

Humans choose. Every day of their lives, time and again, they look at circumstances with their tiny eyes and decide somehow. They make their decision, knowing next to nothing, then they stay on course for enormous spans of

time. Sometimes even when they sense that they have done
wrong, they persist. Humans are tenacious souls.

They frighten us with their tenacity. They frighten us
with their clever tools and how they manipulate the worlds
around them. They frighten us with their innate capacity
for intentional violence, within their species and without.
Like when Service went south seeking vengeance against
the Two Sisters grove. Again and again I have heard stories of the fear that event brought . . . Service telling the
story aloud, just once, his voice and manner proud, his
eyes never blinking as he explained how he had brutalized
an entire grove of Remarkables . . .

Yet the adults loved Service at the same instant. A great
sweet love was mixed equally with their fear. It was like
the love felt toward a great cretin. A respect for his talents. An admiration for his single-mindedness. The Old
Ones, following endless debates, had decided to send Service to his death in a foolish, impossible attack; and the
Pitcairn had not just survived. He came home as a legend.
His will and his cleverness became the stuff of myths. No
cretin has ever risen so high. . . .

Humans are our new symbionts.

It remains difficult for us to accept. It is as if the humans
cut off their old hands, trusted and perfectly suited to
them, then replaced them with different hands. Stronger.
More graceful. Quicker and capable of thinking entirely
for themselves.

Our new hands depend on us for their lives.

Now.

We in the Mount Au grove have had these hands a long
time, practicing and improving our ties with them; and
the hands have become comfortable with us, and us halfway comfortable with them. As is right.

Long ago our humans—Service's ancestors—decided to
be exceptional hands. They knew their only hope of survival was the symbiosis, and that has been the ideal for
ages—for almost as long as we can remember.

They make wondrous symbionts.

Yet we ask ourselves:

"For how long?"

We ask:

"Why do they serve the groves so well?"

For twenty thousand of their years, without pause, various groves have debated within themselves and with one another:

"When do our new hands truly belong to us, and we to them?"

For it runs both ways.

Dominion is not our wish.

In this one question we are quite certain. Of one mind, actually. Our ideal is to unite with the aliens, for nothing else will thrive. A union without seams; without tiny, tiny flaws ready to break.

A grand marriage that shall endure and thrive and embrace the Future, with hands and with tendrils both. . . . We hope. . . .

19
MUSKEG

◆

Today's portages look flat on the maps, and we're in a good mood. No climbing today, we think. Eating breakfast at the fire, we joke and sometimes tease one another. Pachel tells Goottich, "Why don't you step back and let five other people warm themselves." Everyone chuckles, including Goottich. Grudgingly. Then Service walks past us, and Goottich tells him:

"A good flat course today."

As if Service doesn't know this country.

And the old Pitcairn grins for a moment, enjoying something. He's wearing his pack, huge and creaking, and he doesn't stop walking. And he doesn't say anything either. Just the grin, and everyone becomes quiet. We look at each other, wondering what that expression meant.

The shoreline isn't a line so much as it's an approximation. It begins with stunted vegetation suspended on watery mud, and my canoe slides home without slowing, pushing the mud deeper and the ground itself shuddering. The slow distinct waves spread out and die. And I'm thinking: *Shit! We're actually going to walk this . . . !"*

"It's muskeg," says Snow, driving us farther inland. She poles with her paddle and makes me do the same.

The Remarkables have no difficulty. They roll off the lake and onward, pausing only when they're too far ahead of their protectors. Service already is portaging, his canoe on his pack and a pair of cretins striding beside him, noses raised. Alert. *Cocked.* Then Service breaks through the crust, one leg sinking fast. The hand with the rifle throws it down, and both hands grab a stunted tree, jerking him out of the black goo with a sloppy wet sound. He never loses his balance or the canoe. He strides hard, picking up the rifle on the rebound, and with one black leg he manages to walk ten steps before falling through again.

He's the expert, I'm thinking. *He know the tricks.*

Bedford climbs from his canoe, not even carrying his pack, and sinks fast. He grabs for the canoe, saying, "Oh, my . . . !"

Snow gives me instructions. Everyone breaks through, she promises, and muskeg is garbage. "Just keep pressing. Don't let it beat you. Don't ever let it beat you. All right, ugly man? All right?"

It's my turn to portage. Naturally.

I swing a leg over the side and stand, the rootbound goo dimpling but not breaking. Instinctively I put my feet apart while untying my pack, then I ease it on and adjust the familiar straps, Snow doing the same.

Pachel teases Goottich. "Good flat country," she says. "Aren't we lucky?"

Goottich isn't speaking. He has a startled, betrayed expression, regretting every gram of his oversized frame. I feel sorry for him, thinking how he looks doomed; pompous, yes, but generally harmless and rather pitiful too.

"Pay attention," warns Snow.

"I am."

"Ready?"

"Go."

She turns and lifts the empty canoe, all in one smooth motion, and I'm under it and taking the weight once I'm sure of my balance. The crust holds. I breathe and feel good, taking one step and another, and the crust changes its mind, splitting under both feet. My fall is slow, almost majestic. The muds under me thicken until they feel like cold vises grasping my feet and shins. Snow helps me climb free, holding the canoe while I struggle. "Use your hands. Steady pressure, then jerk. Like that, right!"

Insects are attracted by our motions and repelled by our alien stinks. They form diffuse clouds around everyone, the air buzzing. Again I put my feet apart. My boots stink of oxygen starvation and sulfurous compounds. Snow stays close, shouting instructions. Where to step, what vegetation is best. But the wrong vegetation is everywhere, and I stop and look at the watery scum, asking, "Now what?"

"Try," she coaches.

I sink fast this time. Part of me remembers the maps—there is no other way across this country—but the rest of me blames my partner. What are we doing here? I glare at Snow, and she seems to expect it. A warm callused hand reaches down and slaps me, and she warns, "It happens. Don't waste it on me, okay? Okay. Now let's move."

I learn. A blistering monologue fills my head, dulling my senses, curses piling on rancid curses. Pitcairns are stupid brutes. Fools to live this way, to accept this shit. They're torturing us for the fun of it. I hate them almost as much as I despise this world, brutal and cold and the rain worsening again, drumming on my canoe until I can't hear anything but it and my ragged breathing.

I fall through and Snow helps me out.

I fall with one leg, dumping the canoe, and she says, "Anticipate."

I want to slap her. I'll kick Service in the balls and break his face against stones, I'm that angry. I start scaring myself, I'm so full of a homicidal rage.

Both legs break through on solid-looking ground.

Snow lifts the canoe, her own legs muddied, and when I don't climb free, she asks, "Had enough?"

"Fuck off."

"What was that?"

I climb free and take the load again, and I manage one long walk before dropping through, dropping to my crotch and nothing to do but wait. My view of the world is compressed. Pitcairns are in the distance, Remarkables scattered between them and beyond. Pachel is leading the tourists by a fair distance. A couple Remarkables are near her, rolling steadily and not even dimpling the mud . . . the irony, them mobile and the humans rooted in place, at least now and then.

Pachel falls through.

Briar lifts her canoe, and she pops up like a cork from water.

Finally Snow arrives, her trouser legs freshly immersed. *Good*, I think.

She seems to read my thoughts. "Don't take it personally. You do and you'll get beat. Believe me."

"Let's move," I groan.

She lifts the canoe off me, and the rain soaks my face. My hair. I climb partway free, then one of my boots pulls free of me. It stays in the mud, and I'm staring at the blackened sock hanging limp off my foot. I start to shiver. Snow says, "Find it. Go on." I try. I reach into the hole, water and thin muds up to my elbow, and I grip the tongue and bring up the boot and drain it and put it on again, tying the laces too tight. Then I stand without trusting anything. "Ready," I say.

Down comes the weight.

Again, with a deep-throated gasp, I start to walk.

Service and the all-Pitcairn teams wait at a midway point, sitting on rocks that make an island in the muskeg. Pachel is with them. She's staring with the rest of them, watching my approach and final collapse. It feels as if I'm an intruder. Not a member of their club. Pulling myself up on the rocks, I shake with exhaustion. What I should do, I think, is eat until I'm stuffed. Only it takes energy to open a pocket, find some nectar, and then chew it . . . too much energy, for the moment. . . .

The other four of us are still on the muskeg. They've given up, letting their partners do the work. (*I managed it myself*, I keep thinking.) But Goottich falls through by himself. Then Bedford. Bedford halfway asks Effie for help, but she seems not to hear him; and he scrambles free by himself.

Briar starts to laugh teasingly.

Salo joins him.

I turn and notice Service's frown, his stare fixed on Briar. Service is on the highest rock, legs crossed, his trousers filthy but nothing else showing of his work. He seems rested. At home.

"You don't have country like this?" asks Briar. "Ranier? What kinds of soft-assed country do you build in your Realm?"

We do have swamps and marshes, I mention. As natural preserves. As zoos and parks where cultured people walk on suspended and transparent walkways, lovely in their own right—

"Soft-assed," Briar repeats.

His tone is superior, sharp and pressing.

He says, "Pachel's got the balls in the group. If any of you do, I mean."

Then Service tells him, "Quiet."

I can see Briar's face and Service's face. But Service can't see Briar's. They could be clones, as much as they resemble each other. Even in their intensity. That fiery nature shows now and again in the eyes. But Service can't see Briar's expression. He tells him, "Quiet," again, wanting a response.

And Briar is furious. He doesn't move or make any sound, but his features turn hard all at once. He closes his mouth and bites hard enough to make his jaw muscles tremble. I'm sure he's going to explode. He can't keep the temper buried another instant—

—but he does bury it.

That's what is so frightening. It's the way Briar's face relaxes all at once, no warning given. Every gram of hate and scorn are swallowed, him turning toward Service and saying, "Sorry," with a chastened voice.

Says the old Pitcairn, "That's not our way, abusing our partners."

"Yes," says Briar. "Yes, sir. You are right."

I can't believe what I'm hearing.

Then Briar turns to me, saying, "I apologize. I'm sure you have ample balls, Ranier."

Then he winks at me.

Maybe it's my imagination, but everyone seems tense. Even Pachel. She glances at me, taking a deep breath. Then everyone goes back to watching the others work their way across the muskeg.

They're getting closer, at least. Close enough to hear. Bedford tells Effie to think of Unity circles, to draw them in her head if she needs. Lumiere is slowly and patiently creeping forward. Goottich keeps breaking through, and he grunts and moans and curses the fucking rain and the fucking fucking mud, and it fucking isn't fair!

I glance at Snow. Just for an instant.

She's looking at Salo, and Salo's looking at Briar. Briar just said something to Salo.

With his eyes, I realize.

It takes me a few seconds, but then I see them talking. Just with their eyes. All the young Pitcairns. Quick mysterious looks and telling winks. There's a conversation going on here. I can see it. None of it quite makes sense, but it's there nonetheless. Right in front of me.

20
SNOW

✦

"Tip-tap. Tip-tap."

I open my eyes, remembering how nothing is as strong as the muscles in our eyes, and if I were built of eye muscles, I could jump flealike distances and shoulder ten canoes . . . and it occurs to me that I'm having feverish thoughts. Not for the first time. I'm too tired to control my own mind.

"Tip-tap," says Snow. "Hey there! You home?"

I say, "No."

"Your share is out here. I brought it." Snow's boots crush old leaves. "Want any nectar? Hey there."

An airdrop was made this afternoon. We were crossing one of the little lakes strung amid the god-awful muskeg, and a string of fat floatplanes roared overhead, wagging their wings on their way to the drop site. They'd found us through a radio beeper carried by Service. Snow explained it to me. That was this afternoon, I remember. Ages ago. How can I eat? I'm past mortal hunger. Even my eyelids ache, and I shut them and nearly forget about Snow.

"I'll stick your shares in your pack."

I manage to grunt once.

She wrestles with my knots. I listen, thinking how I should undress. At least I should pull the muddy boots off. But when I lift my arm, cramps seize me. I gasp and lay quite still, begging the pain to subside. Then the flap opens and Snow's looking down at me. "You should eat." She seems unnatural, acting this concerned. Pleasant. Almost motherly. "And get out of those stinky clothes, will you?"

I say nothing.

She slips into my tent, a big cubic brick of ruddy nectar
in one hand, a ceramic knife in the other. The tent is
crowded with two people. She presses against one wall,
mentioning to me that my stakes aren't secured and any
decent wind will knock down everything—

"Leave me alone."

She smiles. I can smell her breath, warm and pleasant,
and she seems incredibly young. I hate her youth and the
energy and that boundless confidence. All day she's told
me to persist, to get busy, to not give in to the muskeg.
A banter of endless encouragement, and she drove me insane.

"We were impressed today," she mentions. "With you
and with Pachel."

"Who's impressed?"

"Service," she tells me.

She's lying. I doubt if Service has said anything—that's
my intuitive feeling—and she's lying in the same way she
tells me, "Not much farther now. You're almost there."

But I don't care. I like the gesture, I decide.

Snow carves off a piece of nectar, and I take it like an
invalid, tasting her fingertips with the rest of it.

"Strawberry-flavored," she says. With conviction.

But it's the wrong taste. And how does she have any idea
what strawberries taste like? I wonder. A flavor handed
down, generation to generation? People tasting nectars and
telling the Remarkables, "No, no. A little more zip. And
not so sweet either."

She's reaching for the filthy laces of my filthy boots.

"What are you doing?"

Snow's face is serious, tired but focused.

"What do you want?" I ask her.

And she lifts her head, telling me with a soft smooth
voice, "You don't know very much. Do you, Ranier?"

Afterward we talk. I remember Lumiere telling me that
his partner never asked questions, and it's the same with
Snow. I ask questions, and she explains. She uses the same
storytelling voice she used to describe Service's vengeance.
It's a natural talent, I suppose. Words and tones mix with
gestures, building something stronger than the parts. A
piece of me listens. She's explaining how it is to live inside

the Au grove. And another piece wonders if every Pitcairn can tell stories this well. . . .

"Are you listening?"

"You're talking about your house," I tell her.

"So listen to me," she says.

"I am. Go on."

Her house forms in my mind, the grove standing around it. Like every place beneath the canopy, it is warm. Thousands of Remarkables bleed heat and warm the damp air. Even on the coldest winter nights, frosts on the high slopes, the grove's interior is identical to its summertime temperature and humidity. That's why the Old Ones stand near the grove's center. That's where the climate is best, and the soil is its deepest and richest.

"Is it gloomy in the day?"

It's not. The canopy isn't like a rainforest's canopy, after all. Tendrils have no leaves, and her house has windows and skylights. It's nearly identical to every other house, even the one I had for a night. She's lived inside hers since she became an adult. Three years ago, she says. Pitcairn years.

I remember my one-night home, asking about the furnishings.

She doesn't seem to answer me. She tells instead about some huge cretin, semiaquatic and from some distant grove. It had killed several juveniles that shouldn't have been so far out on the spit, on the blind ocean side . . . and she helped hunt the cretin and kill and butcher it. A giant creature—I think of a mobile sea lion. She won pieces of its hide for her work. Its plumage is a gorgeous blue-black, she assures me. With bright strawberry patches. It covers portions of her walls and floor and the huge bed in one corner. She might be talking about her dinner table, as much as she talks about that bed. But it makes a kind of sense. In a world with one basic food— misflavored at that—screwing is a Pitcairn's feast. I shut my eyes and imagine Briar and Salo pumping hard, driving their pricks into my new lover. Then I open my eyes, and she's talking about tables and chairs and the polished wooden floor that shines in the daylight, particularly on bright summer days when the Remarkables lift their tendrils high to let convection currents take away the excess heat.

I see the house and her and now myself. In my mind we stand together, hands linked; and I ask, "What's outside?"

Views are critical to everyone's home, I know. Mine and hers too.

She describes the muscular trunks of the Remarkables. Young ones. The canopy is low, the ground itself a bare lustrous black. The aliens' roots are always churning the soil, working it, and it smells rich. You can never get the odor out of your nose, she says. Pitcairns walk barefoot in the grove, and every step brings the sensation of countless strong worms working underneath the surface.

I'm thinking how those roots interlink, nerve impulses shared.

Then I remember a speculation. It's in the literature on Pitcairn, based on Pitcairn stories. But many experts don't believe in it—

"Can the adults move?" I ask her. "I mean at a slow pace . . . can they?"

She says, "Slowly."

"Can they?"

"Sure." She tells me how the Old Ones become the Old Ones. They're smart adults chosen by the others. Gradually, meter by meter, they migrate deeper into the grove, always churning with their roots. It takes maybe a century to move from the grove's edge to the Old Ones. Maybe more. But since the adults can live for hundreds of years, that's not so long. Not really.

"Do others move?" I persist. "Besides the would-be Old Ones?"

"A few. Sometimes."

"Why?"

She shrugs her shoulders. "Maybe they don't like their neighbors. That or they want a different view."

"You don't know why, do you?"

She says, "Don't waste time trying to understand them." Again the shrug. Sounding like any true Pitcairn, she says, "It's a waste of time and your neurons. It just makes you nuts, trying to decipher them."

I think for a long moment.

"What about Talker?"

She says, "What about Talker?"

"Will it become an Old One? You've said it's smarter than the other juveniles—"

"Maybe. But it has to survive its *passion* first."

"You don't sound very concerned," I remark.

That brings a hard stare. "About the *passion*? I'm concerned. I want to succeed and go home again and be happy. About Talker? Juveniles die, Ranier. No *passion* escapes without a third or more of its juveniles dying somewhere. That's how it is. It's like it is for the babies at sea. The eggs in the bay. Even for the adults. Sometimes, in some of the worst winters, the young adults up on the high slopes are damaged by the freezes and get sick and die."

I say nothing.

"Remarkables don't take death personally," she assures me.

"So you do care what they're thinking. Don't you?"

It's still daylight, but the sun through the tent walls has lost its strength. The rain is cold and peaceful. Sometimes I hear people talking. Sometimes it's as if nobody else is on this planet.

"I have a nice house," she repeats. "I love it."

"So do I," I tell her. "Want to hear about mine?"

No. She doesn't answer, but that's my impression. I watch while she dips her head, kissing my chest and leaving wet rings on my skin. I feel the rings drying, cooling patches of me. Then she takes my penis into her mouth— the entire flaccid thing—and her working tongue sends bursts of electricity up the length of my spine.

"I guess I'm not so ugly anymore. Huh?"

She removes me from her mouth, saying, "Or as old as you think you are, old man." Then she climbs on top of me, artfully positioning herself; and when I enter her, she sighs quietly, looking at my eyes. Then she bends close and whispers into an ear:

"How old are you?"

I simplify the age. I say, "One century young," and laugh aloud.

Snow makes no comment. Nothing shows on her face. She moves faster, then slow again, pumping with her hips and smiling to herself. Her long hair hangs down, covering the small firm breasts. She's firm in my hands. A virtual child, I'm thinking. Then I'm climaxing, withering fast and feeling the old exhaustion filling me again.

Death should be this pleasant, I tell myself.

I shut my eyes; and in an instant, tumbling hard, I fall asleep.

TALKER

◈

We are not builders. We cannot think in terms of tools and architectural plans. I doubt if any Remarkable ever born could design even the simplest human house. We have no talent there. Or rather, we think too much. Too fast. Too many conflicting possibilities occur to us—an endless storm of inspiration erasing both good and bad—and that is why humans strike us as amazing creatures.

They plan and then they act, their slow little minds perfectly focused on whatever the job.

We are too sloppy and grand. Perhaps it is as our humans say. We evolved quickly and carelessly, intelligence cheap to build and easy to misuse. Nature loves success, even if that success means a titanic muddle, and that perfectly describes us. . . .

Yet we have our skills, our potent talents.

Like now. Us in our nightly bunch, eyes watching every person who is in view, and our ears straining to reach beyond.

We gaze at the faces and the stances, absorbing the people, digesting an assortment of minuscule, telling clues. This is our great ability. It is how every Remarkable looks at the cretins. Those-Whom-We-Always-Trust. The cretins cannot communicate deep feelings. They have their aches and limits, but how do they explain themselves? A grove thrives only if it uses its cretins properly. Are they rested enough? Is their nectar keeping them strong, full of energy? Is one of them sick? Because if an infection or disease is seen early, before it becomes contagious, that cretin can be isolated from the rest. An epidemic might be stopped. The

littlest signs can save a grove from disaster; every Remarkable knows this salient lesson. We know it in our blood.

Cretins, simple as they are, show their inner selves
through their motions and subtle manners.

And likewise, so does every human being.

We watch these people now. Particularly the visitors.

Like Goottich. He lies on his belly inside his tent—specially
made to fit his dimensions, that tent—and he uses his flashlight to illuminate a square of toilet paper. With his big
clumsy hand he draws shapes and writes numbers, and we
watch his shadow, following every motion. Tiny numbers,
we notice. Saving as much of the paper as possible. And
sometimes he will mutter to himself, the atmosphere carrying his voice to us . . . every word, as every Remarkable
knows, a little window into the human mind.

"Volume of air. Water," he says.

"Hull stresses. Lighting," he says.

"No, shit . . . start over. . . . "

Then he says, "Tired. Too fucking . . . go to sleep . . .
plenty of time. . . ."

Bedford and Effie huddle together in sleep, more affec-
tionate now than when they are awake. Not once have we
seen the sex act. And tiredness is not a complete excuse,
we know. Twice Bedford has made advances, and his wife
has rebutted him without speaking. With gestures; with a
sharp grunt. With disinterest and anger that we can feel,
even when we are peering through tent walls at the sloppy
heat-images that their bodies make.

Lumiere—the man from Earth—sleeps hard, occasionally dreaming. Speaking in his dreams and us trying to
decipher the Realm words. As always, he is conversing
with someone while dreaming. Every night he gives us
both voices, his and another's, a very slight difference in
tone and pace marking each one. . . .

"Come a long way," he mutters.

"We have," says the other voice.

"It's funny."

"What's funny?"

"How far we've come. In a lot of ways."

The other voice laughs, then vanishes.

Then Pachel rises, her tent set near us. She needs to
relieve herself. We know by looking, noticing the bulge of
her bladder. Walking to the edge of the trees, she drops

her trousers and squats, knees cracking, then she urinates with a strong hot stream, its heat blossoming beneath her, warming her bare rump.

She wipes herself and stands, and for a long while she looks skyward, letting the gentle rain fall against her face and dampen her hair.

This is night, as black as possible at this time of year.

And she is discovering something. It is an understanding that we watch on her face. It shows in the way she relaxes, examining her surroundings. Pachel has come a long way from her home, against her best wishes. She is here on some useless errand, her superiors—humans of great power and ambition—believing against all evidence that she can act as some kind of diplomat. Pachel is suppose to portray New Albemarne as being good and truthful, and would the Pitcairns just consider selling even a portion of their rich Oort cloud? Any portion? Yet she has made no effort to do her job. To whom would she talk? What kinds of diplomatic contacts would she make here? No, she thinks, her presence is useless. She intends to make up any story to satisfy her superiors, but she feels certain that coming here will not serve New Albemarne in the slightest . . .

. . . and she is so very far from home, she realizes. We see the thoughts on her face. Such a distance, yet already it seems as if she has adapted. Pitcairn isn't so awful, she tells herself. Not at all. And with that she climbs into the tent and undresses, then falls asleep again.

And in a little while Service rises, preparing for his watch and the new day. His timepiece makes a single sudden tone—sharp and intentionally abusive—and he turns it off an instant later. He steps into the night air, adjusting his old poncho and walking past us. The face is impassive. Not rested, but not tired either. He only briefly glances at us, and he says nothing.

Service is upset. We know this. We cannot know him as well as the adults do. The adults have watched him longer, after all. But we see what we see, watching a thousand little clues that not even his lovers would find. Like the tension in his skin. Like the persistent dryness of his lips. The way he marches. And the way his hands close around his rifle too tightly, unconsciously strangling the butt and barrel.

He stops to wake two other Pitcairns. Tintoil and the young man sharing her tent tonight.

Uncharacteristically, Service makes no comment about their tardiness. He merely tells them whom they are to relieve on the perimeter, then he vanishes, out past our vision's reach. Down to the lakeshore and Briar later returning from that direction. And Briar is angry too. Words must have been exchanged between the men. Quietly, but with intensity. As always.

They are so much alike, Service and Briar.

Too much alike, we decide once again. That is part of the problem and much of what interests us. Two Pitcairns with that shared intensity. Different applications, but the same basic emotions. Scalding. Ambitious. Almost tireless.

And finally I decide to sleep, nothing more to watch just now. I let my siblings watch for me. I relax and begin to dream at once, my wonderful mind disgorging chaotic images and sounds and sensations, refreshing me for the new day.

Passions have many functions.

Not least among them is the chance to observe your symbionts under stress, learning everything you can about their natures and limits and their capacity for surprise.

Remarkables know more about their symbionts than their symbionts know about themselves, cretin or human.

This is our great talent. And our ceaseless crystalline hope too.

21
LONG CLIMB

❖

Snow wakes and rolls over, saying, "Morning."

"Good morning."

She pulls herself from her bag. The improving light shows me her dark nipples and the cinnamon-colored skin, those stained teeth begging to be straightened. Dark veins run through the undersides of her breasts. Her neck scar seems to glow with its own light, and she's nothing like any woman I've ever known. In the Realm the body is part of the wardrobe. It must be perfect and oftentimes exceeds perfect. Poreless and firm, every feature balanced with one another . . . the effect ultimately boring. . . .

A sour odor hangs on Snow, sweaty and mixed with morning breath. Her expression seems cheerful, yet it isn't. Not really, I decide. I'm watching her, and something occurs to me.

She sees something in my face. "What?"

"I was wondering," I begin. "When your ancestors came north . . . why did they? What brought them here?"

The thin mouth closes, then opens. "Why go anywhere new?"

"Service said you were escaping some war."

"We were," she lies.

"Were you the only survivors from your grove? Was that it?" When she doesn't answer, I charge ahead. "A handful of you. It doesn't seem like any organized mission. Wouldn't you want hundreds of people? Good boats and plenty of supplies? And why leave behind your Remarkables? You could have brought some juveniles with you—"

"Ranier," she moans. She sounds wounded and looks angry.

I consider stopping. But she's my lover and I'm comfortable this morning, ready for anything. I wait a moment, collecting myself. Then I ask her, "Were they banished?"

She says, "Banished," as if she doesn't understand the word. As if she has never heard it until now.

"It's something I've heard about. Experts back in the Realm . . . well, they've been studying Pitcairns. All the old data, all the tales told by visitors. And they claim that Pitcairns are banished from their home groves at certain times. It's your capital punishment. Sure death. A minimal amount of supplies, of nectars . . . and the criminals wander until they find a new grove that will take them. New Remarkables who want human symbionts, like the Au grove did. . . ."

"Most of them die," she tells me. The voice is calm and self-assured, a spine of righteousness in its middle.

I feel like a schoolboy who's just unraveled a complicated quantum problem. "Am I right?" I ask her. "Service lied, didn't he? Your ancestors did something wrong. They were banished. Why? Some sort of political trouble, maybe?"

Snow places her fingertips on my lips.

She's embarrassed. I know from her eyes, noticing how they never quite look at me, and how she tells me, "Shush," through her clenched teeth.

I'm being impolite, I realize.

Yet I can't stop myself. I ask her, "What happened? Why did your ancestors come north—?"

"Nobody knows," she whispers.

I feel I should believe her. . . .

"Long, long ago," she mutters, her eyes hard and glassy. Then she leans toward my face, and I wait for what she'll tell me next. Some secret? Some telling clue into Pitcairn nature?

But instead her uneven teeth clamp down on my lower lip, biting me until I moan.

"What?" I ask. "What?"

"Do you have a perfect family, Ranier?"

I blink and start to shrug my shoulders—

—but she rises, gathering up her clothes and bag and stepping out into the chill rain.

* * *

We left the rainforest yesterday, and I never noticed.

I'm standing with the other tourists, unfamiliar trees around us. No more steelwood. No high epiphytes and clinging mosses. The canopy itself is thin, and through a gap I can look back across yesterday's lakes, their surfaces gray and flattened by the distance.

A new storm is bearing down on us. Those westerly clouds are black, dense and low. A good thing Service kept us moving across the muskeg, I decide. If we were caught in the open today, navigating across the mud with a full-scale gale raging . . . well, I don't want to think about it. I blink and shake my head, our leader now coming up the wide trail toward us.

Service looks small beneath his pack, his legs working fast and his weathered face focused. A sideways glance, and he says, "Come, come." A cretin is galloping after him, its nose working. *"Hunt,"* he tells it. Then he says, "Let's move," with a different voice. He means us.

Our trail winds upward, merging with other trails. Remarkables stretch far ahead, maybe eager to start and maybe fleeing the weather. A second cretin gallops past— the gray-legged one—and it weaves between the Remarkables, almost making a game out of it.

Goottich is in a good mood this morning. He starts telling us how the Pitcairns used to mine these mountains. How the trails are little roads reclaimed by the forest. Copper. There was a vein of the metal up above us. They use copper for wiring. For alloys. He's talking on and on, and why is he happy? He took a thorough beating yesterday. Yet today he's the picture of effervescence.

"Rough night?" Pachel asks me.

She's teasing. A smile, a light laugh.

"Brutal," I tell her.

"So how are the local pleasures?" she continues. "Worth the price of emission?"

What can I say?

"They must be," she decides. "Judging by that grin—"

"Am I?" I touch my mouth, wondering if I'm wearing a lecherous look. Unseemly, it would be. But honest.

Then Goottich continues with his lecturing about metals on Pitcairn. They seem to have been depleted in its early history. It was born as a double planet, he says. But its mate collided with another protoplanet, and the impact dislodged the mate's crust and mantle. There was a fiery rain of rock and ash, he says. And left over was the dense metallic moon—the exposed nickel-iron core—plus the swollen rock-shrouded world beneath us.

We pass the leading Remarkables in short order. Their breathing is thin and labored, and they have difficulty rolling uphill. Maybe it's the mountain air. Maybe the terrain. Nobody's ahead of us, except for Service. The rest of the Pitcairns are scattered among the aliens, walking with a practiced patience.

My legs start aching, and my back, and my arms are spent.

But not like yesterday, I remind myself. I stick my thumbs under the padded straps, shifting the weight and feeling even stronger.

Rain becomes mist, cold and blinding. The trees around us become milky white with gray-black rings on their trunks. Nothing grows near them. Each one is surrounded by a circle of barren ground. There must be some kind of allelopathic effect here. The trees use toxins on their competition. A quiet, enthusiastic chemical war. Between the trees are brief stretches of grassy plants, thin like hairs and knee-high, and sometimes little piles of weathered stones crusted with things like lichen. Low growing. Tough.

I walk up beside Lumiere, and he says, "Hello!" brightly.

I mention the biology that's roaring around us. Isn't it a shame we can't linger?

The old man seems distracted. Thinking about Earth?

He says, "We'll linger in other places," with the red eyes lifting, following our trail into the mountains.

The country above opens up, becoming intensely green. The clouds are close and showing details, vapor pulled into ropes and inverted hills, and the high slopes vanish into the heart of these clouds.

We'll outrace the storm; everyone senses it.

Pitcairn's gravity and the dense atmosphere mean that altitude buys swift changes. We've climbed steadily. The trees around us become more scattered, then stunted. The old mining roadway is a blackish band visible even into the clouds, the mountains gone but the roadway itself suspended in that vaporous white space.

The Remarkables are well below, struggling to hurry. Tendrils grasp at rocks and the weak-rooted vegetation, and their purplish color becomes paler every time I turn and look.

The world behind is all mountains. I don't see lakes or the ocean, and the roof is a leaky mass of clouds.

Service and two cretins sit beside the trail, waiting for us. A dead hunk of plastic stands among the weeds, bleached pale but otherwise intact. It's the hull of a wheeled vehicle, its ceramic engine removed. Two wheels are set on their sides, rich green hairlike grasses bursting through their hubs.

"Take a break," Service tells us. "There's no point in outracing everyone."

Packs drop. Bricks of fresh nectar are dug out, plus water jugs. Mummy bags make comfortable seats. Pachel is on one side of me. She looks at Lumiere. "How are you doing, old man?"

He gives a distant look. "I won't die today."

Effie jerks her head, saying, "Oh, don't talk like that!"

Lumiere chuckles. "I doubt if it matters. I've said it every day, almost forever."

Service is feeding the cretins. Their nectars look odd, black as oil and stinking of wrong-smelling amino acids and such. Hungry dogs would fight, fed that way. Side by side. But the cretins seem to ignore each other, bolting down their lunches and expecting nothing but fair shares. Then Service lets each one lick one of his hands clean, their muscular tongues missing nothing.

Eventually the Remarkables reach us. I've never seen them so vegetable, so passive, and I'm wondering about their physiological limits. They're adapted to a narrow range of temperatures and oxygen. They're not gifted climbers, I'm sure. Their pigments have faded; they resemble gray twists of cloudstuff, thin and depleted.

Yesterday was our misery; today is their turn.

The lead Remarkables are in front of me. A mouth opens, sucking in the air, and a clumsy too-quick voice says, "Re . . . re . . . resssst. . . ."

Service rises to his feet and puts on his pack.

With a gesture he says, "Hunt," and the cretins bolt off into the silky mists.

"Noooo!" moans a second Remarkable. "NNNNOOOO!"

A murmur spreads down through the line of aliens, swelling into a muddled roar. Service pauses, not so much listening as he's simply waiting for quiet. Then he tells them, "If you want to rest, rest." He's wearing his stony face, and his voice is devoid of sympathy or patience. "But the humans are walking. Come if you want. Your choice." A brief pause. "I wouldn't wait, though, if I were you. With a cold night and this humidity, the frost will kill every one of you. We've got to get higher." No hedges; no debates. Then he gives a knowing smile, telling everyone, "It's not much farther. Just a little more."

Service strides off into the mist.

And we go after him. Tourists and Pitcairns, cretins and finally the Remarkables too. I hear the aliens talking. I'm wondering if they're cursing Service and their circumstances. The awful weather; these frightful grades. I have never felt so close to the Remarkables, I realize, and I'm wondering about their pain.

But I can't feel any of it.

I try and there's nothing. And maybe for the first time in years, I'm sorry to be immune. To be safe.

The roadway narrows and quits. The old mine is nearby, but I can't see it. We're walking inside a brilliant white fog. The ground is barren in places, and the vegetation seems hardier and less vibrant. A patch of brighter whiteness floats to one side and above me, and it takes me a moment to realize that it's ice. Old ice left over from winter, I suppose. The Remarkables still struggle to keep close. I hear their motions, but they don't seem to talk anymore. Mostly I walk with my head down, eyes judging distances and the slipperiness of rocks; but every time I look up, I notice that the fog has brightened. It's not lifting, nor can I see any farther. But the vapor itself is suffused with sunlight seeping down to us.

I find myself beside Pachel, and I ask, "How do you feel?"

She gives my question consideration, then says, "Good," as if surprised. "Strong."

"Good genetics," I vote.

"Maybe so."

The slight remaining trail narrows, and she gets ahead of me. I watch her boot heels for a while, then remark,

"The bureaucrat is evolving, isn't she? Becoming an entirely different creature. . . ."

She says, "Maybe so." Her backpack seems insubstantial, stuffed full of clouds and vacuum. "I'm learning to appreciate this place."

"Are you?"

"Each in our own fashion," she teases.

I laugh to myself.

Then she slows and walks beside me. "I hated coming here," she confides. "You know that. But I had orders, and I'm a good bureaucrat."

"I'm sure."

"A lot of this . . . what we're doing here . . . it's drudgery. It means keeping control of your feelings. Your true nature. And that's what's odd, Ranier."

"Odd?"

"We portage and hike," she explains. "Pretty scenery, but we're too busy and much too tired to notice most of it. And Service has his timetable. Each day has its specific goals. See what I mean?"

Not exactly, I admit.

"This is my normal work. A different office, and the demands are more physical. But otherwise I know this place. This kind of life." She pauses a moment, laughing and then saying, "I haven't even come all that far, Ranier. Not really!"

22
HIGH CAMP

✦

The Remarkables are stacked two deep, constantly moving for position. None of them want to be on the outside, feeling the thin air or the cutting winds. Next to nothing remains of their purple coloring. They look mold gray and infinitely weary.

Maybe they're digesting their symbiotic bacteria, Goottich hypothesizes. In reaction to the stresses. As a source of extra energy, maybe.

Bedford makes noise about this being an honor, us able to watch this ancient, holy rite of theirs.

Then Effie asks, "Are some of them going to die?"

It isn't the question that causes faces to turn. It's her tone. It's the hopefulness. Maybe she wants all of them to succumb, then we can turn and retrace our course, the *passion* finished.

Nobody answers her.

The Pitcairns shrug their shoulders and glance at each other. Except for Service. He watches our little camp fire, chewing on nectar, the dark eyes thoughtful. Distant.

Bedford makes neutral sounds and pats his wife's knee.

Pachel looks at me, rolling her eyes as if to say, "What a fool! Who invited her along?"

The sky is a hard cloudless blue with the smallish sun dropping toward a nearby peak. Everywhere are rocks with patches of old ice in the sheltered places, a little mountain lake toward the north, and I'm thinking how this landscape looks like my home. It's the same harsh sterile beauty. Life has a marginal hold on this ground, and I feel relaxed. Reassured.

"This would be a perfect place for a house," says Goottich.

As if he can read my thoughts.

The big man looks exhausted. Yesterday's tortures and today's climb have caught up with him. Yet he manages to smile weakly, breathing through his teeth and nodding.

"You must have a gorgeous house," Effie speculates. "Inside your enworld, I mean." She hugs her knees to her thin face. "I can't imagine such a life."

"One hundred and twenty-three rooms," he relates, "with sixty-six robot servants, antique furniture and rugs from fifty worlds, and a dozen rooms just for my art collections. I even have two paintings from Earth. Authenticated! Plus a lovely bust of someone's emperor."

"Who are the artists?" asks Lumiere.

Goottich names them, neither familiar.

"Do you enjoy them?" asks Pachel.

"What . . . ?"

"Are the paintings any good?"

The round face grows puzzled, and he replies, "They came from Earth." His voice sounds testy. A little shrill.

There is an uncomfortable silence. Off in the west, where the land falls away, I see the knotted tops of the storm clouds, brilliant and remote. Service says we're safe up here. Only the worst summer storms can push over these mountains, and somehow he knows this one won't.

The old Pitcairn is throwing bits of dried lumber into our fire, sparks rising in arcs and dropping fast. Someone carried this firewood up from the forest. Maybe years ago, judging by its dryness. Its eagerness to burn.

Goottich continues talking about his house. Has he told us about the views from his thousand windows? How he can look over his private little ocean? His house is perched on a mountain ridge, and below him is a little bay, deep and green. The greenness comes from reflecting the forest straight overhead. A giant cylinder filled with species chosen by him. Tailored by him. Diverse communities, particularly considering the finite amount of land and water and air . . .

. . . and he pauses, aware of how he sounds. He blinks and almost smiles, telling the Pitcairns, "Sweet luck. All those people in the Realm, and not more than a few tens of millions are in my position."

They understand luck. Briar shrugs his shoulders as if to say, "Someone has to be blessed. Why not you?"

Then Goottich's eyes become round and simple. His mouth drops open, his tongue licking his lower lip. Finally he rises to his feet, grunting before telling us, "I've got to go. . . ."

"Good night," says Effie, enthusiastically.

He waves a distracted hand at her, and he says, "No. No, I've got work . . . quite a lot of work. . . ."

What does that mean? We watch him walking across the rocky ground. Goottich's tent is a tiny bit of geometry set beside the turquoise-colored lake. He pauses and pees into the water before slipping from sight.

"Imagine living that way," says Effie.

The Pitcairns watch us. Snow is one of the ones off guarding us. But Salo is here. And Briar and Tintoil and others. Service is chewing on a lump of colorless nectar, sucking down its juices, his gaze intense and his wiry figure framed by the yellow flames.

"I wouldn't," says Pachel.

Effie asks, "Wouldn't what?"

"Live in any world of Goottich's." She compresses her mouth into a thin bloodless line.

"Why not?" says Effie, sounding injured.

Pachel says nothing.

The tiny woman decides, "You're just jealous—"

"Remember," Pachel snaps, "I knew him before. We were in school together, in some of the same classes."

"So?" Effie persists.

Service stops chewing, the nectar giving one cheek a sharp corner.

"I know stories," says Pachel. "I was halfway friendly with him. And maybe it's hard to imagine, but not a lot of people were friendly with our dear sponsor."

Effie fidgets nervously.

"Tell a story," says Service. "If you want."

And Pachel says, "Okay," while tilting her head, her mouth opened and waiting for her to gather the words.

The New Albemarne University is a city unto itself, she explains. For the benefit of the Pitcairns, she tells how it's the oldest and largest and easily the most prestigious institution in its portion of the frontier. Most local terraformers are products of its honored classrooms. The basic teaching methods haven't been changed in twenty thousand years. And, she adds, the professors themselves might be twenty thousand years old, judging by their looks and their unblinking worship of tradition.

"There's a mandatory project," she says. "Sophs— second-year students—have to design and construct an enclosed biosphere. Any shape, any size. The single requirement is that the biosphere is stable over a proscribed time, no species going extinct and no radical instabilities."

Every terraformer nods. This is one of our common denominators; some of us even smile at the memory.

Pachel tells how most students keep the assignment simple. A single hyperglass sphere enclosing water and oxygenated air, plus minerals, plus some durable blue-green algae and protozoans, then tiny crustaceans acting as predators. That's a proven, time-honored scheme. Grades are given for success, not scope. And if an odd virus hadn't slipped past her sterilization procedure, she would have had a perfect score. Her crustaceans wouldn't have started dying, and she wouldn't have been docked 10 percent.

"I know the feeling," Bedford reports.

"Quiet," snaps his wife. "Be quiet."

Goottich was the wealthiest student on campus. Perhaps in the entire history of the school. He lived in a luxury apartment near the Albe River, not in the dormitories. Rules had been bent on his behalf. Pachel rarely saw him anytime but in class or lab, and as chance would have it, they were stationed side by side for the biosphere project.

"Imagine a giant model of the chlorophyll A molecule," she tells us. "Each atom is a chamber, every bond is a connecting cylinder, and the bonds are opaque where the atoms are transparent. All made out of hyperglass. The actual work was done by artisan robots, according to exacting demands—"

"A soph project?" says Effie. "It sounds *lovely*!"

Her husband mutters, "Quiet."

It was a thing of beauty, Pachel informs us. She wishes she could do it justice with words. Of course there were rumors of improprieties—some famous, cash-poor terraformer had supposedly helped Goottich with the difficult parts, and the dull ones—but nothing was ever proved.

Pachel saw him do the actual work, handling the robots; and the dusty professors gave him a perfect score, although to a person they seemed shocked that anyone would take so much trouble and time. They were much, much more comfortable with simple competent work, thank you. . . .

"It was beautiful," Pachel says again. "Glass and that fragile ecological webwork. It didn't matter who designed it." She swallows and says, "He hung it over the courtyard in front of his apartment building, suspending it with a single hyperfiber thread. In daylight, under New Albemarne's sun, the water inside would turn a lovely green that was nearly black by dusk. At night the water would glow. Bioluminescent creatures consumed the stored sugars, producing light, and different species concentrated in different chambers. Very slick, all in all."

I shut my eyes, imagining the scene.

"Oxygen atoms were blue," she reports. "Carbon was straw gold. Magnesium, green. Hydrogen atoms were fierce little bits of salmon, turning pink by dawn. Then the water became clear again, dormant algae waking, and they'd eat sunlight and produce new sugars. And so on, and so on."

"I'd love to see it," says Effie. Her big eyes are distant, her features relaxed. "It sounds gorgeous."

Bedford stares at her. His expression is concern mixed with fear. What's been obvious to the rest of us finally occurs to him, yet inertia and his stubbornness keep him in control. With a reasoned voice, he says, "Our friend might not have done the work himself. Dear."

"Jealous people make up stories," Effie replies. Then she turns to Pachel, adding, "I don't mean you. You're just reporting the mood, right?"

"There was jealousy, yes." Pachel nods. "Goottich fueled it. He acted proud and made certain everyone knew about how clever he was. He told everyone in class that his chlorophyll molecule was on display and come see it." She grins and looks at each of us. "But you can imagine how he acted. A younger Goottich, even more obnoxious and proud. Maybe a jealous person did the deed."

"What deed?" asks Effie.

"Either someone made a partial cut of the hyperfiber cord," she tells us, "or Goottich never bothered to check the cord's integrity. His lawyers argued the former. 'Vandals. Hooligans.' But my guess is that he was just too indifferent, too sloppy, using old hyperfiber and never once thinking what it might mean."

"What happened?" Bedford presses. "Will you just tell us?"

Pachel breathes through her nose and shakes her head. "It fell. The cord broke and the hyperglass fell some ten or fifteen meters, and it exploded when it hit the flat stones of the courtyard. I heard the impact. My boyfriend was walking with me. It was night, and we ran in the direction of the explosion. We arrived in time to see the glowing water flowing, the colors mixing, night birds and bats drinking their fill. We saw Goottich come out of his building. Maybe a hundred people had gathered, and I was one of the closest ones to him. I saw his face, his eyes. How he moved. He looked almost identical to how he looks today. That same huge frame, that pink ball of a head. He didn't have any expression on his face. That's what I remember best—"

"He was in shock," Effie volunteers.

"No," says Pachel. "No way."

"His big project had been destroyed—"

"He didn't care that much about the project. Knowing Goottich, I think he was becoming bored with it anyway." She shakes her head. "No, he was staring at one particular spot in the wreckage. He could see something, maybe because he was taller than anyone else. He could see a body. Some student. A boy had been standing under the molecule when the cord broke, probably watching the pretty colors."

"I remember that story," interrupts Bedford. "It was after I graduated . . . a tragedy!"

"But I don't see any reason to blame Goottich," Effie adds.

"The courts didn't," Pachel explains. "His family lawyers blamed vandals, and there was some private payoff for the grieving family. But that's not what I'm talking about. That's not my point."

Nobody speaks.

"I liked Goottich," she goes on. "No, I tolerated him. And maybe I felt sorry for him. 'Poor little rich boy.' That sort of thing." She shakes her head. "But I keep remembering his face. He was the first person to step into the shattered glass. He went out to the body and kicked the wreckage from the boy's face. What a mess! And I could see Goottich's face lit up by the glowing water. He just stared. Nothing in his face but curiosity . . ."

"Shock," Effie repeats.

"No!" Pachel snorts and says, "There were a hundred faces in that courtyard. Some of them were in shock, some were sad for the boy. A few were glad they hadn't been under the thing when it fell. I saw every possible expression, but with Goottich . . . there was nothing. I'm not talking about evil. I'm talking about an absence. An emptiness. Cold and nearly dead . . . his gazing down at the corpse and the water glowing with those mixed-together colors—"

"You don't trust him," Service remarks.

Pachel looks at him, then says, "Never."

The old Pitcairn seems satisfied, nodding slightly and leaning back away from the fire.

"That's a ridiculous story," Effie starts to mutter. "What can you tell from a face? Next to nothing. Next to nothing. That's what *I* think."

23
UNDER THE GLACIER

❖

The tongue is shockingly wet, in my ear and then around it. Then Snow says, "No more sleep," with a distorted voice.

I clamp a hand over my ear, hunkering down deep inside my bag.

"It's late," she warns, "and you look like a needle-snail in there. Get up! Get dressed!"

The air in the bag stinks of my farts. I come out willingly, and Snow kisses me once on the mouth. Was she guarding all night? Of course not. I say something about missing her, and she says, "Really?" as if she's never heard anything so strange. "Did you?"

"Don't you ever miss people?"

"I don't know. I've never been alone."

I can't think of a response. Snow slips outside, and I dress and follow, stiff in my joints and bruised where rocks gnawed at me through the night. I dismantle and pack my tent, my hands knowing the routine. People are talking in the distance. My breath curls and dissipates into the chill air. I'm strapping my tent to my pack when Service approaches me, saying, "Today you'll walk with the juveniles. Carry this." He hands me a long stick of firewood. "Hold it this way." He shows me how with his rifle.

I show him my technique, asking why.

"We're being shadowed," he says matter-of-factly. "Half a dozen cretins, maybe more."

I grasp the stick until my hands ache.

"Not like that, no," he warns. "The cretins are trained to recognize firearms. They won't attack in the day if there are too many guns. So pretend your stick has a trigger. Right. That's better." He spins and leaves, walking fast, and he glances down at his timepiece.

"Come on, come on!" he shouts. "We're getting off this fucking mountain!"

The Remarkables extrude a thin white vapor as they climb the last slope. I walk among them, brandishing my stick with authority. They roll stiffly, slowly. Overnight they've turned fragile, and only rarely do they find the strength to talk to one another.

Up ahead the aliens slow to breathe, bunching together.

"Talker?" I say.

One of them says, "Ranier," weakly.

It's like trying to converse with a choking friend. I feel bad, but then Talker asks, "How did you sleep? Well?"

I lie, saying, "Very well."

"Walk with me?"

"Of course."

"Slower," it warns.

"Okay." I concentrate, stepping and stopping and working on my patience. The morning sky is high and cobalt blue, patches of thin clouds in the east. We're climbing toward a ridge of bald stone. After a little while, feeling some vague obligation to make noise, I tell Talker, "This reminds me of my world. Quite a bit, actually."

"You built yourself a hellhole," it responds.

I start explaining no, that Rye's World isn't finished. That's all. But Talker probably realizes that much already, and it was making a joke. I grin and chuckle to myself, and for a little while I lament how emigrants come every day and the natives have big families, even the hard raw places starting to fill up, as always.

We conquer the last ridge, a strong wind at my back, pulling my trousers snug against my legs. Before us is a long curling valley dropping between high mountains, spilling into a larger valley. That's where we're going, I think. Down to where the rocks are covered with green, shaggy little forests clinging to the damp places.

This is a gambler's country. Its inhabitants are generalists. Large litters; blizzards of tiny seed. There's a brief growing season and probably irregular bad years. Toughness and versatility must be sewn into their genes. Not a

lot of species, chances are. Not a lot of complicated struc-
turing in the community.

The juveniles are gathering below the ridge, out of the
wind. I hear them talking. Singing. I start to ask Talker
what's happening, but it has rolled down to the others,
gray tendrils interlacing, eyes lifting, almost every one of
them pointed in the same direction.

Goottich and the other tourists stand together, everyone
holding a long stick. Goottich says, "There," with certainty. He points with his toy rifle, telling us, "That's it."

I look at Pachel.

"Mount Au," she tells me. "At last."

Goottich sets the stick under his eyes. "Between those
peaks." A distant shape seems to hover, almost invisible
behind a thin milky haze. "There."

"I don't see it," Bedford complains.

"Look harder."

The last Remarkables come past us. Their singing seems
excited, but maybe I'm bending what I hear into what I
expect. I really don't have a clue as to what they're feeling.

"How far away is the mountain?" asks Effie.

"On a line?" says Goottich. "Perhaps a couple hundred
kilometers. Give or take."

"And we can see it?" she replies. "From such a distance,
imagine!"

"Oh, okay," says Bedford. "There it is."

We can see only clouds. Self-made weather, I remember; and I start to turn, ready to ask Lumiere what he
thinks. But I stop myself. The puffy face is streaked with
tears, his free hand pushing them back toward his eyes.
He stares at Mount Au with an intensity—a hunger, really—that startles me. I step backward, and he gives a
little moan. Then he settles to the ground, almost falling,
and I'm too surprised to react.

Pachel says, "Hey! What is it—?"

"I'm all right," moans Lumiere. "Just tired."

I ask, "You're sure?" What if he gets sick in these mountains? Our shuttle needs a runway or open water. Can we
carry him somewhere—?

"He'll be all right," says Goottich, his voice careless and
loud.

"I will be," Lumiere promises.

"See?" The big man motions. "There's Service. Down there, waving for us to move. Let's move," and he marches away with a clatter of loose stones.

"Prick," says Pachel.

"He is not," Effie replies.

Bedford says, "He does seem rather insensitive."

"He's a great, great man," she counters, "and all of you are jealous. That's what you are."

"I feel better now," Lumiere tells us. He offers me his hand—dry and too cool—and he says, "Just put me on my feet again, will you?"

"Jealous," Effie repeats.

"He's still abrasive," says her husband.

"You have to look past his bluster." Effie smiles and starts walking downhill, using her stick like a third leg. "He's just a big sweet little boy under everything. That's what I think."

"Effie—?"

The Remarkables are scattering now. Any ceremony has concluded; we are under way again.

"Effie!?"

"You're all right?" I ask Lumiere.

"Absolutely," he proclaims.

"You're certain?"

"I couldn't feel better if I had to," he says.

"*Effie?*"

Bedford starts after his wife, but she moves too fast. She looks weightless, skipping down a long talus slope.

"Watch your step," she tells the Remarkables. "Watch those tendrils. Be careful. Careful! Easy, easy, easy . . . !"

Sometimes Remarkables slip and roll too fast, colliding with the rocks below. Only their flexibility saves them, I decide. They absorb the blows with their tendrils and screech loudly, and that must be their cursing. That's how it sounds.

Talker doesn't slip. It waits for me and stays with me, and after a time, on more forgiving terrain, it says, "Tell me more, Ranier. About this home of yours. How will it look when you're finished finishing it?"

I try. I have no idea what it knows about the technologies, much less what its mental limits might be. Yet I don't want to sound as if I'm talking to a child. I assume an informed layman's familiarity. I describe comets being brought from the surrounding Oort cloud, water ices melted and injected into the growing sea, and different ices vaporized to bolster the atmosphere. Eventually Rye's World will appear quite Earth-like. Particularly if the observer chooses to ignore the eroding craters and the absence of recent mountains. People will settle thick around the equator—the zone of the mildest climates and the best lighting—and eventually there won't be room enough for new emigrants.

"Your children?" it asks. "Are they living there?"

I'm not embarrassed as I might be with people, I discover; that's part of the charm. I don't mind admitting, "At least so far, my only children are here. With the Pitcairns."

"Such skills you possess! To transform whole worlds—!"

"The same way we've been doing it for millennia," I reply. "It must seem astounding, I'm sure. But the basic technologies haven't changed . . . I don't know in how long, honestly. . . ."

"The sky full of green groves," it says. Then a pause—what for Talker must seem like an age—and it asks, "What about a million seasons from now? What do you see in that future?"

"Well, I don't know." I blink and consider the question.

"The future," it repeats.

"There are speculations," I tell it. "Since these worlds aren't naturally habitable, we might have difficulties. Some experts think we'll have to melt their interiors with sunken reactors and radioactive materials. Otherwise the rivers and whatnot are going to erode away the continents. Key minerals will get buried at sea, no natural cycle existing—"

"No no no no," it says. Then comes a strange cackling noise, and it explains, "I meant what's important. With the future, Ranier. You people are so clever, I'm certain you can answer those problems. But what about what matters most?"

I blink and ask, "What do you mean?"

"How does the future look to you, Ranier?"

Maybe it is me, but I sense gravity in the voice. I want to pause and consider my answer, making my best attempt . . . only Talker thinks many times faster than I, and I'm not eager to seem completely stupid.

"The future," I tell it, "looks like now. I suppose."

I pause, then add, "At least to me."

The alien continues rolling, making no sound but the creak of its tendrils and the constant wet breathing.

Finally it tells me, "You are right. And wrong too."

The voice is almost sharp, and I think that must be intentional.

Talker says, "Sometime we must talk, Ranier. About serious matters." As if terraforming is a pleasant distraction, nothing more. "Important matters, my friend. If you are willing."

It surprises me that I'm a little offended.

Terraforming . . . the mass transmutation of the universe . . . less than important . . . !

"Ranier?"

"Fine," I say.

"One day," it promises.

"Whenever."

Service remains ahead of everyone. Sometimes I see him amidst the sudden green vegetation, one or two black cretins hunting nearby. We are being shadowed, I recall. Dangerous cretins are watching even now, and I feel a cold damp pressure building on my neck. I feel them watching me, hiding in shadows high above and not even our Remarkables able to see them.

Above us, filling a tiny hanging valley, is the bluish ice of an active glacier. There are very few glaciers in the Realm. Just on the occasional high peak, and then only as a means of storing surplus water. I wonder if the enemy cretins are hiding in those deep crevices, warm in their plumage and using their streamlined minds to decide when and where to attack us.

I can't see Mount Au anymore. We are too low.

The air has turned warm and humid, thickening as we lose altitude. On my right is a gorge and a little river, water flowing from the high glacier. I hear it, and sometimes I can smell the pounded vapors. Shrubs start to grow taller, standing in little clusters. The breeze rustles the small inflated leaves, the sound dry and pleasant.

We catch up with Snow in the afternoon. Or she allows us to catch up.

I'm thinking about my incredible circumstances. How many people can claim to have spoken to aliens *and* to have slept with an authentic Pitcairn? How many would pay anything for the novelty of this life?

Snow hears my approach, turns and smiles.

I ask about her day.

"How is it?" She laughs. I'm asking another silly question. "Don't you know?"

I shrug my shoulders, unsure of myself.

She gives me a peculiar sideways glance, then asks, "What are you doing with that stick?"

"It's my gun."

"Is it?" she says with a grave expression.

I tell her what Service told me. My associates and I are pretending to carry weapons, trying to worry enemy cretins.

"He's teasing you, Ranier. He's playing a game."

I look at the stick as if it's betrayed me. "Really?"

"Service is famous for jokes. I should have warned you."

"Service?"

"Yes."

"Has a sense of humor?"

She laughs and says, "Why not?"

Someone is having fun with me. That much I know. Maybe it's Snow, maybe Service. Maybe I should discard the stick. But when I glance at Talker, just for an instant, something occurs to me. This simple piece of lumber is a greater tool than any the Remarkables have ever produced. I feel a sudden pride in my phony gun. I actually grip it tightly, almost cutting my thumb on a ragged knot. I won't give it up now. No, I will not.

This perhaps is the original weapon carried by my ancestors, perhaps for the first million seasons.

I should handle it with pride and a certain flare, I decide.

With a sense of life.

As a symbol of great and honorable history!

TALKER

✦

Sometimes he will stop just to stop, just to stand motionless and speak while half looking at one of his cretins. "A slow sloppy ugly *passion*," he will say. "Nobody's working hard enough. Not even the poor clod of dirt who's in charge." Says Service. The poor clod himself. Talking to his cretins and to himself, but knowing that we can see his face, his mouth, reading lips and adding the hard flat sound of his voice. He knows his real audience, saying, "How can I work hard enough? Half of the time I'm watching the others. Who's working? Who's pretending? And these visitors . . . spoiled and ignorant . . . I have to keep an eye on them. Particularly Goottich. Pachel's right. The man has no soul that I can see. Just fancy ideas, just as the Old Ones warned. . . ."

My siblings, in contrast, talk about the Au mountain. They know better, but they cannot help themselves. It is their obsession, the poor things.

Passions have near-laws, and the first near-law is that juveniles may not comment excessively about their own *passion*. Particularly in the early stages. Particularly when the ultimate destination is remote. Better to concentrate on surviving and on the history of this endeavor. Each juvenile is supposed to recall past *passions*. Great ones, tragic ones. The ancient ones of legend. I watch my siblings talking about the look of Au and their excitement . . . already past the high ground, we are, and every one of them can scarcely wait . . . and I shout at them—a single high tone—then I tell them, "Quiet. Can you be quiet?"

They obey me, knowing I am right.

Then I wave tendrils, saying, "We should tell the story of the first *passion*. To each other. Right now."

The first *passion*.

Every grove has its own version, none authentic. That Past is too remote to be known as a whole. But our grove's telling contains many of the common elements. There was a little grove, for example. This was millions of seasons ago. One clear moonless night, without warning, the grove's adults saw a tumbling body high above them. Above the atmosphere, we know now. The body was shaped much like a mountain, sharp-edged and dark. It was an asteroid, we know now. But the ancient grove took it as a sign from the All-Answer. A mountain streaking across the sky above them? It must be some message, and the grove's Old Ones talked and talked, trying to decide what it meant and how to respond.

Eventually they made their decision.

Knowing our Old Ones, it probably took them seasons to feel sure enough.

There were mountains inland, a brief range of them, and they had noticed how the largest peak had a glancing resemblance to the asteroid. Thus they dispatched juveniles and some cretins. Those juveniles made the first *passion*, and the survivors returned and told about the bright sunshine in the interior. They told of praying to the All-Answer. They claimed to have had visions while at the holy mountain's base. And in these visions the All-Answer told them a portion of the Future.

"Every grove must make a yearly *passion*," they reported.

As if to prove their story, those juveniles thrived in the next seasons. They grew faster than the older generations, surpassing them and eventually becoming the grove's Old Ones, and as the Old Ones, they ordered more *passions* . . . but those are different stories, most of them long forgotten. And I stop my telling.

We will travel to the base of the Au mountain, and there we will pray to the All-Answer. This is how it is done. Prayer and perhaps the All-Answer will enter our minds, instructing us in the mysteries of the Future.

The Pitcairns leave the All-Answer to us.

They claim—Service would claim—that a *passion* is a

biological watershed. The strong light and dryness of the interior are essential for us to mature and grow; key enzymes will be released as we wander about the Au plains. As always, the Pitcairns treat us as they would any complicated machinery. Genes and enzymes; exhaustion-induced hallucinations. We are products of countless molecules, each one a tiny tool, and if we wish to believe in our god . . . well, that belief is another tool. One that motivates, and who are they to argue with it?

That is what Service believes.

Motivation is what he wants, stopping again and looking back up at us now. Knowing we can see him saying, "I need help." Saying, "Don't waste eyes on me," in warning. "Study our guests, will you? Try to see inside them."

We have been trying—

"Harder," he says. "Try harder. I need to know everything about every one of them. How they think. How they will respond."

It is not easy work, I am thinking.

"Can I trust any of them?"

Trust.

"At least a little," he says to us, anticipating our thoughts. "Not forever and not everywhere. But enough."

What is enough?

"I need an ally," he tells us. "If you want to make the damned mountain, that is."

24
MOUNT AU

✦

Cowardice is the heart of nature.

A squirrellike something stands nearby, angry at my presence. It's up on its haunches, clicking at me, the plumage green with bright white throat patches. I approach and shout, "Boo!" Some sudden equation plays itself out inside the creature's brain. Stand or flee? Stand or flee? It clicks once again—this time for pride, I assume—before diving into a hole at its feet.

I return to pitching my tent, laughing gently. The sun is dipping below a mountain ridge. In the cooling air I finish my work, then I strip and change into my last clean clothes, putting dirty ones over them to keep warm. Once, then again, I hear a muffled click from underground. "Go away!" says the squirrel. "Get away from here!"

I'm building my own fire, using small sticks and most of my patience. I'm thinking about cowardice and how most animals will flee from most serious challenges, avoiding violence. It's not because they're tenacious pacifists. It's a question of loss-versus-gain. Eons of rigorous natural selection have taught their genes to avoid self-destruction. A good deal of any brain is devoted to these calculations. But if I decided to dig at this ground, following the burrow through its turns, the cornered squirrel would fight with teeth and claws. Another part of the calculation: Is it worth a predator's effort, accepting that work and the eventual risk?

Lumiere finds me and a nearby place for his tent, and I welcome him with a sweet brick and water filtered from the alpine lake.

He looks sad. I'm eating, watching his puffy cheeks and the broken veins and the very red eyes that seem withdrawn. I feel sorry for him, and I don't know why. His sadness has a comfortable feel, as if it's reliable. Expected. I don't ask questions or press him. But maybe he reads something in my expression.

He nods at me and smiles, then says, "Look there."

One of our cretins is running on the slope above us, passing in and out of sunlight with the black plumage bright and the miscolored leg brighter. We watch it splashing across little streams of meltwater; then suddenly Lumiere starts to talk, his voice quiet. Steady.

"I met her on Earth," he says. "She was eleven years my senior, and she told me I was adorable. We were neighbors. Next-door neighbors. She had a private pond, deep and scented, and she was swimming with me. Seducing me. I was fourteen years old, and she was my first lover."

I say nothing.

He smiles, rolling the nectar brick in one hand. "We were married several months later. It was deemed a good move for both families. We belonged to wealthy lineages. Financial holdings would be mutually enhanced. Her parents assumed I was a plaything, a temporary and useful lust. Eventually our relationship would open up. A child or two might come from even better bloodlines, they hoped."

"You really do come from Earth," I whisper.

He nods solemnly.

"When?"

He deflects the question with a shrug. "Two wealthy families joined," he repeats, "and we lived comfortably. We had little country estates on Earth and private parks on half a dozen nearby moons and asteroids. Since hundreds of billions of people live in and around Earth—"

"Sure."

"—we were unusually blessed. Either family had maybe ten times the wealth of Goottich's family. Plus a good deal more power." He almost smiles with the memory, or maybe he's amused to find a flickering pride remaining after so long. "We had enough wealth to afford as many children as we wanted, and that's incredibly rare. Four children in all. Two boys and a girl, plus a girl who insisted on a sex transformation. That's a good way to dilute any fortune, I should add. So many heirs. So many slices in a finite pie."

I nod.

"We loved each other," says Lumiere.

There's emotion in his face, and his hand turns the nectar brick faster, its surface becoming dull and sticky.

"We loved each other," he repeats.

I say, "You're fortunate," and breathe deeply.

He says with a flat private voice, "Our children were killed in an accident. They were the only fatalities. An utterly reliable deep-dive submarine failed. We were at our Callisto park. We watched the wreck brought up to the surface, and my wife collapsed. She very nearly died with the grief."

"I'm sorry. . . ."

Lumiere waits a moment, then continues. "She was a beautiful woman. Did I mention that? Beautiful but flawed. Erratic. Sometimes argumentative, and always demanding of me. Probably spoiled by her wealth, but who isn't?" A pause, then he says, "She tried suicide three times, in three different ways. And of course I gave her the best possible care. Yet there comes a place where you can't help someone so thoroughly committed to self-extermination. The doctors could destroy her personality. Drugs and electrical implants could guard her behaviors. But being a robot was no answer, and I was so afraid for her."

Doctors don't know everything, I want to tell him. To agree with his hard assessment.

"We reached an agreement, she and I." He frowns and then laughs, and he looks at me. "No more suicide attempts until we gathered all the evidence possible."

"Evidence?"

And Lumiere sighs, telling me, "This was long ago. Listen, if you want. I feel like telling it. And today, after seeing Au . . . it's something that I've got to tell. If only for me. . . ."

His wife was named Twyl, and her babies had died. Cold seawater had burst through a faulty hull, acting like a sawblade. What horrible god could allow such a thing?

To Twyl it seemed infinitely unfair, and cruel, and what if there wasn't any afterlife for her babies' souls?

Questions made her ill. She couldn't sleep, couldn't function. She promised to stop trying to murder herself, then she and her husband set out across the solar system, visiting holy sights and kneeling before God in its myriad forms, hands clasped or set on the floor and her tired voice begging for instruction. Evidence. She craved the compelling evidence that would lead to answers, then peace. She was searching for something fair and just, and Lumiere was the patient husband, attentive and quiet and tirelessly supportive.

He had grieved for their children too. But he had recovered, whole again and able to laugh. Afterward the worst part for him was the guilt. He hadn't suffered like Twyl. He felt as if he were flawed for being too resilient. And maybe that's why he was so patient. He went with Twyl to the ice cathedrals on Pluto and the simple Muslim prayer halls in Mercury's crust, plus the countless shrines on the green asteroids, those tiny faiths proving as empty as the giant ones.

Twyl was still a young woman, but the anguish played hell with her looks. She grayed early and then denied herself cosmetic treatments, even when Lumiere suggested free-radical purges. He never pressed her. Over things so trivial as her appearance, how could he press her? But still he began to miss his lovely wife, feeling temptations from everywhere.

Eventually Twyl decided that there were no answers in their solar system. They talked and decided to liquidate their considerable assets, ignoring their families' protests, and they used a portion of the money to build a small and fully armored torchship.

Their course was selected by computer, through random means, Twyl deciding that if God or Whatever had some direction in mind, influencing the minuscule circuits of a machine seemed as easy a trick as any.

They put themselves into cold-sleep, the torchship accelerating to the highest safe-speed possible, avoiding the mapped hazards as they moved from green world to green world.

Centuries passed. Every kind of religious and philosophical site was visited. There was fuel to buy at each stop.

Each jump meant damaged armor, the little impacts unavoidable. Several times they just missed death to comet shards; and Twyl, during her strong moments, took this as a sign that the gods were overseeing their journey.

Lumiere rarely offered his opinions. And there were good times, he wants me to understand. He describes the rare jupiters with airborne cities, their populations worshiping the titanic winds; he mentions perfect worlds with changeless climates and vain, overly pretty citizens worshiping themselves. In one peculiar enworld, nobody ever quite died. Aging citizens had portions of their brains removed, then transplanted into healthy offspring. Neurons were interwoven, and some kind of coexistence was formed. In principle, even the original citizens still remained as knots of neural tissue. But it wasn't an afterlife. It was clever medicine. Twyl saw through the cleverness quickly enough, cursed their hosts, and announced that she was leaving. Immediately.

Unity churches were everywhere. *Of course.* Lumiere talks about a few sects, minor and peculiar. Twyl herself had no interest in the mainstream branches. People are perfect? Death making room for life? But death was a horrible waste, she argued. This was a vast universe, virtually empty of life, and it seemed criminal to her that experience and wisdom were thrown aside with death. Which was what most Unity Faiths demanded from their believers, even the odd little sects. "Death makes room for life. For renewal." As if nobody could think of any better fate.

Lumiere pauses, then confesses that I remind him of Twyl with my cynicism and my humor. We're different shades of the same color, Twyl and me.

Then he continues with his story, covering huge distances in moments. He talks about his wife's declining health and the relentless depletion of their resources, the torchship aging and their mutual energies on the downswing. They spoke of selling their ship for whatever money it would bring. Lumiere offered to become some kind of terraformer. He already had a good deal of self-taught skill, caring for their ship's simple ecology; and terraformers were always valuable on the edge of the Realm. Even if you were an old man with a limited résumé. . . .

Twyl listened, and at the appropriate times she nodded, saying, "That sounds fine. That seems reasonable." Finally she said that they should sleep on their situation—a small joke—and with that she set the autopilot for New Emerald and helped Lumiere into his sleep chamber, kissing him and smiling and kissing him again.

She did something to the controls. Lumiere awoke as they approached New Emerald, climbing out with the stiff gait of any body suffering from too much time near absolute zero. The first thing he saw was Twyl's recorded message to him, the tired gray face explaining how one person could move better than two. Particularly when one of them was too worn down to continue. Particularly when they had at their disposal a means to achieve what they both wanted . . . and with that she told the trembling, naked Lumiere, "Good-bye, love." Her face at peace.

A despairing, exhausted peace. But peace nonetheless.

"She killed herself?" I mutter.

Lumiere shakes his head, saying, "No." He looks at his hands, at the nectar in them, then puts it down on the matted grass.

"She was mostly dead. Just as she had planned, I believe. Twyl had used the cold-sleep process to selectively kill her living tissues. Only portions of her brain had been frozen alive, in suspension. I saw that and remembered the enworld where nobody was allowed death, and I did what she knew I would do. With the shipboard autodocs, I transplanted her living neural tissue into my own soggy cortex, meshing them with my mind. Since memory and personality have a holographic design, every fragment mirrors the whole. Twyl survives, in a fashion. Clever medicine made it possible to continue our journey. Which I have done. For more years—more than I ever thought possible, I confess—but now I'm near the end. Very, very near . . ."

I stare at him. Smoke curls around his face, eyes watering.

"How does it feel?" I have to ask. "Having someone inside you? Can you feel her presence?"

"I hear her voice . . . all the time." He laughs pleasantly, his tone self-deprecating. "But of course when you live with a spouse for centuries, waking and asleep, you're going to hear her voice anyway. You're going to have overlapping memories. You'll find yourself carrying on long,

rambling conversations, and people will think that you're . . .
colorful."

He examines one of his hands, his expression curious and
detached. "I know Twyl influences my thoughts and actions. But why? Because part of her is inside me? Or because I just know her that well?" He shrugs and says, "I
don't know. I can't tell you."

I say nothing.

He lifts his gaze. "I'm such an old man, Ranier."

I uproot a plant, nervous hands needing to feel busy.

"When the Remarkables were discovered," he tells me,
"I felt an electric surge coursing through me. When I heard
about their All-Answer and their holy sites? That's the one
time when I knew I could feel Twyl's presence. Her life.
Before me, she recognized that here was something new.
Wholly different. An alien god worshiped by intelligent
beings. . . ."

I nod.

Lumiere cries. Tears streak his face, and he blinks and
blinks, staring hard at both hands and rolling his fingers
in the air.

"You've come all this way," I begin.

"I've tried a thousand times. I've contacted groves just
like Goottich did, and I was rebuffed every time. Who
knows why? Maybe because I asked to join a *passion*.
Maybe they don't approve of humans chasing after their
god—"

"Ask Talker," I suggest.

"It doesn't matter. Either way . . . I'm here and I know
what I'll do, and now the reasons for everything else don't
matter."

Higher up in the valley, on flat ground, the juveniles are
in their nightly bunch. In the gloom they seem blackish
and immobile. Then I notice eyes pivoting, and I realize
that some of them are focused on us. Nobody else is camped
near us.

"Have you read about the Remarkables' ceremonies?"

I blink and admit that I haven't.

"They ask the All-Answer for instruction. For glimpses of
truth, for hints as to the authentic Future. What only the
All-Answer Itself can perceive with its all-seeing gaze—"

"What'll you do?" I ask.

"Pray." He waits, then says, "I'm going to kneel at the

base of Au, and I'm going to wait for some kind of answer. About existence. About the purpose of life, and is it worth what we endure?"

I know this question. There was a time, I'm thinking, when I couldn't rest until I learned the answer to the question.

Until nine years ago, that is.

"After so much travel and sacrifice," says Lumiere, "anything that happens is the message from the All-Answer. If a bolt of lightning cuts a tree in two, that's the response. If there's a voice between my ears, talking to me . . . well, that would be better. Contingent on what's said, of course."

He laughs for a moment, his face dry and the bright red eyes serene.

"And what if nothing happens?" I have to ask. "What then?"

The smile persists, and he informs me, "If nothing? If nothing but the sound of my own blood running inside my double-mind? Then that's a telling answer too. Don't you think, Ranier? One way or the other, I'll know enough by then. . . ."

25

SLEEPLESS

❖

"Down," says the familiar voice. "Stay." Then she crawls
inside with her mummy bag under an arm, saying nothing. I lie on my clumsy pillow of dirty clothes, watching
while Snow undresses. People are built for the night, I'm
thinking. In the Realm we worry ourselves into perfection
for the hard, uncompromising glare of daylight; but here
in this colorless gloom every flaw is diminished, every nose
and nipple are just as we wish to see them.

Snow unrolls her bag and then ignores it, undoing my
bag's zipper and reaching inside.

She kisses me, and I ask, "Are you done guarding us?"

She says, "Done."

"Did you do a good job?" I ask, just making noise.

And for an instant she freezes, seemingly offended. Is
she? It's been a couple days since I last made noise about
the Pitcairns being less than the best—

—but her mood changes back to pleasant. To horny. We
make love in a careful, almost practiced fashion, the whole
event pleasant yet oddly detached. Afterward I stay inside
her. I lay quiet. Snow's breath smells like nectar—I can
almost guess what flavor she ate last—and she acts as if
she wants to fall asleep.

I don't let her.

I put a hand around her neck and wait a moment, then
ask, "What do you know about us?"

She opens her eyes.

"What do you really know about the Realm?"

She stares at me with her neck feeling hot and damp,
and with a quiet voice she says, "We know a lot."

"Do you?"

"Groves talk to groves all the time. By radio. In person. Boats meet out at sea."

"Pitcairns talk to each other—"

"Oh, sure."

"And you've heard stories?"

"We know you're insane," she informs me. "Crazy as goon birds, you are. That there are more of you than even you can count, and you can never be alone. You're all packed so close together that you have to be insane—we don't blame you—or you'd tear out each other's hearts."

Maybe that's right, I'm thinking. From the Pitcairn perspective—

"And yet you're lonely people. You have no groves where you belong. Your families are spread out and indifferent. Sick." Snow seems proud of her knowledge, grinning now and moving closer. "Isn't that right, Ranier? Where are your parents? Your brothers and sisters?"

I start to tell her, and she interrupts.

"When did you see your father last?"

I count years and confess, then add, "But we're not close. And besides, I've had some troubles traveling. I'm an exception, really."

I'm starting to feel offended. I growl and move slightly, falling out of Snow at last.

"Oops," she says.

"You're better than us," I offer. "Aren't you?"

And she accepts that verdict. "We are. Yes. Every one of us is superior to every one of you—"

"And why?" I snap.

She almost laughs, then says, "Because when you're Pitcairn—when you live in any grove, helping one another to survive—you learn to press yourself to your limits. You don't accept sloth or clumsiness. From the day she is born, a Pitcairn is inside a great, ancient family which cares for her and her for them. Always and always."

"The Remarkables make you so perfect?"

She says, "In part. But only in part."

I remember the inbreeding, the extraordinary relatedness between every one of them. Even between Pitcairns on opposite sides of this world . . . and I'm remembering the similarities between them and bees in a hive. They aren't entirely human. Twenty thousand years of selection

pressures . . . ! Snow has helped me forget that lesson.
Sleeping with her has distracted me, and I feel a flicker of
anger. Angry at what?

"You asked," she tells me.

"I did."

"You can't help but be insane," she assures me.

"You think I'm insane? Is that it?"

Snow nods with authority. "All of you are. We see it all
the time—"

"When?"

"When you fight with each other. When you try to impress us and degrade your companions at the same time.
When you ignore so much of what you're seeing, never
asking questions—"

"What questions? I ask questions."

"Not enough," she warns me. "Because you're arrogant.
You think you already know everything you need to know
about us. You and your Realm . . . nothing there has
changed in thousands of years. You can't get used to being
outside what you understand, Ranier. Which is part of
your insanity. Your ignorance—"

"Hey," I interrupt. "I know a lot more than I let on."

In the very poor light I make out her amused grin and
the way her long hair bunches in one hand.

"What do you know?" A challenging tone—

—and I respond by saying, "You're scared. All of you
are scared of something, and you're doing your best to
hide it."

She moves away from me, making no response.

"The Realm is huge, and you are tiny. A speck standing
against a great wave," I assure her, "and without even
trying we could wipe you into oblivion. Gone. *Poof.*"

For a moment the smile lingers, then Snow says,
"Right."

I regret what I said. I want to apologize, but there's no
way to retrieve the words.

"When we learn about the Realm," Snow whispers into
my ear, "that's what we learn first, as children. That you
are vast and powerful beyond measure. That you are coming and coming, closer every minute. Every instant."

"And that we're insane," I add.

"The worst goon birds ever born. Yes."

* * *

The darkness completes itself. I start remembering Snow's stories about her life in the grove and the Remarkables standing about her home, and it occurs to me that I was listening in the wrong ways. Two nights ago I was too busy thinking as if it were me living in that tidy little house. I wasn't the symbiont in an ancient partnership; I was an intelligent man from the Realm, accustomed to being in control of my circumstances. Which means that I was blind, the truth told.

I start to tell Snow about my own house, room by room, hoping to flesh out my history a little more. Not to prove my sanity, but to give my insanity clear dimensions. I describe my holo room and my universal library, sonic showers and gel-filled bed. The bed is what interests Snow. "How is it for screwing?" I mention my ex-wives and lovers. Pitcairns aren't the only people who enjoy varied sex lives, I argue.

She watches me, her face a featureless oval against the darkness, and I'm letting myself think too much. I keep seeing Snow with Briar and with Salo, perhaps at the same time, and I stop to breathe. To gather myself.

"What do you do, building worlds?" she asks. It might be the first direct question she's asked about my life. "You're a tailor, right?"

"Have been. I'm basically retired now." I launch into a little speech about sculpting organisms to fit existing biospheres. Pleasing species; minimal disruptions. "For the most part, my clients have been happy—"

"Flowers?" she says.

I blink. "What about flowers?"

"I read about them once." She moves against me. "We've got old, old microfilm books copied from our ship library. I read about colored plants. They're called flowers, right?"

"You've still got Earth books?"

She takes a long breath, then says, "A few."

Then she asks, "What about the colored plants?"

Pitcairn plants and insects haven't coevolved as they did on Earth. What passes for a blossom here, I recall, is very drab, most of its pigments lying outside the human spectrum. "A lot of my own work involved plants and their pollinators," I explain. "I'd tailor orchids and very specific insects. Orchids as big as people. Butterflies are popular . . . big as birds, with colored wings . . . drinking the nectar inside the orchids, carrying pollen from blossom to blossom. . . ."

She says, "I know," and stirs.

I lie close and still, and for an instant it's as if I feel an electric current running between us. She's interested, honestly intrigued with this subject, and that's different. Refreshing. I can't see her face just now, but it's something I can sense. Almost smell. My new lover is trying to imagine these exotic lands.

What else can I tell her?

I start to speak again, then she says, "Wait. I've got to pee."

So do I. I feel the pressure of my own bladder, following her outside. I shiver in the thin chill air. Something moves in the Pitcairn grass, and I find a cretin watching me. Indifferent to me. High clouds hang to the west, but otherwise it's a perfectly clear night. Stars are punctuated with several nearby worlds, their soft glows almost silver. I feel bumps rising on my flesh, aiming and urinating and then shaking myself dry, then returning to the delicious warmth of my bag.

Snow tells the cretin, "Stay," and comes through the flap. For an instant I think she's smiling, then I'm not sure. She settles deep in her own bag, and we hear the cretin rising and then lying down again.

"Flowers are popular," I report, then laugh. "I've wondered if the purpose of humankind is to spread flowers everywhere. All those worlds we build, and the flowers are probably thanking us for making them such fine homes."

"Is that so?"

And I say something stupid. "After the *passion*," I joke, "maybe I can take you away. Show you some flower gardens. . . ."

I mean this as humor.

At least I think I do.

Snow grabs me with her fingers, her strength considerable and her blunt nails almost piercing my skin. Then with a dead calm voice, she tells me, "Don't," and her head dips. She places her mouth against my chest, in the curling blond hairs, and without breath she says, *"Don't,"* then takes a flap of skin into her mouth, biting until I flinch.

The deep pink toothmarks linger through the night.

I find myself waking and touching them, thinking about everything.

TALKER

✦

"What I'm saying is that we're banished. Not in name, but in every other sense. The elders and Old Ones cooked this up, knowing we'd never survive. This *passion* is doomed. A zero for the year. But the grove gets new blood, fancy skyborn genes, and it's losing just a hundred juveniles. Not many at all. A lot of successful *passions* lose several hundred—"

"Briar," says Tintoil. "Shut up."

They are facing one another, standing on the mountainside toward our south, their faces illuminated by starlight. Until now Briar has been careful about being out of sight when speaking to the others. But everyone knows what he desires. Service knows, even without our help. But what can he do? Briar goes out on watch, doing his job well enough. What can Service do but fume and stay alert?

Briar is expert at knowing how far he can press the old Pitcairn.

"Listen," he says. "Just listen, will you? We're a lot alike, you and me. We deserve more credit for what we do. We're sick of cowards and fools winning our glory—"

"Shut up."

"Listen," he warns. "Now hear me out!"

She says nothing, glancing in our direction.

"Don't worry about *them*," he says. *Us.* "They'll go where we go. What choices do they have?"

"What you're saying—"

"No, that's wrong. You're wrong." He tells her, "I'm not going to do anything like that. I'm a Pitcairn. All Pitcairn. And I'm not talking about overthrowing any leader. Is that what scares you? No, no. Service is in charge. He's boss. I'm not making real trouble for him."

"Then what is this about? Spell it!"

"We've been banished," he repeats.

She remains silent, her face soft and thoughtful. Taller than Briar, she is. In some ways stronger too.

"The Old Ones picked us. The worst Pitcairns, by their standards, and they've sent us on a hamstrung *passion*. I'm telling you that they don't give us any real chance of surviving. Not even with one Remarkable. We've got these visitors to baby. We've got big cretins shadowing us. And it's a drought year on the Au plains. The worst summer in ten—"

"What about Service?"

"What about him?"

"Is he like you? Is he a criminal?"

The insult flows off Briar, him grinning with a dose of human charm; and he assures her, "Yes. Just like me. In his youth he had a temper, just like my famous temper, and just like him in his youth, I've been put into an impossible task—"

Service's vengeance attack. For the instant, between Briar's words, we relive the whole story again. In full.

"—and I'm going to succeed," says Briar. "Against all odds."

"You."

"He's an old, old man, Tintoil. Admit it."

"This is Service we're talking about. Service."

"A human. Not invincible. I bet he's tired—more than he lets us see—and eventually he's going to have troubles."

"You're predicting an accident?"

Briar says nothing.

"Where nothing can see what happens?" she asks.

"I really don't know," he replies. He won't allow himself to be trapped. "Maybe his heart will die. Who knows? But if it happens, and if we're left with nobody in charge—"

"And if you offer yourself to lead," says Tintoil.

"What's wrong with considering the possibility?"

She knows Briar, and she knows ambition. They do share ambitions, though Briar is beyond her by every measure. This they both understand.

"I'll bring this *passion* home alive," claims Briar. "That's all. I just want to show the grove that we can't be thrown away."

"Banished," she says.

"What's banishment?" he asks. "It's being sent out to die. We haven't done enough to suffer the official banishment—we're not bad Pitcairns—but you know what is going on. You know this *passion's* history."

"Quiet."

"Look at us," he says. "Me with my desires and my famous temper. And you're no angel, Tintoil. And Salo, big and strong . . . you know the gossip about Salo—"

"Quiet."

"—and sweet Snow. The dreamy girl."

"Snow's good. I've never understood why she's here."

"See? Admit it! We're a sickly bunch."

"I won't go against our grove," says Tintoil. "Don't ask me to—"

"I haven't and I won't. Trust me."

"Trust you," she says.

Then he says, "Or don't. But let me warn you, Tintoil. If some bad thing does happen, if Service's age catches him . . . don't even think about going against me. This is fair warning."

His face is calm in the starlight. We cannot read anything in his features, he is so terribly good at hiding himself.

"Fair warning," he repeats.

And we fidget. The ones of us awake fidget.

This is the Future we were shown—

26
THE WHITE RIVER

❖

Big shiny black turds are scattered on the ground, some of them mashed flat by hooves. Trees become more and more common—short but densely packed, leaves already inflated and the sunlight making them glow. Snow is somewhere ahead. I can't see her or Service anymore. Remarkables move steadily, faster than in the last days but never fast. I'm near the back of the *passion*, my stick held high, and the thickening air is warm enough that I pause and strip out of my shirt, tying it around my waist with its sleeves.

It must be noon when the gorge quits. Our valley is broader here, almost flat and heavily forested, and the little river is making its final push into the new valley. I don't recognize the trees. Some remind me of tailored sycamores, their papery bark decorated with fine black rings and the big leaves inflated but partly flattened. Selection pressures have made them tolerant of drought and the dry winds. The sunlight is stained green before it pours down on me, and I'm following a modest game trail marked with turds of different sizes and colors and shapes, big bright flies clinging to them.

The Remarkables won't touch animal wastes.

I notice the curling marks left by their tendrils. Thick coats of colorless dust fill the low spots, and the aliens leave behind maplike swirls. I find myself staring at them, my tired brain laboring to find patterns. To conjure up meanings and overarching principles.

Somewhere ahead is a larger river; my maps make that clear.

"Ranier."

Pachel is crossing through the underbrush, coming from a parallel trail. She smiles. I notice how the smile seems to fill her face, and she says happily, "It's a lovely day."

"A little warm," I grouse.

"Walk with you?"

Of course. I welcome the company.

The Remarkables fill the forest ahead of us. They look huge and substantial in the weak green light—elephant-sized and unnervingly quiet—and I find myself thinking again. Like last night. A lot of things are pushing down my wet neurons, begging for my attention.

"We've taken too long," says Pachel.

"Pardon?"

"This morning. Service wanted us here earlier."

"Yeah?"

"The warmer it gets, the more water melts off these glaciers. These rivers are fed by melting ice. We've got to ford the river as soon as we can."

I feel hungry, finding a dirty piece of nectar in my shirt pocket. I pick off lint and place it in my mouth, and there's a little kick as the sugar and stimulants hit my blood-stream.

"We've got our schedule," she mentions.

"What if we're behind? Is that bad?"

"Service wants us into open country as soon as possible. His cretins keep finding scents. Enemy scents." She's taking enjoyment out of this business. "If we get into the open, attacks are harder to manage. That's why we've got to hurry."

"Before more cretins arrive."

She nods and says, "Right. Before they zero in on us."

Not us, I recall. The Remarkables. Unless we stand in their way, the cretins won't bother with funny-looking people. They haven't been trained to hunt people for their own sake.

"He wants me to do more."

I look at Pachel. "Who does? Service?"

"To help keep the Remarkables moving. And to keep my eyes open. That sort of thing."

"Okay."

"We talked last night," she mentions. Then her expression changes, amused and mystified. "For a long while, really. Service isn't the silent fanatic that he pretends to be."

"No?" I joke.

She grins at the memory. "And you've got to admire these people, Ranier. Their sense of social place and purpose—"

"Snow and I discussed those same things."

"—and how well they work together. For one another. It's the perfect system for them. Hell, it's what a lot of people in a lot of places want in their lives. You know? A huge extended family. Every day full of goals and guts . . . !"

Is that the whole truth? I keep thinking of Salo's punishment and Briar's fiery attitude. Is Pachel misleading herself?

Am I?

For a while we walk together. Sometimes I watch Pachel, her thick legs carrying her without effort, her long stick digging at the forest floor. Sometimes she prods the Remarkables, saying, "Move, move!" One time she assures me, "They'll respond to you. Yell at them, and they will roll along faster. True!"

But they're moving faster on their own. The river is nearby, singing to us, and the aliens start to outpace us, breaking into the glare of a clearing and the sunlight making them halfway transparent, purplish clouds cavorting on barren ground. A strange image, yet I'm so accustomed to it. A glance, a blink, and it's as if I have been watching these creatures for my entire life.

The river is broad and white, and the juveniles are rolling down to it. They pull back their tendrils to expose their mouths, dipping into the water and drinking noisily. Lustily. Every eye raised, pivoting with a useful paranoia.

I'm looking at the river. *We have to cross this thing*, I remember. *Ford it.* I watch the current and the strange thick whiteness of the water, rock flour suspended by the roaring chaos. I listen, feeling the current through my toes. We've waited too long. I remember what Pachel said about the sun melting the glacial ices, and now we'll have to camp here and wait for morning.

I turn to ask Pachel what she thinks, but she's vanished. Bedford is closest. He notices me and offers a weak smile. Something is bothering him, his hands laced in front of him and his feet a little pigeon-toed.

Goottich and Effie are standing farther upstream. Just them.

The big man is talking, smiling, his teeth shining and his voice carrying over the river sounds. He's telling a joke. Four people in a lifepod. A poor person, a rich person. A Unity minister, plus a terraformer. The terraformer knows there isn't enough air to reach port, and he commits suicide. The minister knows that death is inherently beautiful, and he also kills himself. Then the rich man pays the poor one a fortune to do the same, and the newly rich man dies happy.

"Oh, that's funny," says Effie.

Goottich giggles, agreeing with her.

I look at Bedford, feeling sorry for him. I don't want to feel sorry, but he makes such a wonderful picture. That pretty face; the way he insists on acting unconcerned. How each finger of both hands begin to tremble while he stares at Goottich's boots. Not the face, but his boots. As if he isn't noticing anything at all.

Lumiere comes from downstream, approaching me and glancing out at the rushing water. "I suppose it's too much to hope that it's ankle-deep."

"And warm," I add. "Shallow and warm."

We're both laughing when Briar emerges from the forest, a pair of cretins flanking him. The Pitcairn glares at everyone, one after another, then a strange slow grin breaks out on the narrow face.

"The ford is upriver," he tells us.

The voice is accusing. Sharp.

He says, "Did someone tell you to stop?" then continues walking, expecting no answer. Briar carries his rifle in one hand, his manner relaxed and self-assured. "Let's keep going!"

Remarkables climb up the bank, dripping water onto the dried earth. Complicated muddy tracks form as they roll upstream.

Lumiere waits a moment, then mentions, "Briar hasn't been walking especially fast. Have you noticed?"

I hadn't.

Bedford approaches, then says, "It is a lovely day, isn't it? And us without holo cameras too."

The lidless black eyes keep watching us. I'm so accustomed to their gaze that I ignore it for long intervals. Then I notice them. There are moments like now when it's as if hundreds of eyes are examining each of us, weighing us according to exacting means.

What are they thinking?

What do they know?

And more to the point: What do their parents know? The adults; the fabled Old Ones. Those great minds that are so gifted along such odd lines . . . what in the hell were they thinking when they threw this group together?

Because they were thinking something, I decide.

There is a reason. . . .

"Hey!" snaps Briar, glancing back at us. "We've got to move. We can't fuck around now! Hear me?"

He looks like Service, and sometimes he halfway sounds like Service. Only Briar isn't much like the wise old Pitcairn, in truth.

That's one thing about which I feel quite certain.

A green mountain wall stands across the river, narrow bands showing where avalanches have cut long brown gullies. Aprons of loose stone gather at the mountain's base. The rest of the valley floor is almost flat. Our fording point is where the little river flows into the white river. There's a wide channel followed by islands and little channels. Service is working on our side. Salo has already crossed to the first island, and together they're erecting some kind of rope-bridge. It's much too high to reach, and I'm tired enough not to understand at first glance. Then I realize it's for the tendrils. It's to give the Remarkables a secure grasp, sure. . . .

Salo drops from the island's lone tree, then shouts, "Done!"

Effie begins removing her pack, Goottich helping her. Service notices. "Don't do that. Leave it on."

The big man says, "I'm taking it for her. We decided."

Service blinks and says, "No," with firmness.

Nobody speaks.

The Pitcairn looks at each of us. "Your packs are going to push you down and hold you there. You'll need them. Move in a line and use your sticks. And don't get upriver from anyone, because if you do and you fall, you'll take someone down with you."

I manage a deep breath, watching the milky water.

"Snow? Can you lead them over?"

She steps forward and gives me a fleeting glance, sober eyes and her mouth clenched shut. Her rifle is tied to her pack. Both hands hold onto a long stick, and she tells us, "Like this. Don't let go."

Snow splashes into the river, and I hesitate for a moment.

Pachel says, "I'll go," and pushes ahead. Then she says, "Fuck," with a near squeal, laughing loudly. "The blood of a glacier," she screams, and "Fuck it fuck it fuck it!"

It's nearly freezing. I step twice, watching Pachel and then Snow. The quick white water climbs over my ankles, then my calves. The first touch is startling. The cold flows into my feet, making my toes curl reflexively, and behind me Lumiere moans. He says, "My oh my. . . ."

My trousers are soaked. In an instant it's past mere cold. I am in pain. I feel my own pain and the hard knots of it ahead of me, then behind. "Use the sticks!" Service is shouting. "Plant them, then step! Plant and step!" Sound advice, I'm thinking, but nothing is easy without practice. I'm clumsy and tentative. The frigid water is deadening my legs, making the clumsiness worse. River grit has worked its way into my socks, cutting into my heels. Waterworn stones slip underfoot, sometimes rolling suddenly, making a dull clatter that I feel more than hear.

I plant my stick and step and plant and step, finding a rhythm.

Snow's rump is just above the water. Pachel's too. I'm past my knees and dropping, more of my legs going numb. Collars of pain rise toward my crotch. My testicles retreat and shrivel. The current is stronger here, and I lean upstream and start to shiver as my core temperature plunges . . . *the stick, plant it and move* . . . and all at once I'm terrified. There comes that glorious scalding rush of adrenaline, and I say, "Fuckingshit, fuckingshit! Fuckingshit!"

The universe is composed of milky water piling against my legs, my hips, and I sob. I can't feel my legs anymore. My feet have died. I walk sloppily and look up as Snow rises from the water, her splendid firm rump soaked and the river splashing around her; and I press ahead.

My breath is fast and shallow and pained.

Yet I can't feel anyone else's suffering, I realize. *A cure.*

Snow is up on the island, helping Pachel by offering her walking stick. I'm driving my stick into the water, fighting its buoyancy while dropping into deeper water. Suddenly I'm up to my waist. My boots slide sideways. Without the weight of my pack I'd be upended, I realize, and Service was right. Always right. I tell myself to listen to him, he knows what's best . . . and I manage another step, nearly falling.

The soggy end of a stick hangs in front of my face.

I ignore it. More kicking than walking, I drive with my cold dead legs. Somehow the frozen toes find purchase, my crotch in the open air, then my thighs and my knees, and another step puts me on damp sandy ground, feeling a stunned amazement. Some piece of me had conceded to death, and even now it's denying my survival.

Pachel is stomping her feet, smiling at nobody in particular.

I walk stiffly and work at my flesh with both hands, feeling a tentative surge of chilled blood.

Lumiere is climbing out with Snow's help. He looks pasty white and pleased, saying, "Thank you, pretty lady."

Bedford is next. He seems detached in contrast, almost calm. He climbs out on his own and turns to watch Goottich and his wife. He says, "Effie," and then, "Careful?"

Goottich climbs from the water, turns and offers his stick to Effie. "Take it," he shouts, the water rising well above her waist.

The woman is crying, almost screaming. Some of it is terror, but I can feel the pain. It reaches into me, twisting at my insides, and I start to shake and moan.

Bedford approaches, offering Effie his walking stick.

It is an idiotic moment. Juvenile; silly. When Effie starts to fall, for that instant, it's as if both men weigh risks and rewards. These are the calculations every living organism has employed since time immemorial. *What will I risk for this woman?* They hesitate, and Snow is the quick one. She acts out of instinct, thrusting her stick and Effie grabbing hold with both arms, clinging tight and Snow strong enough to fish her from the river in one motion, hauling her to land and Effie collapsing, coughing hard and sobbing between the coughs.

Bedford steps back when Goottich kneels.

Then he walks toward me, and from somewhere comes a strange aggressive smile. Bedford opens his mouth to speak, to explain something. Only he doesn't have the words. He can't find them. So he steps away and with his boot starts drawing a circle around himself.

"Earth is round," he whispers. "The Realm is round."

I watch him.

"Our Unity is perfectly round," he tells himself.

In the background Goottich is saying, "You're okay. You made it, you're fine. . . ."

Effie keeps coughing.

Bedford is looking straight down, stomping his feet, standing in the middle of his clumsy little circle.

27
ONTO THE PLAIN

◆

Remarkables cross one at a time, tendrils clinging to the high rope; and between them comes the occasional cretin and Pitcairn. Everyone else is on the far shore, sitting in the sun with boots and socks drying. Finally just Service and a pair of Remarkables remain, one cretin sitting nearby. Service is talking, not looking in any particular direction. Is he having a conversation? With Talker? But I can't hear anything except the river and sometimes the people talking around me.

The last Remarkables come across, then Service dismantles the rope bridge and crosses, Salo coiling the rope and packing it away. The cretin cranes its neck until it seems quite thin and snakelike. It smells something. It climbs higher and gives an odd half bark, then turns and runs into the water, swimming effortlessly across the deep stretches.

Service calls the Pitcairns together, and he says something about the cretins that are shadowing us. He tells them, "Three of you walk behind. You choose. Just keep a better lookout than you have been," and his gaze moves toward Briar.

The young Pitcairn grins, saying nothing. He keeps his eyes level and unblinking.

Goottich is sitting with Effie, sharing a flat piece of pink granite. She's talking quickly, and he isn't paying attention. With one thick finger, Goottich draws in the packed sand. Numbers; shapes. I start to approach, curious more than anything. Effie is saying, "Weak. Weak and childish.

You know what I mean?" Then she sees me and stops talking, nudging her companion in the ribs.

Goottich blinks and lifts his head.

It's as if he is coming back from a dream, finding himself here and a little baffled with everything.

"Busy?" I inquire.

He says, "Doodling," and immediately erases the sand with both boots. Then Service is telling us to start moving, and Goottich rises, smiling at me and saying, "Doodling," a second time. For emphasis.

He leaves, Effie beside him, and I examine his little project. I make out mathematical signs and one drawing in the middle of everything—a fat-walled cylinder partly destroyed by Goottich—and I know at a glance what he was doing. Is doing. What the mathematics mean; what the cylinder represents.

An enworld, I'm thinking. *Goottich's home.*

The man was doodling, all right. He's remodeling his home, at least in theory. Increasing its spin rate and its air pressure. More carbon dioxide, I notice. The perfect greenhouse for steelwood, isn't it? And for a good deal more too.

We walk through the afternoon and camp inside a dense forest. Herds of game have eaten away the undergrowth. Their turds have a toxic stink, and I have to sweep them away from my tent. Feeling spent, I go to bed early and Snow wakes me to tell me that she can't stay. Not tonight. Everyone has to pull a double-duty, she explains. I wonder aloud how she survives without sleep, and she says, "It's summer, Ranier," amazed by my weaknesses.

I sleep deeply, remembering nothing about my dreams in the morning. Yet still I feel tired, almost drunk with soreness and mental fatigue.

We walk near the river in the morning. Sometimes I'll watch the frigid water, how it twirls and rolls, bubbles rising from the turbulence. The river seems dangerous but respectful. It tried to kill me yesterday, and I feel something between us. Not friendship, but something similar. There's a mutual appreciation here.

After noon the mountains pull away and the valley broadens. We leave the river; and at one point, for no clear reason, the Remarkables bunch together and begin singing. It resembles the ceremony when we saw Mount Au, and I ask Snow to explain.

"This is the Au plain," she says.

"I know. But what are they saying?"

She tells me how they're probably sharing stories. Remarkables are full of stories, even the juveniles. Particularly tales about past *passions*.

Bedford says, "They must be thanking the All-Answer too."

"For seeing them here." Snow nods and tells us, "The All-Answer doesn't cause things. It just knows everything."

"Everything," Lumiere echoes.

Snow shrugs her shoulders. This line of talk isn't important, she implies. The aliens have their concerns, and we need to think about ours. "This is a dry summer," she mutters, kneeling and running a hand through the browning grasses. "Bad news all around."

"I bet they're glad to be off the mountains," Pachel adds. "Glad to be on good flat ground again."

Bedford asks Snow, "What do you suppose the All-Answer sees for us?"

She doesn't seem to hear him.

"Ranier," he says, "what do you think it sees?"

"I don't know. I barely know what shoes I'm going to wear day to day."

Snow rises and winks at me. Just once.

And with that gesture I feel light and joyful. A wink is all it takes.

The plain is divided into patches of thick wood surrounded by shaggy pastures. There's no trace of game here. Service moves ahead, scouting and then returning to take Snow and Briar on a longer hunt. Tintoil is left in charge. She has us camp beside a clear-water stream, in a little wood, and while I'm pitching my tent, the Remarkables spread out on the grass, becoming motionless, their tendrils outstretched and flattened to the sun.

They are eating sunlight. Their purple coloring has become rich again, almost radiant. Photons alone aren't enough food—they will need meat—but they will help make the fat reserves last longer, at least.

Later Snow wakes me. I watch her undressing, noticing

her sour smell. I washed before bed. The harsh Pitcairn
soap left everything else in the world needing a similar
scrubbing. But I say nothing. She opens her bag and lies
on top of it, casually scratching her rump. I ask if they
killed anything, and she says, "No," and puts her other
hand in her mouth. A nail breaks, then she spits and smiles,
reaching into my bag.

"Are you worried?"

She says, "No," and half shrugs.

"It's early," I offer.

Her hand is warm and calloused, almost slick in places.

"Will you worry?"

She takes back her hand and watches me. I'm just curious, I want to tell her. I want to know how symbiotic
partners look at each other. Is there affection? Is there any
emotional attachment? If Talker died, would Snow feel
any loss? Even a sliver of grief?

Maybe she anticipates my questions, saying, "I'm tired,
Ranier."

I watch her face, trying to read clues.

Then something occurs to me. I hear myself asking, "Did
you have a good time today, you three—?"

"Shut up," she says mildly. Almost softly. Then she kisses
me once on the mouth and pulls herself into her bag, dropping straight to sleep; and I'm left staring at the tent's
roof, its clean geometry too simple for real worlds—a
V-shaped peak made taut, creating a straight line that follows the curving universe all the way back around to here.
To me.

I start to feel pain by noon.

I know the warning signs, and what worries me most is
the distance between me and the source. A dull diluted
pain, but it's coming from some point far ahead of us.

Service returns from another scouting trip. A huge
grazer—a knobhead—is trapped at the center of a tar pit.
Good news; the brief famine is broken. We walk through
the afternoon, and my illness grows worse. It becomes
sharp, familiar, and I try distracting myself with a variety
of tricks. I concentrate on my own aches. I study random
rocks and individual stems of grass. My skin starts leaking
sweat, more than just the warm weather would bring. And
then, as always, the sensation of pain diminishes. The

countermeasures inside me gain the edge momentarily, bringing me back to a false and temporary normalcy.

The tar pit is a giant lake of sun-dried blackish goo, and I feel the knobhead before I see it. Its tracks mark the nearby tar. A flock of hunting moas had driven the creature out there, says Service. He has walked out onto the tar, indifferent to the way it dents under him. The knobhead's tracks are broad and rather deep, the edges smoothed by the sun. Service pulls a crude pair of binoculars out of his pack, then he screws them against his eyes. One more step forward, and the tar begins clinging to his boots. He retreats, climbing the bank and ending up beside me. Again he works with the binoculars, saying, "It's been there a few days. Cooking."

I don't speak, aware of my quick breathing.

"A big old knobhead, and tough." There's admiration in the voice. "It stomped on one of the moas. Care to see?"

I drop my pack and stick, trying to steady my hands. The massive creature has a long head adorned with a blunt yellowish ivorylike horn and a stubby trunk hanging over its mouth, curling and then relaxing, curling and relaxing. The plumage is dark and striped with darker bands. Sometimes the body moves, and the underplumage is a bright pink color. Blood and old tar are spattered on its face. The dead moa resembles a lump of feathers with a single twisted leg in the air.

It never makes sense. Some creatures are worse than others for me. The physicians have guessed it's something in their architecture, the specifics of their neurons and their capacity for misery. Whatever the reason, the knobhead is ruining my day.

I breathe and swallow with a dry throat, then I look again.

A pair of substantial birds perch on the creature's back, dipping their naked heads, tearing holes in the thick living hide. I feel their beaks and the open infected wounds. It's not my pain, no. There is a kind of separation between me and it. I can't explain it. It's as if some phantom fifth limb of mine is being tortured, and I feel the limb only when it aches. That's the only time it exists for me.

"How did it get out so far?" asks Pachel.

"In the morning," says Service. "When the tar's cool and dry. And the knobheads have big feet too."

"Like Goottich," she jokes.

Goottich says, "What?"

The creature jerks its body, rocking and straining against the tar. During the last days it has sunk to its belly, one leg managing to pull up slightly. Gooey black ropes hold tight, and the leg collapses. The agony smacks into me, and an instant later everyone hears the weak low-pitched moan—

—and Effie says, "The poor animal."

Someone coughs. Bedford, I think.

I put down the binoculars, and Pachel asks for them. When I hand them up, she's watching me. Studying me. I start to blink, salt in my eyes, and I wipe at my face with both sleeves.

"Listen to it," Effie moans.

Then Bedford says, "Beauty in death."

"Oh, but it's suffering . . . !"

"Life demands death," he says with a stiff, grieving voice.

I turn and tell him, "Shut up! Will you?"

People look at me. They're surprised by my tone, and maybe they're warning me to ignore Bedford. He just wants to bother his wife. He's not concerned about the knobhead or me or anyone outside his own misery. All of which I know . . . can appreciate . . . anytime but now . . . !

"Death makes homes for the new and the young," Bedford continues, spreading his arms, "and it's holy because life is holy too!"

I turn to Service, "Shoot it!"

He shakes his head. "Tonight. It's too far away, the skull's too thick . . . we'll wait until we can get close."

Service looks at me, his face sober and resolved. He's warning me that he has more good reasons if I press him.

The knobhead has been dying in slow motion for several days, not drinking or eating, the cloudless sun broiling it alive. No human being would suffer such a death. Not in the Realm, at least. Death for us is a quiet and orchestrated event, physicians and autodocs keeping the extreme elderly comfortable every moment, an enforced dignity overhanging the entire procedure.

"Pain is part of life," Bedford tells Effie. "You know the Unity lessons. Are you forgetting them?"

He wags a finger at her.

"But nature doesn't give what can't be withstood. That's a basic, essential Unity principle." His face is severe and obviously tired, the pretty features made sharp. Harsh and strained. "Pain guides every organism through its life—"

"Shut up," I mutter.

He doesn't turn toward me. He simply freezes, staring hard at his wife.

Again the knobhead moves—I feel it—and both feeding birds dig with their twisting beaks, the easy meals probably thrilling them. What a glorious day!

I shiver, then we hear the long cold moan.

Bedford has turned to me. "I know what you mean, Ranier."

I say nothing.

He comes over and pats my shoulder, his gaze wild. Almost blind. He halfway smiles before assuring me, "It's a primitive animal with a very rudimentary nervous system."

I look at Effie, then Bedford.

"The same kinds of drama happen on our worlds," he mentions. "You of all people should appreciate—"

"Quit," I groan.

Bedford stops talking, narrowing his eyes.

"Yes," says Effie. "Please just shut up."

"A clash of philosophies," Bedford declares. "I can appreciate our differences, Ranier. I just wish you could appreciate them as well."

I stand and gasp, wondering if the pain is going to make me pee my pants. It can. Several times I've been embarrassed, losing my round grip on my bladder—!

"Listen to that thing moan," says Pachel. "A tough, tough animal. That's certain."

"I feel sad," says Effie.

"It'll die soon," Goottich tells her. He snorts and shrugs his shoulders, the entire issue inconsequential. "I wouldn't worry about it. One way or the other."

Lumiere grasps my shoulder, saying, "You look awful, my friend."

"Unity is everywhere," Bedford announces. "That's the great lesson I've learned here. Yes, it is! People dominate wherever they exist. On Pitcairn as on Earth, and throughout the Realm!"

I take a weak step toward Bedford.

He blinks, watching me.

Then he says, "I'm glad that I'm young. Young enough to watch this world change, its people growing, taking their rightful ruling position here . . . dominating over the thinking vegetables . . . !"

I nearly turn away.

"Dominion is our duty in this universe," he proclaims. "Our eternal duty!"

I sag a little as the knobhead strains against the tar once more.

"Shit," I whisper.

Bedford says, "I understand pain too."

He sticks out his lower lip, proud and defiant.

And I tell him, "Understand this," and my first swing puts him on the ground. I hit the smug pretty face, surprising both of us, and then it's as if a fever makes me crazy. I kneel and punch him again, harder this time. Then someone's hands grab me and pull me off. Somehow I manage to spin and get free of them. Service is beside me, and I try hitting him. But he sidesteps and drops low, then comes up with his rifle. No hesitations, no doubts. I see the wooden butt coming for what seems like an age, then—

—nothing.

A great blackness; a glorious hard-won peace.

28
MISERY

✦

I wake hearing voices, and I move too soon. I try lifting my head and a voice says, "Gently." Snow's face floats above me. I assume it's her voice, and when my head starts spinning, I drop again and wait for a long moment, then tell her:

"I don't feel right."

She says nothing.

I blink and blink again, fighting my nausea. Someone begins to touch my face, only their fingers feel wrong. They are too thick and smooth, brushing clumsily against my bruised jaw and the swollen lips, then across my eyes, and I look skyward, realizing that tendrils are caressing me. It wasn't Snow who said, "Gently." Again I try sitting upright, and the tendrils restrain me. "Move slowly," Talker advises. "Take your time."

Sound advice, I decide. I breathe and brace myself with both arms, gradually absorbing my surroundings. It's late, not dusk but not far from it. A camp fire burns on a stretch of barren ground. My fellow tourists stand in a knot, watching me. The Pitcairns are more scattered, talking among themselves and scarcely glancing in my direction. Except Snow. She kneels beside me. Behind her is Service, his face rigid and unreadable. I look at the tourists again, noticing Bedford's face, bruised and a little swollen. My temper has broken, but I'm still too groggy to feel any compassion for the man. Then I blink and look past him, noticing how the Remarkables form a ring around us. An inquisitive, mostly silent ring.

I touch my sore places and climb to my knees, asking, "Is this some kind of trial?"

Service responds.

"You started a fight," he says. "Attacking another person might be how things are done in the Realm. I wouldn't know. But not here, certainly not on a *passion*. . . . I'm not tolerating it from anyone."

I am on trial.

I breathe and hold the breath in my belly, and nobody speaks or moves. Even the Remarkables are perfectly silent, and there is no noise but the crackling of combusting wood and the quick, panicky boom of my heart.

Service, as always, will be judge and jury.

I ask about possible punishments, and he regards me for a long while, eyes like hard crystal and his jaw set. "Banishment, at the worst," he says. My first thought is that he can't banish me; I can signal our torchship easily enough, our shuttle descending to rescue me—

—and Service says, "Or corporal punishment. If you give me any good reason not to banish you."

A paddling. Banishment might be preferable, I'm thinking. I barely hear him asking for my explanation, and Snow touches me on a shoulder and shakes me.

"Pardon?" I manage.

"Why did you strike the man?" Service asks again.

I look at the bruised face, deciding that he looks better when he's not so pretty. Bedford returns my gaze, then shudders. It must have shocked the hell out of him. He probably hasn't been hit since he was a boy, if then . . . and I turn back to Service, reporting, "I'm ill, and sometimes I get irrational."

"Because you're ill?"

I nod.

"I don't believe you," he says matter-of-factly. "Explain yourself."

Again I turn to my associates. Lumiere's eyes are the most sympathetic. Effie looks distant, unreadable. Goottich watches me as if I were a specimen in confinement, a puzzle meant to be deciphered. Bedford wants to appear self-righteous, his back ramrod straight and his battered mouth trying to appear smug. But Pachel is the angry one.

She glares at me, making me turn away before I start to talk. Before I try to explain.

"When I was a boy," I begin, "I owned a huge aquarium made from hyperglass. It was as tall as me and ran the length of my bedroom wall, and I stocked it with fishes that I found in the nearby river. A muddy little river running into the sea on Rye's World. I caught the fishes with hookless baits. I fed them and kept the aquarium water clean enough for me to see them, but with enough sediment to make them think it was home. A lot of children in the Realm do these kinds of things. Maybe Pitcairns do it too. Do they?"

Service gives the slightest of head shakes. *No.*

"Anyway," I continue, "I had my pets. Sunfish and little catfish. A big carp and hundreds of silvery minnows. I took care of them and grieved when they died despite my best efforts. I was a sensitive boy, I suppose. I let too much touch me. I mean, they were just fish. Scaly and cold, just like Pitcairn fishes. Yet somehow I managed to grow emotionally attached to them, going so far as naming the largest of them."

Lumiere nods as if he understands.

I tell everyone, "Someone once wrote that there are very few lessons in any person's life, and every lesson happens while you're a child. That is the only time when you're really susceptible to profound learning, and what's called learning when you're an adult is simply the childhood lessons repeated time and again."

"I've read that," Goottich reports.

"Quiet," Service warns him. And everyone.

"Anyway, I had my aquarium. I collected my fishes. And one day I captured a new fish. A rare specimen. It was a tailored piranha newly introduced into the watershed. Piranhas are flat-bodied and sometimes large, although this one wasn't particularly old or large. It had the typical piranha teeth, like razors, and it demanded meat for its diet." I pause for a moment, then say, "Zeus. I named it Zeus. I built an aquarium inside the main aquarium, isolating Zeus from the other fishes. And I fed it from my ample stocks of minnows, none of them having names or identities. I'd put one or two of the little silvery fish into Zeus's home before nightfall, and in the morning they would be gone without trace. They might have dissolved into the grimy water itself. . . . Zeus was thorough with his work. . . ."

It occurs to me what a silly story I'm telling. A boy and his fish . . . how does it sound to a man like Service?

"One night Zeus jumped from his little home. The primitive brain must have made some calculation. The lidless eyes must have been too tempted by the motions of the big fishes, and he made the leap and got into the main aquarium . . . probably early at night . . . and when I awoke, I found Zeus and his leftovers." I pause, then say, "I was a boy, Service. Like any child in the Realm, I was comfortable and unafraid. Insulated, I suppose. That's why it was such a shock for me—"

"What happened?" snaps Pachel.

"My piranha had chewed off the tail fins of every big fish. Without exception. But the fishes were too big to catch and consume whole. They had gathered into a wounded mass in one corner, and Zeus drifted alone in the open. Except for the minnows, that is. The schools of them swirled around with impunity, sensing he was too full to even consider eating."

My human audience moves slightly, but the Remarkables remain still, staring at everyone.

"It sounds silly, I know." I tell Service, "But I was nine years old, and what's sillier than being nine?"

"I don't understand," Effie says. "What's your point?"

"My point? My point is that I was responsible for those organisms. Maybe they were fishes, but they belonged to me and carried names given by me. They ended up maimed. Not only had they lost their tail fins, some of them had lost enough meat that their guts were dislodged, falling loose out of their rear ends. Pink intestines hanging limp in the water; bits of partly digested food leaking from razor-sliced gaps. It was a mess, and I made it even worse by trying to save them. I flooded the water with antibiotics to stave off infections. I actually tried fitting some of them with prosthetic fins and rebuilding their rectums . . . my methods well intended but clumsy, prolonging their suffering, I'm sure. . . ."

"What?" Effie persists. "You felt *guilty*? For *sunfish*?"

Goottich laughs, amused by something.

"A major lesson of my youth," I admit. "It stuck with me for decades. I became a terraformer for some of the same reasons that I kept an aquarium when I was nine. I enjoyed the biology. I had an aptitude in balancing life-forms in an enclosed environment. World-sized, yes. But enclosed nonetheless."

"You loved being in charge," Goottich mentions.

"In a fashion, sure." I nod and look at Service. "I never forgot my pets, sir. It's not as if they haunted my dreams or anything so overt . . . I could think of them without more than a sliver of regret, the truth told . . . but the half-gutted fishes kept reminding me about the nature of life. I worked for decades as a terraformer, and all the while I kept wondering how much pain my creations had to endure. The butterflies I devised, the little birds . . . everything . . . what kinds of suffering were theirs? I'd ask myself that question, again and again—"

"Pain is important," Bedford tells me. "If we didn't possess it—"

"We don't," I reply. "People don't. Not in the Realm, at least." I wait a moment, then tell Service, "The Realm isn't many places. It is one place replicated millions of times. It's not the original Earth, but Earth is the inspiration. Humans rule over green landscapes. Beauty is something serviceable and pragmatic. There are countless species whose functions are to look pretty and sing well and support a biosphere that keeps humankind on top. Which we are. We rein supreme, our lives long and almost effortless. We have very little important pain, and between us and the other lifeforms lies an enormous gulf."

I tell Bedford, "That gulf has always bothered me."

"Does it?" he responds. His voice seems haughty and nearly indifferent. "It's never bothered me."

"Quiet," warns Service.

I look back at the old Pitcairn. "A little more than a decade ago I was hired to do my usual work. My employers were an odd sect of the Unity Faith. They owned a tiny enworld and wanted it filled with a reasonable mix of species. Unique species, but not too unique. A durable, proven ecosystem. Several dozen of the sect's devoted members were going to live inside that enworld, harvesting wild game while pursuing some kind of perfection—"

"What sect?" Bedford inquires.

"The Children of Pain."

The bruised man blinks, obviously stunned, and his wife rocks back on her heels and softly moans.

"What?" asks Pachel. "What are they?"

Bedford says, "Fanatics."

Then Effie moans again, saying, "You joined them." She turns to her husband. "That's what he did—!"

"Not completely," I reply.

Bedford informs everyone, "They're fanatics. I didn't know they were nearby."

"I became friends with one of their members," I tell Service. "She was a low-ranking priestess, young and pretty, and I was recently divorced and perhaps vulnerable. We became lovers during my years on the job. She explained the basics of their faith to me, and through her I became halfway close to the other Children. Like me, they weren't satisfied with the gulf between humans and their biospheres. Their answer was to embrace the pain that surrounds everyone. That misery is vast and instructive, they told me. By employing certain novel technologies . . . by injecting minuscule robots called nanots into their flesh, allowing them to interface with their nervous systems—"

"That's illegal technology," Pachel informs me.

"And immoral," I add. "And rather appealing too."

"Appealing? How?"

I tell her, "I wasn't building just an enworld, you see. I was helping to finish a church for friends, for my lover. And the Children seemed quite at peace with themselves. I will grant you, I was at a low point in my life just then. I'd failed at another marriage . . . probably for the same causes that have always ruined my long-term relationships. I don't give enough of myself to my partners. I'm restrained. Not cold exactly, but too independent to allow anyone close enough. . . ."

Then I say, "But that's not the story. Is it?"

"You joined them," Effie repeats.

"I think any modestly contented fanatic would have looked appealing just then." I nod and Service asks:

"You've got these nanots inside you?"

"Yes." I turn and say, "They're sensitive to certain neural patterns brought on by pain, and they interact with my mind. They can replicate and repair themselves, like viruses, and once introduced, they're nearly impossible to remove or suppress."

"You felt the knobhead," says Service.

Which I can't feel now. Yes. I explain the sensations as well as I can manage. When words fail, I try shivering hard enough that everyone notices.

"Let me understand," says Pachel. "You let them inject you with nanots? Because you wanted to join them?"

"No, no. I took the nanots in lieu of payment. I wasn't actually attempting to join them, not in an official sense—"

"And it worked too well, didn't it?"

I nod, telling the rest of the story. It seems long ago— another person's life, in fact—but my words manage an immediacy. The Children of Pain apologized to me when they realized that I was unable to cope. They should have made more tests. Different people respond differently to the nanots, they admitted. Only a few people had the constitution to embrace and grow from this technology—

"Fanatics," Bedford repeats. He shakes his head, full of scorn, and seems genuinely sorry for me.

"That's why you're retired," says Pachel. "And why you're living on an almost-empty world."

"But why did you come here?" asks Effie.

"Because I've always wanted to visit," I reply. "Ever since I was a boy and heard about Pitcairn and the Remarkables." I glance back over my shoulder, noticing Talker's large black eyes. "And because my physicians have made great strides in controlling the infection. There aren't any cures, but I can tolerate most of what I feel."

"Besides," says Lumiere, "this is an alien world."

"I don't feel the Remarkables," I admit. "But knobheads and sometimes cretins. . . . sometimes everything but the Remarkables. . . ."

Goottich wears a strange smile, telling me, "I bet they seduced you on purpose. The Children, I mean. Seduced you so they wouldn't have to pay you what they owed you. I bet so."

I have had the same cynical thought myself. Many times.

Pachel says, "Oh, Ranier," and shakes her head in disappointment.

Then Service steps closer, lifting one hand. "All right," he begins, "we'll pretend you were sick when you hit Bedford. Sick and out of your head. You won't be banished, but you'll get a stick to your butt. You know the routine."

I'm not banished; and I'm surprised how relieved I feel. I nearly smile.

"Help him," Service tells Briar.

I glance at Snow. She rolls her head, implying, "It could be worse."

Briar walks up to me and remains standing. "Can you move?"

I say, "I think so," and rise to my feet, shuffling forward and Briar walking beside me. He doesn't hold me in any way. We pass through the ring of Remarkables, the ones in front of us parting and talking among themselves. They roll fast enough that the darkening air is full of a thin clinging dust.

"It won't be bad," Briar whispers to me.

I glance at the young face, noticing an odd little smile.

"Now I'm like you," I mention. "A criminal."

And he laughs loudly, hands to his stomach and his thin face rearing back with the mouth opened wide. I couldn't have said anything funnier, I sense. Not in my entire long life.

TALKER

What we see in the midst of the punishment goes unnoticed by the people. What we see is a single starlike object slipping across the darkening sky, too faint for human eyes. Almost too faint for our eyes too. We can barely discern the fuel tanks and the crew's quarters, plus the shuttle sleeping in its berth. The great torchship circles Pitcairn, adjusting its direction now and again in order to pass above us. To watch us with its machine eyes. And as it moves, in those places where the sky above any grove is clear, the adult Remarkables share their eyes with one another, through their roots, examining details we cannot begin to perceive. Looking into the little windows, into the empty rooms; and wondering how this *passion* is making due.

As with the great Au fort, the torchship is a symbol of human skills and accomplishments.

We cannot decipher how its machinery operates, nor can we pretend to build such wonders with human ease and economy.

And the punishment—the methodical whipping of Ranier—still is another rich symbol for us to ponder and to cherish.

What we see is every Pitcairn and visitor taking his or her swing at the bare rump. They use a stick in place of a canoe paddle. And like several nights ago, the sufferer is sprawled across a substantial log, holding tight and fighting the urge to scream.

The visitors find this business distasteful, even disgusting.

But most of the Pitcairns seem joyous. Maybe they resent Ranier and what the visitors represent. An intrusion; an encumbrance. Maybe for some this is a chance to show authority over the strangers. The strangers might be able to reshape whole worlds, but they can suffer a spanking like anyone. Yes? And certainly everyone resents being on this *passion*, selected on the basis of their past weaknesses and failures. Why not enjoy inflicting pain? It is under the guise of Service's judgment. Why not take revenge on one of those who came here and turned their world on its proverbial head?

Punishments are always symbols, we know.

Humans dispense human justice. That is the immortal rule.

There are stories of the ancient Past—every grove knows these stories—where inexperienced groves tried to discipline their humans. They felt the humans were working too slowly or without the proper loyalty . . . thus they withheld their nectars as a warning. Or they lowered the quality of nectar. Anything to show their collective displeasure—

—and the humans, the fledgling Pitcairns, responded at once. They went to sea in their boats, out of sight of land, then returned with only half-filled holds and spoke of the poor fishing. Wasn't it terrible fishing? The water seemed poisoned by something. Maybe it was the ill will carried from the land, the ill will and mistrust. They only hoped that the sources of these awful toxins could be turned off somehow. . . .

We depend on each other, of course.

We are eternally tied into our symbiosis, neither partner ruling over the other.

Human law reins over the Pitcairns.

And our role is to observe and learn, absorbing every clue into the nature of every participant. We watch the faces, particularly the eyes. We measure the force with which the stick strikes the bare rump. Who swings softest? Lumiere. Who uses the most force? Snow, we realize. *Snow*. It is an attempt to fool everyone, perhaps even herself. She is the last one to hold the stick, and afterward she tells him, "You're all right. Stand up and pull up your trousers. Come on."

She has no joy in this task.

Service hated it too. An unnecessary, gruesome chore.

And now Snow and Ranier are alone. The other visitors have moved away, pretending they want to go to bed. The other Pitcairns are going on watch or hauling pieces of the butchered knobhead across the cooling tar. And the torch-ship has long ago vanished into the northern glow of sunlight.

Ranier moans and says, "I can't stand up."

"It helps if you move," Snow promises him. She wants to help, yet she wishes she was elsewhere too. "Try, Ranier. Just try."

And a thought occurs to me.

I roll forward, approaching the people as Ranier fights for his balance; and with my most careful voice I say, "Humans and Remarkables. Humans and Remarkables."

The man leans against Snow, one hand grabbing at his trousers and the expression dumbfounded. "What? What are you saying, Talker?"

"Humans," I say, "and Remarkables."

I say, "We live in each other's aquariums, my friend."

Then I wait a moment before saying, "My friend," once again. With great, honest feeling.

29

THE ROUTINE

The plain remains flat for several days. Then we reach a low eroded chain of hills covered with new trees, their inflated leaves finger-shaped and rattling in the dry breeze. We camp at the base of the hills and climb them in the early morning. By now the Remarkables are wonderfully purple—a shade of purple that lingers when you look away, in the eye and mind—and they didn't appear this way before. Not even on the coast. Unbroken sunshine does them wonders. They're even climbing with renewed life, rolling between trees and pressing for the final crest.

Mount Au surprises me.

I reach the hilltop and halt, my mouth ajar. Mount Au is distant but unobstructed—a great snowy mound of tortured stone adorned with blue-white glaciers and lesser peaks. The summit is invisible, thick clouds gathered around it and nowhere else. A fitting symbol for any god, I think. Au covers the horizon to the south and east, the plain between quite flat and green in several shades, laced with rivers and patchy forests and the faint bluish streaks of cold lakes.

This is another occasion for ceremonies. For stories. The Remarkables bunch together and sing, tendrils waving with a peculiar almost-rhythm. I try not to project human emotions on them, but they do seem happy. Maybe they're relieved to have made it this far. More of them come up from behind me, joining the moment, and I notice people dropping their packs and digging out bricks and jugs. An early lunchtime, I gather. I select a warm flat stone and sit gingerly, basking while I eat my fill.

I keep watching Mount Au. Sometimes I catch myself seeing faces in the ice and the clouds. Craggy ones; bearded ones. The smooth lines of a baby's new face. I nick myself with my ceramic knife while watching, my hand jerking free and shaking itself.

"Careful," says Lumiere.

I turn around.

The old man has arrived, his shirt soaked and the face grinning. He sits beside me, saying, "Weeks and weeks away still." He sounds disappointed, yet he looks like someone spellbound, eyes never blinking and his breath making a thin whistling sound through his nose.

"The hunting will improve," I mention. "Service says it's wetter near the mountain."

Lumiere doesn't answer. Maybe he doesn't want to jinx us.

I finish my lunch and drink my fill, watching Au. It never looks quite the same twice. It's too large to embrace like ordinary scenery. I keep staring, maybe a little spellbound myself. Through the rest of the day I watch the clouds changing, and the sunlight. I have an image of Au in my mind, perfectly rendered, but every time I look again, the minor peaks seem aligned wrong and the cloud faces have changed their expressions and there is more blue glacial ice, or less . . . and the mountain always is larger than I expect . . . my soggy brain incapable of reducing the scene into an electrochemical pattern that is true and that I can hold. . . .

Our routine has its own rhythms and life, building momentum with the days. We wake, eat and pack, and we walk among the Remarkables. There are kills. Pitcairns return from the kill sites, others left to guard the fresh meat. Several major kills happen daily. Most of the prey are little grazers resembling muscular deer wearing jade-colored plumage; larger quarry bear glancing resemblances to camels and cattle. The largest kill of all is the easiest one. A pair of sprintbears are wrestling over a patch of barren ground, standing on their hind legs and driving at one another. They are giants . . . my first impression. They're idiots . . . my second. Snow explains that the ground is saturated with urine. The stink brings females, and the winner normally would gain this prime breeding ground.

Dust rises, and the long-legged creatures roar to intimidate. I don't even hear the first shot. Briar hits the closer bear in the brain, and it folds and drops without pain, instantly dead. Yet its assailant is too involved in the fight to give up. It throws back its head and screams, then it charges and somehow lifts the corpse upright, holding it secure between its forelegs. Service takes the second shot, and both sprintbears collapse into the twisting dust cloud.

I smell the dried urine on the wind.

"Is it always so simple?"

"No," Snow assures me. "This is just sweet luck. Nothing else."

Every midday has its long break. The Remarkables eat sunlight and speak among themselves, moving their tendrils in the bright dry air. We watch them and Au, and sometimes we sleep for an hour or more. My naps are deep and dreamless. I must be horribly tired; one afternoon I wake to find tiny bits of limestone half-buried in the backs of my hands, each one leaving a little pink pit surrounded by tanned flesh.

One midday brings an airdrop. Service has deployed his radio beacon, hanging its antenna from a nearby tree. We expected the drop yesterday, but it never arrived. Weather problems, Service explained. Today there aren't any delays. There's the grating roar of propellers, and an instant later there's the flash of wings followed by plastic cylinders raining down, little parachutes making them straighten and slow.

They hit the ground to our south, bursting open.

Then the planes—half a dozen of them—come back over and tilt their wings before climbing into the clear sky, turning into specks and gone.

Our routine gathers around us again. We walk and camp, eat and sleep, then wake again to eat again and pack and walk farther south.

As always, I carry my stick as if it might be a weapon. I don't know if it does any good, but it's my habit now. My hands have worn through its bark, my fingertips feeling for their accustomed places.

Remarkables surround me. The bright purple flesh glistens under coats of dust, and they roll at their usual pa-

tient pace. Only rarely do I see other people. Since my
fight my associates, save Lumiere, have kept a certain distance. I'm welcome to join them in the evening, talk, and
even joke. But when we're traveling I'm left alone. Which
is fine, I tell myself. I notice more of the country without
them.

Sometimes I sense pain. A little bit; a lot. The sensations
are uncomfortable, but manageable. Sometimes I have to
pause and wait, sweating hard until the feeling passes.
The Remarkables watch my spells with their bottomless
eyes, always talking. Discussing my condition, I suppose.
But I've given up listening. Their voices are too complicated, fast and fluid and beyond me.

We pause one midday, and Lumiere offers me a seat. I
take it and thank him. We're facing Goottich and Effie,
Bedford sitting nearby but not close. Goottich is telling
about an enworld he built as an investment. He gives sizes
and costs, then mentions that it was a zero-gee enworld.

Effie watches Goottich as if every utterance is blessed. I
have never seen such admiration from one person to another.

"A floating lake at its center," Goottich explains, "full
of duckweed and elodea. I strung the houses on spiderweb
cables. I planted free fall oaks and ginkos. Then I adver-
tised the enworld, painting it as a luxury residence. There
are always wealthy people deeper in the Realm. People
who think the frontier is different. People tired of stale air
and elbows—"

"And who can be fooled," says Bedford.

"It sounds *wonderful*," Effie responds. She doesn't look
toward her husband, adding, "I'm sure they're happy, all
of them. . . ."

Goottich shuts his eyes and nods, amused with something. One great palm is upturned, stained with a melted
nectar—a thin chocolate color—and with his eyes still
closed he lifts his hand, his broad pink tongue licking it
clean.

Effie and Bedford are still sleeping together inside their
cramped tent. Sometimes she stays out late talking to
Goottich, listening to his endless stories about his wealth
and cleverness; but nobody thinks there's a physical component to the relationship. Which is a surprise for every-

one but Pachel. Pachel has said, "It's because the behemoth doesn't fuck. Can't. Won't. Is afraid."

"Think so?"

"The poor girl is going to have to do everything herself," she told me. "Which is against the nature of things. The female should lure. Men worth having should take."

I watch Effie and Goottich. If I were an alien and found them in some sample net, my first instinct would be to separate them. They don't look like the same species. I'd be afraid one would try to eat the other whole.

Suddenly Effie asks, "What are you going to build next?"

Goottich is gazing up into the sky. After a moment he says, "Something new," and sucks air through the square teeth.

"What's that?" Bedford asks from a distance. His voice is shrill, and he's mastered a victim's status.

"Oh," says Goottich, "something special."

I watch the teeth.

The little eyes squint, pale and delighted. "Never mind. It's my business, and never mind."

I walk beside Talker, and it asks:

"What people live in a 'zero-gee' world?"

Only Talker asks such questions. Snow and the other Pitcairns wouldn't waste the breath.

"Basically," I explain, "ordinary people. They've got a few more tailored genes, and they're adapted to free-fall conditions. But their ecosystems are familiar. Earth-norms apply. In some places they've got huge populations . . . particularly in some of the long-settled Oort clouds."

Talker says nothing.

"They look like us. Basically. Not as much muscle and bone, and they wouldn't be able to cope with your gravity—"

"They have legs?" it interrupts. "Like you?"

"Sure."

"But why? Why not remake themselves? Why not look like spiders or like birds?"

The images are almost disgusting. With a measured voice, I explain how humans work hard to keep to certain norms. The Realm survives in part because of . . . . well, because of its unity. That tireless sense of belonging together. Of being part of one species.

Talker makes an odd sound, then says, "I know that, Ranier. I was just teasing you."

Was it? I glance at the pivoting eyes. "Do you miss your grove?"

"I miss it and I don't. In equal proportions."

"All right. . . ."

"Emotions for us are tangles. Not so clean and trimmed as for you, Ranier." A pause, then it adds, "By *us* I mean juveniles. Once we are adults, nothing is even that simple anymore."

Great minds full of conflicting opinions . . . and I tell my companion, "I know that. I was teasing you."

Again the odd sound. A buzzing, I think. *Laughter?*

Looking ahead, I notice a greatnest hunting over a wide stretch of grass and low brush, dark wings and its body silhouetted by the vivid white mass of Au. The image sticks in my mind. A hundred years from now, I'll be able to shut my eyes and see the greatnest again. As if for the first time.

A perfect moment.

The greatnest moves off, and I turn back to Talker. "I wonder how your grove is. Doing well, do you suppose—?"

"Very," it states.

The quickness and certainty of the answer are unnerving.

"There was a tremendous catch at sea, and a feast just before the last storm, and after the storm the sun stood screaming in the bare blue sky . . . lovely, lovely, lovely, and lovely. . . ."

"How do you know?"

The inner tendrils lift as high as they can stretch, and the voice makes a muddled sound before settling into a clear word:

"Wind."

I stop walking. "What?"

"In the wind," says Talker.

And I ask, "How?" while thinking, possibilities crowding into me and my mouth hanging open.

"When the wind is right, like now, and dry like now . . . I taste *everything*—"

"How?!"

"Words come to us in the wind. Now and again."

I ask more questions, but Talker refuses to answer. It

chatters with the nearby Remarkables, moving tendrils at the same time, and I settle on drawing up my own explanation. 'Words come to me in the wind.' All right, I think, what about aromatic compounds? Highly specific molecules are synthesized and released into the atmosphere, then absorbed by receptors on the tendrils. It's done to a limited degree by earthly lifeforms. Pitcairn has thicker air, which might help, and the Remarkables certainly can synthesize unique compounds. A sophisticated alphabet? An airborne language? The molecules would have to assemble into meaningful symbols and hold together, riding on winds over the mountains and only a tiny, tiny portion of them actually touching these tendrils. An occasional channel of conversation, at best. And entirely one-way—

"I've never heard about this trick," I sputter. "We never guessed—"

"A secret. Tell nobody. Nobody." A single tendril reaches for me, its tip brushing across my lips. "We know we can trust you, Ranier."

I feel more confused than honored. "You do?"

"We tell whom we trust," it declares; and I realize that *we* encompasses more than Talker and the Mount Au grove. "Some visitors know," it assures me.

But not the official researchers. They came here and missed an entire phenomenon. But how could they recognize alien compounds as being words in some language? Then I think about cretins with their hypersensitive noses. Do they *smell* the wind talking? Do groves control their symbionts at a distance? And what about from grove to grove? Here's another function for the aliens' intelligence—the deciphering of aromatic languages. Pitcairn is a world bathed in language. Thousands of groves can eavesdrop on each other at irregular intervals, perhaps even converse . . . according to the shifting winds. . . .

Again I stop walking, wrestling with the possibilities.

"Think hard," Talker advises.

I swallow and look into its airy self, the central organs rolling past me and its mouth remaining in view.

"The Pitcairns know—?" I begin.

"Yes, yes, yes!"

Of course. Why wouldn't they know?

"We trust you, friend."

Several other Remarkables say, "Friend," clumsily, oftentimes too quickly.

"Do you?" I mutter.

And Talker says, "More than we don't trust you, at least." Then comes the odd buzzing sound—Remarkable laughter—and my friend quits speaking to me. I ask questions and more questions, but enough has been said already. That's what the silence tells me.

30
NIGHTS BETWEEN

•❖•

Part of my routine includes the nightly walk into the brush, a shovel and toilet paper in one hand. My wastes have to be buried. It's the custom, human bacteria killed when entombed in Pitcairn soils. Another *passion* might happen past here, and nobody wants an infection brought on by some strain of mutated *E. coli*.

What began as an indignity has become ordinary. I find a suitable place, dig and squat, then stand again. The burial completed, I start for camp again. But tonight I hear voices, close and softened. I pause. I turn my head. Pachel says, "Please."

I step toward a wall of greenery, reaching with my free hand and pushing back the branches. There's a clearing and sunlight, and I peer into it without thinking. I see Pachel's black hair and her face and how her silvery flecks enlarge and link, covering her chest with silver. The breasts are tipped with comet-black nipples. A single hand massages one breast, and a gray head rises to suck. *Service.* I gasp loud enough to make Pachel turn her head, eyes finding me. Then she does nothing. She merely watches me while moving her hips, and Service drops from view as I back away.

"Who?" he says.

"Ranier," she answers.

And he says, "Ahh," while I retreat, feeling foolish and careless and a little sad.

Pachel moans.

Service says, "Ahhh!"

I walk faster, up on my toes and close to running.

* * *

We built four fires in the evening, surrounding the sleeping Remarkables with their flickering light. Enemy cretins continue to shadow us, we hear. But we've heard it so often that the threat isn't something real anymore. It's like the bogeyman to children too old to fear the dark anymore.

One evening there are four of us around one of the fires. Lumiere and me; Bedford and Effie. I ask about Pachel's whereabouts.

"She's with Tintoil," says Lumiere. "They're having target practice."

"With guns?" says Effie.

"Rifles. Yes." Lumiere nods. "I saw them walking that way. Pachel says that she got permission. Ten bullets worth of practice . . . that's what Service is allowing her."

"How does she win the honor?" grouses Bedford.

Faraway expressions show that the others know. Or at least they sense the reasons.

Then Bedford asks his wife, "Where's your friend tonight?"

"My friend," she answers, "is sleeping, thank you."

"What? He exhausted himself with all the boasting?"

Effie warns him, "You should be more appreciative. He did invite us here, after all."

"Because he needed bodies. Sperm and eggs." Bedford can't help but sound petty, and I feel like taking him aside and explaining that righteous rage is more appropriate. Unless he doesn't care, in which case he should get over his sourness.

"Listen," says Lumiere, "can we change the subject?"

"Can and will," I say.

Bedford gives a little snort, glancing my way. The yellowish bruises are healing fast, the original face reemerging.

"So what do we talk about?" asks Effie.

We must seem like peculiar creatures. At each other's throats, yet nobody wants to be alone on this splendid evening.

"What do you miss?" I ask the question, looking at no one. "I'm just curious. What are you craving about the Realm? Something we don't have with us. . . ."

"Meat," Bedford responds. It must have been on his

mind, judging by his tone. "I miss cooking meat, and the smell of it cooking, and how it cuts and tastes." He gives a half giggle. "Is that what you want?"

"Sure," I say.

"I miss being comfortable," Effie admits. "I'd like to be able to sit somewhere and not feel my back aching, or my knees. . . . I just want to forget about my body for a little while. . . ."

"That too," says Bedford. "I get sick of hurting."

I glance at Lumiere.

"Youth," he answers.

I nod and hear a distant *pop*.

Everyone turns and listens, but there's nothing else. Then Lumiere says, "I don't want my youth back, I'm not greedy. I just want to be a couple weeks younger. . . ."

We start to laugh.

Then Bedford asks me, "So what do you miss most?"

"Trash." I say the word as a joke. Then I elaborate, giving the joke body. "When I'm walking at home? On the empty highlands? I'll find bits of hyperfiber that dropped from space. And plastics preserved by the dry cold. All kinds of human trash." I wait a moment, then say, "There's nothing like that here. This country . . . we could be the first humans to walk on this ground, and I guess that's a little disconcerting . . . if you see what I mean. . . ."

We hear a *pop* and then *pop*.

"I think I understand," says Lumiere.

The others make no comment, both watching our fire.

Pop.

We listen to the echoes of Pachel's shooting, then the breeze in the tallest trees. Then I announce, "I'm tired," and rise to a chorus of polite "Good nights," making for my tent.

Pop.

I am in bed.

Pop. Pop. Pop.

Sometimes Snow tells me that she's guarding all night, and I know better. Even Pitcairns are granted sleep. "I can't visit you tonight," she tells me. I used to believe it was Salo or Briar. Then I decided it couldn't be Briar, that Snow kept a certain distance between her and him. And maybe it's nobody at all. The girl just wants to be apart—that's my current suspicion—sleeping without a tent and without responsibilities. Does she find me to be a burden? I'm beginning to believe so. It's nothing I can point out, but I can feel it nonetheless.

When Snow does come to visit, she's never anything less than alert and attentive. She calls me, "Rainy," and tries tickling me. We make love and talk afterwards. The nights are warm, and we lie flush against each other, slowly drying. Sometimes I talk about the places I have visited—worlds and enworlds and comets—and she seems to listen. Several times I describe the holos made of Earth, and they interest her most. But what can she make of her home world? I describe crystal towers ten kilometers tall and seas laced with cities, submerged and not, and five-hundred-plus skyhooks standing on the equator . . . and all the while I'm wondering if she's impressed by the engineering, the sheer vibrant scale of things. . . .

What interests Snow most are her stories about her grove and her best friends and their various adventures. She tells me about famous fishing boats and famous airplanes. She tries to teach me how to fly a Pitcairn airplane, using imaginary throttles and making childish explosions when we crash. She loves to read, she admits. Too much. "What's too much?" I interrupt. Too much means too much. That's all. Then she tells me about ancient books that are copies of copies of copies. Some of the stories seem to be happening on Earth, except there are Remarkables and sweet green clouds of plankton. She gives me brief story lines, and sometimes they taste familiar. A boy and an escaped slave raft down a huge river, moving from grove to grove until they find theirs. Two lovers come from warring groves, and of course they're wrong and banished for their deeds. Of course. And one of her favorite stories—a silly thing, she admits—tells of a young girl finding an enchanted bottle that grants one wish. After many adventures and much thought, she decides on the only reasonable wish. She asks the bottle to give her wish to—

"The Old Ones," I interrupt. "Right?"

"Wrong!" Her face turns sour, then she tells me, "To an elder. Not to a Remarkable . . . that's silly . . . !"

I ask about her first lover, and she tells me about a boy several years older. Very handsome; very experienced. He

had his own house, and they did it in the middle of his
huge bed, the sun streaming through the skylights on a
clear summer's day.

"Where's the boy now?" I inquire.

She says, "Dead."

I feel a thick spot under my sternum, watching her face
in the near-darkness. Snow seems more thoughtful than
saddened. "His fishing boat was over the Ghost Banks. In
the winter. Real shitty water, and a storm caught him.
Them."

"I'm sorry."

She shrugs, telling me, "He was very brave. Not smart,
but he was always hard at work."

"A good person."

She nods, saying, "Luck turns bad. It always does."

"A morbid thought."

She ignores me, talking now about recent lovers. Boys
and men. And sometimes with several men, plus other
women. Her first "group" was in a little pond in the middle of the grove. The water was clear and made warm by
the heat bleeding off the Remarkables, and all I can think
about are the black eyes gazing down at the orgy, absorbing every clinical detail.

Snow asks if such things happen in the Realm.

"Probably somewhere," I admit. "But not often. Not
openly."

"No?" She seems puzzled, perhaps even offended.

I feel an obligation to defend my culture. I explain, "In
the Realm, we believe in the freedom to do as we choose.
Anything is permissible so long as nobody's hurt by our
actions."

"Is that so?"

She is grinning at me, pleased with something.

Finally she says, "We believe the opposite here. We're
free to do anything so long as it helps everyone else," and
with that she kisses my damp forehead, smiling dreamily.

A superior code, I realize. *Altruistic, even saintly. . . .
Provided one knows what actually helps.*

I wake one night, feeling my dream-stiffened penis
against Snow's rump. I push a little bit, and she pushes
back against me. Snow's awake. I wrap my arms around
her and kiss an ear, then ask, "How'd you get your name?"

"It snowed."

"When you were born?"

She says, "When I was conceived."

I reached down her belly, knowing its feel and the precise position of her navel and the first stiff pubic hairs. Familiar terrain. With every lover of mine there has been a point where familiarity balances with lust, and this is that joyful point now.

"It fell on the grove itself," she says, "then melted when it touched them. Big midwinter flakes of it."

"Were they scared? A hard freeze—"

"—could kill a grove. Yes."

I say nothing.

"Have you ever noticed," she asks, "how smart people worry more than anyone?"

"Maybe so."

"Remarkables spend a lot of their time worrying. Particularly the Old Ones. . . ."

I shut my eyes, wondering how it would feel to have those alien eyes. I would watch every snowflake tumbling from the clouds, following their chaotic paths down to me and then melting. I would hope they'd melt, at least.

Snow and I make love, then I climb outside and pee. Stars glitter to the south. In the north, above the lumpy horizon, I notice the diluted glow of the sun and the slight colored gleam of the northern aurora. I turn again. Mount Au is starlit and beautiful in different ways than in daylight, its slopes vague and the clean bright snow ethereal and the very highest of the shrouding clouds catching a sliver of the sun's glare, shining with a muted golden color.

The campsite is quiet, four fires burning around the interwoven Remarkables.

I kneel and return to bed, finding Snow asleep.

Maybe I sleep too. I'm not sure. Then suddenly I hear the *pop-pop* sounds in the distance, and my first thought is:

Pachel is practicing. She is shooting again.

So rude! At this hour! Then I notice Snow sitting upright, naked but for heavy socks. In my confusion I decide that Snow's angry too. She has picked up her rifle from beside the tent wall. Is shooting Pachel any answer? Then Snow is talking to me, and I can't understand her. Suddenly gunfire is coming from everywhere, and she wants me to do something. What? What? Finally she shakes her head and rises, bursting from the tent without dressing, her bare rump shining in the starlight.

Bullets skip past me and make me drop flat on my belly. "Down!" she was telling me. "Get down!"

31
A BURIAL

◆

The Pitairns form a line, and each of them shoots with deliberation. A certain delicacy. Some are dressed; some naked. This might be a bizarre form of target practice. *Pop pop pop pop pop.* I follow the gun flashes with my eyes, and something is moving. Several somethings. Sprintbears, I think; then I realize they're cretins. Five or six of them. Or seven. Or eight. They have long, long legs rising to thick bodies, and they gallop and weave, charging from a nearby wood through which they must have crept, using darkness as a cover.

The lead cretin drops hard, its head driven into the ground. There's more gunfire and a second one collapses, rolling onto its back with a single fluid motion—boneless and limp and eerily graceful.

Their speed is incredible. That muscle can carry anything so quickly seems wrong. Against Nature itself.

Another drops, then a second one jerks its head sideways. I feel a searing pain rising to where I nearly scream . . . and the pain vanishes abruptly, the cretin dead while upright, the dead legs collapsing and the head plowing up grass and earth.

I count three left. Three. They're fast but they can't reach us over this open ground, I decide, and aren't they stupid creatures? Trained by their groves, yes. By alien intelligences . . . yes. But they can't face rifles and win, that's silly . . . and now I hear them roaring from deep in their chests. That's all I hear. Nobody is firing now. The ammunition is spent. The Pitcairn line dissolves, people running and shouting, and too late I remember Snow's pack. It's set against mine, and I climb outside and slap the pockets, hunting for spare clips.

The shooting starts again. From beside me. *Boom boom boom.* I wheel around, Service not three strides away. He's fully dressed. He must have been guarding elsewhere and run here, kneeling now and his gun flashing and the sounds slapping at me. Another cretin feels agony and drops, dying in front of the aliens. Stinging tendrils deploy, threatening the last two cretins. And suddenly there's a high-pitched noise from them, a soaring and brittle agonized screech. My ears start to ring—

—and there's a sharp concussion as a bomb detonates. A single cretin is illuminated by the yellowish flash. A naked figure stands in front of the cretin—a woman—and she lifts her arms, not moving, holding her empty rifle like a club and the cretin running through her without slowing, the woman evaporating and the cretin driving into the Remarkables, swatting at the first of them with one paw, then another. Shreds of tendrils and then whole Remarkables fly free, and our cretins—tiny and supernaturally quick—rush in from several sides and clamp hold of the monster.

Service slams home a fresh clip and aims and shoots. The cretin tilts its head and drops. Then he shouts, "Where's the other one?" He looks at me, then turns before I can answer; "I don't know."

The Remarkables are trying to pull apart. They cry and screech, the outer ones rolling away from the center. Eyes pivot. They're panicking. The last cretin is in the midst of them, swatting and clawing and chewing as it moves. Pitcairns are shouting, pointing. They aim but don't fire. How can they chance firing? Dozens of Remarkables still are packed tight, and I begin feeling the cretin being stung and bitten. Its pain and another organism's pain too. . . .

I start to trot, some voice warning me that Snow is the injured woman. I prepare myself. A fool, letting herself be caught in the open. For what? All at once I feel distant and incapable of sadness, my insides made of stone.

Service is beside the Remarkables, yelling at them. "Keep still! Keep the fuck still!" And with his rifle in one hand, he climbs among their tendrils and vanishes. Just like that. Not an instant's hesitation.

I reach the injured woman and kneel. Her face is bloody.

Her pain arcs through me as I touch her belly and navel
and then the large, almost-soft breasts. Service is shooting.
I feel bullets impacting on flesh, at point-blank range, then
the sudden warmth of death. Of no-pain. Two deaths, I
realize. The cretin and woman pass on simultaneously.
With both hands I wipe away blood, making certain, then
I turn and see Goottich behind me. He's staring at me.
"It's Tintoil," I inform him. "Your partner."

Effie approaches, saying, "The poor, poor woman."

"Death begets life," says Bedford, and he makes a show
of drawing circles in the air.

Pachel slaps his hand, saying, "Stop that!"

Lumiere touches my shoulder and helps me to my feet.

And all the while Goottich stares at the corpse, intrigued,
one of his hands wiping the sweat from his face. He looks
like a titanic little boy much too much impressed. I stare
at his eyes, noticing the emptiness behind them. Intellect
without compassion. And the big mouth betrays a little
smile, slight and brief and something about it infinitely
cold.

Pitcairn grief is easy and intense.

Service oversees the funeral, standing at the head of the
fresh grave. As the sun rises in the northeast, stained orange by dust, I notice the cuts on his face and hands and
how everyone cries, wishing their friend well in death.

Tintoil is on her back, still naked, and Service says a
few words about her surviving in the memory of the Au
grove. About how the good stuff in her blood lives on forever. As do her good works and her bravery. And with
that he tosses the first clod of moist earth on top of her.
Everyone does the same. Snow and Briar remain behind
to bury Tintoil, and Briar says something. I can't tell what,
but Snow straightens and says, "Quiet," while pushing
tears across her face.

We'll stay here today, I learn. The cretins will be
eaten—an expensive feast for the surviving Remarkables.
The cretins came from the Two Sisters grove, says Service.
The one he attacked as a boy. He eyes us, griping the worn
stock of his rifle. He says, "This isn't the fun you wanted,
is it? Is it?"

Nobody answers him.

"This is real," he promises. "This is the most real thing you'll ever know."

Eight of the Remarkables died outright. Their real corpses are pale and insubstantial, left where they died. Their brethren show not even the faintest interest in a funeral. By afternoon their dead flesh is covered with insects, the sour stink wafting across the campsite. But the survivors continue basking in the area, absorbing sunshine and apparently indifferent to the losses.

I start looking for Lumiere, thinking I can talk about my feelings with him. But I happen upon Talker, and it says:

"My friend Ranier."

I turn reluctantly.

"You think . . . what? That we should have a funeral for them? That we need to act *human* and earn your respect?"

It makes me uncomfortable to think that my thoughts are transparent. I move my weight from leg to leg, holding my walking stick close to me. "You don't know what I'm thinking," I mutter.

"You're saddened by Tintoil's death. Perhaps for a moment you thought it was Snow, not her—"

"Perhaps."

"—thus you feel guilty too. Guilty because you're secretly glad that Tintoil died. Not Snow."

I turn my head, looking for Lumiere. Where is he?

"Lumiere's at the other end of camp, friend."

I try not to show my surprise, turning and remarking, "I'm not angry with you. And I can understand how you must look at death. All those eggs and almost none of them surviving . . ."

Tendrils point, and the familiar voice says, "Lumiere is sitting on a downed tree at the far edge of that wood. He's looking at the Au mountain and speaking with his dead wife."

I say nothing.

"You were going to speak to Lumiere, weren't you?"

I say, "No," and force a laugh. "Not at all. Not for a minute. No."

I wait through the next night for another attack, none coming, and it's the same for my associates. In the morning we're standing around one smoldering fire, faces tired and nervous and nobody speaking.

Service comes to us, reporting that he can't find any signs of other cretins. That means they must be clever ones. Understood?

We nod, impressed with his paranoia.

He glances at his timepiece, telling us how long we have before we leave. Then he drops his wrist. "Questions? Any?"

He wants something specific, I realize. What?

Pachel asks, "What about Tintoil's rifle?"

Service nearly grins. His face is clean, the cuts healing fast, and he seems absolutely calm.

"Let me carry it," she tells him.

"Unloaded."

She hesitates, then says, "Fine."

Service nods and looks at the timepiece again, and Bedford asks, "May I see that for a moment?"

An old hand undoes the band, and he tells Bedford, "Pass it around." Bedford holds it gingerly, acting as if his grip could fracture the case. Then he gives it to Lumiere, and Lumiere gives it to me. The device looks old and partly melted at the edges. The band is made of a soft thin leather stained white with sweat salts. The time is scarcely visible through the clouded glass window.

"My father's," says Service.

I look up.

Bedford asks, "How was it damaged?"

"It spent time in a cretin's stomach, in the acids and rot." He waits for an instant, then says, "It was the cretin that killed my father."

Bedford says, "Oh."

I hand the timepiece to Effie, and she quickly passes it to Goottich. But before he can so much as read the time, Service snatches it away from him. In an instant; without hesitation. Then he straps it on his wrist again, saying, "Why don't you put out this fire first."

Something is happening. Or is going to happen.

He says, "Before anything. Please?"

The smoke curls around him and us, and I can't shake the feeling that something is close. Something that I'm just too blind or too stupid to perceive.

TALKER

I lived the horror again, helping Service.

It was the night after the attack, and he approached us and called for me and settled once he found me, asking what had happened. What happened exactly? And what could I offer him about the others? What was their mood now? Collectively, singly. Was Briar still plotting? Was Goottich still laboring with his numbers? Which Pitcairns were watching Briar, taking cues from him? Then he said, "Shit, if he'd just been the one killed. Briar, not Tintoil."

"Briar fled," I told him. Which he knew. I lived the horror again—the charging cretins; the fierce gunfire; the savage deaths of my siblings—and I told Service, "Everyone but Tintoil ran away."

"Cowards," he said, then he glanced all around. As if I were not watching for intruders. As if I would allow Briar to see him speaking to me. Service is a nervous man for countless good reasons, and he has to maintain his vigilance. His hyperalertness. It has to be a habit, I understand, and that is why I cannot take his glances personally.

"Some of them were cowardly," I admitted. "But others were making earnest attempts to find more ammunition—"

"Lousy, lazy shooting," he complained.

Probably so. Yes.

"Firing fast like they did. Like children!"

"Snow searched for bullets," I informed him.

His head cocked, and he nearly smiled. He nearly said, "Did she?" then suppressed the urge.

I continued with my description of events and emotions. We have talked this way several times lately. I relived the horror for him and then its aftermath too. What did I see during the day? What about this evening? Which people were angry, which ones scared? Who among the Pitcairns were sure to back Briar in case some "accident" took Service? A lot of them, I admitted. But not all.

"Salo?" he inquired.

Briar trusted no one more than Salo. Yes.

"Shurgar?"

She was not sure of her feelings. Not yet.

Then he had to ask, "What about Snow?"

I waited a long while—a human instant—before saying, "As it stands now, Snow will back you. And should something happen to you, she'll leak honest tears at your funeral."

"That's something," he grumbled.

"Our other problem is finished with his fancy calculations. He's decided on his means—"

"Goottich."

"—and waits only for the perfect instant."

Service never shows despair, nor fear. Nor anything but his usual tenacious desire to succeed against all odds. Yet in that moment I could see behind his eyes; I could make out flickers of panic that he probably couldn't sense for himself.

"All right," he said mildly. "All right."

"Watch for accidents," I warned. "But Briar is being patient. For him, he's showing amazing restraint. Probably because he has time. Because so far all he wants is to gain control of this *passion* and return home victorious. He can't imagine that more is at stake here."

Service seemed deaf, muttering to himself, "I can trust Pachel, I think. But what about the other visitors? Which ones would help me, if it comes to that?"

We discussed each one. Lumiere is trustworthy, in ways. And perhaps Ranier. Both men have heartfelt reasons for seeing this *passion* to its natural conclusion. Unfortunately Effie is Goottich's ally, and unless vengeance was an attraction, Bedford will likely remain neutral.

"Shush," Service interrupted. "Did you hear something?"

His voice was calm and strong, dry and slow; but between the syllables was the telltale panic.

I said, "Nothing. I heard nothing."

"I didn't either," he added, talking more to himself than me.

And I wondered—every waking sibling wondered—"Is this great old man going to last out the storm?"

32
AN OFFER

◆

The day is hot and cloudless, the thick air absorbing our sweat without warnings. Dehydration is a risk. I make a point of drinking before I feel thirsty, draining two jugs in the morning and filling them at midday. Then in the afternoon march I drink them and a third jug, eating little and feeling no trace of hunger.

Mount Au swells in the distance. At one place we cross a low ridge and find the countryside sinking toward the south. This is the first time I've seen the entire mass of Au, down to its base—blue-green forests watered by melting snow and rains and dew—and I feel weak and happy. The beauty of it all, I suppose. And through the rest of the day I'm smiling without planning to smile, and sometimes it's as if I can smell the mountain's cool breath.

"There you are!"

I turn and find Goottich watching me. Smiling, he says, "Listen. I want to talk to everyone tonight, including you. It's important."

"What about?"

"I've got an offer," he replies.

"An offer."

"Just let everyone know," he says, "I've been telling people, but I'm missing some. Will you tell?"

"You want to talk. Okay."

"Great!" he says, walking past me and down a narrow trail. The hair-like grasses stand tall and brown on both sides of him. Quick yellow birds flush from the grass, wheeling and lighting farther downhill; and Goottich keeps walking, flushing them a second time. Then a third.

* * *

Only four Pitcairns are missing—ones to whom I have never quite put names—but everyone else is present. We're sitting near the largest fire, the Remarkables bunched nearby. There is a mood of expectation and curiosity, plus emotions that I can't quite pin down.

The big man wears a clean shirt and trousers, and he smells of soap. Pacing in front of us, he seems pleased with the suspense. He loves holding court in this way. The big round face turns and turns, and for a moment he stares at the aliens.

"A lovely night," says Talker.

Goottich says, "It is," and turns to face us. "As you know, I own an enormous enworld. I am blessed in many ways. And being blessed with room and resources, I can afford to dream in spectacular ways." He pauses, then tells us, "I want to make an offer to everyone. Every person; every Remarkable."

Nobody moves.

The Remarkables' eyes are directed at Goottich and at us; and for an instant it feels as if they are, in some peculiar fashion, nervous.

"I will gut my home," says Goottich. "My enworld . . . I can raise its interior temperature until its soils and air and well-boiled waters are thoroughly sterilized . . . then I can introduce a variety of new species. That's my plan. Unusual species. Steelwood trees and ribbon fish, for instance."

"Pitcairn species?" Bedford responds.

"Oh my," says Effie. "Really?"

Goottich nods with authority. A thin veneer of perspiration begins to drip from his forehead, making him blink, and he wipes at his face with the big wet palms. "What I intend to do—what I've been planning in no small detail for these last weeks—is to collect a wide range of native species. Yes, Pitcairn species. From this plain. From the coast and mountains. Even from the ocean itself. I have enough room in my enworld, enough for a representative sampling. Money won't be any problem, either. And since this involves a huge amount of work, I'll have to hire experts to help me. Quality terraformers. People with experience in the Pitcairn biosphere."

Nobody moves.

He breathes through his mouth, almost shivering.

I say, "Goottich?"

The round face finds me. "Yes, Ranier?"

"What you're proposing . . . I don't know if it's legal. Pitcairn organisms are restricted, and the transportation of restricted species—"

"Oh, it's all legal. Absolutely!"

Terraformers glance at one another, more puzzled than anything.

Goottich nods with conviction. "I have all the permits required. Believe me. And what's more, my enworld meets all Code A factors for biological isolation. If we travel straight there, avoiding New Albemarne, we'll have no problems whatsoever."

"It sounds wonderful," says Effie. Wringing her hands in her lap, she declares, "It's an impressive plan!"

I'm remembering his writing in the dirt beside the river. I had a strong impression that this was coming, yet I still feel stunned. Does he mean it?

"Just a minute," says Pachel. "You can't take anything off Pitcairn without permission. There's the Pitcairn charter to consider. We've got an assortment of treaties—!"

"What about them?" Goottich responds.

"Any transaction involving any part of this solar system . . . first there must be permission—"

"Exactly. Permission. Exactly!" He taps his forehead, saying, "I know every code and every bylaw, Pachel. I memorized these rules before I came here. And what I need is the permission of an existing Pitcairn governmental unit. That's how it's written. When it comes to a specific place on this world, we require its owners' permission. Which means the Mount Au grove, *or* some equivalent."

Pachel looks at Service, puzzled by his silence. His apparent distance. Then she growls and says, "The grove isn't going to allow you to haul off trees and whatnot—!"

"No, no." He wags a thick finger at her, parent to silly child. "It's in the bylaws. Any *passion* is considered a legal Pitcairn nation. It's a nation ruling its surroundings. A fine legal point, I'll admit, but I'm sure my lawyers will make a tight case in my favor."

The Pitcairn faces seem flat and very simple, at least at first glance. But Service acts as if he's not surprised to be hearing any of this craziness, and the others cultivate a

strange faraway gaze to hide what they must be thinking.
Which is what? What? I stare at them, unable to even
guess.

"You'd destroy your own home?" asks Lumiere.

Goottich blinks and says, "For this, yes. Of course."

I remember how he talked about the place, full of
pride—

"To make some Pitcairn zoo?" says Pachel. She snorts
and forces a laugh, shaking her head in disbelief. "So you
can have some odd-looking trees? Is that what this is
about?"

"No, no. No!" He shakes his head, frustrated with her
and maybe by the Pitcairn indifference. "We're going to
return to our torchship, and from there we'll collect seeds
and eggs from a full range of organisms. All environments.
It might take years to replicate this biosphere. I know that,
Pachel. But that's why I'll gladly pay everyone for their
help and guidance."

He's greasing us with praise. Goottich wants our com-
pliance more than our help. Otherwise we might make
noise and legal problems for him. A shrewd shit, that man
is.

Then he gestures at Service and the other Pitcairns. "I
mean you too. Each of you."

The air seems too still. Unnaturally so.

And Goottich wheels around and says, "And all of you!"
The Remarkables.

I grow cold inside, my reaction immediate and visceral.

"Do you know what you're suggesting?" says Lumiere.
He sounds a little angry and quite worried. "Transplant-
ing an alien species into the Realm—"

"Pitcairn," says Goottich, "is going to be surrounded by
the Realm in a few more centuries. One way or another,
old man, it's going to be inside us. It's going to be part of
us eventually."

"So," says a voice, "what kind of work would we do?"

Everyone turns, eyes focusing on Briar. He smiles without humor, almost without life, but the voice seems curious. Even intrigued. "Okay," he says. "Suppose we leave
with you—"

"You'll live there," says Goottich. "You'll help me es-
tablish a smaller version of Pitcairn. Then you and your
children, and eventually your grandchildren . . . you'll live

as you live here. What I'm offering . . . it's a huge opportunity. A first!"

"Oh my," says Effie.

Bedford asks, "What about gravity? The air and lights, and the chemistry of the soils—?"

"Technical issues, easily fixed." Goottich makes a sweeping gesture, proud of his confidence. "We'll change the spin rate, the mixture of air, and by increasing pump size we can enlarge the tides on my little sea. We'll even produce horrid winter storms, for the sake of authenticity. Which is what I want. I want to capture every sharp facet of this place."

The Pitcairns move, looking at one another.

Snow turns and stares at the Remarkables, her mouth slightly opened and her teeth just showing.

Goottich continues. "We'll transport people and Remarkables inside the empty fuel tanks. They can be made into cold-sleep chambers . . . it's done every day. . . ."

"This entire *passion* is invited?" says Briar. "That's what you're telling us, isn't it?"

Goottich says, "Yes."

Briar's eyes seem to blaze up with their own fire. He has coals stuck into his narrow face, not eyes, and I feel an instinctive pain cutting through me.

"What I want," Goottich proclaims, "is an established and mature grove. A thriving community of Remarkables. And I'll pay a fortune to acquire such a treasure."

Pachel glances at me, her mouth clamped shut.

Lumiere moans softly under his breath.

Goottich turns to the Remarkables, saying, "Without you, I'm not interested. I'll be honest. You're the main attractions for me."

The Remarkables make no noise, and they scarcely move.

"You'll have your grove in a lovely bay. A perfect place, believe me. An ideal climate and plenty of airborne planktons, if you want them, and *passions* every summer."

The Pitcairns stir quietly.

"And I can replace Mount Au too. From hyperfiber foams. I'll build an artificial mountain against an endwall and dress it with glaciers and clouds." He walks toward the Remarkables, waving the thick arms and his boots kicking up tufts of dust. "I'll even breed cretins to

attack you. Just like you expect. Your *passions* can be as
awful as you need them to be. Believe me. Trust me! I
mean what I'm telling you!"

"Enough."

The voice is dry and quiet, and everyone hears it.

Even Goottich. He turns and looks at Service with his
face changing to confusion. "What was that—?"

"Stop talking."

The old Pitcairn rises to his feet. His face is sharp and
self-assured. I notice the darkened teeth and the gleam of
the horizontal scar, and he takes a long breath and says,
"It won't happen."

Goottich approaches him, then remembers to smile. In
a clumsy way he tries to charm Service, asking, "Are you
certain? I mean, do you know what you're turning down?"

"The discussion is done. Now shut up." Service glares at
everyone. "Am I understood?"

A few Pitcairns nod their heads.

Briar shrugs his shoulders, then whispers, "Sure."

But Goottich keeps coming, the smile dissolving into a
kind of panicked anguish. He wants Service to bend. To
compromise. He says, "Put the proposition to a vote. I'm
sure if everyone voted—!"

"This is my *passion*!" Service warns him.

"Yes, but—"

"Shut up."

"Except this is such a wonderful chance . . . for everyone. . . ."

Service picks up the nearest rifle and sets the tip of the
white barrel against Goottich's sweaty forehead, and he
taps at the forehead while saying, "Understand. This is a
passion. I rule. It's my responsibility, no one else's, and
there won't be debates or votes here. So shut up. Not another word. Hear me? Yes? Yes? Yes?" Every time he says,
"Yes?" he taps the forehead again. "Yes? Yes? Yes? Yes?
Yes—?"

"Yes! All right!"

"Good." Then Service turns and walks away, not so
much as glancing back at us; and Goottich reddens, blood
filling his face and his lips mashed together and his eyes
outraged by his helplessness. The big hands grasp at one
another, slipping free and then grasping again. But he says

nothing. He swallows the words and his anger, then turns and marches off in the opposite direction, passing the Remarkables as they start to buzz among themselves.

Their voices almost sound excited to me.

When I'm careless; when I let them sound that way.

33
HEAT

❖

Morning feels cool with a dry wind from the east, but soon the wind shifts and dies away and the climbing sun sucks at every gram of moisture. Drinking just seems to make my thirst more real, more immediate. We keep walking toward the giant frozen mountain, and sometimes in the distance are columns of dust kicked up by grazers. Sometimes I taste the dust against my tongue and teeth, working to find spit enough to moisten it. We don't break until midafternoon, and that's not for long. I sit on a flat slice of rock, cool to the touch, and Snow sits beside me, offering me a partial brick of reddish nectar. The strawberrish stuff, I recall.

I tell her, "Thanks."

She shrugs her shoulders, implying, "No need to thank me."

"How long since it rained here?"

She takes a slow studied look at the plain. "Maybe since winter," she allows. Then she adds, "That's why we have to keep moving. The closer we get to Au, the wetter it'll become."

I pull a map from my pocket and run my fingertips over rivers and the long thin lakes, then I look up and notice a single greatnest hunting above a little wood. Remarkables are singing. Maybe I'm imagining it, but they seem to link their singing with the giant bird's motions. The greatnest circles and then folds suddenly, diving and extending its talons at the last instant. I feel a faint distant pain, then the chill dissolves. The bird rises on long wingbeats, a limp black something beneath it. It passes near us and cries out.

Such a majestic creature, yet its voice is thin and brittle. Thoroughly unlovely.

People wouldn't let them have those voices, I tell myself.

If I was hired to tailor greatnests, I'd probably have to improve their cry. Making it bold. Creating something impressive, even stunning. That's my job. . . .

"What are you thinking?" Snow asks me.

"Nothing."

She shrugs, settling for that answer.

I'm glad Service cut off Goottich. That's what I'm thinking. I'm relieved that whatever was started was finished a moment later. The big man could have caused problems. Who knows what kinds?

Reaching into my pack, I produce a lump of sour green nectar.

Snow tries smiling, saying, "Thanks," with a stiff voice. Pitcairns don't thank each other for sharing food—it's like sharing oxygen—and this is a joke. She wants to be funny. She watches me, waiting until I chuckle, then she breathes and looks at nothing, delicately chewing on her lower lip.

We camp late in the evening. Everyone seems spent, including the Remarkables. There's not much conversation around the fires, people eating and walking to a little spring to fill their jugs, most of us in bed early and hard asleep.

Snow is on guard tonight, but she promises to come see me later.

She makes a point in saying, "I'll be there."

But I awaken in the dark and reach, my hand finding the cool slick fabric of the tent floor. *Oh, well.* I think the worst because at times like this, feeling comfortable and rested, the worst never seems too awful. Snow and her Pitcairn boyfriends must be having fun, I decide. Then I drift back to sleep, dreaming and waking and needing to pee.

Dawn is beginning. I step outside, and someone is trotting toward me. I finish, shake and tuck, then I notice two others walking through the nearby wood. Salo, I'm sure. Large and muscular. And beside him is Briar. Or maybe Service. But there's a youthfulness in the motions, a certain quickness. No, it's Briar walking beside Salo.

Snow is the first figure, walking toward me.

"Good morning," she says.

I say, "Good night," and climb back into bed.

She brings her mummy bag, spreading it out while I say that there's only a little time left for sleep. I sound angry, I realize. Parental.

"Then sleep," she tells me.

I say nothing. I keep still, jealous and scared of my jealousy. My self-control isn't in danger, but I can feel my limits. I'm not going to let her split her affections, not like Effie does with her two men. . . . I make that promise to myself.

"Ranier?"

I pretend to have fallen asleep.

She touches me and then pulls her hand away, making a soft odd sound. I feel her watching me. Sometimes I feel her breath against my neck, very light and warm. Then I'm asleep without warning, never dreaming; and I wake in an instant, Service shouting, "Up and out! Up and out!"

I reach again, reflexively, my hand flat on the empty floor.

The planes find us at midday, on schedule. They resemble enormous greatnests as they pass over the open country. I watch their flight and how the clumsy flaps move, their propellers making noisy blurs. Some have cumbersome floats stuck to their bellies. Once, briefly, I notice one of the pilots glancing at me. That face and the long hair: she might be Snow's twin. They look that much alike. I wave to her; then the engine screams as the plane climbs, buying altitude so it can cross back over the green mountains.

We claim our shares, as always. I've got more than before, I notice; and it takes my brain a moment to realize the obvious. I have a fraction of Tintoil's share. I count the bricks a second time, thinking of her. I've never been much of a supporter of afterlives, yet I can't help but think of her as lonely, dead and buried and lonely in this enormous wilderness.

We walk hard through the endless afternoon.

Dust collects on the Remarkables, softening their color. There aren't any streams or working springs. Service has warned us. He warned me twice. "Conserve every swallow," he told me. But I drink without discipline, emptying my jugs. Then my thirst starts nagging at me, and my tongue thickens and grows raw.

Eventually it's as if I have always been thirsty. I can't remember any other state. My concentration suffers. My thoughts start to wander. Every subject leads to water—its feel and taste and perfect musical sound—and sometimes I catch myself watching other people, wondering how many full jugs they're carrying and how many sips I could beg from them.

I was stupid to drink everything.

I knew better. This is justice. Suffering is justice.

Then Lumiere comes up to me and says, "Here," without prompting. He hands me a sealed jug, the clear plastic filled with sunlight and warm clean water.

"Your last one?" I mutter.

He says, "Take it."

I'm already unscrewing the lid. "Just a sip . . ." But then I'm drinking and I can't stop myself. Intellect shouts, "No more!" but the reptile parts of my brain are in charge. Finally I peel the jug from my face, handing it back to him. Less than half the water remains, and I apologize.

"Keep it," he tells me.

Dehydration has narrowed his face, not giving him youth but instead producing a different kind of old age. I smell Lumiere's years in the hot dry air, sour and vivid and probably embarrassing him. He can smell himself, I realize. The poor gentleman.

"You need it more," he says, touching me with a cool hand.

"All right. I suppose." I drink the rest of it and lick my lips. They're still badly chapped, almost sharp to the touch, but I feel stronger now. Handing back the jug, I belch and say, "I owe you."

He pockets the jug and says nothing.

"We're making good progress," I offer. "Don't you think so?"

"I hope we are," he replies, smiling and then moving away.

We drop into a shallow wide valley, trees rising from the dusty earth, and a breeze comes from no clear direction. Small half-inflated leaves rattle against each other, and I think of sloppy music. I'm watching Mount Au with its silence and bulk and the snows like the cleanest white frostings imaginable, the clouds always forming around it and blowing westward, becoming distant and silvery before breaking apart and dissolving.

I nearly miss the splashing sounds ahead.

Then I pause and hold my breath, trying to find a direction. Straight ahead, isn't it? I break into a trot, my pack jerking at my spine. The Remarkables are rolling into a shallow stream. This is some bizarre vision of paradise. Water! I peel off my pack and kneel on the rocky bank, dipping my face into the chill of it. I nearly forget what is what. I suck in a mouthful and taste the wrongness, the sediments and alien bacteria; then I spit it out and mutter, "Filter it, idiot. Think. Think!"

It takes time and an amazing patience. I didn't know I could be so patient.

Meanwhile the Remarkables are drinking themselves sick. They submerge their mouths and gulp, the sounds sloppy and boisterous; and afterward they lift themselves as high as possible, tendrils stretching and their central organs above the water, and they drain their stomachs. Water is thrown up in geysers. They miss drinking so much, it seems, that they want to do it again and again.

The purging doesn't disgust me after a while.

It's part of the scenery, the ambience, and I've drained three jugs of my own. I feel strong enough to pitch twenty tents in the trees, I'm thinking; but first I open my pack and carefully eat Tintoil's dinner.

Almost nobody gathers at the fires tonight.

It's the heat, maybe. The general tiredness. I'm happy just to sit in the shade of a great old tree, bark like pink granite and strange seed-sacks strewn across the bare ground. Pachel comes past, carrying Tintoil's empty rifle. She says, "Hello," and nervously flexes her meaty forearms. I envy those genetics. She notices my expression, pauses, and asks, "What are you thinking?"

"I'm hoping we'll reach the mountain soon."

"Won't," she snarls. "It's a long walk still."

I'm thinking how the Pitcairns must be thrilled to have her eggs. Her gutty genes. In a few generations, with sweet luck, the Mount Au grove is going to be strong in countless ways. Salo would be a weakling. And what about the rest of our talents? We must have a few, I reason. Various flavors of intelligence; doses of creativity. And meanwhile other visitors will come to Pitcairn and leave their seed, every grove changing itself over time . . . over decades and centuries and longer. . . .

"Well," says Pachel, "good-bye."

I watch her walking away. She is going to meet Service, I realize; and with that I say, "Give him your best."

Maybe she's laughing, not looking back at me. Saying, "I will," and walking faster.

I watch the rhythms of the campsite—Remarkables absorbing the last of the sunshine; Effie and Goottich sitting under another pink-barked tree; Pitcairns in twos and threes bringing firewood and sharing dinners—and I hear someone walking up behind me. I turn slowly, seeing Briar. He doesn't notice me. His face is taut. He stares straight ahead, carrying his rifle up high. There seems to be nothing in his eyes.

I belch softly—

—and he wheels, his mouth dropping open. We scare each other; then he regains control and stares. Almost glowering at me.

"What?" I manage. "Were you scouting?"

"Hunting."

The man makes me uncomfortable. The feeling only gets worse when he breaks into a smile, telling me, "You picked a good place for tonight." His voice is friendly and well shined.

"I thought so," I tell him.

He says, "I was hunting upstream," and points.

"Any luck?"

"Plenty." He smiles again, saying, "The bad kinds of it."

"Tomorrow," I offer.

"There's that," he says.

Then he says, "I need my own tent up," and leaves.

I don't bother saying, "Good night." I watch his back, sweat soaking through the dusty shirt; I follow him into camp and then lose sight of him.

After a while comes the distinctive sound of tendrils on the ground, and Talker says, "Hello, Ranier."

I greet my friend, watching the eyes lift on their stalks.

"I can't tell you from the others," I admit. "I've tried, but you look the same to me. Almost exactly."

The eyes are watching everything, but most of them are pointed at the campsite. Not me; not the mountain. But at the Pitcairns.

"What do you think of this weather?" I ask.

"Many things, I think." Then it says, "But mostly it's just too damned hot."

34
DARKNESS

❖

I sleep on top of my bag, escaping the heat, then I awake and find the play of the light has changed. It's later in the evening, quiet and a little cooler. Where's Snow? On guard duty again? I can't remember, my eyes drifting shut and dreams beginning. I find myself standing before Mount Au, only the sky is the wrong blue and the barren land is reddish. This is Rye's World, I realize. New Albemarne is in the east, the black wafer of the jupiter is above, and what's Au doing here? Except it isn't. I blink and look again, finding nothing but scattered rock and rotting ice. Then I set to work, stacking rocks on top of one another. I'm building my own mountain, I realize, every rock huge but weighing nothing. After a while clouds begin collecting around its summit—

—and I awaken again, lifting my head and blinking.

Snow is kneeling beside me. After a muddy few seconds, it occurs to me that she's talking. I must be her audience, but my impression is that she has been talking for a long while. She says something about Remarkables. I'm still fighting sleep, forcing myself to breathe and clear away the remnants of the dream. And she says, "He spoke to them, before the selection—"

"Who did? Who?"

She almost looks at me, her eyes wrong and her posture stiff, and I can't tell just why I'm uneasy. I keep very still. It's dark enough outside for stars. I can barely make out her face, and Snow tells me, "They helped select us for this *passion*."

"The elders picked you," I manage. "You told me—"

"Twice," she says. "They picked me twice. But *they* helped the second time."

A different *they*, I realize.

"The elders made the first list. Service was on it. And me. Plus a lot of people qualified to go on this *passion*. It was going to be a small one, and the elders wanted the very best of us."

I look for pride in her face. A faint silvery light flows through the tent flap, but I can't see pride. Her face is blank. Impassive. Again she says, "The best of us," then shakes her head for a moment.

"Was Briar included?"

"No."

"Salo? You said he once went on a *passion*—"

"No, no." She shakes her head. I notice a thin sheen of perspiration on her forehead and the high cheeks. "Both of them were working on the piers, helping to unload the freezer ships."

I nod.

"This wasn't long ago. You were almost here, in fact, and we were planning our route and getting our equipment. It was like any *passion*. Service in charge, everything falling into place . . . and one day we were meeting, discussing plans, when an elder came. We were inside a common house, and she told Service, '*They* want to talk to you, now,' and we could see who she meant. Who was *they*. And of course Service left right away. When the Old Ones want to talk to you, you don't move slow—"

"The Old Ones?"

She makes a frustrated sound, quiet and restrained. "You don't really know how we are. You don't know . . . can't . . . that we have fun. That we laugh and joke, that we have songs and sometimes dance. When we're in the grove, in our homes—"

"What are you talking about, Snow?"

She shivers and explains, "Everyone was happy. People were coming from other worlds, from the strange Realm, and we were excited because we were the ones selected to take you to Au—"

"Excited? I haven't seen—"

"Listen," she warns me. "Will you?"

I shut up.

"Like it was yesterday, I remember seeing your pictures

and reading the little biographies Goottich sent us. Service had them and passed them around, and we joked about your funny faces and how you didn't look too crazy. Even if you were from the Realm, all of you looked sane." She pauses, hugging her knees close to her mouth. "I was thrilled to be selected. And surprised. For weeks I was practically floating, and my lovers teased me for daydreaming even worse than normal." Another pause. "Then we were in that meeting, in the common house, and the elder came and told Service that the Old Ones wanted to speak to him. And everyone became worried. Just like that. Not saying a word to each other, but everyone knowing that something was very, very strange. . . ."

I say nothing.

Snow tilts her head, and the silvery light shows her features more clearly. The cheeks aren't wet from perspiration, I realize, and her mouth quivers as she fights emotion. Her sadness is infectious. I feel it come into me, and I manage a ragged little breath, holding it deep inside.

Someone is walking past my tent.

I hear a branch crack underfoot, and Snow jerks her head. I'm looking at her profile, the mouth and tears. What's happening?

Whoever it is moves past, walking into the wood. We listen to the steps and then silence, apparently waiting for something, and maybe I'm afraid and maybe I'm sure this is nothing. I don't know what I believe. Then Snow turns to me, and she says:

"After a long while Service came back again."

He returned and said, "I'm sorry. There's a change of plans. We're going to use different people on this *passion*. Except for myself and Snow, we'll make a complete change."

Nobody is as good as Service at hiding emotions, and he almost managed the trick. She tells me how the corners of his eyes twitched while he spoke. Then someone interrupted, asking:

"Then who's going? If it's not us—"

He named names. The Au grove is huge, and some of the names were unfamiliar. But a few weren't. A few were authentically famous. This was unheard of, changing a *passion*'s people at the last instant; and when Snow knew who would be traveling with her and Service . . . well, she was stunned. Speechless and weak and cold.

"Criminals," I mutter.

"Yes," she says. Then, "No." Then finally, "Maybe. I don't know."

"What do you know?" I ask.

"Tintoil was supposed to be lazy. Shurgar is a thief. Most of us are one or the other," she claims. "Those aren't real crimes in the Realm, I bet. But for us—"

"I understand, Snow."

"Good Pitcairns are brave and selfless."

Like bees in a vast hive, I think. *Admirable for the same reasons.*

"Salo?" I ask. "What about him?"

"Salo." She shakes her head. "He may have done something awful. Something . . . awful. Remember that he went on an earlier *passion*? Well, he fought with another man. Like you fought with Bedford, only worse. Both were punished accordingly, and afterward Service made them scout ahead together. This was close to Au, in the green forests, and Salo came back one evening and said there'd been a tragedy. He was cut and bruised, telling everyone that his partner had fallen into a gorge and been killed—"

"Murder?" I whisper.

She says, "Maybe. Nobody knows."

Pitcairns killing their brethren . . . it seemed incredible. Against the natural order, wasn't it?

"Some think murder. Some think he just didn't warn his partner about the gorge. But nobody *knows* what really happened."

"And Briar?"

"Briar on a *passion*," she says. "That seemed too incredible. When I heard his name, my first thought was that we were all being punished for crimes. Even Service. The Old Ones remembered when Service tried to kick them, and they were finding a justice years later."

"What about Briar? Is he a murderer too?"

"No, no." She shakes her head. "But he has a temper. He's got ideas about being famous and admired by everyone, and he resents any person more important than him. That's why he's been in so many fights. That's why he's been close to being banished maybe a dozen times."

"Has he?"

"Only he slips free at the last instant. Does something good. Talks nice to some elders. Whatever it takes." She sighs and says, "He's very clever, Ranier."

"He looks a lot like Service," I mention.

She says nothing.

"Is Service his father?"

She acts shocked, gawking at me. "They're not even that related. No. You're talking about . . . he's not Service's son . . . that's silly—"

There comes a sound—a distant almost-soft *pop* followed by silence—and Snow sits straighter with a hand running through her long hair. Once, then again. Then a slow third time.

I say nothing.

She says, "What I think, and what a lot of people think, is that the Old Ones became too scared to keep quiet. Taking visitors like you on a *passion*, living with Pitcairns for months on end . . . they imagined problems coming from it. You bringing the wrong ideas. And them not trusting us enough. The best people in the grove, and they decided that they couldn't let us go with you—"

"They talked to Service."

"And the elders too. The Old Ones named names, and the elders made their choices. Nobody but them knows just what was said, but that's what we guess happened. 'Please take criminals,' they said. 'People the grove won't miss, if they die. Or listen to, should they come home again.' "

Or listen to, I think. *People unadmired. Sure.*

I hear more gunfire in the distance. I flinch, sweat rolling into my eyes, cool and sudden, and I wipe at them. Then I'm hearing the Remarkables talking to themselves, sounding like a flock of agitated birds about to burst into flight.

Snow touches me, her hand wet.

She's crying, telling me, "Briar has been making trouble. Even before you came, he was talking to people, warning that we'd have disasters and the visitors would be weak and slow. That if something happened to Service, then people would have to choose."

"Choose?"

She tries to speak, to explain, but there comes an explosion. The concussion makes my tent vibrate, and I hear shouts afterward. Then nothing. I listen and wait, and Snow says:

"I should have stayed home."

Her voice is plaintive. Weak as I have never heard it.

"We've got to choose," she whispers; then there are more shots, quick and sharp.

I start to move, finding my trousers and her grabbing one leg, telling me, "Don't. You're safer here."

I jerk free, climbing outside and finding my boots. Then I'm running toward the smoky little camp fires, the boots loose on my feet and flopping.

"Stay down!" calls Snow. "Ranier—?"

Figures gather about one fire, and the Remarkables are moving behind them. Tendrils and eyes seem agitated. There's one last squawk of gunfire, and the echoes fall away. Goottich stands by the fire. All my associates are waiting. I move more slowly, watching them and everything else. Nothing seems too unusual or out of place. Mount Au covers the southern horizon. The Pitcairn moon is nearly full, hanging beside the mountain with its cratered face gazing down at us. I was dreaming about Au, wasn't I? What was I dreaming? The first thin trace of dawn is illuminating the high clouds, golden and showing the delicate vaporous folds within them.

"Do *you* know what's happening?" asks Effie.

Snow isn't behind me.

Effie says my name, her voice sharp and anxious.

I'm smelling smoke, but the camp fire smells wrong. Then I realize it's the smoke of munitions carried by the warm night breeze. My associates are watching me, waiting for some answer. Again Effie says, "What's happening, Ranier?"

"I have no idea," I lie.

Bedford says, "It's a little attack."

The words sound practiced and fragile.

I turn to the Remarkables, gazing at the eyes.

"There's no need to be scared," Bedford tells Effie.

She's standing beside Goottich. She tells her husband, "Just leave me alone. All right?"

"A cretin or two," Bedford continues. "That's all it is."

Then Goottich is smiling. Maybe he was always smiling, I realize. But I notice the expression now; and quietly, between deep wet breaths, he tells everyone, "No, there aren't any cretins. And this isn't an attack . . . believe me . . . !"

TALKER

Every sibling was talking fast, with noise and with tendrils, with their nervous voices telling each other, "As foreseen! As the Old Ones described it! Rebellion among our own dear people . . . treachery as never known, never imagined—" Untrue, untrue. "—and this is the Future. Disaster! Ruin, hopeless and infinite . . . !"

Hysteria is what it was.

Hysteria. I warned them, "We still have countless Futures, siblings. None are assured. The Old Ones described a tapestry of them—"

"Murder! Murder! Murder!" They were terrified by what they imagined as real. Sounds are real, but beside the sounds we knew nothing. Know nothing. Everything happens beyond our sight, and I cried out:

"Silence! Silence!"

But they refused to stop moaning, some actually cursing the humans. And cursing their own imagined fates. "Just as the Old Ones promised," they said time after endless time. "Briar is leading the rebellion against Service!"

"SILENCE!" I screamed.

Then I informed them, "Or I return home with nothing but tales of your cowardice. How the most important *passion* was at its most important juncture, and all you could do was bemoan what might be. Things only the All-Answer sees with certainty. That is my promise—!"

"If you somehow survive," snapped one of the siblings. "If what follows spares you!"

And I said, "It will."

I told them, "You are stupid children. Be quiet."

Then I said nothing more, leading by example. Culturing a watchful silence, I made the others calm down. As they are now. The panic is past; we accept our duty here. Like me, my siblings absorb everything they hear and see. The people and the land. What was once the Future, almost unknowable, and what is now Now. And now, an instant later, the Past.

35
NEW COMMAND

✦

People are approaching. Briar, I realize. And Salo. Then Shurgar and several others. I can tell from their postures and motion that something has changed. They hold their rifles with purpose, ready for anything; and they keep apart as if nobody wants to walk in anyone else's tracks.

Lumiere is beside me. He touches me and says nothing.

"Was it a cretin?" asks Bedford. He's nervous and forcefully cheery, rubbing his hands together as if warming them. "We heard noise. Did something happen?"

"Something, all right," Briar answers, nodding gravely.

The Pitcairns come around us. Their nervousness seeps out. Fingers twitch; eyes dance in their sockets. They start turning in circles while Briar says, "A big cretin . . . and we had a casualty." He's intense, as always, but the voice is too quick. His words seem to slide together, him telling us, "Someone got themselves killed. . . ."

"Who?" asks Pachel.

Briar says, "Our dear leader," and gives a great sigh.

Pachel doesn't seem to hear him. Maybe her face stiffens, but otherwise she doesn't speak or move.

Effie moans aloud.

Bedford draws some quick circles.

What's Goottich thinking? He's gazing at Briar, his expression sober and calculating. The tiny eyes smile. Then he asks, "So who's in charge?" with his voice anxious, the smile spreading from the eyes.

"We'll have to vote," says Briar. "Vote in a new leader."

Salo begins waving his rifle in the air, shouting, *"Come! Come!"* His sleeves are rolled up past his elbows, his forearms and triceps massive. I feel intimidated, hopelessly out of place. One and then two and then several cretins streak across the grass. Our cretins. They come straight to Salo, and he says, "Sit." They stop and sit. Five of them, I count. The one with the odd gray leg is missing.

"Where's his body?" asks Pachel.

Nobody speaks.

Salo steps in front of the cretins, and I feel my heart against my ribs. It pounds and twists and lifts inside me.

"Where is Service's body?"

I turn as Briar says, "Lost." I notice that the Remarkables are silent, bunched into a single mass and motionless. They look as if they are specimens dipped into some night-colored glass.

"Lost how?" says Pachel.

"The cretin grabbed him, then ran."

"Ran where?"

People start to watch Pachel.

Briar tells her, "I've got people hunting for the corpse." Then he steps closer to us. I hear his breathing, thin and quick, and he watches us while saying, "Salo? Where's the other one?"

He means the sixth cretin.

"Lost," says the big Pitcairn. "The same as Service."

Nobody speaks.

I feel sick. My guts are full of nectar and nervous gas, and I start massaging my belly.

Then Briar says, "Don't wait. Do it now."

Salo shoots a cretin in the head. It drops hard with its skull shattered, the entire body limp and down and Effie giving a little shout, backing into Goottich.

The other cretins stay seated, eyeing their dead comrade.

Salo shoots again.

The three survivors begin to fidget, and he tells them, "Stay," and shoots a third one.

Finally someone interrupts. Bedford asks, "What . . . what are you doing . . . ? I don't understand. . . ."

"We don't need them now," says Briar. His voice is calm and knowing, and he makes sure that we see him shrugging his shoulders.

Salo places the rifle barrel between bright red eye patches, and the yellow eyes gaze at him without blinking.

He shoots again; I jerk with the *bang*.

One cretin remains. Its simple obedient brain struggles with what it sees. It starts flipping its head from side to side as Salo aims. He says, "Stay," once again. He says, "No . . . heel!" The cretin neither fights nor tries to run; but at the last instant it yelps and drops its head, the bullet tearing through flesh and the top of the skull. I feel the impact, the searing pain. The cretin howls and shakes its head in agony, a thin warm spattering of blood everywhere. Finally it rubs the head into the long grass. As if the blood is an annoyance; as if it's trying to dry its head.

Salo says, "Fuck," and shoots twice. Then his rifle *clicks*, and he reloads with a new clip.

Briar watches, his face stony and his mouth set. Yet the eyes seem lost. It's as if he's working to remember what needs to be done next. *What?* Then he finds himself, gesturing and telling nobody in particular, "Give them the carcasses. Don't waste the meat."

A murmur passes through the Remarkables.

Briar glances at them, his eyes changing. Then he says, "Goottich," and slowly turns. "Come here, Goottich. Walk this way. Just you. Right now."

Snow appears. She carries one of my shirts and asks if I want it. Am I cold? I take it while watching her face— the thin sad smile and her eyes focused on the ground— trying to guess her mind. Then Goottich returns and I forget to put on the shirt. I stand with it pressed against my bare chest, arms crossed; and Goottich tells us, "A change of plans."

What scares me most is the transcendent joy he extrudes.

He holds a much-folded map, saying, "There's a deep long lake several days from here, toward the southeast. Since we'll need a lot of water for the shuttle, we'll go there and make the signal—"

"Now?" says Bedford. "Why do we need the shuttle now?"

"Because," he says. "Because they've decided to accept my gracious offer."

Pachel says, "With Service dead."

Goottich shrugs. "I know, and it's too bad." He shrugs again. "But since Briar's in charge—"

"Is he?" Pachel approaches Snow. "Aren't we supposed to have a vote first? Are those the rules?"

Snow rocks where she stands, then says, "Yes," with a flat voice.

"And we're part of this *passion*. We have votes!"

Snow opens her mouth to answer; then Shurgar starts to bang pots together, the noise rhythmic and insistent.

"This is shit!" Pachel declares.

Snow looks past us, finding Briar and saying his name one time. Her voice is weak, more a whisper than anything. "What happened out there?" she asks him.

He looks at Snow, blinks, and says, "I don't know. It was a mess, but we're out of danger. Everything's taken care of."

How can Service be dead? I feel sadness, the sourness in my guts worsening, and I belch and taste something awful at the back of my mouth. Salo and another Pitcairn have dragged the cretins to the Remarkables, but they won't eat. Their only motion is to pull themselves into a denser mass of interlocking bodies.

I mutter, "Shit," under my breath.

"You shot Service, didn't you?"

Pachel is talking to Briar. She doesn't hesitate, stepping toward him and placing a hand on his chest, his rifle between them and her arm pushing at him. "You did, didn't you?"

"No, I did not."

Briar's reply is followed by his own shove, then he makes himself laugh in disgust and look our way. "A crazy, irresponsible lie! That's what that is . . . !"

Pachel knows something. I sense it.

Again she presses against Briar, using both hands this time and giving him a hard push, grunting once, saying, "You murdered him. It was staged, this attack was . . . for you to take control . . . asshole!"

Salo grabs hold of Pachel, almost lifting her from the ground.

"Careful," he warns. "You'll get in trouble, making crazy noise."

She pulls free, snapping at him. "Let me go!"

I glance at Snow, and I think: *Enough*.

She dips her head, gazing at her toes.

I turn to Goottich and tell him, "This is going to stop."

"What is?"

"First of all," I say, "the gloating."

"I'm not gloating," he says through an enormous toothy grin. "And don't imply that I'm in any way responsible—"

"You fucking started this mess! That's responsible!"

He looks at me as if amazed. "And how, Ranier? What did I do to bring a cretin down on us? Tell me that."

"First, by offering what you did. Enticing these people with stories about building some new Pitcairn."

He laughs and wags the thick finger at me. "I resent your assessment. I made an offer in good faith, to people and to aliens alike, and it just so happens that tragedy has made this possible. By the sheerest chance."

"Before," I remind him, "you said it wasn't an attack."

"I misinterpreted the evidence," he claims. Then he looks at everyone as if horrified, asking, "Do you believe that *I* wished anyone any ill? Any ill at all?"

Pachel approaches him, saying, "I think so. I know so—"

He's more frightened of her than of me. His expression changes, the gloating smile subdued and his big legs moving backward.

"Oh, yes, you're happy. Shitass . . . !"

"Leave him alone," Effie tells her. "You've no right to judge."

Stepping between them, the tiny woman looks fierce and maybe startled by her fury. Bony fists swipe at the air, and she says, "This isn't our business. Quit it! It's between *them*, not us. Them!"

Bedford says, "Dear," and approaches.

"Go away!"

He halts and then hugs himself. I expect him to draw circles, either in the dirt or the air; but he does nothing except back up and stand close to the fire.

"It isn't happening," says Lumiere. "Are we walking to this lake . . . getting on board the shuttle, just like that . . . ?"

I want to tell him, "No."

"This isn't happening," he sobs.

I can't speak now.

"But we're taking Pitcairn with us," Goottich replies. He seems ready to dance for joy. Effie grabs one of his arms and squeezes, and he engulfs her and kisses the top of her head, saying, "Think what this means! The history of it!"

Pachel starts for Briar once again.

He stands motionless until she reaches for him. She wants to shove him off his feet, but he moves too fast, grabbing a wrist and pulling her over his leg, onto her butt while keeping hold of the wrist. He works at twisting it, telling her, "You're right. You can vote, old lady. You and your friends belong here. Select who you want in charge. Be my guest."

I feel the pain shooting along her arm. She has no position, not a bit of leverage. But Pachel refuses to make any sound or in any way submit to him.

Then Briar lets go, screaming at the Remarkables.

"Eat that meat! Go on!" He gestures at the dead cretins, telling them, "You've got two choices. A long life in the sky, or a shorter one here. So why not chew on them, huh?"

Tendrils extend, grasping at the carcasses and pulling them out of sight.

"Yes, yes!" he laughs. "I knew you would! I knew!"

Dawn spreads down from Mount Au, over the plain, darkness becoming a translucent green that fades fast in the heat. The other Pitcairns return from their patrols, no body discovered; and something vaguely resembling an election is held. Briar is the sole declared candidate. Every Pitcairn votes for him. Even Snow, I realize. She seems sick at the thought, yet compliant. Silent, yet aware enough to lift one hand head-high.

Goottich makes a show of voting for Briar, and Effie happily does the same. "A few more days, and we're gone," she crows. "The best news in a long time, if you ask me!"

Briar squints at the rising sun, then announces that we are breaking camp immediately.

"I think everyone is tired," says Bedford.

Briar glares at him, learning that's all it takes to intimidate him. Then he smiles at the man, suggesting, "Eat your way awake. Whatever. Because we are leaving now."

His expression seems hard and cutting.

I pack in a blur, my hands knowing the routine and my head aching. I want to sleep. I want the safety of unconscious dreamless long sleep. I'm furious with Goottich for dangling his carrot. I knew he had something in mind, but I should have guessed it. I should have preempted this somehow, I decide. Yet my mind can't come up with any scenario where I convince him to think again. Where I make the slightest difference in these events.

More than I would have guessed, I'm affected.

Service ambushed by his own people . . . by Pitcairns! What an incredible, impossible mess!

We start to leave. A single greatnest is hunting in the south, again perfectly framed by the mountain. I'm walking fast, and Pachel is beside me. Not close. But after a while, when everyone is spread out on the plain, she closes the gap and says, "Look at their faces. When they aren't looking at you."

"Whose?" I'm stupid with exhaustion.

"Briar's or anyone's."

The aliens are rolling gracefully, and I smell the kicked-up dusts and sometimes their rich farts. I can't find any Pitcairns who are close enough. Not just now—

"They're scared," she whispers.

"Are they?"

"Why do you think they're scared?" she wonders aloud. "And why do you think they killed the cretins? As a precaution, maybe?"

"Really?"

"He *knew*," she promises me.

"Service—?"

"The cretins would listen to Service first, given a choice. Out of habit, they'd obey him." She is speaking almost too softly for me to hear. "And he knew what Briar was doing."

As did Snow, I think.

Pachel glances at the countryside, nodding with a certain eerie calm. "I can feel him watching us now," she assures me. "Waiting. Planning his revenge."

36
SILENCE

❖

We stop at midday, the sun above Au and the mountain's clouds brilliant and thick, sculpted into endless shapes by high cold winds. The Remarkables begin basking, as always, and people seem determined to reacquire routines. We sit and carve up bricks of nectar, eating mechanically, then lie back and try sleeping. But Briar comes past, saying, "We're leaving. Up! Move!" He seems to hover over me, hands on hips and his expression touching frustration. Only when I'm standing do I realize he's not looking at me. Several Pitcairns are halfheartedly climbing from cover in a shadowy crevice. Once in the open they move like nervous targets, trying to use the Remarkables as shields.

We move steadily, but never as fast as Briar wants. And Goottich has trouble even holding our pace, taking impromptu breaks by propping himself against treetrunks, hands on the meaty thighs. I walk past him once, him gasping, his face soaked and the perspiration coming through his shirt; and I can't resist saying, "We'll leave you behind."

"You won't," he growls.

I stop and stare at him. The eyes are tiny and bottomless and thoroughly amoral. Squirrel eyes, I think. I try to hate him but fall short. He scares me and keeps me anxious, but something is lacking. Hate doesn't stick to him. It's like trying to hold an animal responsible for its essential nature.

"I don't care what you think," he warns me. The laboring voice is thick and a little angry.

"You'll have legal troubles," I warn him. "The courts aren't going to like this mess—"

"Service got eaten. That's the story."

"I'm promising you, Goottich. I'll make trouble."

The amoral eyes grin, and the big mouth clamps shut. He shakes his head for a moment. Then he tells me, "You're too far down the trophic levels. You can't do anything."

Probably true, but I don't so much as blink.

Then Goottich makes a satisfied sound, jerking himself upright and asking me, "Did the tree leak? You see any sap?" As if we were friends. Or more likely, as if he can't take my hostilities seriously. "Anything?"

"Nothing," I say. "You're clean."

Sap from the tree has made a huge glossy stain on his pack, soaking through the fabric, and I'm smiling to myself. Petty victories are all that are available to me now.

I'm thinking about the Children of Pain. About my priestess lover. About the lessons she would give me as we walked inside the enworld church, her compassionate voice giving encouragement and then little hints about how to tolerate the suffering around me.

I could feel every ache then. The tiniest simplest worm writhing in a bird's mouth, and it felt as if a piece of my flesh were captured. There were no countermeasures, no buffers. Sometimes the enworld seemed to be brimming full of agonies; and we'd have to stop our walk while I knelt, hands over my ears and her assuring me, "That's no way to come to terms with Pain. You must face it. Embrace it. Accept it and let its purity work into your soul, purifying you."

I hated her when she spoke that way.

Once or twice I cursed at her, trying to wound; and afterward, with the frustratingly patient voice, she told me, "Try to listen between the Pains. To the silences between . . . will you, Ranier? Focus on those silences. . . ."

That is what I'm thinking when I happen upon Salo. The big Pitcairn stands motionless, his gaze fixed on the Remarkables. "The silences between," I mutter to myself. And he looks at me, his face not as young as I guessed, lines in the skin and something deeper showing in this light.

"What did you say?"

He is watching the Remarkables. *Why?*

He says, "What did you tell me?"

"You're looking for Talker, aren't you? You want to know which of them—"

"Shut up," he snaps.

Then I understand. "Talker is a problem," I say. "Am I right? It's an enemy of yours. A Remarkable, so it knows its people. Its symbionts."

He shuts his eyes and opens them again.

"Maybe it's working on your associates," I speculate. "Right this minute, Talker is saying the right words to the weak Pitcairns. The ones who are having second thoughts. The ones who are wondering if Briar can lead us anywhere—"

Suddenly Salo grabs me, squeezing and twisting. I drop from the pain, gasping but satisfied.

"You've got little bones," he says as if amazed. "Little damn bird bones."

"And you're scared," I whisper.

He walks off without another word, and I rise and brush at my trousers. *Which one is Talker?* I wonder. *And what if they find it? Another accident? Or maybe they'll just force it to sleep in the open, alone and exposed? Sure food for any sprintbear. . . .*

I whisper, "Talker?"

Nothing responds.

Joining the general flow of people and aliens, I think about the priestess and her advice about silences. It has been years since I bothered remembering any of this. But what was nightmarish before suddenly has a beauty, a sense of purpose only slightly twisted. I find myself missing the priestess and those circumstances. In memory, pain is never as big as it is when it happens. Time softens. I'm learning that. A century old, and finally I'm learning.

Our campsite is beside a little spring, the country open on every side and a strong dry wind blowing through the grass. For a little while I try sitting at the lone fire. Nobody speaks. Half the Pitcairns are walking the perimeter, protecting us from unspecified terrors. Bless them. The others maintain their durable silence, faces tired and something not unlike fear leaking out of them. Something I can smell more than see.

Eventually Lumiere says, "Sleep time," with a thick voice. He rises and glances at me, his expression sick with worry.

"Good night," I offer reflexively.

He wants to talk. I know from the tilt of his head. He's hungry to voice his despair, perhaps asking for my advice. What will he do? If we leave for the torchship in a few days . . . what are his options . . . ?

I don't want to talk about his dead wife now.

That's why I don't join him, and when Lumiere is gone, I rise and head for my tent. I pass the Remarkables on the way. I say, "Good night, Talker." They pivot their eyes, following me. The wind blows through them, making soft-edged whistling noises. That's all I hear. Then I climb into bed and watch the tent walls lift, the gusts inflating my little home. I'm too tired to sleep, I'm certain. Too nervous. Too hot. But then I shut my eyes and vanish from this world entirely.

Snow wakes me, kissing my forehead with dry lips.

I jerk awake—"What? What?"—and she sits above me, watching my panic without trying to comfort me. In the pale gray light she looks spent, the pretty face drawn out and one lip tucked into her mouth. She chews on the lip; my composure returns. Then she matter-of-factly reaches into my bag, stroking me while staring at my eyes.

She quits after a little while.

"Did you see Service?" I ask.

And she replies, "Service was killed last night."

"Snow." I sound deeply disappointed. Shaking my head, I tell her, "You know what's happening. Don't lie."

"Do you hate me?"

She asks the question as if it is data. Not something that injures.

I tell her, "No," but I'm not sure what I feel. I'm on my back, watching her, and I realize that the wind has dropped to nothing and outside is a strange new stillness, the grasses rigidly upright and the cooling night air punctuated with insect sounds—buzzes and murmurs and cricketing noises in the distance.

"I didn't know what they were planning," she begins.

"Suspected, yes. But Briar decided not to include me. He knew better."

"You told Service what you suspected?"

She says, "No."

"Why not?"

"If I think something's wrong, the Remarkables know it. And so does Service. He had to know."

"Then why didn't he do something?" I inquire.

"Like what? Banish everyone? Destroy the *passion* himself?" Snow places her hands on her face, pulling at the skin while making a quiet keening noise. "All he could do is wait and watch Briar, hoping to ruin him in front of the others. That's how he would think."

"And what do you think?"

She seems ready to cry and then doesn't, sniffling and pulling her hands to her lap. "I want to go with you," she remarks.

"Pardon?"

She stares outside, chewing on the lip again.

"You want to go where with me?"

"I don't care."

"What do you feel for me?"

"When I saw you? The picture of you?" In my file, I recall. She drops her face to her knees, her head turning away; and after a minute she says, "I knew you. I already knew you."

"How?"

"And then I saw you on the boat, and it was strange. Confusing. I could barely keep my face under control—"

"How did you know me, Snow?"

"I had a book . . . when I was a girl. A children's story that I'd read over and over. It was about an angel who brings good luck to good Pitcairns. An angel with your hair and almost your face. Almost. I remember the pictures in the glass pages. I'd read that book every day, sitting on my mother's lap. And the Remarkables would read it over our shoulders. Every day. Just like they notice everything."

I say nothing.

"The Old Ones saw me looking at your picture," she explains, "and they know me. Not perfectly. Nothing knows anyone perfectly. But I'm . . . I'm famous. I daydream much too much. I do my work, but sometimes a lot of me is off somewhere, I'm not sure where. . . . I'm just not a very good Pitcairn, in some ways. . . ."

"What do the Old Ones have to do with this?" I ask.

"They guessed how I'd feel about you, Ranier. That I'd be tempted. My angel comes, and the elders decided to let me be tempted. To test me. And Service made me your partner to make it even worse."

"Honestly," I declare, "I never sensed any of this."

She breathes deeply, holding her breath.

"Why sleep with me?"

She sighs.

"If I was such an awful test—?"

"The sex?" She looks at me until I nod, then says, "Sex made it better. It really helped."

"How?"

"You snore in your sleep, and angels don't snore. You aren't as sweet a lover as I'd hoped—"

"Oh?"

"—and up close . . . well, you don't seem angelic." She starts to laugh without conviction, then stops and presses her hands together. She straightens her back, then says, "Nobody has died. Only poor Tintoil, and she would have died on Goottich's fancy world. The same way. Goottich wants to make it all the same."

Nobody has died.

The logic gnaws at me, weakening my resolve. Service is alive and safe. With one cretin? And whatever he can carry, I suppose. And in a few days we'll lift out of his reach, safe as well.

"Nobody has even been hurt," she tells me. "And nobody needs to be hurt. This could be for the best."

I keep trying to think, trying for clarity or at least something resembling it.

Finally I tell her, "I don't know."

She looks at my hands, saying nothing.

"It isn't over," I say. "Service is going to try something. I mean, this is his *passion*, and he's serving the grove. If he's half the Pitcairn people seem to think, I think you'll have to kill him sometime."

She looks ill. Shaking her head, she sobs and says, "I don't care anything about Goottich's world. Not at all."

"Good," I reply.

"And I'm not going to kill anyone."

I say nothing.

"And everything might turn out for the best, with sweet luck. It might."

I watch her face and reach out, gently running my fingertips along the horizontal throat scar. I don't know this person. I could sleep with her for a hundred years, never seeing past what she allows me to see; and maybe that's part of her attraction. That sense of never comprehending—

—and she glares at me, saying, "It's not easy. Believe me, this couldn't be any worse for me!" She slaps down my hand and crawls through the flap, vanishing, her boots crunching on the grass and me keeping perfectly still, listening to her being swallowed by the insect sounds and the dark cool silences between.

37
SIDES TAKEN

◆

Bedford hangs near me like smoke.

We've walked hard for several hours, without breaks, and sometimes he moves close enough to speak to me, saying nonsense about the weather or a blistered toe, or sometimes saying nothing. He smiles without life and seems to float, and I don't say anything meant to chase him away. I can't. This morning, in full view of everyone, Effie climbed from Goottich's tent wearing nothing but a long shirt and boots. Then Goottich emerged, resplendent in the afterglow. We watched him buttoning his shirt as he walked toward the fire, then he tucked it into his trousers, saying, "My waist seems thinner." He grinned, asking his audience, "Do I look lighter? Can you tell?" and the grinning eyes ended up on Bedford. "Or maybe it's dehydration. What do you think?"

I feel sorry for Bedford, even when he's a pest. Even when he starts to apologize for not appreciating . . . well, my condition. "I just should have been more sensitive, Ranier." He wants to form a pact based on mutual sympathy. Nodding, he tries a weak smile, asking, "Do you feel anything? Any nearby pain?"

"Nothing important," I say with disinterest. Flickers and flutters. "Not since the last attacks, really."

"That sect, the Children of Pain . . . I guess I don't see their appeal."

"I don't want to talk about this now."

He says, "Oh, sure," and moves his walking stick to the other hand. "What shall we discuss?"

"Nothing," I suggest.

We walk in silence for a little ways, dust in the air and the liquid-thick wind holding the heat. The Remarkables are rolling steadily, then they halt as if on some signal. We stop as well and stand motionless until Shurgar comes back, telling us, "A quick break," as she passes.

Bedford waits, then says, "I'm working not to be bitter, Ranier."

His voice has changed. His expression is desperately sober, lips pursed and the changed voice saying, "I don't want to be angry with them. That's important to me. I know I'm not a profound being. And I know you don't approve of my beliefs. But I am struggling here, trying to do what's proper."

"Good for you."

"Effie hasn't loved me for a long time, I think." He drops his face and blows air through his pursed lips. "She's entitled to improve her life. Everyone has that right."

I feel uncomfortable, gazing at my own boots.

"New beginnings, new possibilities."

I warn him, "This isn't my kind of pain."

"No?"

He sounds as if he doesn't believe me. Looking for an escape, I dig my shovel and toilet paper out of my pack, and he tells me, "Maybe we've been insensitive about the pain around us. Terraformers have. I think you might be right, Ranier."

"Just a minute—"

"Maybe we can minimize the suffering somehow. What do you think? Nanots of different kinds implanted in every nervous system, making the miseries go away. . . ."

"Bedford," I say, "all I want now is normalcy. Nothing bigger than that."

He nods as if trying to comprehend.

And I feel as if I told some lie just now. That tinge of guilt; that sense of being transparent to someone. Am I lying? I honestly don't know. Walking away, I think about it and think about it. Then I push the whole issue deep into my mind.

There's wooded ground nearby. Entering the shadows makes me feel better, the cool damp air seeping into me and refreshing my senses. I walk just far enough to be out of easy view, then kneel and dig my latrine.

Something moves when I set aside the shovel. I lift my head slowly, with a surprising composure. Yellow eyes stare at me without life or heat, and the glossy black nose sucks up my odor and holds it. I notice the gray leg, the eye patches and throat patch and the vivid red tongue swirling in the air. *Service is close*, I realize. *Probably watching me.* I start to look through the undergrowth and up into the trees, knowing I won't see him. He won't let me. But I want to show him my face, if only to make certain that he sees the earnest concern.

No one has died.

Then the cretin hears something. A whistle, maybe. A bird. I don't know the sound, but suddenly it turns and pads away. It floats into the underbrush, suddenly gone; and for a few moments, in an unexpected fashion, I wish I had followed. I feel as if I missed my last chance.

"When the time comes," says Lumiere, "can you give me your rations? Once we reach this lake . . . ?"

I look at him for a moment. "You're going to go on by yourself?"

He nods. He says, "I don't have any choice. One way or another, I at least have to try."

Alone. Walking alone toward the mountain, carrying his dead wife inside his head . . . and I know better than to speak of reason and other chances. Watching his eyes moisten, I promise him, "I'll give you whatever I've got left. All of it."

"Thank you," he whispers softly.

Pachel approaches the little fire. Tonight our campsite is at the base of an eroded cliff, and we quit early because of the general exhaustion. The Remarkables haven't basked for any time, nor have they eaten. Their pigments are fading again. Almost every Pitcairn is scouting the local terrain, chasing shadows. Snow told me that someone found tracks left by the gray-legged cretin. She's scouting with the others, only she won't do anything if she finds Service. She told me so. "I'm just protecting us from enemy cretins. That's all. I've told Briar, several times. . . ."

"We need to do something about this mess," Pachel informs us.

Lumiere also knows about Service being alive, but it gives him no hope. He won't let it.

She says, "We need to help him!"

"We're not in any position," I warn her. "What can we do?"

"Try to think. Give me that much effort."

But nothing seems workable. Lumiere is resigned to setting off by himself. Making legal problems for Goottich is my best strategy. Bedford joins us, and he responds to Pachel by saying, "Both sides should declare a truce, then meet to discuss compromises."

"Compromises?" Pachel laughs scornfully. "I don't think anyone's in the mood for negotiations."

"But maybe the Remarkables would like to leave," he counters. "Has anyone asked them?"

I can't envision Talker agreeing to any compromise. Nor would Service. I don't even know where you'd begin to heal the wounds.

"We need something," says Pachel.

"But we could make things worse," Lumiere cautions. "If we do anything foolish, we could pay."

"We're part of this *passion*," Pachel responds. "We're accountable. We help Service, or we're against him."

Lumiere shakes his head helplessly. "What can the man accomplish? Can he call for help? All he's carrying is that radio beacon, and the next airdrop isn't for many days. He has a rifle and some bombs, perhaps—"

"And he knows this terrain," Pachel adds.

"Don't the others?"

"Not like him," I interject.

"Just watch Briar." Pachel grins. "He's always referring to his maps. And asking Salo questions. Only Salo's never been in this area, and he's just as lost as the others."

I look at the dark eyes and the proud secure angle of her mouth. Pachel drives the blunt end of a stick into our fire, scattering bright coals. I smell smoke and my own filthy clothes. I want to get away from these people, yet I can't find the juice to lift myself to my feet.

"People fighting people," says Bedford. "It's horrible."

"You know," warns Pachel, "Service will do *anything* to stop us. I know him that well. Don't doubt it!"

We say nothing.

"Sleep on it," she advises. Then she rises and marches away without another word.

"How much harder can it get?" asks Lumiere.

Bedford coughs and rises as well.

I look at my hands, finding that they're shaking. How

long have they been shaking? I try wiping them on my
trousers, then on the ground. Then I rub them against one
another, hard enough to make them sweat and make their
calluses tear into softer flesh, a comfortable ache reaching
down to my bones.

Effie climaxes.

Goottich's tent is nearby, and I look outside, half expecting
her groans to have knocked the snow from Au. Then they're
done, and I hear nothing but quiet talking too soft to understand. There's no tone of endearment. Just talk. I wonder if
the big shit feels anything for the girl. Maybe she's a convenient bit of plumbing. Another repository for his sperm. Her
intrigued by his wealth; and him glad to be intriguing. A perfect disaster accelerating out of control: That's them.

I try sleeping, but I can't. I start to relax, eyes closed,
but there is a sudden bright chill and the telltale shivering. I recognize the symptoms. My first thought is *Knobhead*, but the feeling is wrong. It's familiar, but in a
different way. Then I think about Snow. Where is she? I
haven't seen her since we made camp. I climb outside and
pull on my trousers, running into the gray near-night.

The pain worsens, gaining body and brightness.

I pick up my pace, forgetting my bare feet. A long figure
sits beside the fire, entirely unaware; and I come up from
behind, cutting my heel on the rocks. I can scarcely see through
my sweat. I blink and blink, crying out, "Where's Snow?"

The girl turns, asking, "What do you want?"

I look at Snow, breathing and feeling relief build.

She asks the question again. What do I want?

I nearly tell her that someone's in agony. I don't know
who—I can't discriminate that well—but she sees my face
and understands.

Leaping to her feet, she shouts, "Wait here. Wait."

She runs and pauses, then whistles sharply. Then she
vanishes, and I look up at the sky. More people are whistling, a ring of them. But one direction is silent. It's where
the pain lies, I realize. Above the pain the moon is dipping
behind the high clouds, filing them with its weightless silvery light; and suddenly I'm feeling nothing but my own
skin, the heat of the fire, and the heat of my poor cut heel.

TALKER

❖

Service stands on the crest of a knoll, knowing each of us can see him. Speaking to us with his face illuminated by reflected moonglow. Talking fast and his hard determined eyes telling as much as his words.

"This is what I'll do," he says to us.

I will succeed, say the eyes.

"This is my plan," says the mouth.

Briar is doomed, the eyes promise.

The Old Ones described countless Futures to us, creating a tapestry of possibilities. Now the tapestry is simpler. Our *passion's* future has new boundaries, clearer prospects. Some good, some awful. None of the Old Ones' stories seem to be embodied here. But they are not the All-Answer, after all. They were guessing, and guesses are by their nature wrong. The simplest vibrant circumstances lead into grayness, and grayness into the unknown.

"Starting tomorrow," says the mouth.

The eyes close and open again, drawing energy from the man's great will. Then he waves an arm at us—a human gesture meant to reassure—and we notice myriad details. The rolled-up sleeve, surprisingly neat, and the wiry forearm muscles. The timepiece always worn on the wrist—I read its numbers and watch the slow transformation of the seconds—and the hard old hand clenched into a fist. The fist holding the hilt of Service's hunting knife. The knife's fat blade gleaming in the moonglow, but not as usual. Not with the familiar white shine. A darker gleam, we realize.

And several of us say, "Blood," aloud.
　And with that Service retreats.
　Off the knoll.
　Out of sight.
　Even to us, *gone*.

38
INTO A FIRE

❖

Salo retrieves the body. I recognize the boy's face, eyes mercifully closed, and I learn the ways that a knife can mutilate flesh. Then Snow tells me, "Bween was the youngster." I can't decide if she's outraged by Service's attack, or if she's merely impressed by the finality of it. *Bween.* I vaguely recall the name. Some part of me wants to paint him as a terrible criminal. Like Salo, perhaps. A possible murderer. I want justice, only Bween looks too young and too horrible to suffer this way.

"At least it's not another woman," Goottich mutters.

I turn and stare at him.

He smiles, realizing that I heard him. Then he giggles and says, "I'm not the one butchering people. So quit it!"

The sun is rising, stars fading and the high clouds brilliant. Salo and a couple others dig the shallow grave. Then Briar leads the ceremony, sensing the mood and trying to inspire. Poor Bween wasn't alert, he warns. Staring at the Pitcairns, he reminds them that they should work for the common good. As always. He says, "This *passion* was designed to fail. The Old Ones and elders became scared, and with good reason. They put Service at the helm, sacrificed with the rest of us. A tiny *passion* spent to buy our new blood . . . only they never guessed the charity of our friend Goottich. Our friend is our salvation, and our future is assured."

He reminds them that their ancestors came from a distant place, banished for forgotten crimes. "In a thousand years," he proclaims, "our descendants will have forgotten our supposed crimes too. And they will rule their own

world. With their Remarkables, of course. A new world
and perhaps a new order"—he pauses, the smoldering eyes
never blinking—"and each of us will be revered by our
descendants. They will remember our names and deeds for
twenty thousand years, and by then our Remarkables will
have decided this was a very good thing."

He says, "You know Remarkables."

He waits for a moment, nodding, then says, "They'll come
out of their muddle and see what's obvious. This is good,
what we are doing. And Service, tired and old, is nothing
but wrong."

Is. He finally admits what everyone knows.

Snow sighs, holding onto herself.

Then Briar kicks a clod onto the body, saying, "He is
the criminal here. Service is our only foe."

Mount Au is brilliant in the sunshine, symmetrical without being predictable, rising and rising and still distant.
The plain beneath it is brown and then green, streaks of
whitish gray in the country ahead. We eat as we walk. I
consume two bricks in the morning, not tasting them, feeling their stimulants working on my muscles. They lend me
a rough endurance. My pack rides me as if it's part of me,
and my walking stick is an extra leg. Sometimes I'll press
into a stretch of rising ground, feeling capable and in control. There is exhaustion inside me, but not too much. It's
as if I know my limits—that precise point where I will
collapse—and there's a strength in knowing my frailties.
A certain odd and seductive power.

Nobody walks with anyone else. The new routine means
nervousness and a hyperalertness, and it's not just the Pitcairns who feel it.

I watch everything around me. Little nameless birds flip
through the grass, and my heart kicks. Grazers run into a
wood, and I wonder who spooked them. Even the tangled
vegetation seems dangerous. Has Service devised booby
traps. Would he claim a few visitors if it means stopping
Briar too?

We wade through a clear warmish stream, then climb
out of the valley. Briar and Salo and Snow stand together
on a ridge, halfway hidden inside a knot of trees. The
inflated leaves glisten, their waxy exteriors throwing sunlight in rainbow sparkles. I approach the trees, and the

dry wind gusts, leaves rattling and the air smelling like an old camp fire.

I turn, hunting for blackened coals. That's when I notice the wall of dark clouds upwind. Yet somehow the clues don't connect. I lean against my stick, blink, and breathe deeply; and Snow says, "They're growing," with a worried voice.

What are growing?

I squint at the distant clouds. They seem motionless, but that's an illusion. Orange flames are consuming the woods in the next valley, and the flames are being driven by the wind. They're as tall as the crowns of the trees, I realize; a terrible blaze. I wonder how it was set. Then I know. The burning woods become sun-dried grass, and if the wall of fire keeps coming . . . judging its distance and speed and the lay of this land . . .

"Tell everyone," says Briar.

He is talking to me as well as Snow and Salo.

"We're running across—"

"Running?" asks Snow.

"Service is trying to cut us off," he explains. "Slow us down. Take away our cover." Briar squints at the wildfire, his expression a mixture of anger and weary despair. "Go back and tell everyone . . . tell them to hurry. Don't say why. Just get them here. Go!"

He has Service's voice, I realize. Just not so old and worn.

Except Service wouldn't tell me not to tell the truth. He would say nothing, demanding nothing from me but honesty and honest effort.

At least the grass makes for good running. People trot, their packs flopping against their backbones. There isn't panic, at least. The burning valley is small and easily crossed. Plenty of time, I tell myself. Sometimes I stop to rest for a moment, looking upwind, watching the swirling black clouds and fire.

I climb a modest ridge, Remarkables on all sides of me. They don't want to be left behind. The hunting moas and sprintbears would make quick meals of them. Their tendrils clumsily grab at anything. They uproot grasses and gulp at the smoky air, sometimes coughing as the stench grows worse. I cough too. I press with my legs and the long stick, but near the ridge I stumble and drop. *There's still ample time*, I tell myself. I roll onto my back, my legs tingling and a thousand little cramps making muscles twitch. I stare at the high porcelain-blue sky. Wouldn't it be fine just to stay here? Just to rest and bake in the day's heat? I could catch the others later, I'm thinking. A dose of solitude sounds lovely. . . .

A Remarkable rolls over me. I hear the creaking of roots as it lashes hold of the grass, and the sky turns purple. There's a confused mass of tendrils and eyes and the spherical center with its mouth straight above me, opened wide and white teeth shining. I smell its breath, humid and vaguely like the Pitcairn sea; then it's past and the uprooted bits of grass descend on me.

I stand and finish climbing the ridge, tasting blood in my mouth.

The next valley is wide and shallow. There's no river, but I spot islands of sediment pulled into teardrop shapes. Thin woods stand among the grasses. Sandy soils? Leached by some long-ago flood?

The Remarkables have gathered into a long wall, and they talk among themselves with crisp chittering sounds.

Their eyes, almost without exception, are looking upwind.

The orange flames are moving toward us. I never imagined the fire was so large. The wide valley is filled with tinder, and I can hear the fire working and smell it, and the ash and smoke make my nose sting.

Briar screams, "Move! We're moving! Go!"

He's downwind—a tiny furious shape throwing up his arms, his rifle in both hands—and his voice is thin and shrill.

Someone closer says, "We can't! We should go back!"

I recognize the voice, turning to the Remarkables now.

"Better to retreat," Talker assures me. Its voice is rushed, telling me, "We can't cross in time, Ranier!"

And with that the Remarkables begin moving backward, voting en masse, my legs reflexively doing the same.

Someone shoots.

It's Briar. Pointing into the air, he fires twice.

Talker says nothing. Which one is Talker? I look at the purple wall, trying to decide. Then someone is beside me, and I turn to find Shurgar's grim face. Her tongue licks at her lips. She seems to shiver for an instant. Then she turns, about to say something to me, her mouth opening and something hitting her, driving her off her feet. I watch her fall and hear the faint *crack*, nothing more, and her chest is covered with blood. I can't believe all the blood pouring from the wound. I step closer, then realize that she has to be dead. Numbness spreads through me. What's going on? I keep staring at the hole and wide-eyed startled dead face, then someone is shooting nearby. *Boom. Boom.*

Briar is shooting a Remarkable.

Cornered by the firestorm, he's panicking. He'll try anything now. *Fuck the taboos.* He aims at a second Remarkable, at its exact center, and fires twice again. The Remarkable sags and makes a strange graceless wheezing sound.

I can't feel even a hint of suffering.

Briar comes closer to me, then shoots a third Remarkable. Then he shouts, "Move!" He brandishes the rifle, threatening every alien. "Now! Move! Move!"

Snow approaches, then stops. She seems unsure of what to do.

Even Salo looks stunned by the scene.

Briar tells his people, "Shoot all of them!"

Snow looks at her rifle as if surprised to find it in her hands. Then she looks at me with a helpless despairing expression, noticing Shurgar's body beside me . . . her mouth dropping open. . . .

Briar continues the slaughter. He kills three more Remarkables, aiming with deliberation. Becoming more expert. Their bloods are scalding purple goos, and the ones beside them panic, rolling downhill to escape. I hear high whistles, sudden and quick, and the entire line bolts. It's like a strange tremendous race beginning, the Remarkables surging forward and using the slope to gain momentum. I almost forget to follow. I watch their airy bulks in motion, awestruck. Then Effie says, "We have to run! Run!"

She's standing beside Goottich. Goottich is standing over Shurgar, and he says something.

"Darling?" moans Effie.

Goottich shakes his head, some pale twist of sadness in him. Then he looks up at me, the big mouth saying, "This isn't good. Not at all."

* * *

I run despite aching knees. I'm alone when I reach the valley floor, the Remarkables ahead of me and a burning ironish taste in my mouth. I start to cough. The sky is darkening, and the air itself seems unnaturally hot, forced from a furnace and making the grass swirl. It's as if the grass wants to uproot itself, trying to escape. Blades bend and sway, and I cough harder, swallowing with a dry throat and pressing on ahead.

I'm going to die. Talker was right; we should have retreated. Briar is wrong—why didn't Service shoot him? But he was down among the Remarkables, I remember. Shielded. Service is a good Pitcairn. He could never bring himself to kill one of them. I keep remembering the woman's dead face, and I try to make him into Briar. In my mind I want to see him shot through the heart.

I run with my eyes ahead.

I won't look sideways, I promise myself. I don't want to know too much.

We reach one of the teardrop islands. Remarkables and humans flow around it rather than climb it. The Remarkables almost wobble as they roll, drunk with fatigue. All I see is them and the grass around them. The smoke is dense and low, the fire roaring—a titanic living sound that makes the heated air shake—and I feel creatures dying upwind of me, cooked alive. Before now my countermeasures were working. Maybe I was too distracted. But not anymore . . . agonies mounting on top of agonies, the slow and unlucky ones having their skin blister and boil and finally explode, death a godsend . . . !

I start to shiver, pain washing over me.

A brief thick wood stands on my left, not far upwind, and I can't help but see it in my peripheral vision. It bursts into fire and ash. There are a string of soft explosions, huge balls of orange light engulfing whole trees. Inflated leaves detach and fly like clumsy balloons, shriveling and falling to earth and spreading the fire, a few hitting in front of me and me weaving between the little black plumes.

Remarkables and the Pitcairns vanish into the blowing smoke. I guess what is straight ahead and run hard, new life in my legs. Every tiny event seems majestic and overdone. Every breath tastes hot and sooty. There's no more sunlight. There's just the colored light of the fire and blowing embers. An ember strikes my long hair, and I knock it loose. My hair itself is hot to the touch, and I'm bathed in ashy sweat.

I run and stumble, then rise, seeing a solitary figure in front of me. Standing, just standing. He holds his rifle in one hand, and his narrow face is blackened with the vivid living eyes gazing at me. It's as if he has been here for hours, waiting my arrival.

I take a step, then stop and cough. Service coughs too. Then he smiles and gives a little nod before turning—

I want to say something.

—and he vanishes into the swirling hot ash. He's gone before I can speak. Suddenly I hear the piercing wail of a dying Remarkable, and I forget about Service. A Remarkable is burning alive. I've never heard such noise; it's almost as bad as feeling the pain. Almost.

I start running again, and the ground tilts upward.

I'm climbing on crumbling soil, the grass thinning and then gone. There's nothing but gravel sliding under me, loose and dry. Nothing for a fire to consume, I think. A Remarkable looms above me, turning and turning and making little progress. I run around it, stopping at an outcropping of tired old limestone. I make myself grab hold of the rock with one hand and reach back with my walking stick, offering it to the alien. Giving it something new to grasp. Which it does. The tendrils wrap around the stick as the creature pulls itself higher, my shoulders aching and more tendrils grasping at me, then the rock itself, helping it climb up over me with a clumsy voice moaning, "Taaaannk Uuuu. . . ."

I scramble after it, my legs churning out of habit.

And suddenly, without warning, I come out of the smoke. The sky becomes clear and blue, a freshening wind from somewhere; and I breathe hard and cough harder, giggling like a maniac.

39
MURDER

❖

Pachel kneels and whispers, "You should invite me inside."

"So come inside."

She crawls through the tent flap, stinking of smoke. But then everything possesses that leveling odor, thick and clinging. It still sickens me. I keep seeing the fire, mentally unable to escape. The fire will probably infest my dreams tonight.

"Lumiere is better," she tells me. "He'll be fine."

The old man nearly died. How he found enough strength to make the crossing, I don't know. I thought I'd pushed myself to the breaking point.

"That's good," I tell Pachel. "I'm glad he's all right."

She sits over me, her head against the tent's ceiling. She tells me, "Some people didn't deserve to make it."

True enough.

"Listen," she says. Then she says nothing. Her face is strong and quite lean now, the black hair bright with oils. Finally she tells me, "We can do something. We can finish everything if we do one thing."

I wait.

"We kill one person," she whispers.

I glance outside, almost expecting to see the Pitcairns eavesdropping. But they aren't. Briar and Salo are the only ones in view, and they're talking to Goottich, sitting near the camp's center.

"Did you hear me, Ranier?"

"You mean kill Briar."

And she says, "No," as if disappointed with me. How

could I be so dense? "What happens if we do? Salo takes over. And what good would that accomplish?"

Her flecks of silver have gotten brighter with the sun.

"I mean Goottich," she says.

"Kill him—?"

She lifts her hands, unbuttoning her shirt and exposing the clumsy Pitcairn bra. Then she leans down against me, saying, "Pretend we're fooling around. Go on."

I feel the pressure of the breasts.

"Use your hands," she coaches. "Will you please?"

I grope at her breasts and then something else, an angular shape pressed between them. I reach into her cleavage, finding the warmed hilt of a tiny pistol. Made of plastic. Presumably loaded.

"It's got to be you, Ranier."

"How did you get—?"

"Service," she whispers. "It's a Pitcairn toy for children. The bullets are shaped gravel. It's got no accuracy whatsoever. He warned me that I'd have to get very close to use it."

"When? When did he—?"

"Just before he got away," she tells me. Then she nods her head, her expression intense and certain. "Goottich is afraid of me. I doubt if he'd let me get close enough to fire. I thought of Lumiere—"

"Not him."

"—but he wouldn't. Couldn't."

"And I can?"

She looks outside, then turns back to me. "Hit him in the head, maybe more than once. Make sure he's dead. Okay, Ranier? All right?"

Briar and Goottich are having an argument.

I approach and then sit, watching them without staring. Goottich looks awful. Stress and the hard run across the valleys have drained him, and with a shrill voice he tells Briar, "We can't keep losing people. Another dead girl . . . don't you see? We need a reasonable initial population. We need bodies that can reproduce, and particularly women!"

Briar watches the oversized hand gesturing in the air.

"We need to keep your culture intact," Goottich maintains. "Don't you understand? You of all people must appreciate—"

"So we get new blood somewhere," Briar interrupts. "You'll do some magic and give us babies, and we'll make them into Pitcairns. What's the problem?"

"That's not my point!"

Briar shuts his eyes and holds them closed for a long moment.

"I don't want Realm children raised as Pitcairns. I want Pitcairn children. Authentic descendants from the original Earth."

Briar opens his eyes. Anger melds with frustration. He is supposed to be in charge—this is now his *passion*, by rights—yet he doesn't feel the power he anticipated. A lot of Goottich's noise makes him wonder about who will be in charge of whom when we reach the enworld. He's no fool. Young and prideful and ignorant about a lot . . . but not so much of a fool that he's safe from sinking sensations in his gut.

Salo sits apart from the other two. He shakes his head, saying, "We can find other Pitcairns. What's the problem? We can find them while we're collecting samples and specimens. How about that?"

"Yeah, right." Briar nods, trying for authority. "We'll search for people who would want to join us. We can do that from orbit, can't we? We'll hunt for banished souls. . . ."

Goottich makes an uncomfortable sound, shaking his head.

"What?" asks Briar. "What now?"

Either out of exhaustion or his own frustration, Goottich makes his miscalculation. His eyes narrow, and he says, "I don't know."

Salo looks at the ground.

Briar asks, "Is there a problem?"

"If we're going to end up with these banished souls," says Goottich, "then what will we have? A world full of criminals. Just criminals. All this trouble and all this expense, and I end up with a fancy prison filled up with nothing but throwaways!"

Both Pitcairns are furious. I see it best on Briar's face, him rising and then turning away to avoid exploding. He leaves without a word. Without so much as a backward glance. But Salo remains seated, his rifle in one hand and his cold unperturbed eyes watching the countryside around us. If I shot Goottich at this moment, Salo would kill me in the next moment. The best I can do is sit here, waiting for some opening.

Our campsite is beside a shallow glacial river. The surrounding trees are changing again, marking a new climate or new soils. The water itself comes from Mount Au's glaciers. Its whiteness has been diluted by springs and runoff, but it retains its potent chill. Sitting here is cool work. I wonder if these dissimilar men can reach some accord, and I hope it's soon.

"He has a temper," Salo warns Goottich. "Briar's got an angry core that scares *everyone.*"

"So make a new vote. Pick yourself leader."

Salo shakes his head, explaining, "But we need that temper. If he hadn't exploded today—"

"We would have retreated, losing valuable time. I know, I know." The big man snarls and says, "But shooting Remarkables . . . I don't like to see that happen. . . ."

"Neither do I," Salo assures him.

Goottich blinks, considering those words.

"It was an awful crime," Salo continues, "and maybe when we have our own grove, and our own elders, maybe we can manage justice. Killing your own Remarkables . . . it is . . . well, it's. . . ."

He lacks the words.

Goottich keeps quiet for a change, his tongue laid against something bitter.

Salo examines him for a long while, then warns, "Just don't think you know us. Because you don't know us, and I doubt if you ever will."

Goottich sits straighter.

"But I've studied you," he responds. "I know all about the Pitcairn culture and your history and what this symbiosis means to you."

Salo is angry but silent.

"I probably know more about Pitcairn than *you* do!"

Salo groans, his expression astounded and his resistance worn to nothing. Why bother with this noise? Like Briar, he rises and leaves before detonating.

Goottich seems oddly pleased with himself. He has fended off both of them, hasn't he?

I start to approach, and I tell him, "I want to discuss something with you. If you've got a minute."

He shrugs and says, "While we're walking."

We happen to move toward the Remarkables. Ten or fifteen of them died today, and the survivors look ill. Their pigments are a milky purple, and they're much too quiet. Nerves? I wonder. Despair? Or a mixture of many things? Probably many things, I decide; and Goottich says:

"What's this about?"

We'll reach the long lake tomorrow. Late afternoon, Pachel mentioned. Then we'll build the signal out of rocks—

"Hey!" growls my companion. "If you want to talk—"

"I want to ask a question."

He regards me with minimal patience.

"What will you pay?" I hear my voice, only it doesn't feel as if I'm responsible for the words themselves. "What kind of salary did you have in mind? For my expertise with Pitcairn, I mean."

"I knew it!" Goottich acts as if he expected that question. "It's got to interest you, this whole huge scheme of mine."

"Very much," I say.

We're standing between the cold river and the Remarkables. Goottich asks me, "How about five times the average salary?"

"Ten times."

The round face seems amused. "You think you're worth that much?"

"But you'll be making fortunes on top of fortunes," I point out. "The only piece of Pitcairn outside Pitcairn, and it will be your monopoly. You can charge any sum to the visitors. You'll sell holos of the Remarkables throughout the Realm. Plus your books. Plus whatever you learn about Remarkable minds and physiology."

Goottich has a vague, stunned expression.

After a minute he says, "I really haven't gotten into that part of the business . . . not that I haven't considered . . ."

I feel the weight of the pistol in my trouser pocket.

"Okay," says Goottich. "Ten times the average."

And I say, "Thanks, no. I'd rather not be involved in that kind of shit. If you don't mind."

Goottich puffs up his cheeks, turning red-faced.

Then he wheels, offering me a perfect shot at the back of his huge skull. And I don't shoot. I have my hand around the pistol, but I never so much as aim. I watch him storm off, furious and sick of everything; then I glance sideways at the black eyes that are watching me.

And the sky.

And Au.

Everything.

Pachel is angry, and of course she tells me how she feels. "You could have done it. Neat and easy, and you didn't!" She wants to whisper, but emotions keep her voice level up. We're standing upstream from camp, the place preplanned. I was supposed to run here after the murder. She was supposed to give me nectar and water, then work with the Pitcairns until they changed their minds about everything.

"You're a coward," she assures me.

"Probably," I agree. "But that's not why I didn't do it."

"Then why?"

"First," I say, "I don't think this rebellion would be finished if Goottich were killed. These people have done horrible things. By their social norms, they're on the brink of damnation. What can they do? Surrender to Service? Accept banishment from their grove?" I tell her, "I know a few things from Snow. Plus I can make guesses too. What if they could kill Service and then arrange the deaths of the juveniles? They could straggle home and tell lies, and nobody would be able to prove what was true and what wasn't—"

"The Remarkables would see through any lie," she claims.

"But humans are in charge of human justice. Don't you see? If I kill Goottich, they retain options. They're not simple primitives. They've already figured the odds and built up contingency plans."

She blows air through her nose.

"Second," I add, "Goottich was close to me this afternoon, not far from Shurgar. If Service thought he could end this with a magic bullet, why didn't he? Goottich is only the biggest man-shaped target on the planet!"

She shakes her head.

"What did Service tell you to do with the pistol?"

" 'In case.' That's all he said. 'In case.' "

She puts out her hand, palm up.

"Where's the gun? Give it here."

"No."

She stares at me. Her strength doesn't scare me, only her temper. "For now," I tell her, "I'm keeping it for myself."

"He trusted me with it."

"Then report me to someone."

The silver flecks brighten, but she won't speak. She doesn't trust herself not to shout and bring others.

"I'll keep it. Believe me. At the right moment, if there is one, I'll give it to you. Promise."

She moans under her breath.

"Besides," I add, "they might search you sometime. They're becoming a rather paranoid lot."

"Good night, Ranier."

She walks away, and I listen to the water sounds. I'm not thinking about anything definite. Gray formless ideas. Then I turn and walk back the way I came. Beside the bunched Remarkables are a collection of flat weathered stones, and I kneel beside a familiar stone, turning it over and finding nothing.

For an instant I'm afraid someone has stolen the pistol.

Yet there's no cavity underground, just sand and some cold bluish worms. Which stone was it? I rise and look for landmarks. I'm so tired, I realize. I'm a danger to myself.

"Two steps forward," says Talker. "Then a half step to your left."

Okay. I step and step, then go left. Then I kneel and turn the stone, quickly hiding the pistol in my boot.

I flip the stone back over and rise again.

I feel light-headed. Looking at the Remarkables, I'm thinking about everything at once. Questions I had never considered suddenly have answers; the muddle inside me partly evaporates. It feels as if I have dunked my head underwater, the cold shock of it awakening me—

Of course, I think.

"I understand," I whisper. "Everything—"

"Shuuuush," mutter several Remarkables. "Shhhuuu-uuushshsh."

TALKER

✦

There is a resemblance. Of face. Of body. In elemental emotions. Both men possess tempers, and both are capable in their fashion. Yet where Service has learned to control his emotions, using them as raw material and always serving his grove, Briar has lost all pretense, all balance. He lies in the most dangerous ways, lying to himself, making the lies to us all the more transparent. Every one of my siblings—the survivors of this most strange *passion*—sees the man's falsehoods. Easily and often.

"I'm sorry," lies Briar.

"It won't happen again," he lies.

Then he sets his rifle down in a facile bid to appear harmless and chastened, telling us, "You've got to understand. I saved you by forcing you to cross that valley. I'm not bad. Believe me, I'd like to take every last one of you with us tomorrow, safe and healthy . . . taking you up into the sky and to our new home. . . ."

Lying.

With motion, my siblings tell one another, "He almost believes himself." They ask me, "Is that what you see, Talker?" They notice how Briar tries to convince himself of his goodness. His basic purity. After everything, the man is hungry to feel correct. To be the good Pitcairn. "So strange," they say.

They ask me, "What do *you* see?"

Service, I see.

I point with an eye and a single tendril, no motion overt.

Service stands on the slope north of us. Some of us feared that he had died in the fire. Some of us wasted energy and

time debating what we would do, left without him. A few
had hoped, hoped, hoped that Ranier would kill Goottich
with the pistol, canceling one great problem for us. (Yet
Ranier did what was right, I believe. Inaction was best,
and for the reasons he gave to Pachel. Plus more.) Now
we do not have to face an existence without Service. He
lives! Eyes are lifting and turning, maybe too many of
them, but Briar seems not to notice. Talking with motion,
my siblings say, "Look at him!" They say, "Defiant still!"
They tell me, "The man is beautiful, Talker! Look at him!"

I am looking. Service is speaking to us while the lower-
ing light pulls shadows across the plain. While water from
Au's shoulders flows past us. While Ranier sleeps, the
weapon tucked at the bottom of his mummy bag. While
Pitcairns walk the perimeter. While clouds subside from
Au's summit, a little. And while Briar continues his graceless lies.

"I want what's best," Briar says. "And a new grove is
best."

He says, "We're partners, symbiotic mates, and you trust
people's instincts and focus. So why not trust me? Goottich
isn't perfect, I know. He's certainly no Pitcairn. But he
needs us and we can control his excesses. When you're
adults, growing beside this new sea of ours, you can help
with Goottich. You and your genius for reading faces and
character." Then he adds, "But you've got to help me now.
Help us. Please?"

Service is telling us about tomorrow. He speaks in simple human terms, no muddle and distractions. What he
needs of us; what he hopes for from others. A directed,
thoroughly human plan—

—and the faces look alike. Briar's and Service's. A very
similar mixture of genes making the illusion of sameness—

—and Briar says, "Are you there, Talker?"

Did I die today? he means. It would be a stroke of sweet
luck, another possible enemy vanquished. He tries to hide
that thought, but the tired face cannot even pretend to
lie. I am his enemy. He suspects that I talk to weak-hearted
Pitcairns, turning them against his will. He says, "Talker?"
with considerable feeling. All false. And I respond, saying:
"Yes?"

I am deep inside the bunch. Briar will not be able to
single me out, I hope.

Briar gasps, then tells me, "Wonderful! And you're well, friend . . . ?"

I say nothing to the disgusting creature.

Then he asks, "Can you help me? I'm not asking you to forget my excesses, my mistakes . . . but for the sake of the others, for this new grove of ours . . . will you help us?"

"Perhaps," I reply.

The criminal swallows, then says, "Good . . . good. . . ."

"But first," I say, "come closer."

My siblings are still and silent.

"We need reassurance," I tell Briar. "We want you to crawl among us. To trust us. Show your trust by sleeping among our tendrils tonight. Among our mouths."

And with that the criminal takes a backward step, then another, then remembers his rifle and grabs it before turning away. Not running. He will not run. But not walking either.

We cannot see his face.

We watch Service's face as he repeats his plan, making certain that we have seen him and understood.

But Briar hides his face, his fears, every lie bright and shining, hanging about him like some poisonous super-heated cloud. . . .

40
CONQUEST

◈

Our torchship soon will pass overhead. The signal has to be built now or we'll wait until tomorrow, and neither Goottich nor Briar want to wait. The big man has explained how on-board radars have mapped this terrain, storing every feature; the signal is meant to be noticeable and meaningful. An arrow. They're building a long arrow from rocks, and the arrow points at the lake where the shuttle will touch down.

Briar and Goottich are working. So are Effie and Salo. I'm sitting between Pachel and Lumiere, watching the frantic effort.

Goottich wants more help, but Briar explains, "I can't pull anyone from the perimeter." He carries a jagged piece of limestone, veins bulging and his voice coming through clenched teeth. "We don't have enough on guard as it is."

"What can Service do?" asks Goottich. "This is open country—"

"Which means good shooting," snaps Briar. "Which means we've got to make the perimeter bigger. Unless you want Service shooting us from a safe distance—"

"You never should have killed those cretins," Goottich responds. "You could have used their noses."

"And Service could have told them to bite your ass!"

Pachel laughs, nudging me once.

"If you want more help," Briar says, "ask one of your friends for their backs. They're not doing shit."

We aren't and won't. Goottich knows better than to ask us, his sweating face glancing at us with the mouth sneering. Then he drops another block of yellowish limestone on the arrow's long stem, wiping his brow with one sleeve and then the other. Then he turns and starts hunting for a new block, each one meaning a long walk.

The three of us are on a rock pile above the beach. The lake is deep and clear, but the west end is covered with a thin scum of seeping oils and gray-gold fungi. Gleaters are eating the oil and talking to each other. The intensity of the people lend the lake scene a peacefulness, a certain tranquility; I find myself staring across the water, nervous but not as nervous as I would have guessed.

Effie approaches, searching for her next stone.

The Remarkables are bunched together on the beach. I glance at them, wondering what they're thinking now.

Then Effie asks, "Where's Bedford?"

She doesn't sound concerned, nor even curious. I realize that she's making noise to avoid her work.

"He went down the lake," Lumiere responds.

The old man looks completely spent. If he was to shut his eyes and keep motionless, he'd resemble someone boiled, left soft and limp, the muscles scarcely able to hold on to the tired bones.

"He's playing tourist one last time," Pachel tells her.

Effie is a different color of tired. She acts nervous and too energetic to concentrate, yet the little face seems ready to cry.

Goottich shouts, "What are you doing?!"

Effie straightens, then turns around to face him.

"Get a goddamn rock, will you?"

She nods and turns back, grabbing a block that's too large and not lifting it. Instead she gazes up at us, saying with a confidential tone, "Sometimes he scares me. He really does."

"*Effie . . . !*"

She jerks the block off its perch, then she shuffles across the open ground, bending and bending but somehow making the arrow without ever stopping.

"Dumb woman," Pachel grumbles.

"Now, now," says Lumiere.

I say nothing, moving my right foot and feeling the precise shape of the toy pistol. Then I look at the lake again, and the Remarkables, and after a while I discover that I'm smiling. Just a little. Just for the briefest of brief instants.

* * *

The torchship has passed overhead, unseen, and Goottich says there is nothing to do now but wait. The shuttle will come in an hour and a half. Unless the arrow wasn't big enough, of course. Which means we'll have to wait for tomorrow morning.

Lumiere starts to make ready. Pachel and I give him bricks of nectar, her aware of his circumstances. His guest. He explained himself yesterday, I learn. He asks for advice about his route, the voice distracted, thick, and slow. A puffy fingertip moves across a landscape of folded paper and curling lines, and we do our best to help, relying on positive words and basic advice about taking his time. About not pressing too hard. About taking his time.

Gleaters fly past, their fat bodies skimming over the smooth water. It's a windless evening. The air feels cool beside the lake. Back and forth move the gleaters. They probably have nests somewhere nearby. I mention that to Pachel.

"I wish I knew if it was coming," she says. "I'm sick of the tension. This waiting shit."

Her gaze is intense. Driven.

I tell her what I think Service is doing—biding time; waiting for his opening—and she says, "Remember your promise."

"I will."

Then she says, "Huh? Look who's here."

Snow. Briar must have pulled her from the perimeter. She stops above the beach, then sits with legs crossed and her rifle on her lap. The Remarkables are below her, quietly singing. I've scarcely heard them make any sounds today, I realize. Then I breathe and watch the girl nervously tugging at her ponytail.

"So go talk with her," Pachel suggests. "You want to."

I want to. I approach, and Snow smiles, not quite looking at my face. It's as if we're meeting after many years—brief good friends who've lost their comfortable familiarity—and I feel unsettled, a little confused and mostly guilty for not caring enough. I do like the girl, but I don't love her. She isn't the same as Briar and Salo, yet I can't say that Snow is *this*, Snow is *that*. We're strangers, scarcely in the same species. A symbiont and a citizen of the Realm. *The title of my book?* I think. *The Symbiont and the Citizen. Maybe so*, I tell myself. *Maybe.*

I sit beside her, the ground's dampness bleeding through my trousers. After a long uncomfortable silence, I manage to ask, "If I'm your angel, what do you want me to do for you?"

She glances at me, then drops her head.

"If you don't want to live in Goottich's house . . . you can live in mine," I say. "I've got room enough." I'm an adolescent boy stumbling over himself. "Or I can give you money. Or lend you some. We can put you into a school, teach you our language and customs . . . if you want. . . . Whatever you want your angel to do for you, I'll try. . . ."

She is crying and has been crying for a long while. I notice the puffy eyes and their redness, her face gazing at me and the hands limp on the worn wooden butt of her rifle. What kind of Realm citizen would she make? From symbiosis into our strange self-gratifying freedom? Twenty thousand years of selection pressures and culture swept aside . . . can it be done?

"Tell me what you want, Snow."

I don't mean my voice to be shrill. I feel betrayed by the harshness of the words, as if they've shown something to both of us.

The Remarkables are singing louder; they have been for a few moments.

Snow says, "I don't know . . . what . . ." Then with a rising disgust, she tells me, "If you were my handsome angel, you'd know. You'd know exactly what I want. What I need—"

The whistling voices cut into my ears, and for an instant I'm almost glad for the distraction. The tension breaks into a new tension. A larger one.

Snow says, "Their eyes," and gestures.

The Remarkables' eyes are focused on the same moving point, panning across the sky as they shout to one another, tendrils waving and unwrapping from one another while the outermost ones of the bunch begin to roll down the rocky beach.

"The shuttle?" she asks.

I squint and admit, "I don't know."

Every Remarkable is moving. For an instant I believe they must be maneuvering for better views. But then the first ones are on the lake, air sacs filled for buoyancy and their purplish shapes churning at a sprinter's pace. I never guessed, never suspected this . . . and I stand, coming to my feet without thinking, Snow standing beside me.

Goottich and Briar are nearby, sitting on the arrow while Effie keeps a respectful distance. Briar tells Goottich to be quiet, noticing us and standing too. He starts to trot closer, curious and then concerned. Then he can see the juvenile Remarkables scattered across the lake, and he cries out, a fist threatening the air and his voice full of bile. "Come back!" he shouts. "Are you crazy?! What are you doing? What are you doing? Shit, shit . . . *shit*!!"

He never thought this possible, juveniles acting this way—

—and now comes the lone voice, speaking Pitcairn as well as any human. But louder. "To the mountain! To the mountain! To the All-Answer, my friends! *Come with me!*"

The shuttle roars as it flies above the lake, its autopilot digesting the scene and calculating against prewritten programs. A trained swimmer could cross this water in minutes. A narrow runway. The Remarkables are maybe a third of the way across, spinning slower now. They're tired after their initial burst. They look like tufts of cottony seed, gray in the low light and the glare; and Briar is firing at them, cursing steadily the whole time.

Snow says, "Don't," each time he shoots.

A Remarkable collapses, and she says, "No," almost too soft to be heard. "Not this way . . . no . . . !"

"How far can they go?" screams Goottich.

Briar lowers his rifle, saying, "It's rough ground over there. Ravines and rock. Not too far—"

"Then we'll find them."

Briar glares at his ally, saying, "Sprintbears and cretins will get them. When they don't smell us, they're going to come from everywhere. And juveniles alone . . . they can't defend themselves for long."

"So we'll find them first." Goottich pulls a hand across his face, and he says, "We wait for the shuttle, post a couple guards, then you'll take a group around the lake and hunt for them."

Briar says nothing.

"These are workable problems," Goottich assures him.

Yet Briar looks lost, perplexed and aching with despair.

Thousands of years of biological marriage are dissolving. The Remarkables are refusing to go with us. He can't believe they would commit this suicide, but how can he stop them? By restraining each of them? With ropes and knots and more threats of being shot? To keep them, he senses, he will have to enslave them. And despite everything he has done, Briar cannot make himself accept such a future. . . .

Pop, pop. Pop, pop.

We hear the gunfire, distant and almost soft. Briar turns and tilts his head, listening as if he's not certain what he hears.

The shuttle makes its approach, slowing itself and half-heartedly trying to maneuver around the obstacles on the water. Then it settles, skipping once. Several Remarkables vanish under the blunt front end, and several more wilt as the engines blow scalding air backwards. The autopilot never recognized them as threats or as taboos. I feel sorrow and frustrated anger, thinking of the pseudogulls we struck when we landed ages ago.

The gunfire intensifies.

Briar is running, passing Goottich; and Goottich asks, "What is it? Service, you think?"

"Stay here!" warns Briar. "Stay!"

There is a pain, sudden and familiar. I start bending at the knees, almost gasping.

Bedford appears, touching my shoulder and asking, "Are you all right?"

I wave him off.

The shuttle is turning toward shore, and the Remarkables are more than halfway across, spinning and spinning.

And now the pain subsides abruptly.

Pachel appears in front of me, her hand extended. "You promised," she says. "Come on."

I remove the pistol from my boot and place it on her palm.

"What is that?" asks Goottich.

Pachel starts to run.

I pick up my walking stick for lack of better, and I start after her, no idea what I want. There comes another quick dose of pain, rising fast and evaporating in an instant. Absence is death. Two deaths, and is one of them Service? But there's more shooting, then the hard *bang* of a gre-

nade. I pause, hunting for smoke or people. Pachel has
gone one direction. Briar appears in another, shuffling forward and then keeping still—the slow smooth motions of
someone accustomed to hunting wild game. I start toward
him. Then the shooting resumes, closer now. I smell
burned powder and hear shouts. There's a tall stand of
thick grass past Briar, and someone shoots from it. Bullets
spray over me, then pause, then Briar rises and shoots in
a methodical fan-shaped pattern. He empties his clip and
removes it and starts swatting at his pockets, unable to
find new ammunition—

—and Salo rises beside the grass, aims, and fires once. I
feel the impact. I moan or I scream, something, because
Briar hears me, turning and reading my face. "Salo?" he
screams. "You got someone! He's hurt!"

Salo wades in and vanishes.

The pain worsens. Sharpens. Then Salo cries out, "I got
Service!"

"Bring him!" says Briar.

An icicle is being driven into me. I feel sick. Salo emerges
with his prisoner. Service looks very old and tired, his eyes
waxy and half-dead. The bullet cut through his side just
under the ribs, blood soaking his shirt. Salo twists him,
using pain to immobilize him.

"Where's his cretin?" asks Briar.

Salo throws Service down between them, saying, "Haven't
seen it."

"We'll find it later." Briar approaches Service, saying,
"Look at you. The sweet luck has gone out of you, old
man."

Service says something too soft to understand.

"He killed Wissen," tells Salo. "And Mere."

"Fuck you, old man."

Service's pain diminishes. He breathes fast and sup-
presses the worst of it.

Pachel comes up beside me.

She says, "Shit," once, uncertain what to do. Move
closer? Is there time? No, she decides. With great care,
she holds the tiny pistol in both hands and aims, arms
extended and steady.

Briar takes the loaded rifle from Salo. He's beside Service, glancing back toward us. He sees Pachel and starts

to laugh. "At that range," he warns, "you'll likely hit him. Not me."

Her bluff is called, but she won't drop her arms.

Her hands tremble, I notice. She's learning that it's not neat or easy, using a gun on someone.

Service tries to stand, grunting and rising partway before Briar forces him back to his knees.

More Pitcairns approach. I count four of them bunched together, moving cautiously. Goottich is close, Effie just behind him. Bedford and Lumiere are behind them, and at the rear is Snow. I stare at her for a moment, wanting to see her face.

Then Briar says, "As leader of this *passion*, I find you, Service, guilty of murders and treachery. You will die."

Service's face is stiff and uncompromising.

Pachel fires twice, aiming high. The pistol sounds like a toy, and it accomplishes nothing. Then she moans and throws it to the ground, charging Briar, starting to scream.

Salo steps up, blocking her way.

Briar licks his lips, setting the tip of the rifle barrel at the back of Service's head. There's certainty and fierceness on the old man's face. I'm waiting for the bullet to erase the worn features—

"Kill him!" Salo wails.

—and Service says, *"Coward."*

Resolve shows on Briar's face. He grips the rifle tighter, and just then Pachel collides with Salo. The big Pitcairn swats at her face, then grunts as the woman hits his belly and tries slipping past him. And then comes the shot I anticipated, clear and sudden. And final. Salo kicks Pachel off her feet. Then he turns, and my eyes track sideways, expecting to see Briar standing over a corpse. . . . Only what my mind perceives is Briar on his knees—what's he doing on his knees?—and someone is sprawled out behind him. Not in front, and it takes several moments for me to understand—

Salo moans and runs.

—that Briar is dead on the ground, Service still alive.

And now Service turns around, grabbing for the rifle as Salo reaches him. Both men wrestle. There's a second *crack* as a bullet clips Salo in an arm, in the meat, and I feel that pain as he winces, Service now driving with his legs and twisting the rifle until the barrel slips under Salo's chin, firing and the head jerking back hard, Salo dead before he can fall and Service slumping over with exhaustion and shock.

I turn.

Snow is down on one knee, her rifle starting to lift.

"What happened?" Goottich asks me. "What's happening?"

Pachel is standing over Service, and Service manages to lift himself with an arm, speaking quietly.

Snow starts for the beach, walking without haste.

I watch her, thinking nothing. My mind is nearly blank. Then Goottich touches my shoulder with a wet hand, saying, "Get that rifle—the one in Service's hand. I'll pay you . . . just bring it to me. . . ."

The cherubic face gazes at me, nothing in those eyes.

"A million credits," he says.

"What—?"

"Ten million!" he says. "The man's weak. You can do it . . . for twenty million. For *anything*!"

I say nothing.

And with that Goottich turns to Effie. "You go! Get me that rifle! If you want to live in my house, get me a weapon! Somewhere!"

"What . . . ?" she moans, taking a reflexive step backward.

"Someone! Will someone . . . ?" Goottich swats at the air. "A hundred million credits. I want a fucking rifle—!"

And I remember the stick in my hands. I've carried it since the mountains, learning its balance and weight and the feel of its comfortable old wood; and it's as if I've carried it here for a purpose, clear and pure. I aim—

"Any fucking rifle!"

—and swing. And Goottich doesn't say another word. One good blow to the head, and suddenly he turns quiet as a sleeping baby.

REMARKABLES

◆

. . . growing means to know more, to have more room for knowing, but knowing always teaches how little one comprehends, teaches how next to nothing is predictable—the flights of birds and clouds and raindrops and the tiniest motes of dust—chaos reigning over this great universe that we watch nightly; and what will be is the realm of the All-Answer, its eyes perfect enough to perceive the one true Future, and our hope-of-hopes is just for a glimpse of that Future; that is the ideal for every juvenile's *passion;* a glimpse is worth more than any guess, we teach them . . . every adult in every grove holding that in common—our *passions*—and more; because where once the All-Answer had many glimpses to offer, in ancient times, now now *now* it shares the same vision, something no adult can ignore or debase . . . every grove on Sweetair (Pitcairn) has its holy mountains, ours being Au, and the air in the interiors is dry and clear and warm and sometimes amazingly still, some nights on the Au plain extraordinarily clear; and sometimes in the night, just briefly, the clouds around Au will dissipate, exposing the summit, and the moon will be down; tradition says such moments are the most holy, the All-Answer most accessible; young eyes gazing upward at the snow and ice and raw dead rock, then even higher, perceiving a sky shot full of a distant and warm and living green light that shrouds stars and the cold gaps between them; the juveniles at last seeing what they have always known, every sliver of green meaning a trillion of *them*, a trillion humans—They-Whom-We-Must-Trust—except how does one trust those who have no allegiance to us? . . . and every adult forever remembers that instant, for each of us at that holy instant have heard the All-Answer's great voice speaking to us . . . this is the vision shared by all Remarkables, with or without humans . . . the All-Answer telling us: this is the Future; you are seeing the Future; Humanity is the sole Future; their great green fire lighting up the cold blackness, soon to wash over you and yours . . . the challenge plain; and by this way, this sight, our purpose is bolstered . . . every grove asking itself and its enemy neighbors: *what can might should we do we do we do . . . ?*

41
BANISHMENT

◆

These last weeks have given our shuttle a newness and a technological sophistication that it didn't possess before. The shiny hyperfiber hull and the steady throb of its engines are out of place. It's a superfluous concoction, gaudy and a little unsettling. I enter its cabin carrying Goottich's right arm and shoulder, Bedford on the other arm, and Snow wrestling with the legs. The interior atmosphere seems alien, thin and wrong-scented. It feels as if I can't find my breath. Half-dragging the unconscious man, we manage to put him into the proper seat, upright and strapped firmly into place

The lump on his head looks ugly, but I'm not too hopeful that he'll die. The torchship's autodocs probably will have him awake and screaming soon enough . . . the old Goottich, wholly unrepentant.

Snow walks around the cabin, examining the floor and running a hand over the transparent wall. Grief shows on her face. And anger. Plus a dose of resolve. The *passion* is in Service's care again—he has made his pronouncements about guilt and punishment—and while shooting Briar was a partial atonement, Snow can't be excused. She voted for Briar as a leader. She made no overt effort to help Service. His verdict, as always, is final; and while he spoke, I watched her face move from sadness into resignation, sometimes nodding with a very tentative relief.

We walk back outside, down the deployed ladder and onto the beach. Pachel is adjusting Service's bandages. He drinks water and eats bits of an odd yellow-white nectar, looking generally improved. Not strong, but stronger. The bullet struck nothing vital. He claims he can walk. With his stained teeth, he breaks off a sliver of the nectar—"For the pain"—then shoves the sliver directly into the blood and torn meat, wiping his fingers clean on his trouser leg.

I feel his discomfort, then it fades away.

"Finished?" he asks.

Bedford says, "Yes, sir."

Snow walks down the beach, joining the other four Pitcairns. They gave up at the end, emotionally beaten. No interest in fighting. They aren't murderers, just criminals; and banishment, however awful, is the preferable future. At least it holds the faint tangible hope of survival.

I turn and look across the water. There's no trace of the Remarkables. Service says they'll move until night, then pull themselves together and hope for the best. That was the plan, he claims. In that rough country, keeping low and out of view, they won't know what happened here, and it's our duty to find them while there is something to find.

They can't see us, I'm thinking.

For the first time in weeks I'm out of their gaze, and I almost miss them. Their lidless eyes; the all-consuming stares; that sense of being interesting enough to be studied day and night.

Pachel makes a sound and points eastward.

The last cretin. Its black plumage is lustrous in the low sunlight. I see the curling tongue and the telltale gray leg, and I shout, "Come!" with my hands cupped around my mouth. "Come!"

"No, no!" says Service.

I put down my hands.

"Stay!" he screams. And the creature stops. Sits. Then Service gives a second command—a nonsensical word—and the cretin responds immediately. It begins to strain, twisting its neck and sucking in its belly, the long jaws opening as it vomits, emptying its stomach's contents onto the beach rocks.

Four hard lumps are mixed with bile.

Now Service shouts, "Come!"

The cretin gallops up to him without hesitation, and he warns us, "Don't go down there."

"What are those things?" asks Lumiere.

"Grenades." He glances at the half-melted timepiece on

his wrist, then explains, "The stomach acids eat at the pins. Another couple hours, maybe less, and they'd detonate."

We stare at the Pitcairn.

"If I died," he says with a cool voice, "you might have found the cretin and felt safe enough to take it. I might have gotten some sweet luck at the end, the cretin inside the shuttle and boom. Boom."

Nobody moves; nobody speaks.

"It's a trick I invented when I was a kid. I made a cretin eat a grenade, then go off and sit. It sat until it blew up, and I got my butt slapped by my father. Then afterward he told me that he hoped my cruelty paid off someday. That's all you can ever hope when you're cruel, he told me. That someday it pays off."

Among the tourists, only Goottich is banished.

"I can't know what you did or didn't do," Service has explained. "But think about where you're going from here. On the *passion*? Or do you want to take an early sleep?"

Effie doesn't hesitate.

"I'm leaving. I'm tired of this . . . this shit. . . ."

"I'm staying," says Pachel.

"To Mount Au," says Lumiere.

Service looks at me, and I say, "I want my money's worth." It comes out as a thin, unfortunate joke.

Yet he smiles, half nodding and looking at Bedford.

"I think I should go with Effie," says the pretty-faced man. "I really don't belong here."

"Then do us one favor," Service adds. "Watch Goottich. Make sure he doesn't do any mischief."

Sensible, I think.

Bedford says, "I will."

Service glances at his timepiece, then tells us when we're leaving. Very soon. But first we need to claim rifles and ammunition, plus the shares of nectar left by the dead. By whomever. For now the rifles stay unloaded, excepting Pachel's. Nothing else has changed, he reminds us. He is in charge. We have our duty. We have to find the Remarkables as quickly as possible, despite the hour and anyone's discomfort.

I'm making ready when Snow approaches.

"Ranier?"

I won't look up. I try to convince myself that I won't have to look at her.

"I wanted to wish you sweet luck, Ranier."

I can't stop my head from lifting.

"You look so sad," she tells me.

I wait a moment, then tell her, "When it's over? When the rest of us are back up in the torchship? I could find you and the others. Make arrows out of rocks, ration your nectars, and wait for us—"

"—and what?" she asks, laughing mildly.

I'm offering to save her life. Doesn't she understand?

"I could live with you, I suppose." She shrugs her shoulders, then tells me, "I'm curious about the Realm. I think it would be exciting and very strange. Maybe I could learn to like it."

"But what?"

"What about them?" Snow asks.

She means the other Pitcairns. Four similar faces are gazing at us, narrow and handsome. Two men and two women, though in this light they look more like adolescents than adults.

"They don't have any desire to see the Realm. And I'm sure they'd refuse your . . . your generosity. . . ."

"But you could—"

"Abandon them?" She shakes her head, disappointed with me. "Ranier, I'm the only one of us who's had time on the plains. The only one who knows anything about the interior. They *need* my help, if they've got any hope—"

"What hope?" I start to cry now. "Where can you go?"

"Maybe the Two Sisters grove wants humans now." She shrugs her shoulders. "Maybe we can join a boatload of other banished people and go somewhere new. You never know, Ranier. Sweet luck could put us across the sea in some young grove, and in a thousand years our kids won't be able to count themselves." She nods with authority. "You just never know."

All I can say is, "Good sweet luck."

She says, "Thank you," and starts past me. I make a clumsy attempt to kiss her, and she returns the kiss and then grins, her messy teeth showing between thin lips. "Don't be sad."

"All right."

"It wastes time," she assures me.

"Thanks," I say. "I'll remember that."

Snow talks to Service as our shuttle pulls away from shore. A burst of hot wind subsides into a gentle heat, and I make out the vague human shapes inside the cabin, only one of them taking the trouble to wave at us. I give Bedford a wave in return, then hoist up my pack and walk toward Service.

The old Pitcairn is giving Snow an assortment of nectar bricks—colors bleeding into one another—and he gives advice about directions and the best trails to follow. "If you're trying for the coast, which is the smart way."

Snow nods, the dutiful student.

Pachel glances at me, eyes startled. Odd.

Then Snow says, "Thank you," and pauses. She's smiling with all of her will and energy, tears leaking down her cheeks; and she says, "That's all your extra nectar!"

She means Service's shares of Briar's and Salo's and so on.

She says, "Don't—"

"We'll have another airdrop soon," he replies. "Don't worry."

"Thank you."

"Maybe someone else would be gracious enough," he adds, glancing at Pachel and then me.

Of course. I can't dig out the extra bricks fast enough. I have Goottich's share—half again the norm—and Lumiere also stacks his extra bricks on the waterworn rocks. They create a little building, a strange and pretty edible fortification. Then Service rises and somehow takes the weight of his pack, a dull pain subsiding; and with a clean unreadable face he tells us:

"We have to move. Now."

Except something shows, just for an instant. It's as if I can see past his hard gaze, his mind exposed and nothing secret anymore. I look at Service as if for the first time, then blink and jerk my head sideways. Inside him is a stew of anger and pity and such love that I feel embarrassed knowing about it. I feel chastened.

"Come on," Service warns me.

One last look at Snow—on her knees now, deftly partitioning the bricks into five equal piles—and after she offers a weak smile, I turn and walk briskly down the beach.

Only later Pachel asks me, "Did you hear it?"

"Hear what?"

We're walking side by side, trailing the old Pitcairn.

"She called him, 'Father.' "

"Snow did?"

She nods and says, "That's what I heard. I'm certain—"

" 'Father'?"

"That's the word I heard."

And I look back over my shoulder. A single gleater is flying home from the oil slick, fat and happy. Otherwise nothing is moving on or around the lake. I stop and squint, finally discerning a cluster of human-shaped figures walking in the opposite direction. They look identical at this distance. No genders; no faces. For my life I couldn't guess which one is Snow—

—and Service stops long enough to snap, "Let's move!"

Then he turns and marches, screaming, "We've got a long walk tonight! A fucking long walk, and a lot to do afterward! If you please!"

42
THE FUTURE

-❖-

The mountain is a piercing white-on-white mass, solidity rising into the white-on-white etherealness of the sky; and the country beneath the mountain has the clean fine-grained green of jade, folds of ground trailing off into low mists and no sound but our constant wet breathing.

Service pauses, kneels, and examines nothing.

The cretin helps, snorting delicately. Then both rise, and the man reports, "This way." His voice is no more than a whisper. His face is white as the mountain. A small revelation—Service, it seems, has mortal limits.

We move along a ridge, then downhill. The country is scented, damp soils and pungent vegetations that break underfoot. Sometimes I feel a mild pain straight ahead of us. I mention it to Service, and he nods soberly, making no comment. We cross a narrow valley and climb the opposite slope, and the valley itself makes a wide turn and passes in front of us again. The Remarkables show below as a weak bruise-colored stain against the green. Dead ones litter the ground around the bunch, their central organs removed; and a single huge sprintbear sits between them and us, its mouth left swollen from the stinging tendrils but the pain no worse than an irritation.

Service charges, half sliding and half running down the slope. The sprintbear tilts its head and growls, the plumage lifting to expose the crimson underplumage. It takes a few confident steps toward us, pauses, and Service shoots and Pachel shoots, the creature lifting its head higher while slumping, dead in an instant.

The Remarkables start to roll forward. They sing and

gyrate, swarming over the carcass and gnawing at it; and I hear Talker over the melee. "What happened?" it asks. "Tell, tell!"

Service explains in brief, then he sits and lets us add details. He shuts his eyes, appearing to drift into sleep, and when the feast is done, he rises again, a weak old-man voice saying, "We'll move downstream. I know this valley. It opens up nicely. . . ."

Several dozen Remarkables remain alive.

I count them three times, reaching three different numbers.

"Thank you so much for your help, Ranier."

Talker rolls beside me. A few of the stiff outer tendrils are torn, I notice. The dried blood glitters like a purple-black metal. Its eyes examine me, absorbing me. My turn to speak, and I grin and nod. "I do understand. At least I think so."

"Of course you understand."

"Everything was planned," I continue. "The Old Ones knew that Briar would lead some sort of rebellion. They guessed that Goottich would want to create his own version of Pitcairn. The players were set up intentionally. There was a purpose in everything—"

"Such as?"

"I wasn't certain. At first." I shake my head. "I didn't see the obvious answers. You gave me every clue, but I wasn't thinking clearly."

Talker says nothing.

"The Realm is coming," I say. "Everyone knows it. Remarkables and Pitcairns both. One day you'll find yourself surrounded by us, and you're afraid of the consequences. Reasonably so. You and your humans have done your best to minimize contact. You use these structured little visits of ours to improve bloodlines, and since there are no cameras allowed—nothing that captures these scenes or yourselves—you enhance the distance between cultures. You help make Pitcairn more remote and mysterious, and that's all for the good."

It asks, "Why?"

"Distance. You want a certain distance maintained. You realize that the Realm has great powers and specific needs. We'll want the worlds of your solar system. Your comets and moon, and even Pitcairn. The Realm is going to consume this place, if you let it. Us. Populations will swell, factions will covet your resources, and the Pitcairn charter will be broken—"

"And terraformers like you will transform what you steal!"

I nod and shrug my shoulders. "Probably so."

"But what about here? What about now?"

"You almost told me, and I didn't understand." I smile at myself. "We were put here to serve a role. The Old Ones guessed what might happen, given these ingredients. Goottich would make his offer. Service would refuse him. Then open warfare and this victory . . . and the Remarkables and Pitcairns are left with a story to tell. The *passion* . . . it was set up to serve a bigger purpose. The Au Pitcairns will tell others what happened; the Au Remarkables will do the same. Once you return home, the adults are going to start seeding the wind with aromatic words, describing what has happened and using our adventures as a warning—"

"And as a testament to the loyalties of our best people."

"Service," I interject.

"And heroes from without too."

Such as me, I suppose. Though I don't feel particularly heroic, the truth told.

"And you and Pachel and Lumiere shall return home," says Talker, "and you too will tell stories. All the countless people in your Realm, and we must have many friends like you. Friends who will listen. Who will be warned now, and who will work on our behalf. . . ."

I imagine Pachel, the stolid bureaucrat, returning home to sponsor new legislations. To block future Goottiches, she will work to make it illegal to possess any lifeform from Pitcairn. For any purpose. That's one tangible good deed that might come from this mess.

"Insulation," I mutter.

"Insulation," Talker echoes.

"You want to start building barriers now, don't you? While we're still in the distance. While the dramas are small enough to manage. That's what this was about—"

"In part," it says. "Yes."

"A warning for the future."

It says nothing.

"But what I don't understand," I admit, "is the stacking

of the odds. Service against everyone? Wasn't that cutting it a bit fine?"

"The Old Ones and the elders were confident," it replies.

"But what if Briar had killed Service instead of Service slipping away? Or what if some cretin had chewed on the old Pitcairn, killing him for Briar? After all, a lot of wrong turns can happen . . . !"

"What if Goottich won?" it asks.

"Exactly."

"Then the *passion* is stolen. Goottich toys with his enworld, as promised. And then . . . well, you should see what would likely happen. Don't you, Ranier?"

I try to concentrate.

"For years and years, Goottich broadcasted his appeals to visit here. Groves everywhere listened to his voice, to his manners and moods, and we spoke with each other through the wind—"

"He'd fail," I interrupt.

"Yes?"

"Goottich is too stubborn and ignorant to pull it off. Sure! I understand. He would have fought with Briar and the others. Recreating Pitcairn would have taken decades, only he doesn't have the patience—"

"A simple-headed man-child."

"—and that's why he was selected. Some good genes among the pompous ones, but they were certain he'd fail somewhere. Right?"

The alien makes the buzzing laugh.

"Only the All-Answer feels certain, my friend."

I nod dutifully.

Then Talker says, "Ignorance is everyone's burden—"

"I suppose so."

"—and everyone's bliss too," it says. "Burden and bliss. Burden and bliss. Equal doses of both, I think, and I wouldn't have it any other way."

Lumiere wakes me as night falls, his cool hand on my shoulder.

"Your turn for watch," he says, then he hands me a warm cup full of nectar mixed with water.

I sip and say, "Thanks."

"It's getting cool," he advises. "But I built up the fire for you."

"Thanks."

We keep watch, and the waking Remarkables do the same. One of us is supposed to be awake every moment. Service's orders. We made camp at midday, and Service gave us quick lessons in the care and use of our rifles. Then he dropped into a deathly sleep. I check on him before taking my post, his pulse steady and slow. Lumiere was right, I'm thinking. It is cold. I throw another log on the fire, glancing at the Remarkables, then I settle on a convenient stone and hold my hands to the blaze.

Full night descends.

There's motion, and I jerk my head, startled. Then I see it's just Service rising from his bag and approaching.

We trade greetings.

He sits opposite me, boiling water with nectar in a chipped ceramic pot. By firelight I can tell that his color is improving. His vigor is reemerging. He grins at nothing in particular, shaking his head. Then his expression changes, eyes finding me and the strong voice asking:

"Do you feel this?"

He drives his thumb into his wound.

I straighten and admit, "Somewhat. I do."

He nods and asks to hear the story again. Why did I do such a thing? Service is curious, nothing more. He wants to understand, if I could explain. Please?

I tell about my fish again.

I tell about my long hollow life.

Then when I come to my priestess and my attempted conversion, he stops me. He lifts his hand and asks, "How can she manage and not you?"

How indeed?

I mention her attempts to teach me the tricks. "Listen to the silences between the pains," she told me. And I tell him. "As if something so simple could make a difference." Then I groan, shrugging off the whole ugly business.

Service drinks and says nothing.

After a while he rises, telling me, "I think I should sleep a little more. You're doing well enough. . . ."

The compliment makes me smile, secretly.

Then the old Pitcairn pauses, looking at me, finally saying, "I don't believe in profound answers. Not for people, I don't."

I watch him.

"For me," he says, "there's nothing but the simple answers. The test is to apply them every day. For all your life. Work at them and work at them, and if you can count seven perfect days when the life's over, you can feel pretty good about things."

I give a little nod.

"Good night, Ranier."

"Night," I manage; and I continue staring at the space he occupied, unable to move my head or blink my eyes. Thinking:

Only simple answers.

Thinking:

Work at them.

Thinking:

Every day.

TALKER

❖

I sleep deeply and thoroughly, dreams upon dreams . . .

. . . seeing myself in the grove again, beneath the Old Ones again, and them retelling their story of the Future. What-Will-Be. Only suddenly they change and the scene changes with them. The Old Ones are the All-Answer now. I find myself on the plain beneath the Au mountain. What I hear is not the guesswork Future, but it is the true Future. A thousand seasons from Now; a million seasons from Now. I behold the All-Answer and listen, and it sounds like the Old Ones when it says:

"Pay attention, Talker. Will you please?"

I have been trying, I want to say. But I cannot dare speak aloud in its presence, nor doubt the All-Answer's appraisal of anything.

What-Will-Be.

The Realm comes and engulfs our little sun and worlds. As promised. And we have built our insulations using mystery and mutual respect, plus tenacious legal barriers, as promised. Yet no barrier lasts forever. Mountains crumble, even continents, and how can we survive forever inside an alien Realm?

We must embrace these transformations.

Says the All-Answer to me.

We and our humans—the stronger and smarter and even more tenacious descendants of Service—must allow the Realm to gnaw at our outer reaches, taking cold worlds in exchange for gifts. For machines and for trickery.

Our humans must learn how to fly again.

Says the All-Answer to me.

To fly across the void in giant torchships, taking us with them as they streak through the Realm and into the uncharted places. That is the Future. We and our symbionts—Those-Whom-We-Trust-Most—will journey to new suns beyond the reach of the Realm's light and powers. And there we and they will recreate Pitcairn again and again and again.

Says the All-Answer to me.

Many ships will perish along the way. But failure makes successes all the sweeter. New worlds; a new Realm. A different shade of green will grow along some other tendril of the galaxy, expanding and embracing and perhaps someday brushing against the pure human Realm again.

But as equals, this time.

Says the All-Answer.

And in my dream I ask, "Then what happens then?"

Only now the All-Answer has become the Old Ones again, and I stand in the grove again, roots deep in the rich black living earth; and a summer sun stands in a singing blue sky; and I am an Old One too.

In my dream.

I say to myself.

Only in my dream.

43
THE MOMENT

◆

I kneel and touch the milky water, burning my hand in the cold.

Pachel says, "Bad?"

"No," I lie. "Almost hot, in fact."

She laughs for a moment, then asks, "Do you have the rope?"

The extra rope. Yes, I do. I open my pack and open the top pouch, handing her the neat coil, and she takes it to Service. We are crossing here, I realize. I look upriver and down, no better place offering itself. Then I stare across, trying to measure the churning white water with my eyes; and Lumiere comes up beside me, telling me, "The clouds don't seem as thick today. Have you noticed?"

Around the summit, he means.

I look at the enormous mountain. This is more than a week after the fights and banishments; our progress is obvious. Au continues to swell, individual bluish glaciers showing against the whiter snows, and exposed faces of rock betray details invisible just yesterday.

"You're right," I say. "The clouds are thinner."

Pachel starts wading into the glacial water, one rope tied around her waist. We watch her. The Remarkables are scattered around us, enjoying the sun. Service shouts instruction from time to time, keeping her moving on a straight strong line. All of this is routine by now. Instead of nervousness, I feel a quick longing for the woman . . . imagining her in my tent tonight, in my bed, those silvery breasts dangling over me. . . .

I could invite her, I realize.

We're Pitcairns, after all. At least for the time being.

Lumiere says something, and I blink and turn. He acts embarrassed, smiling and admitting, "Not you. Sorry."

"No problem."

I shut my eyes, and for a little while I concentrate on the pains around me, inviting them to me.

Silences between.

Each pain is a star, I pretend. And it's the quiet unseen places between that matter. That I find and I feel. Another week or two or ten of practice, I think, and maybe I could accomplish this trick unconsciously. Automatically. A simple, unprofound solution, and I try applying it whenever I can.

Pachel climbs from the fast-moving river, then into a low tree. Then she ties the rope at the proper height, and Service throws the other end over a limb, tying it off on an exposed root.

We rise, knowing that it's time.

Lumiere says something again. And again, not to me.

I lead. He follows me to the shoreline, Service watching us. He'll wait until the last Remarkable is across, as always. For now he wishes us luck with his eyes, his mind already considering the terrain beyond the river. What course to take; what to avoid; what kind of timetable to keep. As always.

The water grabs hold of my stick, my feet, and the current is amazingly swift. I fight my way into the long middle stretch, wet to the crotch and shivering. Then I happen to look up. I notice Pachel waving her walking stick in the air, the motion frantic. She's shouting, only I can't hear anything over the roaring water. What is it? I squint and try reading her lips, then I think to turn around.

The shallow arc of the rope is overhead. I am in position. But Lumiere is too far downstream, too deep in the water, a bright white fountain surging over him and his stick lost. I can't see it or his face.

I turn around, nearly falling myself.

I drive with my cold legs, the river splashing and me tasting the chill of it and the grittiness of the rock flour. Poor Lumiere. Soaked to the chest and working hard, struggling to keep his place. Finally he sees me. He turns and sees me. I stop above him, boot heels against rock, and I lift my stick and offer it to him, afraid that he'll grab it too fast or too hard, throwing me from my feet.

But he doesn't.

He grabs the cold slick wood and presses against the current. I'm partway blocking the river. He reaches me, trying to thank me, and what I do I do without planning. I force my stick into his hands, telling him, "Go on! Please!"

Lumiere starts for Pachel again. He works his way beneath the rope, leaning hard on the stick, and I follow as best I can. I find myself slipping every so often. Not a lot; not dangerously. But every step has to be done slowly, with unusual care, my frozen toes measuring the slickness of rocks and their tilt. I'm not making progress, I sense; and sure enough, I look up and see Pachel on the far bank, tiny and very still, and somehow I've worked my way downstream. Too far. Much too far.

Service sees my troubles and drops the rope.

The rope is carried by the current, brushing against me. Only I'm so cold that my hands lack purchase. My hands and my feet. I grasp and grope, and I start losing my footing completely now. Bitter cold water slams against my chest, my heart—

—and I am carried, buoyed up and the rope shooting through my curled hands and my tired cold brain shouting: "Grab it! Grab it!"

Somehow I stop myself, holding tight to a fat hard knot near the rope's end. If only I can hold on long enough, I reason, the currents will carry me against the far bank and save me. Yet I am so very tired, so cold . . . like I never knew possible—

—and I reach with my mind, intentionally seeking the worst pains around me. I cherish them all at once. Those tangles of aching suffering life seem suddenly precious. I want to remain with them for as long as possible, I tell myself. Suddenly I'm completely at peace with myself. It's the easiest trick in the world, isn't it? You just have to approach it from the right angle—

—and that's when I start to laugh.

Laugh and tell myself laughing isn't the best course right now. It might even be a mistake. Yet here I am, clinging to a rope with deadened hands and shooting through the cold white roaring water; and all I can do is laugh at myself.

Which isn't the worst sort of end, I suppose.

And with that I start laughing even harder—